SISTERHOOD

ALSO AVAILABLE FROM CHAOSIUM:

King of Sartar
Greg Stafford

S. Petersen's Field Guide to Lovecraftian Horrors
Sandy Petersen, Lynn Willis, and Mike Mason

Edge of Sundown
edited by Kevin Ross and Brian M. Sammons

Mark of the Beast
edited by Scott David Aniolowski

The Guide to Glorantha, 2 vols.
Greg Stafford, Jeff Richard, and Sandy Petersen

Madness on the Orient Express
edited by James Lowder

Cassilda's Song
edited by Joseph S. Pulver, Sr.

H. P. Lovecraft's The Call of Cthulhu for Beginning Readers
R. J. Ivankovic

Daughter of Fate
John Wick

The Arthurian Companion, third edition
Phyllis Ann Karr
[forthcoming]

The Leaves of a Necronomicon
edited by Joseph S. Pulver, Sr.
[forthcoming]

Arthur the Emperor
Book 1: *The Soldier*
Christopher Gidlow
[forthcoming]

SISTERHOOD

DARK TALES
AND
SECRET HISTORIES

EDITED BY
NATE PEDERSEN

CHAOSIUM INC.

Sisterhood: Dark Tales and Secret Histories © 2021 Nate Pedersen. All rights reserved.

This edition © 2021 Chaosium Inc. All rights reserved.

Chaosium Inc. and the Chaosium logo are registered trademarks of Chaosium Inc.

See Permissions for individual story copyrights.

Cover illustration © 2021 Liv Rainey-Smith. All rights reserved.

Cover design and typesetting: Inkspiral Design.
Cover illustration: Liv Rainey-Smith.
Proofreading: Dale Donovan.
Assistant fiction editor: Nick Nacario.
Executive editor: James Lowder.

This material is protected under the copyright laws of the United States of America. No portion of this publication may be reproduced or transmitted, in any form or by any means, except for the use of short excerpts for the purpose of reviews, without the express written permission of the publisher and the copyright holders.

Names, characters, places, and incidents featured in this work are the result of an author's imagination or are used fictitiously. Any resemblance to actual persons living or dead, events, institutions, or locales, without satiric intent, is coincidental.

Address questions and comments by mail to:

Chaosium Inc.
3450 Wooddale Court
Ann Arbor, MI 48104

chaosium.com

Chaosium publication 6058

ISBN-13: 978-1-56882-464-2

First Edition, April 2021
10 9 8 7 6 5 4 3 2 1

Printed in the United States.

PERMISSIONS

"The Wine of Men" by Ann K. Schwader. © 2021 Ann K. Schwader. All rights reserved.

"From an Honest Sister to a Neglected Daughter" by Monica Valentinelli. © 2021 Monica Valentinelli. All rights reserved.

"Étaín and the Unholy Ghosts" by Lisa Morton. © 2021 Lisa Morton. All rights reserved.

"The Barefoot Sisters of Saint Beatriz of the Mountain" by Kali Wallace. © 2021 Kali Wallace. All rights reserved.

"Unburdened Flesh" by Penelope Love. © 2021 Penelope Love. All rights reserved.

"Only Dead Men Do Not Lie: The Trials of the Formosans" by Kaaron Warren. © 2021 Kaaron Warren. All rights reserved.

"Jane, Jamestown, The Starving Time" by Sun Yung Shin. © 2021 Sun Yung Shin. All rights reserved.

"Dorcas and Ann: A True Story" by Molly Tanzer. © 2021 Molly Tanzer. All rights reserved.

"The Resurrected" by S. P. Miskowski. © 2021 S. P. Miskowski. All rights reserved.

"The Low, Dark Edge of Life" by Livia Llewellyn. © 2016, 2021 Livia Llewellyn. First appeared in *Nightmare Magazine* #51, December 2016. All rights reserved.

"The Anchoress" by Lynda E. Rucker. © 2021 Lynda E. Rucker. All rights reserved.

"Siūlais ir Kraujo ir Kaulų (Of Thread and Blood and Bone)" by Damien Angelica Walters. © 2021 Damien Angelica Walters. All rights reserved.

"Gravity Wave" by Nadia Bulkin. © 2021 Nadia Bulkin. All rights reserved.

"The Veils of Sanctuary" by Selena Chambers. © 2021 Selena Chambers. All rights reserved.

"The Sisters of Epione" by Alison Littlewood. © 2021 Alison Littlewood. All rights reserved.

"Red Words" by Gemma Files. © 2021 Gemma Files. All rights reserved. Quotation from "The Treader in the Dust" by Clark Ashton Smith © 1935, 2010 the Estate of Clark Ashton Smith. Quotation from "The Infernal Star" © 1933, 2011 the Estate of Clark Ashton Smith. Used with permission.

ACKNOWLEDGMENTS

Joe Pulver and Nick Nacario for first believing in this anthology and Jim Lowder for shepherding it through.

The team at Chaosium for putting this all together.

The sixteen contributors, for their patience, hard work, and copious amounts of talent.

Tom Pedersen.

April Genevieve Tucholke.

You, the reader.

This book is dedicated to the memory of Joseph S. Pulver, Sr.

TABLE OF CONTENTS

1 "THE WINE OF MEN"
Ann K. Schwader
(ancient era)

5 "FROM AN HONEST SISTER TO A NEGLECTED DAUGHTER"
Monica Valentinelli
(Wales, 1st century; New England, 20th century)

15 "ÉTAÍN AND THE UNHOLY GHOSTS"
Lisa Morton
(Ireland, 6th century)

27 "THE BAREFOOT SISTERS OF SAINT BEATRIZ OF THE MOUNTAIN"
Kali Wallace
(Spain, 14th century)

41 "UNBURDENED FLESH"
Penelope Love
(Italy, 14th century)

59 "ONLY DEAD MEN DO NOT LIE: THE TRIALS OF THE FORMOSANS"
Kaaron Warren
(England, 15th century)

71 "JANE, JAMESTOWN, THE STARVING TIME"
Sun Yung Shin
(Virginia, 17th century)

73 "DORCAS AND ANN: A TRUE STORY"
Molly Tanzer
(France, 18th century)

89 "The Resurrected"
S. P. Miskowski
(Pacific Northwest, 19th century)

107 "The Low, Dark Edge of Life"
Livia Llewellyn
(Belgium, 19th century)

129 "The Anchoress"
Lynda E. Rucker
(Appalachia, 20th century)

145 "Siūlais ir Kraujo ir Kaulų (Of Thread and Blood and Bone)"
Damien Angelica Walters
(Lithuania, 20th century)

159 "Gravity Wave"
Nadia Bulkin
(Indonesia, 20th century)

177 "The Veils of Sanctuary"
Selena Chambers
(France, 21st century)

193 "The Sisters of Epione"
Alison Littlewood
(England, 21st century)

211 "Red Words"
Gemma Files
(America, 21st century)

249 Contributors' Notes

THE WINE OF MEN
ANN K. SCHWADER

By day we mind our shuttles & our looms
With downcast eyes. Chaste wives & daughters all,
We drift like shadows through secluded rooms
In silence uncorrupted by that call
The mountains harbor, ancient & divine,
Its summons irresistible as wine.

Like shadows, too, we crave the waning light
Of sunset as it touches us. Struck deep
In our last secret places, we ignite;
Yet smolder through the hours until sleep
Claims those who claim our flesh, or hold our hearts
Too lightly for regret as we depart.

With moonrise as our guide, the ivy crowns
Our brows & weapons almost on its own,
Bestowing sacred madness. Round & round
The dance begins; each thyrsus with its cone
In token of some trophy still to take,
Still promised by the god when he awakes.

Emboldened by his stolen sacrament
Of grape-blood as it passes hand to hand,
We sing our sisterhood—& our intent
To range unfettered through this changeling land
As huntresses. All hail the quarry's name,
Though none of us perceive him quite the same.

Some seek among the leaders of those flocks
That climb the highest through our Theban hills,
& drag one down. Flayed open on the rocks,
Its flesh suggests divinity that fills
Our mouths & minds alike with fleeting bliss
Intoxicating as a satyr's kiss.

Our bolder sisters seize upon a bull
& bind him to the earth with eager hands
In place of nets, then catch his head to pull
His throat against their teeth. These sharp demands
Are answered in a heartbeat as a rush
Of holy crimson stains the midnight hush.

Yet beasts are not the god entirely. Filled
& unfulfilled at once, our frenzy craves
Some nameless savor. Barefoot, bloody, chilled,
Though innocent of all discomfort save
This greatest, we must find another way
To sate our appetite for choicer prey.

Whatever solitary sacrifice
The god provides—some shepherd huddled deep
In slumber, or some reveler enticed
By loveliness—permits us all to keep
Divinity within. At least a taste
For memory, & nothing gone to waste.

So little of the godhead yet remains
In any man, & that well hidden. Swift
As panthers we reveal it, pulsing plain
Before our faces, dripping with its gift
Of ecstasy. We paint our fingertips,
Then lick the last like honey from our lips.

Dawn finds us at our duties. Once again
The rattle of the shuttle speaks, & we
Slide quiet underneath the thoughts of men
Who take no notice of our sisterly
Exhilaration from the evening's wine,
Or their resemblance to those ravaged vines.

FROM AN HONEST SISTER TO A NEGLECTED DAUGHTER

MONICA VALENTINELLI

THE GROVE IS CLEANSED AND *the fires are lit. Finish applying the blue ochre upon your cheeks, drink the herbal mixture, and let us begin. Quickly now! Disrobe our Virtuous Sister and heed the call of our Sacred Goddess. We must contact the Pale Woman who lives in the Age of the Machine and foretell the fate of our children's children. The Veil is already eroding! We, her ancestors, must reach through the centuries to pull our daughter close, to speak to her in the sacred groves of her own, stolen land of Massachusetts. Take your seat at the heart of our circle and picture this Land Beyond the Great Seas. Call to her now!*

Daughter of Eve, can you hear me?

Call to the woman in white!

Daughter? Are you there? I must speak with you. Can you hear me? Sisters, I fear something sinister prevents me from reaching her. Is it her father? Or the false god?

Her father has only the power the Unspeakable One has given him. He is of no concern to us. It is true, the Lord of a Thousand Eyes can affect men's hearts and is very powerful, but that forlorn deceiver lives beyond our mortal realm. He cannot reach us.

No, you must have caught the eye of her future son, the abomination. He now stands in our way. No doubt the horror senses our presence and considers us a threat. It is we who have the power, and we must reach his mother if we can. We must touch our daughter through the blood of all our line and hope our sisterhood can stop her still. There is yet time to prevent the child's birth. The timeline is still mutable, and her life is not yet a fixed point.

Tell me, Sisters. What do I do?

Turn your Eye inward and speak your heart's truth louder still. Be the Honest Virtue you were destined to represent. We each must relay our visions and boldly send them into the future—six final warnings of a mutable future for a neglected child. Begin again! You are the first and must get through!

The blackness of time is ice cold; it threatens to swallow my consciousness whole. No, wait! My vision is becoming clearer. There is a light—it is . . . green. The grass is lush and thick. There are many trees, but I can see through them. There is a large dwelling, but it is warped. The once-proud wood is rotting and crawling with worms. I see thin cattle. Their bones stick out. They shy away from a bestial man with yellow eyes. This man . . . He frightens me. His wiry hair is wild, and his body is thick and hard where it should be soft. He is hungry—no, ravenous—for power. Is he the one we fear?

Quickly now! Ignore the monster. Let his vision be a fading nightmare and our voices but whispers in the dark. That is the future we wish to avoid. Look away! Travel back in time a few years. Set your sights clearly on your quarry, for humanity's last hope rests in your hands. Call to her now in her youth. Tell our daughter what you've seen. Let your words bite and claw and rend the lies that shroud her, consume her, and damn her to become Mother of Evil.

Sisters, I will. I . . . I worry my words will cut too deeply. Must I do this? Is there no other way?

She must hear you. Be honest! Courage rallies you. Hospitality comforts you. Loyalty stands by you. Honor guards you. And I, Justice, fight for you.

And if she does not listen?

Then, she must die.

Daughter, if you can hear me, follow the witch's light into the woods. Head for the heart of the forest; no one will follow you there. Heed my voice. It is the beacon you need and the source of your hope.

Yes, that's it! Slash through lies and shatter illusions. Speak the truth, and may our Goddess favor us. Only She will amplify your words and allow our warnings to echo through time. Speak and let your words echo through the years, luring her to a new future.

Daughter, though you are loved there are men who will call you ugly. They will say your chin is weak, your cold skin is pallid and veiny, your glistening eyes are red as Devil's fire. These men will not see you and do not measure you. They cannot treat you as a sexual object, a living, breathing body to stick and suck and slime, so they find you worthless. It will not matter you are a human being, a daughter, nature lover, daydreamer, with thoughts and feelings and a mind of your own. You are undesirable, and for them that is enough.

Your fleshy container, the pale hairless covering that stretches over your brittle bones and thin muscles and bloodless organs, is not attractive in their eyes. These men are not fit to banter with you. They are bitter, because they are powerless. They did not make it (you). They did not buy it (you). They did not define or give it (you) permission to live. They exist, only to consume you.

Keep going! We feel a faint presence, a feminine shadow taking shape. It chases butterflies.

And so, these judges of all our sex will claim you have no memory for numbers, no curiosity to sate, no depth for philosophy. Your brain is timid and weak, they'll profess. It is filled with rot. You are not to be wedded. You are not fit to be seen in public. No man would want you and, to these men, that accusation is far worse than being pretty yet arrogant, gorgeous yet vapid, beautiful yet cruel.

The longer you listen to them, the more they will siphon your power away. They fear you, so they condemn you harshly: you are the product of incest, the Devil's spawn, child of Lilith, Yog-Sothoth's chosen. The hollows of your gaunt face are a sign of your father's obsession with black magic—not malnutrition. Your awkward gait is the result of inbreeding—not poor medical care and lack of therapy. As your long years stretch, from Yule to Lammas to All Hallows Eve and back again, you will fight boredom as you would a rabid dog, and your wits will soften. Then, in your prime of womanhood, you will be damned for traits and circumstances you cannot control. You will suffer the curse of the unwanted and forgotten in near total isolation. You will speak to mournful shades expecting them to answer you.

She is coming! The shadow grows stronger still. It takes shape and becomes more defined with each passing word. We can now see the outline of her youthful body, her unkempt hair, her rumpled dress. Please, continue! It is her! We are sure of it.

Before anyone sees your white face, they will fear it. Before they hear your trembling voice, they will learn not to listen. You will think you deserve to be abused; that you were destined to be evil. You'll see scars where there are none to be found and star in a nightmare of your own creation to fill the black void of loneliness and despair.

Then you, my beloved daughter, will lose the will to live. That, child, is the day you will fall, for on that fateful day you will pray to the wrong god asking not for forgiveness or hope, asking not for the means to destroy your enemies, but for the love of a child you believe you should never have. You, a poor creature shunned by men you know, will believe the answer to your predicament is to offer yourself to the only "man" who would lie with you—an eager, malign deity who cares nothing for mortals and hates us utterly.

The lies these men will tell you, my unborn Daughter of Eve, are as numerous as the stars in the sky. They will tell you, as they told my own daughter, slippery half-truths that slither through the folds of your memories, planting love-sucking seeds of unworthiness that grow with every insult. You will be despised not for who you are, but for what your body can do despite the look of you. Despite every mole, every wrinkle, every misshapen pockmark and dimple in your pigment-deprived skin, your body can (and will) produce the miracle of life. And yet, despite this, you will hate every inch of yourself, every month you bleed and every month you do not, for your worth has been weighed by lesser men—but not yet. And, it is this self-hatred that catapults you into the arms of the unworthy, dogs who are not fit to lick your heels.

It is her! The woman in white! She hears you!

"When will this happen? Soon?"

No, not *yet*. Not before I die, and my daughter dies, and my daughter's daughter's daughter's die, and the goddess of our ancestors, the Unnamed and Unknowable One, has all but faded into pleasant memory. There is still time to save you!

"Save . . . me? But who will save my father? Only I can do that."

Your father is responsible for his own choices. That is not your burden.

"Who are you?"

Someone who loves you.

"My father loves me. At least, I think he does."

All men claiming to be just and faithful will whisper falsehoods because they fear us, for the same reason they are afraid of you.

"How can someone be afraid of me if they haven't met me yet? Who are you?"

She Who Can Save You. I worship . . . Ah! Even now, I try to say the name of my Beloved Goddess who granted us this audience, and I cannot—the Vile One has wiped her from human memory.

"I . . . I believe half of what you're saying, but not all of it. I know my father values power over gold, but once he's done with his books he'll be all right again. He promised."

And your uncle?

"He's from the 'other' side of the family, the side that doesn't know magic is real. He glances at my ghostly white skin and threadbare dress and, instead of recognizing I suffer from a rare condition, claims I am a witch and makes the sign of a cross that won't protect him in the end."

Our Unnamed Goddess will never abandon you. It is She who has sent us, She who will comfort you, She who will always wrap Her loving arms around you. Embrace Her and you will never know the pain of loneliness, the burden of carrying an abominable creature, the duty forced upon you as the daughter of a vile man. Embrace Her and find hope.

"I—I—I can't. You don't understand. I *am* afraid. He will kill me."

Who?

"My father. He threatened to murder me. Please! Staying with him isn't my choice."

Daughter, you must lis—

"No! *You* must listen. I know what they say about me, and I know why."

Sister, you are losing her! Stand strong!

"Their words hurt, but I have nowhere to turn. I live in fear of my Dad. Don't you understand? Every day, I wonder when he'll get angry, when he'll raise a hand to me like he does Mother, when he'll kill me."

Why, daughter? *Why* would your father do such a thing?

"I watched him murder my mother. I *saw* what he did. I even called the police, and my dad. . . . He blamed me for her death. He said I made him angry, and his anger was my fault."

So, your mother has been ripped from creation by your murderous father's hand. Then, when you are grieving and most vulnerable, that is when you believe the lies. You don't want love. You believe you're undeserving of love, and think you're worthless. That is why you perform the ritual. You don't expect anyone will save you.

"It's *not* true! It's not. I know what my father wants. He said he would tear my heart out and sacrifice me, that he brought me into this world and he's the only one who can take me out!"

You must know your future son will be a crime against nature, a monster from Beyond, a thing that threatens the purity of air and fresh water, an abominable beast all other beasts recoil from. Why else would you allow your womb to be defiled in such a way?

"Forgive me! I do not want to die! Mercy!"

Sister, tell her. Yes, show her the future of what's to come.

The woman sobs uncontrollably, and her body is wracked with tears. I sense her spirit is frail and the horror of her choice is not unknown to her. If I share the nightmares of our storied ending, they could warp her mind and damage her.

Sisters, I ask you. What have we done? I have not brought her hope; I have forced her into a scrying pool. She sees herself, as she always has, and knows where the blame must fall. Would we, fearing for our lives, make the same choices? Has the truth not done enough damage this night?

Enough! It is dangerous to ask questions we cannot answer. You know this. We have no Will of our own to serve, but that of the Goddess who stands opposed to eldritch beings. Your honesty has sliced her heart's festering boils and allowed the infection to bleed. The woman in white was never destined for greatness, she was never promised a happy life. Tell her! She must know! The woman in white may still be swayed and choose to die by her own hand to unravel this foul plot. Speak!

"Mercy! P-P-Please, mercy. I can't take it anymore. It's too much."

Daughter, what would you have me do?

Do not give her that power!

Silence, Sisters! These words are *my* choice to speak. Daughter of Eve, I ask again: What would you have me do? I come from your past. Now you see into the future and know how all creation ends. Watch flames rip the sky, bodies bloated in the streets, the foul stench of charred corpses piled higher than the tallest building. The air is thick with gritty smoke, the soil is sickly gray, and all water has been replaced with a greenish-yellow ichor. All living things have died. The trees you love, the butterflies you chase, the cats and hounds and horses—all gone. The sound of a child's laughter, gone. Two lovers kissing, gone.

"Is there anything left?"

Only greed. Some panic. Little bread. And relief when another mortal dies quickly. But that is all.

"And... And I did this? My son, I mean. He does that? He kills everyone and everything, and I am responsible?"

Yes.

Yes.

"Then, I need your help."

What do you mean?

"I am already pregnant. I have . . . no one. Not even Mamie. This is bigger than me, and I know that. But I want to live. I know that much, at least. I never learned how to read, and I don't have any gifts. Won't you help me? Please?"

We did not know, Sister. We are sorry. There is nothing to be done, and now that the Vessel has been contacted we are not permitted to speak with her again. Worse, we are certain the child will enjoy magical protections until it comes of age, into its own power.

Daughter . . . I do not know what to say. You have been chosen as the Vessel and cannot die until your son is born. Even so, your son will be protected by its father until it comes of age. Only then can a being that matches its unholy power destroy it. Possible, but unlikely.

We have made a grievous error. Now that we are doomed, we should close the sundered Veil. Our Sisterhood is finished. Make your goodbyes, and let us begin mourning.

"I know a little more. I used to sneak into my father's study late at night, and listen to him. He prepared for this, to make sure his god would be satisfied. There is one way to kill it."

What way is that?

"You must kill it by your unseen hand. You must leave your time and space, and channel into my body—just as Yog-Sothoth has already done. Then, when the time is right, I will release your spirit into this grove, so you may begin your murderous work. Then, and only then, will we both—will humanity—be freed."

Impossible! Her fragile body cannot hold two spirits. She will go mad! Who would go? Not I! Nor I! The body here would need to be kept alive, in a trance . . . caught between worlds, between life and death itself!

"You said it yourself, Sister of the Unnamed Goddess. Your deity's name has been struck from history. I understand the risks, but I also know my father.

If your goddess's name cannot be found, if your names have disappeared . . . he won't find you. I am sure of it."

Hush, Sisters. I will go. But I must ask one more time. Are you sure? Do you know what you're asking?

"I do. I am losing my lucidity for one, last shred of hope. And . . ."

. . . I am sacrificing my life to save the future from your son.

"Will it hurt?"

I've already begun. It won't be long now. Goodbye, my sisters! Farewell!

"Oh, what a pair we'll make! What should I call you?"

I don't know.

"Oh, I should call you Mamie after my friend. I don't want to be locked up in Arkham, after all. We can hold conversations then. No one cares what I say. It'll be our secret."

And you? What do I call you, daughter?

"Lavinia."

That's a pretty name. I am almost there now, Lavinia. I can feel your thoughts—they are warm and feverish. You're . . . resisting . . . me. Don't panic, Lavinia. Relax! Take a deep breath. I will make myself as small as I can and hide in the back of your mind.
  Lavinia? Are you there?

"Yup, mah name's Lavinia Whateley, an' I'm a terribul mother. I vaow afur Gawd I am."

ÉTAÍN AND THE UNHOLY GHOSTS
LISA MORTON

Imbolc/The Evening of February 1

Étaín saw the first ghost on Imbolc.

Sister Boann, who oversaw the kitchen, had sent her out for more leeks. The abbey's food was kept in a cave a dozen yards outside the kitchen door. Even though it was a short walk, all the sisters dreaded it in winter, when they'd be forced to leave the warmer confines of the abbey after Terce, the day's third service, to trudge through snow and ice before ducking under a chilled stone lintel to enter the dank cave.

The walk was less dreadful today. The mother abbess had granted them a feast to honor Imbolc even though it was from the old calendar, one of the quarter-days that the people on her father's side—the Celtic side—had celebrated. Imbolc, when the ewes were gravid with the spring lambs and the goddess Brigid provided blessings to her believers. Although the Christians considered Imbolc to be pagan, Brigid, also the name of the mother abbess—whose parents had both honored and diminished a goddess by bestowing her name on a human child—was wise enough to allow the celebration. The nuns under Brigid's care had little other time to enjoy a rare feast of porridge, watercress, beer, and the dark cake known as *barm brack*.

The day was freezing, the sky a solid, gloomy dark gray, and Étaín pulled her robes tighter with one hand, holding a candle close with the other as her boots crunched through the snow. She hated the nuns' schedule in the winter. They awoke just a few scant hours past midnight for Matins Laud, the day's first service, and were only allowed another four hours huddled beneath blankets before Prime, the sunrise service. Étaín frequently wanted to ask the mother abbess what good all these prayers did if God couldn't keep them warm through the winter, but she didn't dare.

Étaín reached the cave, knelt beneath the lintel, and pushed open the wooden door that kept beasts and vermin from the food contained within. She paused before entering, glancing up at the square cross woven from reeds that was mounted above the door. It was originally the goddess Brigid's sign; although it was pagan in origin, the nuns had continued its use as a pretty little symbol of good luck. Its resemblance to their own crucifix surely hadn't hurt.

Just past the door, a short flight of steps carved into the earth led down to the cave floor, where the vault was low enough to make Étaín hunch slightly. Shelves that held various pots and metal containers lined the walls, while wooden barrels made aisles along the floor. Étaín held her candle out, looking for several herbs Boann had requested along with the leeks.

Étaín was just squinting at a jug when her candle flickered, as if rustled by a breeze, but the air in the cave was still. A fresh shiver coursed through Étaín; she had the sudden, overwhelming sense that she was not alone.

Turning, movement caught her eye, and a shallow light.

At the far end of the cave was a man. He was dressed in a white robe and cowl, holding a doll made of twigs and dressed in scraps of clothing. There was no doorway at that end of the cave, no way he could have entered behind her and walked unseen to the other end.

He glowed as he made his way slowly across the room. His feet didn't seem to move, yet his body glided forward. Étaín saw that he was speaking, but she heard only a slight, distant echo; the words sounded familiar yet strange, as if she knew the tongue but not the dialect. She wanted to run, to scream, but paralysis held her like an oaken casket. She could only stand, watching, as the figure made its slow way across the room, muttering barely heard words, to finally vanish through the cave's stone side.

A puff blew out the candle flame.

Étaín was released. She gasped and whirled, heading back to where she thought the stairs were. In her panic she ran headlong into a case, causing bottles and metal implements to clash and clatter. She felt pain in her side but then she found the steps leading up and out. Holding her robes up, she took them two at a time. At the top she threw herself against the heavy door and staggered as it flew open. She fell into the snow, but got to her feet not noticing the cold, and ran to the abbey, her breath leaving her in jagged clouds.

She burst into the kitchen where Boann was directing six other sisters in the preparation of the Imbolc feast. When she fell against a metal bowl and sent it clanging to the floor, they all stopped and stared at her.

"Child," Boann said, with concern, "what is it?"

"I saw . . . there was . . ."

A new voice interrupted. "There was what?"

All heads turned to see that the mother abbess—Brigid—had entered the kitchen. Her eyes scanned the scene quickly before turning on Étaín, who felt even more exposed and anxious in the presence of her superior. "Mother Abbess, I beg your pardon, but there was a man in the cave."

Several of the nuns murmured, but Brigid silenced them with a look before returning her attention to Étaín. "A man?"

"Not a man, or not a living man, but—a ghost."

More whispers sounded. Boann crossed herself, but muttered something from the old Celtic verses. Étaín realized it sounded like the words that the ghost had whispered.

Brigid, still imposing and elegant at seventy, smiled as she laid a comforting hand on Étaín's arm. "Come, girl, you know that ghosts are part of the old beliefs. Our Bible teaches us that our souls find eternal solace after death, that we have no need to return to our earthly dwellings."

"But . . . I saw . . ."

One of the other nuns in the kitchen, Maeve, said, softly, "Aye—I've seen that same man down there, one Samhain. A Druid."

Brigid's brow furrowed as she glanced at the speaker, then she gripped Étaín's arm more tightly and led her from the kitchen, away from the other sisters. "Let us speak further about this elsewhere."

Étaín allowed the older woman to lead her out of the kitchen to an empty chapel, where Brigid seated her on a rough wooden bench before sitting next to her, carefully arranging her robes. "Now, Sister Étaín, tell me exactly what you saw."

Étaín shivered as she spoke. "A man—or not a man—at the far end of the cave, dressed all in white, carrying a doll." Étaín thought of the rough doll and recalled Imbolc traditions.

"No—'tis Imbolc, so it was a *Brídeóg*."

Brigid nodded. "A figure of the goddess."

Étaín continued. "The ghost was dressed all in white, like a Druid, and he walked across the room and then through the wall."

Brigid considered her words before speaking. "Sister Étaín, I believe you witnessed something extraordinary, but our Christian fathers—I'm thinking especially of Saint Augustine—tell us that spirits cannot return to this realm. What you saw was a vision, and you must be wary of the possibility that our great enemy Satan gave you this vision as a way to tempt you from the path of the true faith."

No, Étaín wanted to say, *I know what I saw and it was not Satan.* Instead, she said, "But why would the Deceiver seek to tempt me? Why not you or even Sister Boann?"

Brigid smiled, an expression with a hint of sadness about it. "I have been tempted many times, my child. But as for you—you possess extraordinary skill with words. The verse you've created to honor God, and the history of these lands that you've collected and written down . . . you've truly been touched by the Creator. Don't you know that?"

Brigid cupped a hand beneath Étaín's chin and lifted her face. Étaín saw care there, and benevolence, and something indefinable she could only call grace. It was no wonder this woman had become famed throughout Eire.

"Mother Abbess, sometimes I . . . doubt." Étaín lowered her head in shame. "I doubt that it's God who has allowed me to possess these skills. After all, the stories I record are not those of God. Perhaps my gift comes from Cerridwen, or even the Morrígan." The matriarch of the old gods. As a child, Étaín's family had still practiced the Celtic religion. It wasn't until they'd sold her for marriage to the cruel son of a wealthy merchant and Brigid herself had rescued the sixteen-year-old girl from a public beating that Étaín had discovered Christianity. She'd been happy to convert, to serve Brigid (under the guise of serving God), to learn Brigid's language and writing along with her religion. That was now a dozen years in the past, long enough for Étaín to look back and wonder how much of her life had been her choice, how different it might have been had she been allowed to make her own decisions.

"Étaín, do you not see that the Morrígan is but another name for Mary, the mother of Jesus?"

Étaín had heard Brigid suggest that before, but she'd never been able to understand it. She could see the similarities between the pagan goddess and the Madonna—both were mothers to gods—but the Morrígan was the "phantom queen" who copulated with her consort before heading into battle, where she might transform into a crow to fly over the heads of the enemy troops.

Mary did none of those things.

But Étaín held her tongue as Brigid regarded her with a mix of affection and worry. After a few seconds, Brigid sighed and rose. "We should return to the feast. Being in the company of your sisters and Boann's good food should set you right again."

"Yes, Mother Abbess." Étaín followed the older woman out of the chapel and to the abbey's main hall, where the nuns were assembled, eating and chatting by candlelight.

Étaín took her usual seat next to Maeve, a woman in her fifties with a face like a winsome potato but a kind heart and cheerful smile. As Maeve handed Étaín a plate heaped high with steaming food, she leaned over and whispered, "The ghosts in this place are real, Sister. Many of us have seen them. The spirits of the old Druids. Where else would they go?"

Étaín ate the Imbolc feast in silence.

Beltane/The Evening of May 1

Étaín shoved more branches into her pack, tested the weight, and pulled the straps around her shoulders. It was enough for this trip; with what they'd already gathered over the last week, surely they'd have enough kindling now for the Beltane bonfire.

As she was about to turn and head back to the abbey, something caught Étaín's eye—movement. Someone in the forest, ahead of her. She froze, holding her breath.

It was a figure in white robes and cowl.

Étaín knew immediately that this was no ghost, however. The figure bobbed as it walked into a clearing between oak trees, where it cast a shadow in the late afternoon sunlight. The cowl went back, revealing a bearded face. The man climbed to the apex of a mound that bulged up from the clearing's center.

A *sidhe*. An entrance to the Otherworld.

Étaín shook the heretical thoughts from her head. She started to move off as quietly as she could, but—without turning to look at her—the man called out, "Stay, child."

She froze, her heart hammering. The man set his gaze on her; she saw strength and kindness there, and her heart slowed its frantic rhythm. He lowered one arm, letting his leather shoulder bag slide to the ground as he leaned heavily on his wooden staff. "Please, indulge an old man who just wants to talk for a few minutes."

Étaín stepped forward, more curious than concerned. As she neared the man, she saw he was old, face creased like a dried apple, back bent, hands lined, but his eyes were still clear, young.

"You're a Druid, aren't you?"

The man smiled. "Yes, but please call me Tadg. And you're a Christian nun, I believe?"

She lowered her head, felt her face reddening although she couldn't say why. "Étaín. From the abbey, yes."

"Collecting wood for the Beltane fire?"

Again Étaín felt like a child who had been caught stealing milk in the barn. "Yes."

"Brigid is wise to let the fire go forward."

"You know Brigid?"

"I know of her, of course, just as I know of her male counterpart, Patrick. Lower your burden, please."

Étaín shrugged out of her pack, dropping it to the soft, leaf-strewn ground. "Why are you here?" she asked.

Tadg released a mournful exhalation. "Didn't you know this area was sacred? It's why Brigid commanded her abbey be built here." He gestured in a circle around the clearing. "This place in particular. Sacred—to the goddess Brigid, in fact. There was once a divine fire kept burning here in her honor. Nine women tended it at one time." He gestured to a large, flat blackened stone perched atop the mound. "But it's also a dangerous place."

"The *sidhe*."

The Druid grinned. "There—you *do* remember some of our wisdom."

Étaín tried not to wince at his use of "our."

Looking up at the overhead light, edging toward the indigo of dusk, Tadg said, "I come here on each of our quarter-days. The *daoine sidhe* will only try to leave their mound on Samhain, but it's wise to appease them on all the important days." As he dropped slowly to his knees, Étaín heard them creak like unoiled hinges. "In the past, I came here with novices, all so anxious to learn the rites and invocations. Now, though, I'm alone."

He knelt, opened the bag, pulled out small sealed jugs and fresh flowers. He held up the first jug. "Milk for the Good Folk." He placed the small ceramic jug on the ground at one edge of the barrow and reached for the next container. "Berries." Lastly, the flowers were arrayed artfully. Tadg began to mutter a prayer in the old tongue.

Étaín wished she had quill and parchment; the words were strange, almost alien, but beautiful, provoking memories she didn't know she possessed—of attending rituals in forests with her parents, feeling the communion of the tribe; but then the missionaries had arrived, with better ways of building, smelting, map-making, and the greatest magic of them all—writing. The Celts had drifted away, one-by-one, to the new churches. After the ghost she'd seen three months earlier, she'd wondered if that was all that was left of the Druids, the great priests of the Celts who passed their knowledge orally. If she could talk to this one, write down his words . . .

Tadg finished the prayer and attempted to rise, his movements stiff and painful. Étaín leapt forward to help. "Thank you," he husked out.

"I wish I could write down what you said."

He looked at her with fresh interest. "Do you write now? That's a rare skill indeed."

"Mother Abbess—Brigid—taught me herself. She says I'm quite good at it."

"I don't doubt it. Pity . . ."

"What is?"

"You would have made a very fine *bandrui*."

Bandrui—a female Druid. Étaín felt her cheeks flush again. She hoped Tadg hadn't noticed.

If he did, he gave no sign. Instead he continued. "I could teach you so much. There are secrets that we Druids reveal to no one; even our initiates don't learn of them until they are ready. Secrets of much older gods than the Dagda and the Morrígan, older even than the Fomorians. These Great Old Ones sleep now but will awaken someday, and the fearful creatures that serve them in other realms will shatter all the weak religions." He paused to turn his gaze full on Étaín. "There are secrets much stronger than mere writing can record."

Étaín forced herself to meet his eyes. "My religion is *not* weak."

Tadg sighed before looking up at the sky, now a vivid purple. "It'll be dark soon. You'd best return while it's still safe."

Still safe. . . . She wondered if he meant while she could still see her way or if she should leave before the *daoine sidhe*—or something *older*—were unleashed.

"What about you?"

Tadg used his staff to push open the leather bag, revealing a lantern and candle within. "I'll be fine. Although you might wish me luck, should the Folk decide to celebrate Beltane as well."

Étaín shivered, hefted her sack of firewood, and left, reluctantly. Part of her wanted to stay with Tadg, learn his lore, become the novice he no longer had, but she knew her home was with Brigid and the sisters.

"Leap well through the Beltane fire, Étaín," he called after her as she left the clearing and entered the dark forest.

She looked back once, saw a tiny flame atop the mound, but couldn't make out Tadg.

She wondered if she'd ever see him again. She wanted to believe she would.

Lughnasadh/The Day of August 1

THE FEAST DAY OF THE god Lugh would be celebrated in Kildare Town with games of strength and speed; Brigid had given her nuns permission to attend, leaving the abbey empty, hollow, quiet.

Étaín feigned illness. She had never lied to the mother abbess before.

Once the others had left, Étaín threw back her covers, leapt from her narrow bed, dressed and left. Today was Lughnasadh, another holy day in the old calendar.

She wanted to see Tadg the Druid again.

Étaín wasn't sure why that thought had consumed her since Beltane. She worked furiously, and Brigid had told her that the new verse was her best yet. Something about the quiet dignity of Tadg—going about his Druidic duties as if the world hadn't flipped upside-down for him—filled Étaín with fire.

If Tadg was willing to let the Celtic ways die with him, unrecorded, forgotten, Étaín was not. She had honored his greatest secrets and included no mention of the older gods he truly served, but she'd written of the old quarter-days and the *daoine sidhe*. She felt the work was unfinished, though; she needed more from Tadg. She didn't know where to find him, but she hoped today he would return to the sacred grove.

The forest was fragrant and warm, in the full rush of summer, trees green with leaves, flowers sprouting from moist ground. The day was bright, but the woods were dappled with patches of deep gloom. Étaín picked her way carefully, pausing from time to time to listen to birdsong or to study an especially lovely bloom. Once she encountered a doe with fawn grazing, abruptly stiff as they heard her approach. She locked eyes with the doe, feeling something primeval exchanged, before it led its offspring to flee away from her.

Étaín approached the clearing among the oaks carefully; if Tadg was present, she didn't want to startle him.

But he wasn't there. The sacred space was empty.

It was still early in the morning, so the sun's rays slanted into the clearing, causing the top halves of the surrounding trees to glow while much of the clearing was in dense shadow. Étaín paused at the trunk of one of the oaks when she saw movement ahead. At first she thought it was Tadg with others, but then she realized she could see the far trees through the figures gathered around the mound.

She froze. The scene shimmered, almost as if Étaín were watching from underwater. Shapes—indistinct, slender, female. They moved slightly, performing some task. Among their blue-white forms flashed an occasional glimmer of gold.

A fire. They were tending a fire . . . that didn't exist. That *hadn't* existed for decades, just as they hadn't. Yet they continued here in their sacred duty—*bandrui*, forever feeding the fire dedicated to Brigid, their great goddess.

Étaín was mesmerized. She stood motionless, willing her breath to come and go as silently as possible. She watched for several minutes, discovered she could actually see the ghosts more clearly when she didn't look at them directly, but rather turned her gaze to the side, away from them. At one point the doe and fawn appeared, galloping through the center of the clearing, visible through the ghost women, who didn't respond to them. The deer moved off; the ghosts continued to work, their arms mimicking the action of placing tinder in the fire.

Not much later, the sun spied over the treetops, light bathed the clearing, and the ghosts vanished.

Étaín knew it was possible that Tadg might yet arrive, but some instinct told her it was unlikely. She thought him either dead or tending to some other function today, perhaps leading his last few believers in a ritual to recognize Lughnasadh.

That night, as she slept in her narrow bunk, she dreamed of a great stag that was chased through the woods by grotesque, inhuman hunters, huge things with amorphous shapes covered with dozens of eyes. They cornered the magnificent beast in the sacred clearing, advancing on it, driving the deer to its knees as they tore it apart, all while something unseen and greater than the world stood just outside their circle, looking down dispassionately.

Étaín woke with a start, gasping. Once she'd calmed down, she began to cry.

Samhain/The Eve of November 1

Étaín waited until after Vespers, as the sisters were enjoying their Samhain feast and telling stories of the *daoine sidhe*, before she crept out of the abbey.

She excused herself from the table, went to her cell, pulled on her heaviest cloak, took a candle, and decided to leave by the kitchen door. She half-expected Brigid to follow, or to be waiting at the door, offering wisdom about the glories of God, about the sacrifice of Jesus, about living inside God's love.

But Étaín had dreamed last night of another kind of love. In the dream, she'd been on sacred ground, surrounded by oaks that had faces buried in their boughs and whispered to her. Looking up, she'd seen two immense figures in the sky, intertwined. She'd instinctively understood them to be the Morrígan and the Dagda, the Celts' mother and father gods, merging their energies to renew the world. Samhain would mark the arrival of the new year and would be celebrated throughout Eire with feasting and camaraderie, but Étaín knew there were other, darker passions associated with this holiest of days as well. The eve was a boundary, when the Otherworld crossed into ours, when the *sidhe* barrows opened and things not human came into this world. Even as the Dagda and the Morrígan copulated to create new life, the mischievous ones were afoot, and sometimes their mischief was malicious.

Étaín awoke from that dream planning to venture into the woods alone at dusk. She had to see for herself if the *daoine sidhe* existed, because she had come to believe that Mother Abbess Brigid's religion was pale, suitable only perhaps for those of Roman heritage, who had seen their empire fall and their gods disperse. Christianity didn't accept ghosts, but Étaín knew they existed; it didn't recognize the turning seasons or the reality of physical love. Étaín had known such love only once, and it had been an ugly, brutal thing that she'd been happy to leave behind. But she thought there was something better, something grand and sensual and lasting, something she knew she would never experience as long as her life belonged to six services a day and the endless work of the nuns.

She left the abbey unseen. No one tried to reason with her, no one demanded that she remain. She was alone as she ventured into the woods.

It was full night, so Étaín moved carefully among the roots and deadfalls; it wouldn't serve her purpose to spend Samhain with a broken ankle. Her stomach fluttered with excitement as she ventured deeper into the forest, her ears strained for unfamiliar sounds. What would the *daoine sidhe* sound like? Laughter? Shrieks? Something that was both and neither?

At last she reached the clearing in the oaks, the ancient circle with the blackened stone in the center. She was disappointed to see that she was alone in every sense—neither human nor spirit was present. Was she too early? She pulled her cloak around her and settled down with her back against a broad trunk, waiting.

Étaín started once at a loud cry, but then recognized it as the call of an owl, circling in search of prey. A scuttling noise a few minutes later she suspected to be a fox or hare.

As she sat huddled against the tree, she thought back to her Lughnasadh encounter, when she'd seen the ghosts of the former servants of Brigid's divine fire, and she now doubted her senses. It had been early, when shafts of light had dappled the clearing. Perhaps she'd really seen nothing, had put her faith in yet another illusion. Perhaps the Druid ghost in the cave had been an intruder or a hanging sheet caught in a breeze from the open door.

And she was convinced that the Druid Tadg was dead. He'd told her he came to this place on each quarter-day, but she'd encountered him on neither Lughnasadh nor today, Samhain. He'd been very old, his joints seizing. Perhaps his elder gods had come for him.

She was about to stand and go when a sound drew her attention—wings flapping. As she waited, frozen, a large owl settled atop the mound in the center of the clearing. It was the biggest bird she'd ever seen—nearly the size of a man—with white feathers and vibrant eyes. It regarded her without fear, but instead with something like affection. She held its gaze for no more than ten seconds, but it felt like a century in the Otherworld.

She whispered a name. "Tadg?"

At that it lifted away into the night again, and Étaín knew that Samhain was over.

The Otherworld was not opening for her tonight, no magic or gods—either Celtic or older—would be revealed. She rose, turning to go. She'd felt some kinship with the owl, but if magic had been there it had left her feeling that neither Celtic nor Christian could show her a way forward. There was only here, tonight, a natural night. There was only life, waiting for her beyond the forest, away from the convent. She was still young enough to take risks, to feel the oak at her back, hear the night predator overhead, smell the rich mulch of the woods, see the warm flicker of the candle leading her. There might be things—*horrible* things—waiting to lay waste to her world, but she would savor it first. Eventually she might feel the soft caress of a lover, taste them on her tongue. There was magic to find in the world, if she could learn how to look.

She had never walked to the other side of the clearing, but she went that way now, and kept going. The new year was already promising.

THE BAREFOOT SISTERS OF SAINT BEATRIZ OF THE MOUNTAIN

KALI WALLACE

WE CLIMBED THE MOUNTAIN STAIRS at sunset, my sister and I. Dust stirred in clouds at my feet. The day was hot, the sun a weight on my shoulders. With every step the stench of disease and death faded, and the chanted prayers from the convent grew louder.

The plague had reached the valley well before us, and we had spent the day tending to the sick. They had been suspicious of us, strangers abroad in their little village, having heard the tales of brigands on the prowl, false holy men offering salvation for a price, even ravenous, red-eyed demons stalking the roads, but there were stories aplenty in these dark times and there was nobody else coming to their aid. Everybody who could flee was already gone. Now, as the day softened to dusk, my hands stung with fresh cuts, and my sister was lighter on my back.

Lighter, but no less stubborn. Her voice spurred me up, up, and up, and the constant chatter was a relief. She had spoken little since we left Seville, breaking long hours and days of silence only to tell me which road to take, which path to follow, giving guidance to the promise of our mother's stories, to the lure of her memories I felt as a tug in my gut.

About the convent of Saint Beatriz of the Mountain our mother used to say: *I was very young and very foolish when I lived in that place.* As she spoke she would smooth my hair back from my brow, the tap of her one wooden finger hard where there should be warm, soft skin. I was a curious child and asked her where the convent was, which town it stood near, which river it overlooked, but she never told me. I knew only that she had been there before she wed and that those pious sisters on the mountain had cast her out. Our neighbors in Seville, wealthy wives with sharp smiles, had waited until my mother left the room to pointedly ask me if I knew my age, my *precise* age, as they counted on their fingers and nodded knowingly.

I was the one who had listened to the stories at my mother's knee, but it was my sister who knew the way. That was how it had always been with us. *Follow the road east to Cordova,* she said, when we first left Seville. And when I hesitated: *Turn north to climb from the lowlands.* As I grew tired: *Into the hills. Into the mountains. Into the cracked spine of the land.*

And before I slept each night, hiding in thickets of roadside trees: *Soon, sister. Soon.*

Four hundred steps and more from the valley to the summit, and at last we reached the convent. Below, the hills glowed warm and yellow, terraced with olive groves, and through the valley a river wound like a snake. This valley was where the beloved saint, my namesake, had fled the unbelievers who mistook her miracles for wicked magic, who had named her witch, demon, succubus—this was where she had climbed, barefoot and bleeding, half the bones in her body broken, to die upon the mountaintop, gasping her last prayers, alone. This was also where, according to the apocryphal tales vehemently derided by men who knew such things, tormented Beatriz had woken from that cruel death to a new life. Those stories were, of course, blasphemy. She was only a saint, after all, not a savior. She was said to have left a trail of blood from valley to summit.

Nobody stirred in the village below. It was a restful sight. Our mother had said that view from the top was all she missed of the convent. *Not the sisters, not their judgment, not the pain of their sacred mortification that had left her with nine fingers of flesh and one of wood. Only the view.* There had been sorrow in her voice when she said it, a sadness almost as great as her anger.

The summer fields and golden dusk allowed me to forget, for the time it took my breath to steady and my heart to slow, how much sickness and agony now covered the world. The Black Plague had come to Malaga on Italian ships and burned across all of Iberia, all of France, across the channel to England. Everywhere, men and women were praying and mourning, begging salvation from the pope in Avignon, from the Castilian king on his battlefields, and most of all from God in Heaven who had judged the world so harshly.

As for me, my skin remained unbruised, my blood free of fever, my lungs empty of phlegm. Every morning when the sun rose and every evening when it set I examined my fingernails for black stains, but found none.

Nor will you, my sister said, every morning. I was starting to believe her.

The convent that loomed before me looked more like a fortress than a holy place. The broad stone face was broken only by arrow slits, its corners anchored by high, square towers, and the doors were tall and wide enough for three mounted soldiers to ride abreast. I had never seen such wood before, polished as dark as iron.

Listen, said my sister.

As always, I did as she asked.

Through those great doors, beyond those great walls, rose the sound of women's voices joined in prayer. My skin pricked to hear it; my blood hummed. My entire life I had woken every morning to the Moors calling to prayer, the bells of Santa Ana ringing, the devotions and declarations of the faithful coursing over the city as sure as dawn breaking, but this was different. I did not know the words—my mother refused to teach me even one line of their sacred songs—but still I felt the desperation in their chanting as a quickening in my gut, a tremble in my heart.

"Listen to them," I said. My voice was parched from the long, hot climb. "They sound so frightened."

They sing for us, said my sister, a whisper behind my ear, and her laughter was my own.

A chill caressed my skin, a teasing promise of evening wind. It would be dark soon. I raised my hand to knock upon that great door, and I jumped back in alarm when my knock echoed with threefold strength, a reverberation so strong it was as though I had struck a drum the size of a mountain. The voices sang uninterrupted as the sound boomed, and they sang as it faded. Evening birds chattered cheerily again.

I folded my hands and I waited. I shifted my weight from one aching foot to the other. The voices within sang and sang. I had shed my shoes at the base of the stairs; the Sisters of Saint Beatriz went barefoot in every season to feel their mountain beneath them, as their saint had felt it on her climb. I felt only hot stone and sharp pebbles, not the purifying pain of spilled blood.

Presently I heard a scrape of footsteps inside: *rasp-tap, rasp-tap.* The gait was uneven, the pace slow.

According to the stories, the infidels had broken Beatriz's leg, but a shattered bone had not stopped her escape. *To assume that wound upon oneself,* my mother had said, *was a very pious act indeed.* How she had scowled when she said it, and how she had raged when I hobbled through the house with a feigned limp, dramatically snapping sticks of kindling and howling as though they were my bones.

From the collar of my dress I withdrew my mother's Saint Beatriz charm, a small white medallion of bone with the visage of a woman carved on one side. She had never worn it until she fell ill; I had been surprised to find it about her neck when she lay insensible and feverish in her bed. I had taken it from her when she was too weak to protest, before I gave her the strength to rise again. Even now, with the long days and miles of dusty road between the barred doors of our home and where I stood, I felt a pang of sadness to imagine how frightened she must have been to cling to the saint she hated so much.

The footsteps on the other side of the door stopped. I twisted my hands. Listened to a lock clank, a bar lift and drop. One half of those great doors opened with agonizing slowness. A woman's head leaned through the gap. She was no taller than a child, her face wizened with age. Her eyes, soft brown, set upon me warily.

"Good evening, Sister," I said. "I have come to seek sanctuary with the Sisters of Saint Beatriz."

Show her, said my sister, but I did not need the reminder. I was already holding the saint's medal between my fingers.

"My mother was here when she was young, before she wed. She always spoke warmly of your convent and the kindness of the sisters here," I said.

It was not, in its way, a lie. The anger my mother had carried burned as hot and steady as banked embers.

The nun's eyes flicked over the medal, back to my face, searching for any sign of illness. She glanced past my shoulder to the valley beyond—fields abandoned, gardens untended, and evening sky empty of smoke. She looked at my hands and saw the thin scabs where I had squeezed droplets of blood into wooden cups, but she did not see fingernails blackened with rot.

I went on: "Before she died my mother told me I might be safe here."

My sister laughed, playful and sharp.

"Please," I said. I was soft; I was young; I was alone. "Please. I don't know where else to go. There is nobody in the village who can help."

That, at least, was true, but irrelevant. It was I who had helped them, in the end. From this height, four hundred steps and more, I could not hear them coming awake in their hovels to snap and snarl at quaking walls.

With all the slowness of mountains shifting, the crags of the nun's face broke from suspicion to pity. "My dear child. Did you hear us singing?"

"I did," I said. "I heard your voices before I climbed. They gave me the strength I needed. I hear them still."

"Then you are welcome here."

She shuffled aside to let me in. I helped her tug the great door closed and set the bar back into place.

"We cannot be too careful," she said. "These are wicked times. A young woman should not travel these roads alone."

A tender sentiment, but they had not cared about a young woman alone when they had sent my mother away. Neither had they cared much for the child growing inside her.

The woman's name was Sister Isidora. She had come from Valencia many years ago; she had not seen the sea since she was a child. She wore a habit of wool so coarse it would shame even the most austere Benedictine. As expected her feet were bare. She leaned upon a crutch and dragged one foot as she walked: *rasp-tap, rasp-tap.*

I offered my arm. "Let me help you, Sister."

Sister Isidora smiled. "We suffer as beloved Beatriz suffered, and these pains of the body trouble us no more than they troubled her."

If the stories were to be believed, Beatriz had died weeping and screaming, in excruciating pain, shunned by every priest in every town, every Samaritan on every road, alone with her punishment and her pain—which seemed to me very troubling, even for a saint.

The convent doors opened not into an entrance hall but a large courtyard, Roman in style, with covered walkways on all four sides and a large reflecting pool in the center. The courtyard was so ancient trees had grown into the stones themselves: branches braided over archways, trunks woven into the walls, roots erupting from the floor. Leaves sprouted in rich bursts of green from cornices and pillars, walls and sills, from the cracked center of a stone bench.

At one end of the shining pool stood a magnificent yew tree, the base of which had once been carved into an image of a woman. Bark had grown over most of her; all that remained visible were her bare feet and naked legs below the knee. Her toes curled against the roots in ecstasy or pain. It is hard to know how a saint suffers, judging only from the shape of her toes.

It was in the nest of that yew's hardy old roots that my mother had taken comfort when she discovered she was with child and knew the sisters of the convent would soon send her away. There, beneath a crown of turning leaves, she had prayed for forgiveness from her God and solace from her saint, and she had never quite forgiven either of them for giving her a squalling, unwanted baby instead.

From the courtyard Sister Isidora led me through a pleasant garden, through a smaller courtyard, around the chapel where nuns chanted without pause, and finally to a refectory with a ceiling so high and so grand the room might have been a church itself. The scent of fresh-baked bread was so sweet tears sprang to my eyes. Sister Isidora showed me to a table, and I slid onto the bench at one end, smiling uncertainly. I slipped the bundle from my back but did not let it slump to the floor; I held it instead on my lap and felt the shifting points and knobs press into my abdomen.

"Thank you," I said. Isidora was already hurrying away—*rasp-tap, rasp-tap*—and so I addressed the women nearest me. "Thank you for your kindness and for this offer of sanctuary."

Their smiles were as craggy and ancient as Isidora's, and their bodies bore the wounds of devotion to their saint. Sister Elaine carried one arm in a sling, though a sling was more care than Beatriz would have had on her flight from her murderers. Sister Ines had strips of cloth wrapped around splints on two fingers—those broken fingers being, in the stories, the very first of Beatriz's injuries, inflicted upon her as a taste of the torments to come. Many of the others had crutches or canes leaning against the table or bench. When Sister Estafania offered me a bowl of olives, I saw that she had a wooden finger affixed to her hand with leather straps, much the same as my mother's.

"Is it very bad beyond our walls?" asked Sister Ines, after I had finished one cup of fine summer wine and she had poured me a second. "One of our younger sisters went to help the villagers when the plague first came, but she has not returned."

Not yet, cackled my sister. I pressed a hand down atop the bundle to hush her. In the village the young woman in the coarse wool habit had fought like an animal to spit our gift from her mouth, and she was fighting still when we left her.

"Sister Infanta," said Sister Elaine. "She was a gentle child."

Sister Estafania snorted. "Too gentle. She wept with her first snap."

"We had hoped her gentleness would be comfort to those who suffer," Sister Elaine admitted, and together they tutted sadly.

"There is suffering everywhere," I said.

I told them what had become of Seville, how our bustling streets and markets had fallen so easily to the Italian plague, how voices that had once greeted each other in Arabic and Hebrew and Latin and every language of Christendom had turned to crying only for help, and then wailing in mourning when no help came. I confided that my merchant father had not returned from his travels, and I could not help but believe he had perished. I even shared the rumors racing along the roads: demon-eyed predators, monsters in the night. They gasped and exclaimed and told me how brave I was to have come so far, how blessed I was to have kept so safe.

Of my mother I told them only that she had taken ill and died.

Tell them how she screams, urged my sister, and to the nuns I said, "She spoke of your sanctuary when she was ailing." *Tell them how she threw the candle at your head and cursed your name to cast you out,* my sister taunted, and I said, "She prayed to Saint Beatriz, still, at the end."

My sister, she only laughed.

In truth, my mother had spoken little in her final hours. After she had cursed my name and her saint's, her voice had failed, and it was all she could do to whimper as her skin blackened with sores. She did not even have strength enough to push me back when I squeezed her mouth open and tilted a droplet onto her tongue. She had tried to spit it out, landed a lucky spray of pink foam on my cheek, but I pinched her lips together and held them closed until she stopped struggling beneath me, until her breath slowed, and finally stopped—and held them longer until she shuddered and her eyes opened once again, now red with wild rage.

I fled from the house. My mother's screams would have drawn the neighbors, had there been anybody alive to hear. My sister was laughing as we ran away and my own heart was pounding, my breath short, the giddy flush of victory burning through me.

"She was at peace, I think, when she died," I said.

They did not hear my sister snickering in my lap.

"The plague has not breached your walls?" I asked, and they assured me that no, it had not, and they were certain it never would. "But it has come close—the village."

Yes, they were very sorry for the village, and Sister Infanta—so young, so gentle. They did not see themselves as cowards, hiding behind their walls. They honored their saint for how she had died, but they cared little for how she had lived: wandering, unprotected by stone towers and barred doors, performing miracles so striking and so strange whispers of suspicion hounded her everywhere she went. My favorite story had always been the executed men hanging from the old Roman walls of Barcelona, and how Beatriz had made their bones clatter and dance until their rotting sinews snapped and their skeletons fell to pieces.

"Our beloved Beatriz preserves us," said Sister Elaine. The old nuns nodded, wrinkled faces bobbing over loose-skinned necks. "You hear our song, my child, do you not?" Heads tilted to listen. Tears glistened in eyes.

Sister Elaine patted my hand. "We sing without fail. When those in the chapel grow weary, others will replace them. With Saint Beatriz's words we sing a veil of protection over our sanctuary. You will be safe here."

With the elderly sisters at my side and the comfort of their voices all around, I ate deeply from their bountiful table: figs and dates sticky-sweet on my tongue, red pomegranates bursting with juicy seeds, fish stewed with spices, each bite more delicious than the last. There was no end to the feast.

Sister Ines offered me a third cup of wine—each she poured me was an excuse to pour another for herself—but before she could tilt the first drop the doors of the refectory opened and a hush fell over the room. Voices dropped away to whispers, cups clicked to tabletops, and every head in the hall, including my own, turned to see who had come.

In the door to the refectory stood the biggest woman I had ever seen, as impressive as an Amazon from ancient times, taller than every other nun by at least a head. Her face was as broad and flat as a cart wheel, her shoulders as wide as the cart itself. Her hair was hidden behind the severe line of her wimple, but her eyebrows were twin dark caterpillars crowding her impressive brow. Sister Isidora was as tiny as a child beside her.

We know her, said my sister, and I did. My mother had spoken of this woman, lips curling into a sneer around the words. She was the one who had been standing at the convent doors before they slammed shut, candlelight behind her, her silhouette as towering as the mountain itself, unmoved by my mother pleading on the steps outside.

Sister Isidora hobbled over to me, and that mountainous woman came behind her. They stopped together.

"Reverend Mother Frinolde," said Sister Isidora, bowing out of the way. "Abbess of the Sisters of Saint Beatriz of the Mountain."

I stood, awkwardly clutching my bundle to my chest, and offered my own meager bow. Before her I felt as small as a gnawing worm upon the perfect ripe skin of an apricot.

"I thank you for your sanctuary, Reverend Mother," I said.

"You are welcome here, child," said the abbess.

She knows you, said my sister. How strange it felt, to have her whispers tickling like autumn leaves in my arms rather than humming like bees behind my ear. I squeezed the bundle tighter and wondered if I had imagined the twitch of the abbess's eye.

"I remember your mother," said the abbess. "She was very young when she came to us, and not much older when she left."

"*Left,*" my sister hissed, and I felt it too, the sting of that dishonest word.

Left, as though they had not thrown her and her unborn child from their sanctuary, thundering with indignation as they slammed the doors closed.

"You have the look of her," said the abbess.

"So I have been told, Reverend Mother," I said.

It might have been an attempt at a smile, the expression that crossed her face, but to me it looked only like a rot-softened fruit collapsing in on itself. Beneath the broad cuffs of the abbess's sleeves I saw one hand of flesh, its knuckles knobby, but the other, the other was a knot of five hinged wooden fingers, each articulated like the jiggling legs of a marionette. *How boastful,* my sister sneered. I bit the inside of my cheek to keep from smiling. An entire hand! Very boastful indeed. I could not see if she had five matching medallions about her neck. Saint Beatriz had never lost an entire hand.

"We are so happy you have found your way to us, after so very long," the abbess said. "Please, finish your meal and your wine, and rest for the night. Tomorrow we shall speak of your place here."

She did not offer her hand for me to kiss, so I did not have to find a way to refuse.

I said, "Thank you, Reverend Mother."

When she was gone, Sister Elaine confided in a girlish whisper that the abbess spent every evening chanting prayers to relieve those sisters who had sung through the day. She was the strongest of them, Elaine said, admiration shining in her eyes. The abbess had suffered every wound the saint had suffered twice over, or more, but she stood tall, and still she sang.

When I had eaten my fill, Sister Isidora led me from the refectory. Dusk had fallen over the mountains. The midsummer sky was streaked red and purple, laced with delicate clouds so beautiful my fingers itched to reach into the heavens and touch them. A sliver of moon slipped downward on the heels of the sun.

Isidora showed me to a well where I washed the dust of the road from my face, then to the chamber where I was to sleep. It had been the cell of the young nun who had gone to the village. Sister Infanta, recently lost, already mourned. Here, too, living trees twisted through the stone walls and floor, roots bumping the floor into uneven slopes, splitting the walls along jagged seams. There was a high, narrow slit of a window in the stone wall.

I thanked Sister Isidora again for her kindness, and she bid me good night. I listened to her shuffle away—*rasp-tap, rasp-tap*—before I closed the door. A quiver of leaves rustled; the frame was half stone, half living tree. There was a wool blanket folded over a straw bed. I wondered if Sister Infanta had folded it there before she left, if strands of her hair clung to the straw, if I would roll into the depression left by her slumbering body. If she had known when she stepped through that low doorway she would not see this cell again.

She may yet, said my sister, laughing.

"I very much doubt she'll recognize it, if she does."

Four hundred steps and more.

"Not yet. We'll wait until they sleep."

A knock upon the door.

"Be quiet." I lowered my sister's bundle to the floor, myself to the bed. "I want to rest."

A spit upon the tongue.

The first time my sister and I made our cure, my hands trembled as I ground the bone with mortar and pestle and opened a slice in the flesh of my palm. In spite of my sister's whispered reassurances, I was uncertain as I knelt at my mother's side. I asked my mother if she was thirsty, and she tried to knock the cup from my hand. She didn't know what was in it; she would have knocked away anything I offered. She had no strength to speak, but I thought I heard, in her ragged breath, a single word: *You.* She did not say my name. I wouldn't have known if she spoke to me or the saint in any case. *You.*

My hands were not trembling by the time I mixed the concoction in the village below the mountain. I had practiced on the road—a widow here, a peddler there, never more than one at a time. I was a young girl, harmless, and there were so many people desperate for hope. Drops of blood, dust of bone. My sister in her bundle was shrinking, but then she had never been very big, never having cried even a single infant's wail.

"Wait," I said to my sister and the darkness. Through the window I could see only a slice of stars. "Give them time."

She hummed to herself as I rested. The song was a lullaby, one our mother had sung when I was a child. It had been years since those comfortable winter nights when my father boasted and my mother laughed and only I knew that the thing growing in her womb had the shape of a girl like me rather than the boy they had prayed for. How very happy they had been, and in my childish innocence I had been happy too. A child never sees until too late the way her parents' eyes turn cold and hard when they look upon her. A child has no armor against that.

Perhaps my sister thought it a comfort, to hum that song, but the words crawled over my skin like rats, and even worse than the lullaby was the chanting of the nuns. That ceaseless prayer, that needling song, it filled the convent and the night, suffocating all other sounds. I could not hear wind through the trees outside, nor insects or birds. I heard no groans, no snarls, no clumsy hands scrabbling on stone. I could not hear them at all, my villagers, for the nun's voices had no beginning and no end. I felt every pause as a gathering expectation at the back of my throat, a certainty that this time, *this* time their breath would fail, their devotion would falter, and a moment of silence would fall over the convent, and that moment would stretch, and that moment would harden like a soft spring vine growing coarse and brittle, and when it snapped, a hot wet crack like bone breaking, the veil of their prayers would split and tear—for a veil was not so different from a net, and a net could catch all manner of things, and here I was.

Go to them, said my sister, her whispers rising seamlessly from her lullaby.

I threw back the wool blanket and gathered my sister into my arms.

I moved as quiet as a wraith through the convent, through gardens sharp with the scent of bitter herbs, through archways of rustling leaves. I found the courtyard with the pool and the yew, passed them by and found the doors. I lifted the bar and set it aside—softly, softly. I pulled open one of the great doors, then the other.

I walked to the edge and I looked down. There was no firelight in the village. The river was a black ribbon.

Saint Beatriz had climbed this mountain with armies raging at her back. She left a trail as she climbed, or so my mother had said, bloody tracks from the base of the mountain to its crown. Here upon the summit her blood had mingled with her tears and her sweat, seeped into the ground, stained the stone and the springs below.

The day my mother told me that story was the day my sister spoke her first word.

Blood, she had whispered, an echo beneath my mother's voice.

I had answered, "Hello? Baby sister? Hello?" and pressed my ear to my mother's belly to hear it again: *blood,* and a giggle with it, so I giggled too, delighted. I had thought the look on my mother's face was indulgence. I did not know then how well she hid her fear; I never knew until she could not hide it anymore. I did not know that her suspicion had already taken root, long before my sister woke and whispered. I did not know that my father was already finding reasons to travel farther and stay away longer. I did not know yet, that happy day, how vividly my mother would remember later, when my sister was born blue and still and silent. After my sister's stillbirth my mother flinched whenever I spoke, as though it was my greeting that had seeped into her womb and shriveled the child growing there. She might not have been wrong. Since I had heard that first whisper—*blood,* a laugh—I had wanted to keep my sister only for myself.

 Even in the scant light I could see the villagers climbing the stairs. Four hundred steps and more. I hugged my sister to my chest and watched them. It wasn't fear in my gut, but a coiled snake-eager impatience. Some of them came swiftly, springing on bent knees and strong hands, breathtaking in their speed. Others came slowly, plodding as I had that afternoon: lift a foot, rest, wheeze, and step again. I had not thought at first they would need to breathe, but a wheeze is not so different from a scream, and my mother had certainly screamed.

 The first to reach me was a young woman with a whiplike braid of golden hair. Sister Infanta bounded up the stairs with astonishing speed, her new claws clicking excitedly on the stone. She still wore her tattered habit, but her wimple was gone. She stopped when she saw me, poised only three steps below. She had been homely before, her expression dull with hopelessness. They sent her to the village to face the plague armed with only gentleness and prayers, but bruises had bloomed on her youthful skin, a fever had risen, and by the time I arrived her blackened fingers were too rotten to help anybody at all. There hadn't been fear in her eyes. There hadn't been anything except the aching empty hole where her faith had once been.

 But now, now, poised beneath the midsummer sky, she was magnificent. Her eyes flashed red in the starlight. When she grinned her teeth were red too. The stains on her habit looked black, but her plague-bruises shimmered like polished stones. Swaying back and forth, she watched me. She lifted her head with a predatory sniff.

 I gestured: an invitation.

 She was a flash through the open doors, and the first startled shout followed shortly. The others flowed around me, an unstoppable river around a single stone, and one scream turned to two, to dozens. *That interrupted their song,* I thought, and I waited for my sister to agree, waited for the butterfly flutter of her laugh in my arms, but she remained silent. When the last of the villagers were inside—a stooped old man who tripped on every step, a young boy who was not slow but easily distracted—I closed the doors and barred them again.

 I went to sit beside the yew in the courtyard, in the same nest of roots where my mother had once wept and prayed. I slipped my feet into the water; it was warmer than I expected. This water, if the stories were to be believed, had the blood of Saint Beatriz in it. The springs fed the convent wells, the gardens and the orchards, the trees that grew so hardy and strong through the stones of the fortress.

I leaned against the tree, I breathed in the night air, and I listened: screams turned to pleas, to prayers, to babbling fear. Bones cracking. The rainwater splatter of blood. The heavy thump of bodies falling—the clumsy scrabble of them rising again. My sister was quiet. I rested my hand on her bundle. Through the cloth I could feel the knobs and bumps of what remained. She was so little now, a tiny fragile thing made even smaller. It had always been so hard to tell her whispers from my own anyway.

The convent was nearly quiet when the first blush of dawn kissed the eastern sky. The villagers and the sisters gathered around me, returning from far corners of the sanctuary one by one. Red eyes, red smiles. Sister Estafania and Sister Isidora crawled to the edge of the water and lowered their heads to slurp thirstily; ripples spread, stained pink. Sister Infanta prowled the courtyard restlessly before finally curling up beside me at the base of the yew, so close I could feel the heat of her body warming mine. Her breath came from deep in her throat, a low murmur almost like a purr. I smelled blood where she had smelled of sickness before. She watched me. Patiently, calmly. Watched, and waited. All around pairs of red eyes did the same, perched on the roofs and benches, crouched beside the water, clinging to the wood veins of the walls with claws as long as knives.

The last to join us in the courtyard was the abbess. She lurched through a doorway and tripped over the little boy from the village. He snarled and snapped at her ankles. Her broad shoulders were twisted in pain; her arm with the wooden hand dangled uselessly at her side. Twin trickles of blood traced lines from the sides of her mouth. She stumbled over a crooked stone and fell, slowly, a tower toppling.

She lay still for a long time. I could hear her breathing, a sucking wheeze in and out, in and out.

I started when she spoke.

"*You,*" she said, the word wrenched from the ruin of her face. She turned her head, her blue eyes dull, fading, and she said it again: "*You.*"

When she lay her head on the ground again, she was not looking at me but across the pool to the great polished doors, still barred, and I understood that it was both an accusation and a question. The answer to the first was, of course, obvious. Their prayers had never changed. There had only ever been me.

The answer to the second—the doors were closed, the doors were barred. Within were my creatures, gathering and waiting. Without, the world and the plague.

The sky was brightening overhead, the clinging wisps of cloud burning away. A breeze wandered through the courtyard; the air was already warm. I had not been listening for birds before, but I heard them now, their gleeful, chaotic song filling the silence where the grinding chant had been. It would not be so bad, to leave the doors barred, to stay here for a while, with the sisters and the villagers all around me. I could hear them, every one. Breathing, drinking. They watched me with such trust in their eyes, such childish devotion.

I leaned against the yew. The trunk was rough on this side, not polished and smooth. I trailed my feet in the warm, warm water.

It would not be so bad, to open the doors again.

UNBURDENED FLESH

PENELOPE LOVE

In January of the year of our Lord 1348, the abbess of the convent of Sant'Apostolo on the island of Ammiano in the Venetian lagoon saw a plague ship drift past with slack sails and no one left alive to steer. She at once brought in stores and forbade visitors except for old Bernardino who ran the convent's errands. Her prompt action, and the nuns' unflagging prayers to Saint Brigid and Saint Sebastian, kept the plague away, but now the convent's supplies were low and old Bernardino had failed to arrive for the third morning in a row.

The island was remote and the half-ruined building too large for the eight souls who inhabited it. The nuns had all taken the vow to remain within the convent walls. Their novice was a ragged orphan named Arcangela. As the only one who had not taken her vows she was the only one free to leave.

Arcangela was a skinny girl with large, dark eyes and black curls cropped short, dressed in a prickly, coarse brown habit that itched so badly that she sometimes thrust a hand down her back and scratched. She was sleepy, having risen at 2 a.m. for Matins and 5 a.m. for Laud, and she was hungry. It was Friday, a fast day. Besides, her first duty of the day, emptying Sister Teresa's chamber pot, always put her off breakfast.

Arcangela knew enough Latin to get through her prayers, but the abbess told her she must learn to read and write so she could copy the holy books. As she busied herself with mundane tasks in the scriptorium, grinding ink and cutting quills, she cast scared glances at the ranks of books, chained to the copying desks or locked behind the bars of the book vault. What a terrible labor it would be to copy even one.

The summons from the abbess came shortly after the daily office of

Terce. Arcangela answered it quaking, convinced that for her sins she was about to learn Latin. Her fears seemed confirmed when she found the abbess with a richly decorated psalter in her hand. She edged gingerly into the abbess's holy sanctum, prepared for the worst. The relief on hearing that she was being sent to find old Bernardino was exquisite. The abbess was a tall, dark, severe woman. Arcangela worshipped her. In the novice's eyes her abbess stood as high as the bell towers, and even closer to Heaven. Now she took Arcangela's hands in blessing and forbade her from taking even one step on shore. Bernardino's house backed onto the Castello canal, the abbess explained. Arcangela could call to him from the water. The injunction had the force of canon law.

Arcangela flew on dancing feet to the convent's rowboat, delighted to escape the island for a few hours. The convent was damp and cold, and they only allowed one fire—in the kitchen. It was guarded by the prioress, a sturdy woman with a hard hand. To row across the lagoon was a heady luxury after months inside, enduring the endless round of religious offices: Matins, Lauds and Prime, Terce, Sext, None, Vespers and Compline.

During that terrible winter the city had become more and more remote, its bell towers and domes floating in the mist like a dream. Only as she rowed into the Castello canal did she realize that distance had added glamor and hidden the grim reality. The church bells rang and the waves lapped against the embankments as before but the gondolas and barges had vanished. The merchants' ships sat empty and rotting at anchor. There were no hawkers' calls or music, or the noise of brawls, and she heard only inarticulate sounds, a distant scream and nearby muffled sobbing. As she approached the campanile of San Domenico she finally heard a human voice.

Two men poled a barge laden with corpses straight for her. "Dead bodies! Dead bodies!" they cried.

The encounter occurred just at the worst place, over the deep water at the mouth of the canal, where no fishermen would fish. Here the city dumped the bodies of suicides, damned to the Abyss forever for the sin of Despair.

Frantically she thrust with her pole to fend off the barge and its rotting cargo. One of the corpses shifted over with the bump. She saw pallid eyes in a blackened, distorted face. Everything she knew of the Great Malady flashed through her mind. It was caused by miasma, so foul air must be avoided at all costs. Some who breathed the miasma died quickly, an entire household dead overnight. Others screamed in agony as the plague pustules swelled and blackened in their necks. At the thought of such horrors her spirit quailed.

She held her breath until the barge passed. *Saint Irene and Saint Sebastian, preserve us,* she begged inwardly.

The bargemen poled on toward the Lido, the plague burial ground. "Dead bodies! Dead bodies!" their doleful cry continued without pause.

She arrived at the back of Bernardino's house to find all the shutters barred. She stood in the boat and shouted until she was hoarse but no one stirred. She sat, undecided, and scratched.

A filthy old woman with matted hair beckoned from the narrow alley between the house and the church. "You are looking for Bernardino? He's here. Come."

Arcangela eyed her dubiously.

"He wants to talk to you."

Arcangela stood in the boat, but hesitated. To disobey the abbess surely meant a speedy descent into Hell. Yet Bernardino, the gentle, devout old man, was her friend.

The old woman disappeared into the dark alley.

"Wait!" Arcangela sprang from the boat and ran after her. She splashed through shadows and filthy slime as the bells of San Domenico rang out overhead. The sky was a crack of blue between the tall, blank walls of the buildings.

A dozen rats scuttled past. She jumped aside with a prayer that was half a shriek: "Saint Irene, have mercy on us!" The rats dived into the canal and swam away into the lagoon, all but one that convulsed at her feet. Fleas crawled in its matted, putrid fur. It kicked blindly, squealed in despair, and died. Its glazing eye fixed on her as if in divine rebuke.

For a moment she stood in panicked silence. People gathered by San Domenico on the other side of the square—waiting for Mass, she supposed, for the church bells rang. But one winter's isolation had made her shy of crowds. A foul reek shocked her into action. Miasma! She shied away from the source of the stench—a barrel filled with stagnant water—and ran. She found the old woman waiting by the open door of a house.

The old woman pointed inside the open door.

"This is not Bernardino's house," Arcangela objected.

"Oh, you can't go in there." The hag pointed at her neighbor. Bernardino's door was nailed shut and had a red cross painted on it. "They have the malady and are walled up alive, Bernardino and his wife, their daughter and her six children. But there is a crack in the wall to my house. You can talk to him. He is talking now. Listen. You shall hear."

Arcangela took one step inside and clapped her hand to her nose. The house stank. It must be full of miasma. She tried to retreat but the old woman blocked the entrance and pointed eagerly to the corner by the door where a kind of nest had been made in filthy straw. Arcangela decided to get her mission over quickly. She knelt where the old woman indicated. A crack in the plaster vented a fresh waft of stench. "Bernardino," she called.

There was a mutter, then a low murmur. Was it a prayer? She listened and then froze. A mad voice rambled beyond the wall, soft and low, a mindless moan that cursed God and cursed man.

"Bernardino," she said, doubtfully. The babble halted. "It is I, Arcangela! Mother Mary save you and bless you."

A howl burst from beyond the wall, a frantic, inhuman cry of pain and despair. Something clubbed frantically at the bricks between them. She recoiled in horror, scrambled to her feet, and brushed the filthy straw from her habit.

"You must pray for them!" the old woman said. "Pray. I beg you!"

Arcangela did not listen. She ran for the safety of the crowd. Fortunately the old woman did not follow.

Arcangela sagged against the church wall. Why had she ever disobeyed her abbess? This was her punishment for her sin. She tried to pray for old Bernardino and his family, but no prayer came. The solid brick against her back vibrated with the toll of the bells. The world whirled. Sight, sound, and scent mixed together in a muddled, nauseating cacophony of the senses: the bells, the crowd chatter, perfume, and the sweet herbs that people held to their noses. At last she was brought back to the present by a mundane cause. She itched. She scratched herself vigorously. Then deep voices rose in a dirge:

> "Adieu, farewell, earth's bliss,
> This world uncertain is."

A dozen monks, heads bent and cowled, walked double file into the center of the crowd.

The monks reeked of stale blood. Their arms were folded over whips, heavy scourges with three leather thongs each tipped with metal studs. Arcangela drew an ecstatic breath. Flagellants! With their suffering they would purge the people's sins and save Venice from the plague. She hurried forward to watch them.

At the head of the double file walked their master. He was a tall man with broad shoulders, more a warrior than a monk, bare headed to show his shaved scalp. His eyes burned. He stopped before the church and spread his arms wide as if to embrace the world.

Behind the master marched his lieutenant, a youth whose golden curls peeped out from beneath his cowl. He carried a purple banner on which a three-pronged whip was curled. He caught Arcangela's eye and winked. Arcangela sniffed primly and looked away, in rebuke of his sin of lechery.

"Whoever to save his soul is fain
To pay and render back again."

Still chanting their dirge, the monks formed a circle facing inward. With a swift shrug of their arms and shoulders they dropped their robes to leave them naked to the waist. Every man was marked with the wounds of the lash, and every man bore a tattoo on his arm of the same three-pronged whip.

"Mercy you ne'er to others show.
So none will be shown down below."

As their master urged them, the monks lashed at their shoulders and backs with the metal scourges.

The monks dropped to their knees then sprawled face down, then rose again. They moaned their dirge without halt as they scourged themselves and their skin tore beneath the vicious goads until the naked muscle showed. Blood spurted over the enthralled crowd. The master and his lieutenant moved among them, urging them to deeper repentance and harsher blows.

"With Death the guilty souls atone,
The soul unburdened of its sin
Will leave the wanton flesh and bone
To dance and caper in the skin."

It seemed to Arcangela that a strange gleam rose from the monks' tattoos with each blow, a dull, heavy red glow that yet shed no light. She rebuked herself for her sinful distraction and tried to concentrate more on the monk's righteous suffering and less on the odd effect of the morning light. Then the dirge finished with one last, long discordant tone.

The Flagellants rose, arms spread, whips stilled. With a swift movement they resumed robes and cowl and stood with bent heads. Two by two they filed from the campo and were gone. Their master mingled with the crowd, encouraging them to prayer and penance, Arcangela supposed, although she noticed that he spoke only to the well-dressed.

The master stopped nearby to speak to a foppish youth. She could not help but overhear him. His voice was calm and deep and certain. "If you wish to be free of the plague, come to this church at midnight on Sunday with ten thousand ducats," he said.

Arcangela was scandalized. With that coarse speech she saw the Flagellants for what they truly were: ugly, vulgar souls devoured by vanity and pride. Their corrupt venality only added to their sins. As the master turned from the merchant he met her eyes—and read her disgust. He bowed and smiled, hands outspread, unabashed. Then he stiffened and sniffed like a hunting dog. He eyed her keenly. "You are from the Sant'Apostolo Benedictine convent on the island of Ammiano," he said.

"How did you know?" she sputtered, surprised.

"I can tell from the smell," he said. He sniffed again, savoring. "The abbess of that convent is particularly holy and you have the scent of an angel."

She was shocked by this scandalous talk from a monk. She took refuge in silence and hurried away. She heard his voice behind her, strong and soft. "We will meet again, little angel," he said, and then he whispered an obscenity.

She was so startled and upset that tears sprang to her eyes. Her disobedience had been punished indeed. She fled. She ran to her boat, then rowed fast for the nunnery. She passed with a cold shudder over the black pool at the mouth of the canal where fish-eaten eyes peered up at her from the Abyss.

She returned to the convent consumed with shame, guilt, and terror. It was impossible to confess that she had defied her abbess's order. As she arrived in the abbess's cell her belly itched. She felt something move across her skin. She plucked a flea and squeamishly let it drop. She knelt before her abbess.

"Bless you, my child, what happened?" the abbess said.

"Bernardino has the plague and is walled in," she reported, praying that the abbess would not ask any questions. Fortunately the abbess only nodded, deeply grieved, then took the novice's hands in blessing and dismissed her for Sext.

In church Arcangela's guilty soul cringed at every prayer. That night she dreamed of foul blasphemies muttered in her ear by a devil with hot, hairy lips. She fled her tormentor by leaping from a cliff. As she fell the bells rang for Matins and she woke with a shriek.

After prayers she attended to Sister Teresa, the anchorite who was immured alive in her cell in the wall of the church. Sister Teresa slept in her coffin. She was old and pale and so thin that she looked like one of the skeletons that capered on the painted walls above the altar. Her veins showed blue through the flesh of her hands, and her skin was so fine and white as to be almost transparent.

The anchorite shuffled from her knees. "I can retreat from the world but I cannot retreat from my own sinful flesh," she grumbled as she handed a brimming chamber pot through the window that connected her cell to the church. Arcangela emptied the pot into the convent cesspit and returned it.

Sister Teresa waited for her, one pale hand on the windowsill. "Iterum obvenimus," she cackled. *We meet again.* Arcangela smiled dutifully. The joke was a very old one. She went back to bed, only for her dream of torment and flight to repeat itself.

She sat up with a horrid start as the bells rang for Lauds, convinced that the infernal forces had a foothold in her soul. She must confess. After prayers she followed the abbess across the cloisters until she disappeared into the visiting room.

Arcangela peeped around the door, wondering who the visitor was. The room had been unused since the abbess's decree of isolation. It was a long chamber split in two by a wall with a window barred by a metal grate. At the window, the abbess gave a formal greeting, "Pax tecum." *Peace be with you.*

To her horror Arcangela recognized the visitor: the master of the Flagellants! Shame smothered her. He was surely reporting her dereliction. Unfortunately she could not hear a word he said. She did not want to be caught eavesdropping so she stepped away and looked out the nearest window.

A weak sun rose between the slate sky and steel lagoon. The world smelled of salt and seaweed. The master's gondola was moored on the landing stage below. The purple banner of the Flagellants, with its three-pronged whip, was planted in the center like a sail. The golden-haired lieutenant lounged against the bow.

With a sick sense of shock she saw that the curls she had admired yesterday clustered thick all over his head. He was not tonsured! He could not be a holy monk. What was the meaning of such heresies?

Then she heard a cry from the visiting chamber. "Vade retro satana!" the abbess exclaimed. *Step back, Satan!*

Arcangela peered in. Her abbess had backed from the grate, crucifix raised.

The master rose with a soft laugh. "Pax Vobiscum," he said. *Peace be with you all.*

Arcangela lost all her nerve. He had used the plural. He had seen her. She dived back behind the door. Eventually, she peeped out the window to see the lieutenant pole the master away. They both looked straight at her, and laughed.

"Child," the abbess exclaimed.

Arcangela knelt. "Matrem peccavi . . ." she started. *Mother, I have sinned.*

The abbess ignored her plea. She seized the novice's shoulder. "What did you hear?" she demanded.

"Nothing, Mother, only—" Arcangela stuttered.

The abbess released her hold. "Follow me."

Bewildered, Arcangela hurried after her through the cloisters.

The abbess took her to the deserted scriptorium, and to the book vault at the northern end. Arcangela was swamped in utter despair. Surely she was not to begin reading Latin today.

"Confess," the abbess said, curtly.

"I disobeyed you, Mother," Arcangela said. "Old Bernardino would not answer so I went ashore. I saw your visitor, the master of the Flagellants, in the campo of San Domenico."

"Child, he is no master of Flagellants. He calls himself Draco. He was a monk but he was sent to the Lido for blasphemy. He pretended to repent and in these desperate times was brought back into the Church, but he has not abjured his wickedness. Rather, his sin has increased tenfold."

"And his lieutenant pretends to be a monk but he is not tonsured." Arcangela poured out the rest of her story.

The abbess listened intently. She interrupted only once. "What did the banner look like?" she asked.

Arcangela drew the three-pronged goad.

"Child, this man Draco is evil," her abbess said. "You must avoid him on peril of your soul. He is the last of a cult that held sway in Venice at the time of the Fourth Crusade but by the mercy of God were discovered and destroyed. He has gathered around him a company of fallen monks and loves nothing better than to corrupt a nun. He was here for a reason. Of this I must speak. We have a book in this vault. He wanted it. When I refused he threatened us with the plague. Saint Irene and Saint Sebastian are our staunch defenders yet we must take precautions." She gave Arcangela a heavy iron key. "This opens the vault," she said. "I have made my vow of obedience, as has every nun in the convent. We swore never to open it. Only you have not made that vow. Should we be made helpless by pestilence you must destroy the book. It is called *Sine cum pelle*. You will know it by the three-pronged whip on its cover. Do not let Draco get his hands on it. Promise me."

Arcangela clutched the cold key in hands that felt like ice. "Yes, Mother," she whispered. She tucked the dreadful weight into her belt. "Could you not destroy it now?" she asked, timidly.

"We vowed to preserve it," the abbess said. "Doubtless this book is a weapon against these evil men as much as it is a sword in their hands." Her gaze hardened. "We must tell the patriarch to take it to a new refuge."

The abbess returned to her cell and wrote a letter. Then she sent Arcangela back to the city to deliver it.

Arcangela hurried to the patriarch's palazzo. All the while she puzzled over the title, with her very poor Latin. *Sine cum pelle.* Why, it just meant "without the skin." The book without skin? What, by Saint Irene, did that mean?

There was a long line of supplicants in the palazzo's marble atrium and she had to wait her turn. It was almost dusk before she met the patriarch's secretary. He was a plump, bald, sweating man in red robes and purple socks. He took the letter without raising his eyes from his ledger. "The patriarch is ill. He sees no one," he said in a dull monotone.

"Please, I am from the Sant'Apostolo convent on the island of Ammiano. The patriarch must take back a book he gave us," she said.

The secretary did not glance up. "Tell your abbess her letter merits immediate attention. I have promised."

As Arcangela turned away, the next supplicant in the line stepped up, a hooded monk. The monk murmured a request. "Yes, your abbot will have the swan. I have promised," the secretary said, in exactly the same tone.

Arcangela was scandalized. The secretary had paid as much attention to an abbot seeking a gluttonous feast of roast swan as to her abbess's vital letter. She returned to the convent in time for Vespers, expecting the patriarch arrive before Compline. But no one came. After Compline the prioress locked the convent. No one would be admitted until morning.

Arcangela followed the prioress as she barred the doors and shutters, and hovered as the prioress carefully banked up the kitchen fire for the night. It was the only fire in the convent and could not be suffered to go out. Arcangela told her beads and murmured the Exorcism: "*Non draco sit mihi dux.*" Let not the dragon be my guide. "*Sunt mala quae libas, Ipse venena bibas.*" *What you offer me is evil, drink the poison yourself.*

The prioress eyed her balefully. "Are you so afraid of the cold?" she asked.

"No, Prioress," Arcangela muttered.

"Best pray to shield your soul from the torment of Hell-fire," the prioress instructed.

Arcangela bowed her head and slunk off to bed.

The hard shape of the key beneath her thin pillow made her sleep uneasy. She dreamed of moans and shrieks, and woke with a start. All was silent. At Matins she descended the night stairs sluggish and half-awake. At the end of the office the prioress announced a special prayer for the abbess, who had fallen ill in the night.

Arcangela's heart rose sickeningly into her mouth. "Ipse venena bibas." *You drink the poison yourself.* What cup of poison had her abbess drained? Prayers over, she rushed to the prioress. "What ails her? How can I help?"

"Do your duty. She is in God's care," the prioress said.

Rebuked, Arcangela waited on Sister Teresa. The anchorite shuffled from her knees. "Old ladies cannot move quickly. Old legs are stiff, praise God." She handed over the chamber pot, which Arcangela emptied and returned. Sister Teresa waited for her, one pale hand resting on the windowsill. "Iterum obvenimus," she joked. *We meet again.* Arcangela mustered a thin smile and returned to her bed.

ARCANGELA WOKE ABRUPTLY, SHOCKED, REALIZING it was past dawn yet she had heard no bell for Lauds. She pulled on her habit, tucked the key into her belt, and hurried down the night stairs. The church was empty. She glimpsed the sun high overhead. It was near midday. Demons danced on her grave. She hurried contritely to Sister Teresa's cell. She saw the white hand resting on the sill.

"Iterum obvenimus," Arcangela called. *We meet again.* Then she looked in.

Sister Teresa's face was pressed against the bars. It was blackened and distorted, her tongue thrust from her lips. She had died standing and never made it to her coffin standing open only a few steps away.

Arcangela reeled backward, eyes fixed on the pallid hand upon the sill. She had a vision of the plague miasma sweeping through the convent in one fetid blast, withering all life in its path.

She ran through the convent, crying for help. The prioress was not in the kitchen. The sisters were not in their cells. She rushed through the empty cloister and up the deserted stairs.

The abbess lay in bed. The prioress was at her bedside with a dish of water. The sisters knelt in prayer. The abbess writhed, shrieking. Black pustules swelled under her neck, and her face was bloated and disfigured. The room stank of putrefying flesh.

"Kill me!" the abbess croaked.

Arcangela clapped her hand over her own mouth and held her breath.

The prioress pressed her by the shoulder down to her knees beside the rest. "Pray to Mary, Mother of God, and all the saints," she said.

Arcangela lowered herself without resistance. She knelt, staring at her abbess as the dying woman shrieked and writhed in torment. The foundations of her world tottered. The bell tower crashed. Her heart framed a prayer to Saint Irene and Saint Sebastian but she could not speak. To speak she would have to draw a breath. As long as she held her breath she would not draw in the miasma. She felt the prioress's hard hand on her shoulder as a crushing weight pressing her down to death. Her heart beat loud in her ears and her chest tightened. She remembered the cold, dark pool at the mouth of the Castello canal. She saw herself standing at the bottom, among the lost throng, staring upward toward a drowned golden ring of daylight. Disappearing. Going. Gone.

The last breath wheezed from her lungs. A prayer rushed out: "God, why do you let my dear mother suffer like this? Mercy, Mary, Mother of God!" she shrieked.

The prioress lifted her hand. Arcangela fled the room and slammed the door. She held the door fast, but no one attempted to open it. Shrieks and prayers rose from within, a meaningless babble of despair.

She leaned against the door and gasped for air, frantically clawing at her mouth and nose to scour out the stink. She could not stay in that cell, not for all the love of God and her abbess. Shame filled her. Then she remembered. *Sine cum pelle.*

She fled for the scriptorium. At the book vault she fumbled for the key. The lock was stiff and she wrapped the head of the key in the cloth of her habit as she forced it. Metal grated on metal as, at last, it turned. As she stepped inside she met a gust of musty air, of damp paper and rotten leather. Leather spines confronted her, row on row. She searched frantically, hurling books to the floor, until at last found the one she sought. She knew it, as the abbess had said, by the three-pronged whip on its cover.

The book was small for its weight of wickedness, and it stank of old blood and ancient sin. She did not know why it was called *Sine cum pelle*, for it had a skin, and it was terrible. The whip on its cover was worked from iron, red-rusted with age. The three prongs were ornately fashioned so that they lifted from the leather cover in cruel barbs. The barbs snagged at the cloth of her habit and caught at her hair. She clutched it gingerly, at arm's length, as if she were holding a dead, rotted thing. Shrieks resounded from the cell overhead. She shuddered and flinched, each scream a blow from a three-pronged goad. She ran to the kitchen.

The kitchen fire was the only fire allowed in the convent, and it was out. She raked the coals, searching for a spark. Nothing. She slumped to her knees. How could she destroy the book now? Sink it in the lagoon?

The book slipped from her hands and fell open at an engraving in red ink that had gone brown, of a man who had been flensed so that all his muscles and tendons showed. His arms were outstretched, hands extended, and he smiled with naked bone.

Sine cum pelle. Without the skin. The Skinless One.

At his feet a dragon curled.

Stench welled from the open pages, the foul odor of blood gone bad. What wickedness was this, to gaze with bold eyes on the divine plan of the human body that God in His wisdom had concealed? She closed the book with a slam, flinching backward as the barbs clawed for her skin. She curled herself into a ball and sobbed before insight came.

There was one way to restore her world. There was a cure for her abbess. She had heard Draco promise freedom from the plague. She did not have ten thousand ducats but she did have the one thing he valued more.

Destroy this book? No, she should guard it as though it were her dearest friend.

Shrieks came from overhead as if the angels cried warning, but she ignored them. She rose, filled with elation. Why, she even knew Draco would be waiting tonight at the church of San Domenico. The way to redemption lay open before her.

Yet Hell yawned beneath. Surely eternal torment was the only reward of such disobedience. Her hopes swung in the balance, spiked with abject terror. Then a surge of strong emotion tipped her over—love and reverence, not unmixed with fear. Most of all she wanted her abbess to stand as tall and stern and remote as a bell tower. It was worth the Abyss if she could save her.

A pile of discarded sacking lay by the kitchen door. She wrapped the book in it, trying to ease its bite, but the rusty iron tore through the sacking.

She walked carefully from the convent. Holding the book at arm's length, with the prongs facing outward, she made her way gingerly to the shore.

Evening was coming. The stink of salt and rot lay over everything. A rack of cloud veiled the sky, and the lagoon glittered silver. A crimson sun shone out between clouds and water. Venice was soaked blood red. She climbed into the rowboat, unshipped the oars, and skated over the lagoon, which had been turned into a pool of brimstone by the setting sun.

She abandoned the boat at the Castello landing and tied the book in its sacking over her shoulder, constructing a makeshift satchel with the evil barbs pointed outward. She crept through the narrow alley into the campo of San Domenico. On her left was the plague house. On her right rose the church, and high overhead reared the bell tower.

One man stood before her at the church. She recognized the plump and sweating red-clad figure and the pathetic vestige of earthly glory—the purple socks that he wore. The patriarch's secretary struggled to carry a large and indignant swan. Its wings were tied to its body but it was not taking captivity quietly. It fought against its bonds, struck with its beak, and hissed. Two monks hurried from the church and carried it inside. The secretary followed them, with one last anxious glance behind.

Arcangela halted in dismay. This was how Draco had learned of the book's location. The secretary had sold their secret for salvation from the plague.

She could not just walk into the church and bargain with Draco. He was an evil man with the powers of Hell at his command, and she felt terribly alone. She suppressed a shudder and shinnied up the drain pipe of the plague house. She felt dead eyes watch her as she clambered up the pipe, and she winced with every impact of her hands and feet. In her mind's eye the walls dripped with putrescence; miasma made tangible oozed from the house like black bile from a pustule. She was thankful to reach the roof just as the sun dipped below the horizon. The red light snuffed out.

She looked out over the city; darkness was swallowing domes and towers and canals. The churches and bell towers, palazzos and houses, all turned to mausoleums, besieged by the Great Malady and the Devil. Night fell on city and souls alike.

Down below, sunk in gloom, was the alley where she had first met the old woman. She took a dozen steps backward, braced herself, then made a running jump. She flung herself over the gap and clawed to safety onto the tiles of the church roof.

The sun was gone and the darkness now complete, but she could see a crack of dim light ahead. Guided by the light she found a doorway that led from the roof into the church, and she stole into an upper gallery. Stairs led up to the bell tower and down into the nave. The light came from below. As she peered down the steps, the sound of a dirge wafted up to her. Her back prickled.

> "With Death the guilty souls atone,
> These souls unburdened of their sin
> Will leave the wanton flesh and bone
> To dance and caper in the skin."

She crept down the stairs until the nave came into view.

The church was richly ornamented. Marble pillars adorned the aisle, and gilded statues of the saints shone from their shadowy niches. Yet cobwebs veiled the paintings, dust covered every surface, and the sacred vessels were gone from the altar. The church had been abandoned. A pool of amber torchlight illuminated the altarpiece. Death capered over the altar, leading ladies, cardinals, and peasants, and skeletons in their shrouds. The figure of Death was distorted, more *fleshly* than she was used to. With a shudder she saw words scrawled beneath: *Sine cum pelle* . . . the Skinless One. . . . *Exonerata Carnem* . . . Unburdened Flesh. . . .

In the dim light stood the circle of naked Flagellants. They whipped themselves as they moaned their dirge so their blood rained on the altar. Without their robes to conceal their lust, she noticed with disgust that they were excited by their own mutilation. Their male members were like bulls serving a cow. The banner with the three-pronged whip stood over them, and the golden-haired lieutenant knelt in blasphemy upon the sacred stones. He was naked and his shoulder blades stood out prominently against his scarred flesh. His golden cap of hair glowed in the lantern light, and his whip tattoo shone with weird iridescence.

The patriarch's secretary knelt beside him. "I have brought your swan. I am a poor man. I do not have ten thousand ducats. I beg you to free me from the plague," he said.

Only then did Arcangela see the master. He stood in the gloom behind the altar. He stepped forward, cloaked in his cowl, and spoke in contempt. "You hoard gold and seek to secure salvation on the cheap. Hell has a just reward for misers," he said.

Two of the monks left off whipping themselves and released the swan. The infuriated bird lunged at the secretary, beating wildly with its ten foot wingspan. The secretary was driven back. He raised his arm to shield his face, then stumbled and was flattened by the bird's wings. He cried out in pain. The master and monks laughed at him in an orison of cruel derision. The secretary scrambled to his feet, clutching a broken arm, and fled. The monks brought the swan back to the altar and laid it at Draco's feet.

Arcangela stole down some stairs but she stopped at the last landing. She could see there were no other stairs from the nave to the door in the roof. Her escape route was safe behind her.

Draco spoke again, in a different tone, soft and caressing, to his lieutenant. "You are sure this is what you desire?" he asked. His lieutenant raised his radiant face and nodded.

Draco laid his hands, already crimson and bloody, upon the youth's shoulder blades and began to speak. Arcangela clapped her palms to her ears in horror but she could not block out the dreadful and pungent words that came reeking from the bowels of Hell. Then Draco's hands closed on the scarred flesh and ripped. The lieutenant shrieked as Draco tore the flesh from his back, showing the shoulder muscles moving beneath the skin.

Draco then stooped to the bird at his feet. The swan cried out in agony. The sound of the man and the bird combined in a deranged inarticulate cry of utter pain.

Draco stood, holding a bleeding wing in each hand. The butchered, disfigured bird staggered away, bleeding, dropping and rising, until it fell on its side with its neck stretched out. It was still alive. Arcangela, rooted in horror on the stairs, saw its eyes blink and its tongue move.

Draco worked both hands inside his lieutenant's shoulders. He thrust and pulled, and his fingers forced a path into the living meat beneath. He forced apart bone, and he tore at muscle and tendon, chanting hot, hoarse gibberish. Arcangela kept her hands clapped over her ears, yet she still heard.

He thrust the dismembered wings inside the bloody cavity and twined together the muscles and tendons and blood vessels of bird and man. The dead white wings twitched and stirred. The lieutenant's screams cut short. He rose to his feet. He spread his arms and the wings spread with him so he stood upon the altar like an angel.

Yet something had snapped within him. All intelligence had fled. He giggled constantly, and an idiot grin deformed his handsome face. He leaped from the altar and loped down the aisle, half flapping, half jumping. He vanished through the doors.

Draco laughed and wiped his bloodstained hands. "This city is deserving of its angel," he said. Then his nostrils widened. He inhaled scent like a hound and looked up, directly at Arcangela. "Little one, you are here at last. Come down. Meet your friends."

Arcangela shook her head and retreated halfway up the stairs.

Draco smiled. He paced toward her. He unfastened his robes as he walked, and dropped them at his feet.

He was skinless beneath the robe. Red muscle and blue tendon shone slick. Blood coursed visibly through his veins. The sight of the living, naked muscle, bone, and sinew was more obscene than the male member swinging between his legs. His member was completely skinned, along with the rest of him. Only his face and neck had any hide left, and a patch on his shoulder where the three-pronged whip tattoo shone iridescent in the gloom.

He smiled at her, with hands spread, delivering a sermon with his own disfigured frame as text. "We call ourselves the Unburdened Flesh," he said. "For we have sold our souls to the Skinless One and are free of them forever. Now sickness does not daunt us, nor does age enfeeble us. Injury does not kill us. You have brought *Sine cum pelle*. Give it back and join us. You too can live forever." He held out his hand to her. His eyes glowed with unholy power.

Arcangela clung to the bannister to prevent obedience, so tight that her fingernails dug into stone and snapped and bled. "Mary, Mother of God, and all the angels, help me," she begged.

Draco laughed. "Your saints are nothing," he said. "Your prayers are empty words. There are gods, but not as you imagine. The true gods do not care about you, little angel, which is a pity because I do. I would have you at my side forever and you would laugh and sing and kill." He smiled up at her.

Arcangela was so appalled that her sanity staggered beneath the goad. Then, out of nowhere, she heard her abbess's voice: *He loves nothing better than to seduce a nun.*

Draco had his foot on the stairs.

She recovered her senses just in time. "Stop," she warned him. She unslung her satchel from her shoulder and held it high. The barbs poked through the sacking and pulsed. It was not her imagination. She saw that the cruel spikes fire with a dark, blood-red radiance that emitted no light.

The monks gasped in delight. Some dropped to their knees in worship. Some flogged themselves in ecstasy. Others ran forward to seize their prize. Draco held up a hand. They stopped by his side.

Their tattoos glowed, she saw, with the same blood-red fire as the barbs.

"This is the book," she said, despising the tremor in her voice. "I will give it to you if you take the plague from my abbess."

"I cannot cure your abbess. I have no power over the sickness."

"You do! You threatened her!"

"And that was all it was—a threat," Draco said.

"You said that you could free people from the plague," she wailed like a tired child.

Draco smiled. "A body without a soul fears neither the plague nor any deadly illness. Dear little angel, the plague is carried by miasma. I saw you in that plague house. You carried the miasma to your convent yourself."

She shrank back, appalled. She saw the white hand on the windowsill, the disfigured face of her abbess. She sank to her knees. "Forgive me," she cried aloud.

"There is no need for forgiveness any more. Join us, little angel. Fly free." Draco climbed the stairs toward her, hand extended.

"Stop!" She staggered upright, fighting a tremendous weight. At last she stood straight, clutching the satchel in one hand, holding the book at arm's length. "I'll never give it to you. I'll—I'll climb onto the roof and throw it in the canal," she threatened.

"It will float," he pointed out.

That was when she knew: The deep water where suicides dwelled. It was too dreadful. She gazed down at him, blank with despair. Then she looked anew at the dull radiance of the barbs burning through the sacking. The book knew its master was near. She saw again the Flagellant tattoos glowing as they laid on the lash. At last she understood her abbess: *This book is a weapon against these evil men as much as it is a sword in their hands.* The men and the book were one.

She took the book from its sacking and held it high.

The monks dropped to their knees. Draco alone stayed on his feet. He stretched out his hand to seize his prize. "You are indeed an angel."

She opened the book, ripped out a page, then crumpled it with her hand.

All the monks and their master shrieked. They staggered back, their skin crumpling with the paper. She dropped the crushed page at her feet then stamped on it. Hard.

"No!" Draco shrieked. There was such pain in his voice that she faltered, and in that instant, he sprang forward.

Arcangla shoved the book back into its sack and fled up the stairs.

She heard Draco laughing as he followed her. She skidded to a halt. Her escape was blocked.

An angel blocked the door, an angel with idiot eyes and bloody wings. *He could fly.*

Giggling, the lieutenant grabbed at the novice. She stepped back, then whirled the satchel like a flail and swung it at him with all her strength. It hit him full in the face. The glowing barbs struck his eyes and forehead, and hooked hard. He shrieked and rolled his eyes in ecstasy as blood ran down his cheeks. When she pulled the book free, the barbs tore his face clean off. He staggered two steps backward off the stairs, his butchered visage a grinning red mask. He fell, arms and wings spread wide. Dazed or demented, he forgot to fly. He struck the marble of the nave far below, and sprawled, a broken obscenity. Bloody feathers fluttered down around him.

Draco bounded up the stairs. "I will teach you to enjoy such suffering," he said.

Arcangela looked at the scalped face embedded on the barbs and fled from what she had done. She raced up the winding stairs of the bell tower with Draco at her heels. The way was narrow and the stairs smooth and slippery. Her thoughts were a confused jumble: horror and fear—*You carried the miasma with you*—unholy guilt, useless prayer, sin, and utter despair—*If he can fly then so can I.* Surely Mother Mary would forgive her—*the path to Heaven might yet be open*—these monks were one with the book. If it was drowned then they would drown too.

She reached the top of the tower and wrenched open the door. The wind blew in her face, cold and strong. She raced across the roof and vaulted onto the parapet. The night was striped with black and silver as a swollen moon swam between racing clouds. Her hair whipped over her face and her habit billowed. She glanced down, once, from the giddy heights to the deep water—the black gulf where suicides were denied the grace of God forever. Venice stretched out beneath her, domes and towers and palaces a livid corpse tortured on the rack. She untangled the book from its sacking, willingly letting the skinned fragment fall, then held the book out over the empty air. The iron prongs bathed her in their unholy glow, irradiating her wind-blown hair and robes with dull red radiance that shed no light.

Only then did she dare look back.

Draco erupted from the stairs, his eyes blazing with wrath. "It will float!" he repeated as blood vessels knotted and burst in his skinless throat.

"Non draco sit mihi dux," she cried. *Let not the dragon be my guide.*

The winds whipped the words from her mouth. Her faith was too weak. The prayer did not stop him. Draco stormed across the roof. Yet the words gave her the last insight she needed, the last hope. Crumbling fast in the face of utter horror she held firm to Heaven's grace.

If he can fly—

"It will not float if someone holds it," she said.

Arcangela saw the rage and confidence in Draco's eyes give way to panic. He lunged at her.

She leapt from the parapet.

He missed snagging the cloth of her habit by a finger.

She fell, hugging the book to her breast like a baby. *Saint Brigid, Saint Irene, Saint Sebastian—Mary Mother, save us!*

ONLY DEAD MEN DO NOT LIE:
THE TRIAL OF THE FORMOSANS
KAARON WARREN

I WILL BEGIN MY STORY here and no sooner, because before now lies sorrow and that is a place I do not dwell.

So: In the dregs of the year 1421 I began my walk to the house on the hill. At nineteen I was older than most but I would tell them I was fifteen and an orphan. I would tell them of the terrible deaths of my parents to explain the lines on my face.

I would lie about that, and also my virginity. I would not tell them of my marriage, nor that I was widowed. I would not tell them how my husband died.

It was a journey of many months. I would never feel as lonely again, not in all the decades of travel to come.

I carried very little and dressed well below my station. I covered my face with dirt to hide the glow of youth and I spoke quietly. When alone I walked quickly, but in company I stooped and limped like an old woman. In this way I became invisible. In this way, I walked to the house on the hill unmolested and with my purse of money untouched.

AS I APPROACHED THE HOUSE on the hill, at the very moment I stepped foot on the threshold, the sun peeked clear of the clouds that had lain thick for two weeks or more. I was never a fanciful girl but to arrive with the sun warm across my cheeks meant the women smiled as they welcomed me. They said, "Here is the Sunshine!" and that became my name, and my nature, from that day forward. With all that it was three days before anyone thought to ask me where I'd come from. By then it was very clear they wouldn't take me if I had any living loved ones, because there were no visits, no dispatches, no connections with that world. We had to be neutral.

I did not have to lie about my father, long gone and sadly missed, and I merely sent my mother with him. She had not spoken to me since I married out of her jurisdiction. Not even when my beloved Gerald died did she come to me, or call me home. News of his manner of passing must have reached her; half the world surely knew of his ignominious execution.

I did not speak of him, either. As I said; my life began again in that sunstruck moment.

They made me swear I would never request the disinterment of my father. That I would never seek to put him on trial.

It was a simple matter to agree. I wouldn't ask this; I would not need to. He was a good man. He was not lost in Hell.

My mother was a good woman in the eyes of most and of the Lord, though perhaps not the Lord she professed to worship. She was also alive, so the promise not to dig her up was not difficult.

I settled quickly and soon came to love my new life. It is vital to keep new members coming in so it is an easy place to be. It isn't about suffering (starvation, no sleep, uncomfortable clothes) but the opposite, and a place for a woman to be learned, where we can speak freely, laugh wildly. The inspiration in that is that we need to be healthy in heart, head, blood, and liver, because the work at times is relentless.

So many tortured souls to save.

My first case took place in the months after the death of King Henry V. We took to the road, prepared for busy times ahead. It was always such after the death of a king, with supplicants begging us to free their traitorous loved ones. But we didn't believe that traitors reside in Hell because such a thing is arbitrary. One man's traitor is another man's rebel, and it only depends on who wins the battle for the difference to be known. Similarly men who kill in battle are judged differently. The viciousness of battles long distant did not affect us until we were called to represent the fallen in years future. There are many who go beyond the needs of war and these are the men and women we can help when they have paid their debt.

It is possible we are leaving great legions to burn in Hell but we don't believe so. The plague that raged in the Netherlands meant many souls perhaps would need help there, but we have enough to manage with the sinners of England and Scotland. One of the lessons to learn is that we cannot save them all.

This journey was far different from my lone one coming in. We had horses and supplies, and much to trade for food along the way. A small group rode ahead to establish lodgings each night (and how I longed to be one of those! They were the liveliest, the ones with the brightest voices and the highest laughter) and so there was little hardship.

Sometimes people traveled to us to plead. Other times they found us on our travels. We took very few cases.

I WILL ALWAYS REMEMBER MY first trial. This man had been put to death ten years earlier, a confessed but unrepentant luxuriant. It was not the servant girls who were of concern, but the ladies he left damaged. He believed deep in his heart that he had done nothing wrong; that the blood drawn upon them during intercourse, the damage wrought, was all part of the natural endeavors between men and women. We needed to wait a number of years, depending on the crime: Thirty years for murder. Ten for rape. Ten for adultery. Seven for theft. They need to spend that time in Hell; it makes them speak truer words than they ever spoke in life.

We approached the unconsecrated grave where the rapist was buried.

"I warn you," my new friends said. "This is a deeply unpleasant stage of decay." The worst, of course, are the first years, when putrefaction is at its work. We rarely dug them up before ten years.

We began at dawn. We hammered stakes in a perfect circle around the grave, then danced ribbon in and out until we wove a basket of privacy around ourselves. Already onlookers gathered on the outskirts. We affixed mirrors, each facing a predetermined direction. This moment felt thrilling. We carried these mirrors carefully, folded into soft cloth. It was strange to see my face. I looked younger. Brighter.

The rapist's mother, who had entreated for him, was given a stool to sit on within our large woven basket.

We were finished with this work by the noon sun.

It was cold most of the time, so the moments of warmth are much delighted in. At sunrise, all the warmth of the day is ahead of you. At twilight, you only have the cold of night to look forward to. The darkness. I do prefer the dawn.

They had me stand by the mother. I wanted to help dig but they were cautious about the ritual and my place in it. I had studied hard but never yet observed and I did understand the need for patience.

The grave was dug using scoops made from metal from the Basilica of Saint John Lateran, where our patron Pope Formosus was tried. With each scoop the earth was purified.

His coffin was raised and the lid levered open. I heard a small, strange hiss and thought a snake was at our feet. But it was his gases, released. The women nearby wrinkled their noses at the stench. His mother beside me stiffened, but held her breath. No parent should ever smell that of their child.

They lifted him out and settled him into the judgment chair we carried with us. It was light but sturdy, and needed to carry little weight. It was a foul thing, though, because of all who'd sat before, dripping and dropping. Fashioned from the coffin of Pope Formosa, for whom we are named, it is our most precious item.

They had described how a corpse would look and I had seen the tapestries, but still the shock made me shake.

He was identifiable as a man: four limbs, withered and black, with what looked like knotted string between his legs.

WE WAITED UNTIL DAWN FOR the awakening and judgment.

As the time approached, one held his shoulder back while another anointed his forehead with holy myrrh. For a while nothing happened. I had never doubted my belief in the miracle of the Formosans, but in that moment I wondered. Then he shuddered as if in revulsion, and his mouth, previously open, clamped shut. He had no eyelids or eyeballs yet somehow there was movement there as well.

His mother sobbed, and I placed a hand on her arm to hush her.

"Daniel Carpenter, you stand charged guilty of the sin of *luxuria*. You took without consent and with great violence. . . ." And the examiner, our mother superior, listed a dozen names or more. At each name his mother shuddered.

"I shall go to Hell," she whispered, "for having this son."

I was annoyed at being left with her. Surely a more experienced person should be standing here.

"Do you repent?"

"I am sorry. I regret every wrong action. I say to my mother and to the Lord forgive me."

They nodded at me and I let the mother rise and stumble to him.

"It is not for your mother to forgive, only to love," the examiner said. "Her love has given you this chance at redemption and Mercy. It is the Lord who will choose to forgive you."

The mother said, "I failed you," the words drawn hard between sobs.

"No, Mother. I failed beyond all you did for me."

At that moment, magic happened, although it was only the sun and our mirrors. A ray shone directly onto his chest, where the seat of repentance lives.

The examiner said, "The Lord forgives. You will not return to Hades."

His shoulders shook, a memory of crying. His mother wept openly, thanking us.

We carried him to sanctified ground and interred him, feet to the east.

WE TRIED A DOZEN MORE on that journey, men and women. Murderers, thieves, adulterers, rapists. Those guilty of *accidia, superbio, ira, avaritia*. All but one were repentant.

That one . . . with each scoop, our hands clenched up, as if the earth itself fought against us. When we reached the coffin, it was cracked open. His fingers emerged, black, curved, split at the ends like overripe plums.

We lifted him out of his coffin and set him upon the judgment stool.

After his awakening he laughed without cease. It was like a foul, cold wind bringing the stench of dead meat. That time after winter when the dead lie frozen; as the ice melts, the bodies decay all at once.

He would not say sorry. He was lost to the Devil.

Satan lets no one go willingly. But if they confess and repent, he loses the power to keep them.

AFTER OUR LONG JOURNEY, THE darkness of home was palpable. We lit the place, brighter than others would have, and we began the trial tapestry. I already had set in my mind what I wanted to sew and I hoped they would let me. I wanted to depict that first mother, because she represented our mission, our reason.

Love seeks forgiveness. Mercy triumphs over judgment.

For now, we are above whatever law exists. No need for the bailiffs, notaries, or stewards who clutter up all matters. Our work is simple. There are times when we are frightened, such as when the girl Joan was burnt for hearing the word of God. We do not hear the word of God. But we hear the dead. There are some who say we commit heresy, and we wait for the time when officialdom agrees. Perhaps that time will never come, though, because we have the blessing of Saint James: "*For judgment is without mercy to one who has shown no mercy.*"

Our Bible tells us that if souls in Hell outnumber souls in Heaven, the world will end. It is Saint John this time, calling: "*Satan spake to me and he said thus: If my house fills before that of the Lord above, then all will descend to me.*"

We do important work.

I LOVE THE TAPESTRY HALL more than any other place beyond the church and beyond God's natural wonders. I love it for the color, but also for the history, dating back hundreds of years.

The first represents the trial of King John, who repented the murder of Arthur of Brittany. Our tapestry shows that John did repent, but with his few sentences he accused a monk from Swinstead Abbey of his own murder. That monk, the tapestry told us, was disinterred under great secrecy, and wept so hard, cried so deeply at the horrors he had seen, that he is depicted in a puddle of tears.

He, too, repented.

Other stories in the tapestries are of the Peasants' Revolt in England. Many died during this time but there we do not judge traitor or rebel. We do show mercy to a man called Watt Tigher, who murdered a mayor. He took on the guilt of all that went before, and all that followed. In his repentance, he asked that he should suffer for those fools who came after him, who did not know what they did.

The answer is not recorded.

And the Peasants' Revolt in France, where there was much vengeful rape and murder. These were mass graves and that tapestry is one I do not like to look at. Amongst the guilty are the looters, who perhaps are forgotten in the grand scheme of things, but who deserve mercy, too.

Others chose bright colors for the hose, robes, and cloaks in their tapestries because they depicted the wealthy. I took grays and browns and yet I made that mother live.

Our tapestries brighten our gray stone walls. We sometimes make them for the rich, if we need the money, but those are brief things, quickly made and without real history.

I sewed myself into a corner, wanting somehow to be remembered.

IN THIS WAY OUR DAYS passed. I would wait thirty years before seeking mercy for my husband and in the meantime, I am ashamed to admit, I felt grateful and most glorified to be living my life in this way.

Many of our cases were memorable, for the sinners themselves and for the journeys.

We traveled across rivers and over mountains and through vast forests. We went hungry and thirsty, at times. There was little delicacy about the food we ate on the road. Our sister cook brought her pouches of spices and these she doled out to us with a great sense of benefaction.

We rode past scenes of horror: battle-sites, starving villages, dying children. We could do nothing. But we couldn't join the joyous occasions, either, nor allow ourselves to be feted. This was not our purpose of being.

We did accept reward, though. We needed the funds.

Our sinners can only speak if they have been in Hell. Only the guilty go there. So those who don't speak were innocent and proclaimed as such.

We took secret petitions from loved ones, sitting in a darkened tent waiting for the desperate to join us. We needed to remember the words; there was no light to record them. Just one glowing ember to show the petitioners where to stand.

We judged the evil of lesser men. The greater men are already judged; history shows that.

It is the man who beats his wife and servants. The one who takes his daughter when the room is dark. The ones who kill quietly, who murder the dispossessed.

It is my secret, lost husband, whom I promised not to forget. I joined these women so I would be ready when the time came, but this life is one I will never regret.

It is the woman who uses her hairpins to kill.

I stitched her into the tapestry with a colorful butterfly headdress and over-large pins to emphasize her crime.

SOME OF THE SINNERS TALKED all day, until the moment we snuffed their candles again. This was a simple manner of laying them into their coffins and placing sprigs of pennyroyal across their chests.

One of these talkers was a young man in the prime of his life. He reminded me of my husband but his crimes were even worse; he was charged with the murder, defilement, and devourment of his young friends.

"I am too young to lose my life. Keep me imprisoned in a hole in the ground but let me see the sun at times. That is what I miss most."

He did seem to turn with it as a flower does.

"You are not begging for your life. You have already lost that. You are hoping for the chance to ascend to a glorious eternity."

Does even a moment feel like eternity? Do they have an idea of time passing in Hell?

"How long have you been in Hell?" I asked him. I liked to ask them all this question.

"One hundred twelve years," he said. Others would answer *forever* or *two hundred and nine years.*

I wept harder for him than I did for others and my friends looked at me oddly. "Caution!" I told myself. "You are Sunshine, not that other."

WE SPEND MUCH OF OUR LIVES traveling to trial. We need to ensure the bodies are disinterred with proper ceremony and prayer.

I remember (though it is not in the tapestry) the man who dragged to us his son's body, hoping to save money.

"A sinner disinterred thus has no hope of speech. We do our work with reason. All we can do is bury him with full ceremony and try again after a decent interval has passed," Mother Superior told him.

"And what will that cost me?"

I would have disliked him if he hadn't been so genuine. His clothes were worn and his hands rough, so he still worked hard day by day.

"What it would have cost you if you'd allowed us to work properly, and you will have to make amends to the church for insult and interference."

We buried his son feet east, head west. Even sinners deserve to face the Lord when they rise. I will not live to see him on trial; neither will his father.

Another time we had to re-bury a career thief who was finally caught during a spate of wolf attacks, when focus came to his village. That wolf pack killed and ate a number of visitors before they were hunted down by paid aggressors.

We rose this man from the dead, all of us feeling he had spent long enough. He had more to confess, though.

"I took advantage of the wolf attacks and I strangled my enemies, one-two-three. I thought I would be pleased with this but I have never been sorrier. I would give up eternity to bring those men back to the life."

"Still and all you need to spend your time," Mother Superior said. "We will return for you in many years and then you will be ready for an eternity of bliss."

"Will I remember this? Will I have this solace?"

We did not know.

I NEVER FORGOT MY HUSBAND, waiting for mercy, and as time approached when I could safely put him on trial, I became ever more alert.

I waited for the time someone came to me with a foolish confession, begging for the trial for someone clearly not in Hell.

Finally, it came.

"It's my poor husband. He did not give me a baby. He could not . . ." In the dark I couldn't see her movements.

"That is not usually considered a mortal sin," I said. I quietly rejoiced; this was the foolish petition I had been waiting for.

"You wouldn't understand. If you have never known the physical love of a man, you don't know what is like not to have it."

I had known it. My husband and I spent many glorious hours in the pleasure of God's beautiful creation.

"That man committed cruelty and deprivation on me."

I had to be sure.

"Did he seek elsewhere?" Because adulterers did indeed take a place in Hell.

"Him?" she snorted. "No other woman would give him the slightest glance, let alone lie down with him. He had lips like a dead fish and he smelled like one, too."

In the dark all smells are increased. She was no sweet flower herself. I wondered how she looked.

"We will consider your request." Of course we wouldn't accept it; it was not a serious application.

I SHARED DIFFERENTLY WITH THE others, though. I told them my husband's story as if it were the petitioner's husband.

"How long has he been burning?"

"Thirty years." The allotted time for the killer of one person. Any more and the years are multiplied. Men like Tamerlane would not see release in our lifetimes.

I sometimes wondered why I didn't just petition them when the time came. But it was simple: I had to be sure he would be chosen, that he would not be one of the many hundreds rejected.

AND SO WE TRAVELED BACK over the route I had taken thirty years earlier.

I would be giving up life as I knew it for this. Once they found out I was lying all this time I'd be banished.

But not to act would be a sin that would send me to Hell. The few years left to me, decades perhaps, in the life I've loved, or my husband saved from eternal fire?

It was never a question. I had to do it.

My mother was long dead, I had discovered with little pang and now, truly, I had no loved ones left.

My husband was buried in his father's ancestral village, not the one where we had lived, so hopefully no one would recognize me. I chuckled at that, the idea that anyone would recognize that sweet-faced girl in me. I still felt young on the inside, and will say my eyes were still lovely when I took time in vain to look in the mirror.

The night before we reached the village, we found lodgings in a grand building. I had hidden in its stables to sleep, long ago, hiding from a lecherous trader who thought I should be grateful for his attention. Now, of course, we were respected and no one would consider such a thing.

I looked at these laughing women, their mouths full, their hands reaching for the next morsel, and I already felt great loss.

I knew that I would not sit with them again. They would not, they should not, accept me at table again.

I looked at their beloved faces one by one, each of them betrayed and yet not so. Because the person they knew was true and real; it was only a few short years I'd lied about. All we'd shared was true.

I HAD SEEN THIS PROCESS many times before but I could hardly breathe. I would see him soon! My great and only love, the man of my future and my past. Would he know me as others have known their loved ones? Or had the decades burning seared me from his memory?

There was little left of him.

No scent. No gases. Simply bones, and these mottled, with nothing left to keep them together but grave dust. I wept as I helped them set him on the chair, and they looked at me oddly. Already, they knew.

They must know.

"Gerald Montaigne, you stand charged and guilty of the sin of murder through sorcery. In your endeavor for unholy power, a life was lost in wasted sacrifice. Is this so?"

For minutes there was nothing but the faint sway of the breeze over all of us. I wondered: Was he innocent all along? Would he stay silent and then we could bury him and clear his name?

But then his voice. I would not have known it. In life he spoke loudly, drowning out others with his joyful tones. Now, there was the merest whisper.

"My sweetest love," he said, and at that I fell to such weeping as these women have never seen. I was the first, the very first thing he thought of.

"My sweetest love," he said, lisping through gapped teeth set in a yellowed jaw, "forgive me my sin of arrogance and disobedience, my sin of murder, my sin of loving you over the Lord. I repent deeply of all I have done. I cannot repent of loving you."

If he had lips they would have twisted now. I could see he was trying to keep silent, but they have no power to do that.

"Who will speak for you?" he said. My blood ran cold. "Who will speak for your lie that led to his death? He is not here, Jean. He did not sin as you said he did. And so that sin lies on you. Who will speak for you?"

He fell silent then and would not speak again.

I had lied. It was true. The man my parents wanted me to marry, who was old and fat and smelled of horse, he did not take me cruelly. And yet I had led my love to kill him, because what else could I do?

"Jean?" Mother Superior said, using my real name for the first time. "You may have one moment to speak."

I couldn't look upon this bony face and see my love; I had to close my eyes.

"We will find each other when I join you," I said. "And that will be as it should be."

With that, they placed his bones in the coffin. They didn't ask me to place the pennyroyal across his ribs, for which I was grateful.

MOTHER SUPERIOR HELD ME CLOSE, but I could feel the weakness of her embrace. When first we met, her hug nearly squeezed the life out of me. Now, there was little but a memory of that strength.

"I'm sorry to leave you but I will go, to save you asking."

"One day, perhaps, our law will change and you will be remembered as the great woman you are." She leaned close. "And we will give you the benefit of trial when the time comes."

I AM HAPPY KNOWING MY husband is no longer suffering eternal torment, and that I helped so many others out of that pit.

I live in the village close by to the house on the hill, taking in sewing and giving counsel when it is needed.

I sew my own story, this story, beginning with my walk up the hill and ending with me, no longer a small speck in the corner.

JANE, JAMESTOWN, THE STARVING TIME

SUN YUNG SHIN

. . . 1608, leagues and leagues of sea from the lavish bishopric of London . . .
It was a wide, white hunger, hardened arms open
Blank ribbon running taut through the town
Belly to belly, navel to spine, any body grown
Reverse—naught to eat but the crone's bony curse.
Time to bake your prayer, boiled stones
Roll on the tongue's blank bed.
My young body unbroken
Under sun, under wind—no groom—
      only rough hunger to lay me asunder.
Objects sharpened to the quick; my face, my fingers;
Words stuck in our throats:
    hollow, famish, ravening,
      something,
        anything
Eyes glassed and glittering followed my figure
Me, but a girl, ever filling the trough, oiling the bridle
But my maidenly hipbones Death's secret white saddle—

They came for me in the night (axes sorrowing the air)
Found my small cross on the wall, diary open
Me sleeping peaceful, five full fathoms deep,
True face in my pocket—
        Metal parting the dark,
My first, and last, kiss, that man's hatchet
Shrill iron split my dreams down their center
My last meal my own blood, fragrant as summer . . .
Time closed like a closet. It drained down a basin.
Then, me, not—me, no more awake than Jesus Christ.
No more alive than the moon's bright heist.

My drowned heart,
My fine cut of liver,
        red medal for my mother
        memento for my father
As they filleted—rinsed—dried—and—salted—
Everything blessed, said the priory's sisters,
        and everyone pardoned
I was a girl who was good, and now I'm their garden.

DORCAS AND ANN: A TRUE STORY

MOLLY TANZER

> "There is a little girl of about thirteen, upon whose Mind I shall have it in my Power to make the ... Experiment."
> —Calais, November 1769

DORCAS RETCHES AS SHE CURLS into a little ball on the quay. The cool salt spray chapping her freezing cheeks does nothing to settle her stomach. How could it? The earth is rocking as violently as the boat in which they'd crossed the Channel. The birds must feel dizzy, too, for they cry and wail as they whirl overhead.

As warm tears mingle with the cold spume, Dorcas feels sure she is dying, that her rolling stomach will never come to rest. She feels sicker than when she came through the typhus—but when she had typhus, her foster-mother had watched over her, her gentle voice a guide back from the strange lands of Dorcas's fever-dreams.

Now, Dorcas has only Ann. She loves the girl as a sister, but Ann is scarcely a year older, and the whispered reassurances and gentle touches of one with twelve years of life experience to one who has but eleven can scarcely be as reassuring as a mother's, even a surrogate one's.

"Lucretia," whispers Ann. Dorcas cracks an eye and sees Ann's sweet, narrow face framed by a cascade of chestnut curls. "You must get up. *He* says the—" Ann utters some French word that Dorcas has never heard, and definitely doesn't want to learn "—won't wait, and our luggage has been loaded. He says we must go or be left behind with nothing but the clothes on our backs."

Dorcas *hates* being called Lucretia, which was what their mutual guardian Mr. Day—the he of whom Ann had spoken—had renamed her after taking her away from the Orphan Hospital at Shrewsbury. Ann, likewise, Mr. Day had rechristened Sabrina, but Dorcas still thinks of her as Ann.

Sabrina and Lucretia! Ridiculous names, hardly suitable for two wretched foundlings without anything more to their name than a Bible, a Book of Common Prayer, and the orphanage's own publication, a pamphlet titled *Instructions for Apprentices*. Why Mr. Day insists on calling them by these elaborate titles is obscure to her—as obscure as why he would seek a "future housekeeper" in an orphanage, and then spirit his two potentials away to his chambers in London, and now to France. Dorcas's stomach twists in a new direction as she thinks about that . . . she is now in a country she knows she couldn't find on a map, a sea away from everyone she's ever known. Anyone who might care what befell her.

Dorcas wants to get up, to do what her guardian—and more importantly to her, what Ann—is asking her to do, but when she tries to move she only manages to retch again. She cast up her breakfast into the sea hours before, and now she can only bring up white foam tinged with pink. She gags on it, spits before Ann can pull her salt-crusted golden locks away from her face with her slender, clever fingers.

"You poor thing," says Ann.

Dorcas moans. "I can't get on the . . . the whatever-you-said."

"It's just a stagecoach," says Ann, her tone urging Dorcas to recover.

Dorcas sighs, curling up tighter into a ball.

"Please, Lucretia!" whispers Ann, more desperate now. Dorcas knows why; she hears heavy, stomping footfalls approaching, and suddenly fear overwhelms her nausea. Almost.

"What is the meaning of this? Did I not say we must go?"

Dorcas can hear the impatience in his voice as his shadow falls across her shoulders. Without the afternoon sun upon her, and with Mr. Day looming over her, she shivers.

"*Lucretia.*" He is sterner than a vicar, their guardian, and just as obscure. "Why are you on the ground?"

"She's ill," says Ann, standing, moving between them as if her slender body would protect Dorcas from the towering giant if her pleading does not. "Please, Mr. Day, just give her a moment. . . ."

"She'll feel better once she's up."

Dorcas feels her stomach roll again, just like the unending swells of the awful sea. She is terrified of him, but cannot move. She would fall, she knows it, if she tried to stand.

"If we want to make the inn, we need to leave *now*," he says, his voice flinty and precise. "This waywardness is simply unacceptable."

"It's not waywardness. She's really ill," says Ann with a fierceness that surprises Dorcas. But Ann is less afraid of him than she is, perhaps because Ann likes him more.

Dorcas also suspects Ann doesn't quite realize just how precarious their mutual situation really is.

"Never interrupt me again, Sabrina," he says shortly. Ann gasps as he pushes her aside and squats down beside Dorcas. "I will help you to stand, Lucretia, but then you must come along. Do you understand me?"

Dorcas looks up and into his plump, strangely young face with its small eyes and pouting lips and shock of wild black hair that hangs lank and damp over his shoulders. It occurs to her that he is only one and twenty, just ten years older than she. Though she has seen little enough of the world, she knows he cuts an unusual figure, wearing no wig and dressed in his austere black clothes. If she had seen him in the street, back at the orphanage, she and her sisters would have laughed at him.

But she isn't at the orphanage. He took her away from there, and made it very clear that they would not take her back again—she was, and is, *his*. She belongs to him now.

It is that thought that prompts her to try a little harder. After all, if he tires of what he considers her "waywardness" and discards her, there will be no way for her to return home . . . and there had been enough whispering at the orphanage that she knows *exactly* what will become of her should that come to pass.

She offers him her hand. He takes it, and she feels him shudder when they touch.

He does not often touch her.

"Good girl," he says, as she crawls to her knees, then gains her feet, shaky as a newborn lamb. "Come along, now. Both of you."

Ann brightens to be remembered, and Dorcas sees her almost skip as she follows the departing Mr. Day—before stopping, turning, and running back to Dorcas's side.

"You're doing wonderfully, Lucretia," she says, smiling, shining from their guardian's attention, "and I'll help you the rest of the way."

My name is Dorcas, thinks Dorcas, but she doesn't say it aloud. What would be the point? She would only hurt Ann, and she loves Ann.

As for their guardian . . . it is difficult to say what she feels for him, but fear is a large part of it. She will, at least on the surface, comply with his odd requests. She has no choice.

> "Her Understanding is naturally good, I believe, her Temper remarkably tender & affectionate; she is yet innocent, & unprejudic'd; she has seen nothing of the World, & is unattached to it."
> —Paris, November 1769

"Lucretia, your lack of diligence is nothing short of dismaying."

Mr. Day holds a book before her eyes, his finger marking a page very, very close to the beginning. Dorcas trembles. The book, by a man called Rousseau, seems to be a story about a little boy who grows up learning things in decidedly odd ways, but ways that make him superior—says the author, at least—to other little boys.

Dorcas usually loves stories, but the words in this one are hard and interspersed with so many lessons and philosophies that it feels more like a sermon than a story when she can understand it at all. She prefers the fairy tales her foster-mother used to tell her.

Plus, the boy is French, and the author is French, and though they have only been in Paris a few days she is sick to the teeth of the French. Their ways, their food, even their clothes are all hateful to her. She hears them now, outside the window, their conversation as grating as the cries of a flock of peacocks, and every bit as unintelligible.

"You will finish this book. . . ." He looks her up and down where she stands, her breath coming fast and her palms sweaty where they're clasped behind her back. "You will finish this *chapter* before we leave for Lyons," he amends himself. "And, you will produce for me ten perfect alphabets in your hornbook. Do you understand?"

"Yes, sir," she mumbles.

"And Sabrina . . ."

Dorcas glances up to see Ann smiling, happy to be noticed.

"Just finish your book," he says, almost dismissively. "I haven't determined what you will read next. Perhaps it will come to me while I walk. Good day to you, girls."

"Good day, sir," says Ann cheerfully, as Dorcas mutters her farewell.

Ann dutifully returns her gaze to the page. Dorcas, however, does not;

she runs to the window. Leaning out, she watches her guardian trotting down the street, a plump crow waddling away on its own business among more brightly colored birds. It makes Dorcas furious that he should be so free, while she is trapped, and she grabs the shutters. Scarcely glancing at the busy street below, she shuts them with a sharp rap.

Ann, startled, looks up from whatever book she's reading.

"I can't *stand* their incessant chattering," spits Dorcas.

"The people of this city?"

Dorcas, in spite of herself, smiles to see her dear friend so confused. Ann likes Paris—well, what she's seen of it. More often than not they are kept cooped up in their rooms. But Ann is as happy sitting in a strange chair to study as a familiar one.

"There's only one person in Paris worth talking to," says Dorcas, "and I have her right here."

"Lucretia!" Ann sets aside her book and rises to embrace Dorcas. "You are so sweet and so kind." Taking hold of Dorcas's hands, she spins her around the little sitting room, which their guardian has declared their temporary schoolroom.

"I'm neither," says Dorcas, releasing her friend. "You're the one who's sweet and kind. I'm amazed roses and jewels don't fall from your lips every time you speak." She smiles ruefully, and without ire. "And toads and vipers from mine. I can never think of anything nice to say."

"You're just homesick," says Ann.

"You can't be homesick if you haven't a home."

Dorcas regrets the words as soon as they leave her mouth, almost as much as if seven toads and three vipers had fallen out instead.

"Don't you feel *this* is your home, Lucretia?"

Sometimes Dorcas thinks the only lesson Mr. Day has actually taught her is how to smile with her teeth clenched. The thought that this suite of rooms in this terrible city might be home makes Dorcas want to smash everything in it to pieces. But, for Ann's sake, she resists.

"Of course I do," she says. "I'm just bored."

"It is ever so much duller when Mr. Day goes out. But, he has business to attend to."

Dorcas makes a noncommittal noise. She actually likes their chambers far better when their guardian is absent from them. Dorcas doesn't like the way he hovers and frets, the way he stares and rages. But most of all she hates when she notices him watching them—but mostly her—with her head bowing low over her book in the flickering candlelight. The look in his eyes is so very strange, as if it thrills him to see her cramming knowledge into her mind.

It is a hungry look, and it always strikes Dorcas as strange that she, rather than his more diligent pupil, is the one favored with more attention.

Dorcas throws herself into a chair. She knows she is being petulant—and knows, too, that if she has made no progress by the time he returns, he will stand over her. He will raise his voice. She will be threatened with being cast into the street and abandoned.

"Why not work on your hornbook?" suggests Ann, with all the earnest, trusting simplicity she adopts when discussing the will of their guardian.

"No." Dorcas hates writing more than she hates reading.

"But Mr. Day—"

"I know what Mr. Day wants!" She doesn't mean to, but the sentiment erupts out of her.

Ann looks troubled. "You don't like him," she says.

Dorcas shivers. "I'm afraid of him."

"Afraid!" Ann is genuinely astonished. "But why?"

Ann is smarter than her in all but one way, Dorcas decides. "Because I don't understand why we're here," she says.

"Mr. Day is educating us," quotes Ann piously. This is exactly what Mr. Day says whenever questioned. "He wishes us to learn all he can teach us, and away from the distractions and temptations of London."

"To be his housekeeper." Dorcas does not bother to keep the skepticism from her voice. "Ann—" She sees the other girl flinch at the use of her real name, and repents. "*Sabrina*, why would a housekeeper need to know the position of . . . Heaven's body?"

"Heavenly bodies," answers Ann. "The stars and planets, Lucretia. You really ought to listen more; it's so interesting."

"As you say."

"I *do* say."

"And what do you say to my question? Why should a housekeeper know such things?"

Ann shrugs. "I love learning what he thinks I ought to know," she says, very quietly and with such obvious sorrow in her thin, keen voice that Dorcas thinks her heart might break.

It isn't fair. Why Mr. Day is so focused on his less impressive pupil escapes Dorcas entirely. Ann is so convinced of his absolute wisdom and authority, but it seems to Dorcas he is misplacing his attentions. Surely it would be more reasonable for him to lavish himself upon the one of them who actually has potential? If as he says he wants a whip-smart girl to take charge of his household, Ann is the clear choice.

Ann would never say so, but she knows it's true. She must!

She looks so downcast Dorcas is moved to pick up the dreaded volume and turn to where she had last given up. Perhaps if she corrects her behavior, pays attention, does what she is told, Mr. Day will find himself possessed of more energy and come to regard to poor Ann as she deserves.

> *"Is it possible to prevent the Impressions of Prejudice & Folly in a Mind like this? Will it be possible to fortify it in such a Manner, that the Pleasures of the World will make no Impressions upon it, because they are irrational?"*
> —Avignon, December 1769

DORCAS MANAGES TO BEHAVE AS they travel to Lyons, applying herself to lessons and speaking respectfully when spoken to, but the journey to their final destination, Avignon, tries her sorely. The jolting wagon bruises her bottom, and the bad food in bad inns troubles it still further; the cold makes her miserable and the uncertainty over their situation bothers her during the long hours on the road, as much as she tries to keep her mind on the present rather than the future.

And, worst of all, her plan has not worked. Dorcas's attention to studies was instantly noticed and praised, yes—and Mr. Day's threats of chucking her out in a bin, reduced—but Mr. Day's interest in poor Ann was also reduced. He continues to throw books carelessly at Ann, scarcely noticing how she devours them, only to give Dorcas a gift, a book of fairy tales about the Greeks and Romans, unfamiliar to her but far more interesting than *Emile*.

It's awful to witness; Ann is obviously withering for want of his notice. Dorcas can see it in her eyes, in her bearing. Why she should want it, Dorcas doesn't know, but she does, and it is agonizing to watch her seek it so fruitlessly, like a houseplant growing toward a shuttered window through which it sensed there might one day stream some sunlight. Any time Mr. Day calls for anything, Ann is there, as though there could be no greater pleasure in life than fetching him a glass of wine or building up the fire when he is cold. She adores him, wants nothing more than to please him, but among all the tasks set to the girl, this she could not do. Mr. Day finds fault with everything she does, and the unfairness of it distresses both girls considerably.

"I ought to have been more graceful," whispers Ann, one evening after they'd settled into their new chambers in Avignon. She's fretting; earlier that night, she spilled a bit of soup while ladling it out for their guardian, and he had faulted her for waste. "I'll do better in the future."

Dorcas takes Ann's cold, slender hands in hers, trying to warm them under the thin blankets of their shared bed. They must be quiet, conversing—if he hears them, he will separate them, and neither wants to chance cold as well as lonely nights. "You act beautifully no matter what you do," she assures her friend. "If he can't see it, it's because he's blind."

"No, no," says Ann, protesting just like Dorcas knew she would. "He is just . . . demanding, as is his right as a rich man who wants a perfect housekeeper. After all, a housekeeper should lead the servants. She cannot spill his soup."

"Anyone in England would be happy to have a housekeeper as intelligent and capable as you," hisses Dorcas, trying not to let frustration and dismissiveness creep into her tone. She cannot let herself become angry at Mr. Day; when she is angry at him, she snaps at him, which leads to rows and the danger of being cast into the snow. It is so hard, though, for she loves this girl who is so devoted to excellence in every part of her life, whether it be walking and speaking with grace, learning her letters, doing maths or figuring out lessons on natural history, geography, and moral philosophy.

Dorcas feels nary a hint of jealousy over this. She has no desire to do any of those things well—she feels lucky that she is happiest when knitting, mending, or just being left alone. Still, it pains her to see Ann so unhappy, and that is *exactly* why she's been thinking quite a bit about this problem, instead of paying attention to her lessons, as the dressing of the shops and the passersby beyond their casement has turned more seasonal.

"Christmas is coming," says Dorcas. "You should get him something nice."

"Mr. Day cares nothing for fripperies," says Ann.

To Dorcas's mind, this was yet another example of the remarkable difference between what Mr. Day *said* and what he *did*. While he might condemn the pleasures of the world, the man absolutely loved luxury. Why, he'd bought himself a new wardrobe, still black but cut in the French style, and as much as he spoke about the virtues of simplicity in eating, kept a fine table.

"I'm not speaking of *fripperies*," whispers Dorcas. "I think you ought to write a letter. He keeps going on and on about us writing letters to his friends. I think he wants to show us off to his acquaintances, as we were such ignorant little savages when he acquired us."

Ann considers this, her thin face drawn and serious in the moonlight that streams in through the cracks in the shutters. "Perhaps you are right," she admits. "Though I fear my penmanship will not be up to his standards."

"He'll be *delighted*," says Dorcas, grateful that the need to be quiet takes some of the spite out of her tone. It's infuriating to see how Mr. Day's treatment of her friend has made her incapable of seeing her own accomplishments for what they are. In six months, Ann has gone from being an ordinary foundling with a basic education to a well-read young woman who could not only sign her own name, but write lists for her guardian and presumably compose a passable letter if she had enough time.

"I hope so," says Ann, so full of doubt it makes Dorcas doubt herself. Thankfully, Mr. Day is, actually, delighted. By Ann, at least. . . .

On the 25th of December, he presents the girls with parcels of plain but sturdy material for them to make new dresses for themselves. Dorcas knows it is a gift befitting a future housekeeper, but she still feels it's a bit stingy—given how much time they spend reading what he tells them to read, studying what he tells them to study, writing what he tells them to write, cleaning his house and doing all the washing, he could have gotten them something nice. Something fun or beautiful, like a doll (Ann said they were too old for dolls, but Dorcas disagrees), or perhaps felt for one of the fanciful hats popular with the young women of Avignon (Dorcas didn't need Ann to weigh in on this opinion; she knows Mr. Day's opinions of young women's fashions: the Whore of Babylon had been invoked more than once in their presence, to Dorcas's giggles and Ann's horror).

Pleased with their "pretty thanks," he settles in before the fire. He obviously doesn't expect them to have anything for him—how could they, not being allowed to leave the house without his supervision, or make anything when his schedule for their education is so demanding?—so when Ann approaches him in their modest parlor, presenting him with a small tube of parchment, bound with a scrap of string, as there was no ribbon to be had in their house, he looks surprised and, actually, a little touched.

"What is it?" he asks, taking it gently from Ann's bony hand.

"It's for you," manages Ann.

"From both of you?"

Ann nods, but Dorcas speaks up. "From Sabrina," she says.

"It was Lucretia's idea," says Ann, to Dorcas's admiration . . . and annoyance.

Mr. Day looks at Ann, considering, blinking like an owl before pulling the string and letting the parchment unfurl in his lap. His brow furrows as he looks it over, then his eyes widen and a smile turns his plump lips up at the corners.

"Sabrina," he says warmly. "You wrote a letter."

"I left the address blank," she says shyly, blushing from his obvious and long-desired approval. "And I kept it general, in case you had someone in particular you wanted to send it to. Lucretia told me you wanted to send someone you knew a letter, so . . ."

"And Lucretia? Did you write one, too?" asks Mr. Day, cutting Sabrina off and turning to her. His expression is hopeful; she has his full attention. Just off to his side, Ann's countenance crumples to be so soon forgotten after such a triumph.

Dorcas tries to remember Christmas, but she is too angry.

"No," she says sourly, looking at her feet. "I *hate* writing."

"Lucretia!"

"I wish I hadn't so much as a name, so I wouldn't ever have to write it." She looks up at Mr. Day, who is now on his feet. He is looming over her, as he is wont to do. She imagines herself shoved out the door into the Christmas darkness, alone, then swallows her fear. She is tired of him, tired of his treatment of her friend—more tired than she is afraid. "And anyway, if I was to write my name, I'd write *Dorcas!*" she cries, and flees up the steps into her shared room.

"Lucretia!" she hears him cry. "Lucretia, come down at once!"

She will not. She is too angry.

She sits on her bed, shaking all over with rage. She's done it; she's made her feelings clear. She's finally, clearly put herself forward as the opposite of Ann in terms of the shape of their hearts—a shape not so easily seen as that of their features or figures.

The only question is, what will Mr. Day do now?

Perhaps an hour later, Ann comes to bed, looking troubled but also healthier than she has in months.

"I wish you'd come back," she says, getting under the blankets. "We mulled some wine. I had scarcely a thimbleful, but it was so pleasant."

Dorcas bites her tongue to stifle the urge to say that she'd rather drink poison with the Devil than wine with Mr. Day, but her friend is so happy, and she doesn't want to spoil her joy.

"You should apologize to him," says Ann sleepily.

"I won't," says Dorcas.

"Lucretia, you *must* . . . you must. What if he. . . ?" says Ann, and then she falls asleep.

Dorcas watches Ann for a time, her cheeks rosy with wine. She is right, of course—Ann has the measure of their master, just as she did. She must apologize, and soon. If Dorcas reveals too early that she is completely unfit to be his housekeeper, why should he retain her? Why keep wasting his money on her room and board?

Slowly, quietly, she creeps from their room. She knows she should be pleased that light is still spilling from under Mr. Day's office door, but instead, terror takes her by the throat. She feels it squeezing her there. What will he do to her, if she goes in alone, this late, when he had been making merry? For some reason, she recalls the feel of his trembling fingers whenever he dares put a hand to her shoulder, the back of her neck, her hand.

This, she feels certain, is not how men ought to treat their housekeepers, but then again, she knows so little of the world.

She knocks.

"Come in," she hears.

He is scribbling at his desk, the same focus apparent in his eyes that Dorcas sees in Ann's, when she writes.

"Sir," she begins.

"Wait," he says, and keeps writing.

She is cold in her shift; she only threw a shawl over her shoulders. She walks to his fireplace. There, she warms herself until he says, "Lucretia . . . come here, child."

She obeys, standing before him. He looks her up and down, and though he sits so close, and the light from the candle is clear enough, she cannot not read him.

"So you hate writing, do you?"

"I do, sir," she says. "I'm sorry." The lie tastes bitter in her mouth, like lime rind in a slice of Christmas cake.

Mr. Day hesitates, then pats his thigh. Lucretia stares at him; it seems almost like he wants to dandle her on his knee as if she were a girl half her age. He pats his leg again, and she acquiesces, taking a seat.

"Writing will serve you well in life," he says, gesturing at his desk. She looks at the piles of papers before her, the incomprehensible ink scrawls swimming before her eyes. Reading printing is bad enough, but the loopy letters done by hand confused her further. She scans the page closest to her and can recognize only one word: *Pygmalion*.

But that word threw the rest into sharp focus.

"I favor you . . . for my housekeeper," begins Mr. Day, awkwardly, but Dorcas's attention isn't on him. The name is so familiar, but so strange. Where might she know it from?

"I have always thought you the superior choice," he continues, sweeping her unbound hair away from her shoulder. She shivers to feel cool air prickle the skin there into gooseflesh. Still, she stares at the paper.

You will Think me a greater Pygmalion than the Original when you see what is Enclosed, it says.

"And yet, you defy me," he says.

This is a Letter written by an ignorant Foundling & Orphan, but I think it tolerable good for a First effort.

"I cannot have defiance in my life, not from my . . . a . . . helpmeet."

Unfortunately, it comes from the Hand of She who was first chosen, but second loved.

Ann had been picked first from the Orphan Hospital. . . .

"I wonder if knowing you are the one I love best will inspire you to do better," he says, his breath hot, close on her neck.

Suddenly, Dorcas remembers where she's read that queer name. "Happy Christmas, Mr. Day," she cries and, leaping from his lap, she flees back to her room.

The full moon outside makes the snow shine, and by that blue light Dorcas pages through the book of Greek fairy stories until she finds the right page.

So disgusted with the painted women of Cyprus, the sculptor Pygmalion fashioned himself a woman of ivory, pure, simple, and ignorant of the world. But, created by his own hand to suit his own pleasure, so beautiful was the sculpture that Pygmalion fell in love with her, and begged Venus to make her real. The goddess, pleased with his prayer, brought the statue to life, and Pygmalion took her in his arms. Soon after, she bore him a girl-child, Paphos, who—

Dorcas shuts the book and returns to bed, but it is a long time before she sleeps.

> "Will it be possible entirely to exclude the Idea of love? Love I am firmly convinc'd is the Effect of Prejudce & Imagination; a rational Mind is incapable of it, at least in any great Degree."
>
> —Avignon, March 1770

DORCAS HIDES HER KNOWLEDGE LIKE a dragon his treasure all through the winter, pretending ignorance of what she knows Mr. Day's plan must be.

A housekeeper! No, he wants a wife—a wife fashioned by his own hand. One unprejudiced by the world and educated to his specifications. Why else would he have taken them to France, where they could be influenced by no one but him, given their ignorance of the language? Why else would he favor Dorcas, with her plump, pretty face and blond hair, instead of the fine mind and subtle fingers of her almost-sister? Yes, he might wish for an ideal young woman to scrub floors and do the washing and pour his wine, but he also wanted her for other matters. Matters more relevant to personal beauty—beauty Dorcas would have given up in an instant if it would stop Mr. Day from looking at her, craving her, touching her.

Spring brings not only warmer weather, but a garrison of soldiers to Avignon. Rude and boisterous, they throng the streets in their smart uniforms, harassing women and making comments at men. Ann hates it, and fears to go out on their daily walk, even with their chaperone.

Dorcas, however, sees some merit in their rudeness—well, at least she sees a use for her beauty. Again, she concocts a scheme, a more dangerous one than the last, but she must get away from this town, this country. Mr. Day has been speaking of leaving, of longing for home, but he is an idler. Dorcas believes she can force his hand by studying these wild men every day, seeing who she can count on to be where. When for a week in a row she sees the same officer, distinguished by his mustache from the rest, and whom she hears speaking a bit of English here and there, she makes her move.

"A stone in my shoe," she cries, and lurches over to the stoop of a café where the officer sits with his friends in the pale spring sunshine. Unlacing her shoe quickly, so that Ann and their maid cannot not drag her away too soon, she leans in.

"Can you speak English?" she asks.

"A little," he says, as his fellows elbow one another and chatter. It does not sound as if they speak of nice things.

"Tomorrow, will you be here?"

"Lucretia, come away!" cries Ann, gesturing. Dorcas nods, pointing at her foot.

"Maybe, if I 'ave reason," says the officer.

"We will walk here, with a man," says Dorcas. "I want you to . . . to speak to him."

"Of what matter?"

"Of her," she says, pointing at Ann. "Say you wish to . . . marry his daughter."

The officer raises an eyebrow at her. "Marry daughter? But *you* are the fair one, *mon cherie*."

"No, *she* is. Tell him that. Say she is beautiful, even if you don't believe it."

"But I do not wish . . . to *marry*." He leers at her.

"He won't accept your proposal. I promise. Please! Do this?" Dorcas is getting desperate.

"I will do it . . . for a kiss," he says. "*Now.*"

Dorcas glances at Ann, who is deep in conversation with their guardian. They are motioning at her, clearly unsure how to get her back without approaching the men, their conversation clearly impeded by Ann's ignorance of French, and their chaperone's, of English.

"One kiss," she says, and leans in to peck his cheek.

He pulls her into him and, gripping her head in his, presses his lips to hers. Her heart beats a wild tattoo as she pulls away, disgusted. But she senses the sacrifice will be worth it.

"If I do what you say . . . maybe more next time?" says the officer, raising his eyebrows.

Dorcas nods, but only because she is fairly certain there won't be a next time.

"He outraged you!" says Ann, as Dorcas flees back to her side. "Oh, Lucretia! How did you bear it?"

"It was terrible," she says truthfully, "but I got away."

"Well, I won't tell Mr. Day," says Ann. "But as for Marie . . ."

"It can't be helped."

Indeed, she does not wish it to be.

Mr. Day flies into a rage when he hears from the maid what happened.

"We will go tomorrow and see what the scoundrel has to say for himself," says Mr. Day. "Let's see what he does when he sees who protects you, Lucretia!"

"Surely he doesn't mean to take us along," says Ann, her eyes wide.

Dorcas just shrugs.

Dressed in their most modest attire, they are brought by Mr. Day back to the café the next day. Dorcas feels a sense of relief when the officer is indeed there. He winks at her, and Dorcas's breath comes a bit faster—he *must* remember it is Ann he is supposed to admire!

Mr. Day begins berating him in French, and the two girls wait in his shadow as their guardian gestures at them. The officer raises his hands in supplication, then points . . . at Ann.

Mr. Day looks over his shoulder in surprise.

Dorcas would give everything she owns to understand what the officer says next, but all she can catch is *belle*. Mr. Day seems surprised and looks at Ann in a new way after the officer finishes his proposal. Or proposition—who can say?

Surely he isn't considering . . . Oh! Dorcas curses her impetuousness. What if their guardian decides to unload his less pleasing ward, rather than what she had expected?

"*Belle,*" repeats Mr. Day, in wonder—and he has eyes only for Ann.

Dorcas feels her heart leap like a deer; no, she's done the right thing. It is difficult, but she does her best to look sullen and uninteresting as Mr. Day marvels, seeing Ann as if for the first time.

After few words to the officer, who readily agrees to whatever it is Mr. Day says, presumably that he would not indeed be marrying Ann, Mr. Day leads them away. But it is to Ann whom he turns first.

"Sabrina, come along," he says. "We must select your next book, and I wish to look over your penmanship. It is much improved even since Christmas."

"Thank you, Mr. Day," she says, and truly, she does look radiant in that moment.

"And you come too, Lucretia," he says.

Ann looked over her shoulder to Dorcas, worried, but Dorcas cannot pretend at feeling any disappointment whatsoever.

"Is my scheme practicable? If practicable by what Means?"
—London, April 1770

"Apprenticed?"

Tears stand in Ann's wide eyes as Mr. Day tells them the news.

"Yes, to a milliner, a fine trade for a young woman," he says, almost carelessly, shoving his arms into his black coat. He is going out, to finalize the agreement. If all goes as expected, Dorcas will begin tomorrow.

"But that means Lucretia will have to leave us, and we've only just returned to London!"

Dorcas keeps all the snakes and toads in her mouth, where they belong—and wonders if the sister in that fairy tale had ever managed any success in that regard. It is a skill that has served her well already, and likely will continue to do so, in her new life.

Her new life! She's escaping. She will never see Mr. Day again, never feel him looking at her. She will never again be forced to endure his touch.

Her only unhappiness is Ann. She will miss the girl so much . . . and she is worried for her, too. She still believes she is to be Mr. Day's housekeeper. But, it is obvious to Dorcas how well she loves him . . . surely she will be happy to have more of him, as his wife.

"Better to have her begin sooner rather than later," says Mr. Day, looking with tender fondness upon Ann. But to Dorcas's dismay, his attention does not make her shine.

Mr. Day does not notice.

"Put your shawl on, Lucretia. They want to meet you."

Dorcas obeys, though as they leave their former chambers together, she looks back at poor Ann, hovering ghostlike in the doorway. What will her almost-sister do without her? She is so tender, so ignorant, so sweet. She is in reality the innocent ivory girl craved by their strange and pompous Pygmalion. But ivory was not a strong substance, as she had learned through their lessons. It could crack under pressure, yellow with age and ill-use.

She waves to Ann, but Mr. Day scolds her for lack of attention and Dorcas must turn her eyes forward. She'd been feeling so certain that she had done everything for the sake of her friend's happiness . . . but now, she fears it has all truly been for herself.

THE RESURRECTED

S.P. MISKOWSKI

"*Then said Jesus unto them plainly, Lazarus is dead. And I am glad for your sakes that I was not there, to the intent ye may believe.*"

—John 11:14–15

Dear Odelia,

In advance I'd better apologize for the state of these documents. I know how meticulous you are, and this must seem like an awful mess. Bear with me. I'll try to make sense.

Do I sound frustrated? Well, I admit it. Usually I can offer an educated guess re: provenance. Not this time. The whole bundle of documents seemed to fall into my hands purely by chance. I've been on such a strange adventure ever since—whether accidental or guided by an outside force, I can't say. (More on this later, when I see you. I'd rather not go into it here.)

Item #1 in the bundle looks to me to be a journal, possibly a medical record. It's a slim volume, date stamped, maybe to appear more official—but for whose eyes? Was it part of a larger set? Who would benefit from such a record?

Most of all I wonder why the documents were bundled together. Nothing ties the journal to Mount Coffin, or a clinic, or the other items attached. All the same, I have a feeling the "doctor" who kept the journal may be the woman in question. If so, you owe me a martini.

Hugs.

—G.L.

No. 36
(a) 24 (h) 5.3 (w) 89
Admitted—July 15, 1911
Notes
Original complaint (diagnosed by family physician as hysteria) included heart palpitations, fatigue, dizziness, fainting, and shortness of breath. Following two-month regimen, all symptoms have ceased. Daily appearance ranges from fair to above average. Paperwork complete. No further correspondence permitted. Beginning final treatment cycle.

Sept. 1

    Hot tea for breakfast, followed by one slice of bread.

    Half of one (mashed) potato for dinner. Permitted small addition of salt.

    One cup of broth for supper.

Sept. 2

    An orange and a cup of hot water for breakfast.

    Bowel movement.

    An orange for dinner.

    One cup of hot water for supper.

    Usual and expected signs of fatigue, irritability.

Sept. 3

    An orange for breakfast.

    Broth for dinner.

    Broth for supper.

    Subject complained of headache. No salt allowed from this moment on.

Sept. 4

One cup of tomato soup for breakfast.

Determined the subject must not receive dinner or supper. Breaking reliance on physical sustenance is essential to attain next level.

Mandatory exercise before dawn, nurses assisting in a walk to the garden and back.

Sept. 5

No breakfast.

Broth for dinner.

No bowel movement.

An orange for supper.

At bedtime, subject showing color in face and throat. Assured by the first signs of robust health, subject is inclined to follow regimen precisely.

During the night, subject complained of soreness in abdomen. Beginning next phase of purification tomorrow.

Sept. 6

An orange for breakfast.

An orange for dinner.

An orange for supper.

Subject unwilling to take exercise at dawn. No degree of admonishment or punishment made a difference, this time.

Sept. 7

Two oranges for breakfast.

Bowel movement liquid, pale amber.

No dinner.

No supper.

Sept. 8

No breakfast.

No dinner.

Attempted bowel movement.

One cup of broth for supper.

Subject discovered out of bed before sunrise, on stairs. Reported feeling dizzy. Restrained to avoid further incident.

Sept. 9

No breakfast.

No bowel movement attempted.

No dinner.

One cup of broth for supper.

Began enemas. Cramping and vomiting recorded by nurse on duty. Begin dietary substitutions.

Sept. 10

One cup of strawberry tea for breakfast.

Attempted bowel movement. Liquid, almost clear.

One cup of tomato soup for dinner.

No supper.

Subject complains of pain in back, next to ribcage, and soreness in legs.

Sept. 11

No breakfast.

One cup of tomato soup for dinner.

No supper.

Subject continues to complain of soreness in arms and legs. Have instructed nurses on administering compresses. Subject is accustomed to extraordinary material comforts. These are the trying times. Nurses trained to handle attempts at bribery or coercion.

Sept. 12
    An orange for breakfast.

    Diarrhea.

    An orange for lunch.

    No supper.

    Subject complains of increased back pain and sores on back of legs. Nurses administered compresses.

Sept. 13
    Water for breakfast.

    Water for dinner.

    Water for supper.

    Subject refuses water. Enema administered by nurses. Subject no longer expresses discomfort. Breathing shallow.

Sept. 14
    No breakfast.

    No dinner.

    No supper.

    Subject must be prepared. The moment of transcendence will be recorded with a nurse present.

Dear Odelia,
    Next we have Item #2, the letter I discuss more in-depth in my note at the end. Rough guess, mid to late 1880s. All in the most exquisite handwriting—truly a lost art—although we're missing the salutation, the signature, and the address of origin.
    Grrrr.
    —G.L.

Without dwelling on any accusations in your letter, Professor, I must emphasize how thoroughly I have kept my promise, to report any worthy specimens for your private collection, as our party and our scouts may encounter them. Throughout our travels we have met and come to rely upon numerous individuals for transport, for repairs to equipment, and for warnings of weather conditions. We have seen a fair number of injuries and scars among these individuals. No extraordinary physical anomalies have, as yet, come to my attention.

As I anticipated (you will remember) during our final meeting seven months ago, our party has arrived much too late to observe the practices and artifacts recorded by your Lieutenant Warren during his expeditions. I assure you, there is nothing more to be found. Two fires in the past decade caused extensive damage to the spot where Warren first landed. All the known sites we discussed have been raided, and more than once. Remaining materials are in poor condition. The longhouses of the interior have burned to the foundations. Along the coast at all navigable points along the river, burial canoes are nonexistent. According to reliable sources, all have been split open for the ornamental costumes and cadavers inside, and subsequently discarded. We have also run short of bribes to offer, in our pursuit of heirlooms salvaged and hidden by native family members. Oddities are hard to come by and more precious items (your compressed skulls, for example) were stolen or ruined long ago.

You may be surprised at the news that Mount Coffin has become a scenic destination, an innocuous attraction for steamboat passengers. Regarding accommodations farther upriver, in place of the native dwellings you described we found a thriving population of newcomers, with a post office, a hotel, a blacksmith, and a grocery store. No natives were to be seen in the streets. And no rooms were available. We have been forced to move farther north and east, many miles inland, to a sparse, impoverished area, barely a town, where the shopkeepers and homesteaders base their hopes on the rumor of a railroad extension. In this, and all other matters, I resist the temptation to share what I know. Despite the telegraph and a proliferation of broadsides, the residents rely heavily on speculation.

My companions insist that I recuperate before we move on. My continuing poor health is the reason for these repeated delays, which I purposely neglected to state in previous correspondence. I regret my failure to keep you apprised of my true situation. Please accept my apology and consider this my final report until I have regained my strength. We may reside at this location for some time.

Our move inland has been necessary though not ideal. Although we enjoy the rare comfort of beds, in a half-empty boarding house, we find ourselves in the company of a surprising number of amateur healers in place of physicians.

Rather than scratch these lines on a piece of paper destined to travel hundreds of miles, only to disappoint the benefactor whose generosity is responsible for an otherwise spectacular journey, I have decided to relate a story told to me by one of our guides. The tale's anecdotal nature seems to be characteristic of the region, and it may serve some purpose in your lectures.

The man who told it to me spoke perfect English with no discernible accent, although he was fluent both in German and Russian. He appeared to be of European descent but he had lived among natives for some time. He claimed to be the eleventh son of a fur trapper from far north. This style of boasting is common among men with no social standing or lineage. He wore his hair quite long and unbound; his clothes were sewn from deer hide, his boots fashioned out of elk skin. He had the calm eye of an experienced hunter. He swore the tale he offered me was true, though not in every detail.

I hope you find the fellow's descriptions amusing and do not recoil at the events described. I have transcribed the story with some revision for the sake of clarity. The effort has consumed my strength. I feel a deep and irresistible need for sleep.

A window view of the frozen pond is my only reminder of the approaching holidays. Please extend my good wishes to your family—your wife and your beautiful daughters. How glad you must be to see them safe and protected, each day, in the harbor of civilized society.

Dear Odelia,

Despite its introductory manner, my guess is the preceding letter was composed soon after the next document: Item #3. Notice the handwriting is quite different. Did the author of the letter ask a third party to transcribe the story?

Anyway, the backwoods tall tale isn't suited to my taste. As you know, I'm a Jane Austen gal. But I think this particular story might interest you. The final section is vague and it's possible the woman in question started her so-called medical career much earlier than you or Delphine supposed.

Hm.

—G.L.

Beyond the alders and cottonwood, on the north shore of the Columbia River, you can trace the outline of a great rock rising, sharp and black, leaning out toward the water. This stack is the smallest drop in a wide circle of volcanoes and mountain ranges anchoring the region. Its surface was eventually softened by fir trees, and marked with footpaths taken by families placing and visiting their dead. This is how it was for centuries.

The People traveled the river by canoe during hunting and fishing seasons. They camped and they carried home what they needed. Nobody knows how long the ancestors of the People lived this way. No one knows how many generations were buried on the rock. My wife's family says, "If you began to name all your fathers and grandfathers and great-grandfathers, on and on, your hair would grow silver and you, too, would cross into the world of the dead before you ran out of names."

None of the People alive today saw the first European ship come to survey the shore. But they all know what happened. The sailors smiled and waved sheets at the children swimming to greet them, laughing in the splashing water. My wife says the ocean brings everything, eventually. That year, the water brought fever. Sewage from the sailing vessel, released in the tide, polluted the shore. Most of the children swimming out to greet the ship died. They were mourned but no one knew the cause of death until much later.

Soon visitors would drop anchor and explore the land, but only if they received permission. Some wanted to stay; their signs, their clothing and food, began to show up in odd places. When the People broke out in rashes, and fell sick, the visitors were afraid. They disappeared before the People began to die. The visitors returned after the elders and the strongest warriors had fallen.

All of this was many years ago. Most of the People died. Some of the families and languages were extinguished forever. The visitors kept coming, and every journey carried away more bones and the belongings buried with the People on the rock.

When the government offered parcels of land to white couples willing to build farms, they came by train and then by wagon. They cut down trees and burned a path from one home to the next. Their signs appeared everywhere: a cabin, an outhouse, a cedar fence, a barn, a wooden cross, a shed, a corral; none of it bearing symbols the People recognized; the raven, the salmon meant nothing to the new arrivals, nothing to their children. They threw their small houses together in a day, and dug latrines and private wells where the People once farmed and held ceremonies.

The elders of today, such as my mother-in-law, believe the People still exist in body and spirit, in every crevice and every object, in the forest and under the water. They think the place itself, surrounding the rock for miles in all directions, is strong with a will of its own. There are many stories proving this, in various ways. I will relate one. It was told to me by a man whose wife converted to the Catholic faith and confessed her youthful indiscretions, including being a member of a strange community of women. The details of her story may be embellished, or may have become exaggerated with retelling. It seems once she admitted her wayward history, she couldn't stop admitting it to family and friends, until her husband felt compelled to have her committed to an asylum. Bear this in mind while you hear the legend of the Corbett Sisters.

According to recollection and rumor, there was a white preacher named Whitman Graham Corbett who had been jailed and severely punished for his teachings in Nebraska. His church was founded on certain principles the good people of that state found repugnant. He was accused of witchcraft and was incarcerated for a month. A merciful judge allowed him to go free with the understanding that his ministry would cease. Corbett promised never to preach again. He concealed his true nature with shame and led his family away from the site of his disgrace. They followed a trail northwest to escape further persecution.

In truth, this man was on a lifelong quest to locate a path in and out of the world. He believed he was chosen for this purpose. He headed for Washington Territory after a fellow prisoner told him stories of a mythical tribe that practiced a resurrection ceremony. He thought he might learn from the People remaining here.

The preacher was foolish and his intention was wrongheaded. There are things only a shaman can understand, and only after traveling to the spirit world and returning many times, reclaiming the sick and dying and restoring them to health. By the year the preacher arrived, no shaman existed in this place. Some women performed the healing rituals of their families, learned from their mothers and grandmothers. But these were small charms and recipes any clever wife ought to know. The women of my wife's family never share these things with outsiders, for reasons you might guess.

The Corbetts (the preacher, his pregnant wife, and their fourteen-year-old daughter) traveled many miles to reach the Northwest. They slept in their wagon and begged shelter where they could find it. Along the way, the wife gave birth to twin sons and soon lost them to cholera, the kind they call "weaning brash."

The family was quickly running out of water and food. There was no time to mourn, or to rest. The morning after the deaths of their infant sons, the preacher dragged his wife to the wagon and secured her there. She went on screaming the names of her dead children while her daughter said prayers and her husband drove the horses on toward an uncertain destination.

Imagine how the preacher must have given thanks when he discovered this place. He bought a small plot of land with a house deserted by its former owner. The promise of property had attracted a number of homesteaders, who as yet had no spiritual guidance and no sheriff. The preacher mistook circumstance for destiny, and decided to stay.

Whitman Corbett was an educated man. His wife, Josephine, came from a modest family that didn't believe in teaching girls more than the rudimentary skills of reading and writing. Corbett schooled his daughter, Agatha, but not his wife. After his release from jail and his journey across the wilderness, Corbett set aside his bible forever. He would tell his followers he felt the clarity of his mind and soul returning as soon as he broke with the written word. He knew all he needed to know. The men who had incarcerated and humiliated him were well educated, proving the dangerous influence of books.

"For the Holy Spirit seeks oneness with Man," he said. "It speaks directly, as sunlight speaks to the flower, needing no formal language. The written word is an impurity, an object of attainment and sin; it is an obstacle between God-kind and Man. With the barrier of language surrounding him, how can a man commune with the Holy Spirit? The man of letters is doomed to failure."

Corbett counted himself among the most pure of humankind. He counted his daughter Agatha, and Josephine, still suffering the loss of her children, among those who aspired to purity. He called them his shadows. He fed them crumbs from his plate, and cleansed their naked flesh in the icy waters of the stream near their home. He forbade them to speak to one another behind his back.

In a generous frame of mind, one day, Corbett built a pulpit out of cedar in the open air and invited everyone he met to attend his sermons. His voice bellowed all the way into the forest, where the oak leaves trembled. Never did he refer to the Bible. His teachings were extemporaneous and free of influences he considered to be rooted in a desire for material gain. In every way, he rejected the ambitions and beliefs of the men who had punished him for promoting what he took to be the true will of the Holy Spirit.

Initially, curiosity brought a rough congregation of drunks, orphans, and derelicts, men who had lost their savings or their families or both, fallen women, widows, and spinsters. The misfits and the broken wandered in. Most wandered away again, when Corbett's message became clear to them. The men were disenchanted with the notion of poverty for its own sake. Even the lowest man, his boots worn through and his shirt stained with drink, cherished the notion that he would someday live in a mansion and ride a fine horse and marry a beautiful girl from a good family. Women who had lost their place or their virtue and had to rely on kindness were less inclined to believe such fantasies.

By winter of the first year, only eleven women remained in Corbett's church. He opened his home to them as well, told them they were welcome to share his food and shelter, and his bed. A few took on the role of earnest penitents, sleeping on Corbett's doorstep and surviving by foraging and by begging scraps of food from local farmers. But most of the women gave themselves to the preacher in return for his patronage. It was understood that a man's protection was necessary to their survival.

There are many versions of the rest of the story but all of them agree upon one event. Months after settling in with his extended family, Whitman Corbett died. The cause of his death is given variously as heart attack, infection, or food poison. The witnesses to his demise may have been his daughter, a few of his followers, or his wife. He may have been washed and dressed for burial or wrapped in blankets decorated with herbs and flowers. He lay in his own bed for three days or he lay inside an open cedar casket. Rain beat down from a seamless black sky or sunlight gleamed on the rocks and fields.

In every version of the tale, after a brief period of mourning and on the eve of the planned burial, Corbett woke up. He was much changed, his physique considerably leaner and less imposing, his hair longer and grown wild, his beard and his mouth covered with a white scarf. He shook his head as a man might after a night full of demented dreams. He stood and walked among his followers, who fell back in astonishment. Some dropped to their knees and mumbled prayers until the preacher stopped them, and took their hands in his, the warmth of his body proving he was alive.

For three days and nights, while grieving for her dead husband, Josephine had remained docile and quiet. She had been the object of kindness, admired by the other women for her gentle strength. It was Agatha who crept to the darkened bedchamber to inform her mother of Corbett's resurrection, and afterward Josephine never left her bed. Followers were allowed to place small offerings at her door, but never to speak with the ailing woman.

On the first afternoon of his new life, the resurrected Corbett asked for someone to prepare him a bath. Buckets of water were drawn from the stream and placed at his feet. He washed only his hands in the water.

Next he asked for a robe soaked in the blood of an animal. One of the women slaughtered a rabbit and drained its blood over a shawl, which Corbett tied around his shoulders. He still wore a scarf tied across his face, and when he gave instructions his daughter Agatha leaned close to hear him, and then relayed his words to the followers. They were told to form a circle around him and to announce their willingness to sacrifice themselves entirely for the sake of purity.

Finally, the resurrected Corbett asked for a burning branch. When he was given a torch he set fire to the cedar pulpit he had built, telling his followers he had now walked among the dead where no religion reigned and he had returned to set them free. All who were loyal to him would learn the path of purity, regardless of their sex. No matter what they had done, they would be cleansed. Moreover, as long as they walked in his shadow, they need never die.

For weeks after Corbett's resurrection, his followers lingered inside and outside the house, watching and listening to the ongoing tale of their leader's journey through the spirit world, and return to the living. This was the only sermon, spoken in whispers by Corbett and conveyed to the women by Agatha.

"The path is clouded with night," he said. "Black rivers surround us. The dead wander alongside us, on earth and in water, hands reaching into the darkness, straining for a way back to the living. By purification and mortification, you may walk among the dead and return, as I have done...."

While Corbett told of his adventures, and ate hearty meals, Josephine remained in seclusion, never seen by the women. Agatha told the followers how Josephine would tremble when spoken to, and that her words were unintelligible. Agatha described how she had found her mother wandering beside the stream at midnight, barefoot, draped in a white sheet.

Only when Agatha took Josephine's hand would she allow herself to be led home and put to bed with warm compresses on her arms and legs. Then she would be calm, for a time. No one else witnessed these spells, but the women who followed the resurrected Corbett had no reason to doubt his daughter's word. They were dumbfounded on the morning Agatha told them of her mother's demise.

"There she stood, once again, in the moonlight, just as before, with the stream rushing at her feet. She stepped forward. The icy water caught the hem of her garment and she sank to her knees among the rocks, crying out! Crying the names of her dead sons, she fell into the stream and was pulled away! I leapt into the water and reached out but the current was too swift, and I lost sight of her."

A ceremony was held beside the stream. At the spot where Agatha said her mother fell, the women placed a wreath of wildflowers. Every day they expected news but her corpse was never found.

Agatha continued to be her father's shadow. She made his announcements to the followers, and she kept his secrets. She also handled practical and household matters. She assigned chores to each follower, and scolded them if they shirked these duties. One woman prepared Corbett's bath (this included covering mirrors in the house). The follower was under strict orders to leave the room before the resurrected Corbett entered and disrobed. Another woman washed his shirts and darned his socks. Two girls cooked for the family. A small group was given the task of providing food. These women were chosen for their cunning and their lack of fear. Eventually the neighboring farmers began to complain of lost grain and stolen animals but nothing could be proven. There was no legal authority to settle these disputes. And a few of the farmers were on close terms with the "Corbett Sisters," admitting with mild embarrassment to a barter system. The women considered this to be a fair arrangement, as they had not been asked to share a bed with Corbett since his return from the dead.

To calm the followers' nerves, Agatha required them to daily smoke a concoction of herbs and plant leaves, and to fast for as many days as she commanded. She made them drink small quantities of mineral water and bathe in cold water, and she punished them for the least sign of disrespect. This was part of their purification, she told them, a necessary initiation before they could become what Corbett was, a passenger between the night and the day.

Around this time there began to be a good deal of speculation. Some followers truly believed Corbett had discovered a door, an entryway to the realm of the spirits, through a kind of prayer or an incantation, or because he was chosen for this purpose; others wondered if they were witnessing a hoax, a false death somehow contrived by Corbett with his daughter's help. The doubters wasted away, longing for proof.

On two more occasions the resurrected Corbett died of unknown causes, and was laid to rest in his bed. Agatha stood watch, inviting followers to enter the room one by one, and to place their hands over his heart. The women were stunned by the coldness of his touch and the rank odor of the room, despite the aromatic flowers heaped upon the bed and scattered across the floor. Even in the darkened room his corpse seemed flattened and diminished as though he'd been dead all along. It was difficult for the women to remember the robust man of faith they had met so many months earlier.

The second time Corbett returned and repeated the cleansing, blood, and burning ritual, his followers were less attentive than they had been before. They paid respect and performed their duties but they continued to talk among themselves. Some said the preacher was playing a trick to keep them under his spell.

The third time Corbett died, his followers broke into a violent argument. Some claimed the so-called miracles they'd witnessed were part of a hoax. Others thought they were owed a reward for their period of servitude. They felt cheated. Corbett had been resurrected twice and had yet to pass on to the women the secret of death and rejuvenation. There was among his followers a spiteful contingent, and they believed Corbett had been lying from the start.

"Behold the resurrected!" Agatha intoned for their benefit. "The ordeal of the resurrected is not at an end, for he is now and forever an instrument of Heaven." At this point Agatha leaned close to Corbett, who whispered in her ear. Then she turned once more to the women. "His sole purpose is to bring light and redemption and purification to the souls who will follow!"

But the women were still divided. Some who had taken refuge with Corbett had only half believed in his resurrection. They wandered away, seeking shelter and food, unwilling to continue taking orders from Agatha on her father's behalf.

By this time only seven women remained, along with Agatha. When she saw their doubt, she consulted with Corbett. Each follower was given a ceremony of initiation and a new, secret name. Afterward they became more compliant. All the women accepted the rules of purification, fasting for half of each week and then drinking a brew of berries and honey and bathing in cold water. Upon Corbett's insistence, she said, Agatha locked them in their rooms at night to "stifle the hungry and greedy stomach" whose desires might ruin them.

"Beware the temptations of the flesh," she reminded them. "You have come too far to lose heart!"

This might have been the end of the tale, or nearly the end, if not for an odd set of circumstances. One of the people who had rejected Corbett's new church in the early days was a man named Burnham Price, who had since traveled as far as southeastern Kansas. There he happened to stop for the night at an inn run by a family of four, two men and two women, named Bender. Over supper, for the amusement of his host, Price relayed the story of the preacher and the rumors he had heard of the Corbett Sisters and their strange practices.

Price had no way of knowing that his audience was at that very moment planning an escape. They had been under the scrutiny of locals who suspected them of crimes they could not yet prove.

In the days that followed the disappearance of Burnham Price, several people insisted a horse stabled at the Kansas inn had belonged to him. This was not the first time a traveler had gone missing after stopping at the inn for a hot meal and a night's rest. A posse was assembled from a drinking party and set out to investigate. But by the time the posse arrived, the Bender family had vanished, along with their wagon and a team of horses.

Late summer brought drought to the town where the Corbett Sisters lived. The followers, now seldom seen, were held in a strange sort of fascination and contempt. Despite the barter system, local farmers drew a magical association between the Corbett Sisters and their general misfortune. They had heard only gossip about the resurrections, and they didn't believe what they heard or they would surely have taken action against the women.

Surrounded by penitent and devoted females, Agatha slipped further into her role. She was sometimes seen walking the road, speaking in a private language. She kept a record of each follower's progress. The women who remained under Corbett's patronage were the true believers, and they had given themselves over completely. They kept to Agatha's prescribed schedule, fasting and meditating, cleansing and praying, and waiting for the day when they would be chosen.

One day a wagon rolled in from unknown regions, and proceeded through the dust and swelter to the Corbett house. The two visitors introduced themselves as Mrs. Bradshaw and her daughter Kate. The resurrected Corbett was flattered by the news that the sisterhood had attracted visitors from a great distance. Through Agatha, he invited the Bradshaw women to stay.

The pilgrims became a fixture. They set about repairing and adding comforts to the Corbett home. Mrs. Bradshaw prepared broth and baked bread for Corbett each day. Although he ate well, Corbett began to complain of slight aches and pains and took to his bed for most of the day. His followers might have wondered at the coincidence but by this time most were confined to their beds as well.

Kate Bradshaw did the washing. A strong and broad-shouldered girl, she also split logs for the fire and tended the garden.

Agatha was relieved to have help but she was adamant about not taking advantage of kindness. She ate only soup she prepared for herself, explaining to Mrs. Bradshaw that this was part of the dedication she had sworn as her father's assistant.

"He may never forgive me if I allow my body's appetite to sway me," she said. No amount of coercion would change her mind.

Although she had barely laid eyes on the resurrected Corbett and was sworn to secrecy regarding his teachings and state of mind, Mrs. Bradshaw told the townspeople who asked her, "He fares well under the right conditions." Meanwhile, Agatha was kept busy tracking the whereabouts of the Bradshaw women. On occasion she found one or the other listening outside Corbett's bedchamber, and had to remind them that only she was permitted to speak with him directly.

One day, without consulting Agatha, the Bradshaws invited neighbors to hear Corbett preach. A dozen or more appeared, and professed a great desire to witness such an event. These new congregants arrived early and found a new pulpit had been cut from the maple tree that once stood in the yard. They saw Corbett dressed in white, stooped and weak, silent as a mouse, seated next to Agatha. They were mystified by the appearance of the man they had only seen in passing more than a year before. They remarked upon the surprising changes in his demeanor, and were told that he had suffered a great illness and had been bedridden for some time.

Kate Bradshaw handed out small bouquets of daisies tied with string. Agatha helped her father to stand and to address the group. The sight of the two figures with their heads inclined drew murmurs among the crowd. Only a few of the Corbett Sisters were strong enough to attend this strange sermon, and they seemed listless, unable to take in what was happening. The early autumn chill made everyone restless. Yet all eyes concentrated upon Corbett when he began to preach inaudibly to Agatha, who repeated his words until her voice was overwhelmed.

"What is the matter with him?" one man wanted to know.

"Why does he wear a scarf over his face?" another called out.

The townspeople had no interest in a sermon. They had come to view Whitman Corbett. They had heard rumors of people coming from miles away to kneel before this preacher they had formerly mistaken for a harmless fool.

In the light of day, Corbett's physical attributes could no longer be explained by illness. It was all too obvious that the person before them was a fraud.

"Show your face!" someone shouted.

Agatha attempted to steer her father toward the house but one of the men blocked their path. He took hold of the resurrected Corbett and tore the scarf away. The sisters attending the sermon stared at their preacher, their savior, and everything they believed about him unraveled. At first a flurry of movement around the resurrected Corbett was like a flock of sparrows trying to take flight. Hands caught his robe and held him fast.

Agatha broke away and ran. No one tried to stop her. They shifted and sighed, a crowd acting as one body. At the center, held tight, Josephine in her robe and torn scarf buckled under the collective weight. Her mouth opened wide but not to scream. Witnesses said the sound she made was the keen of a mother after a lost child.

The men who broke down the door to Corbett's bedchamber found his long-dead corpse wrapped in blankets. Nothing could disguise the odor of rotten flesh, and in only a minute the men convinced themselves to destroy the heathen site.

The woman who told this story to her husband and friends was among those present at that final sermon, when the resurrected Corbett was revealed to be Josephine. The woman swore that the cry to flog the preacher's wife against her pulpit was spoken by Kate Bradshaw. Whoever spoke first, Josephine was shamed and beaten for committing acts of abomination unspecified by those who proceeded to set her house on fire. This same woman, who would someday be given over by her husband to an asylum, insisted she heard the screams of the sisters who were inside the house, too weak to leave their beds. And she would have us believe the events of the day had scarred her mind. Yet we all know of individuals who have suffered far worse than the Corbett Sisters.

Mrs. Bradshaw and Kate were not heard from after that day. But a sequence of violent occurrences began outside of town and continued in a geographic arc leading away for over a hundred miles. A boy disappeared. He was the son of a sheep farmer, a reliable and hard-working boy who went out to the fields to shepherd his flock home and was never seen again. An elderly spinster who wore her hair in braids was found on her porch with her throat cut, braids tied together under her chin. A drunkard was discovered in a field, his chest torn open and his heart removed.

Josephine Corbett did not recover from the physical strain of her ordeal. She died the next night.

If you are inclined to find wisdom in the words of a madwoman, Agatha was never located by the men who searched in all directions around the charred ruins of her home. If you insist upon a strict moral tale, an eye for an eye, the girl was captured and punished for her part in the abominations performed by her wicked mother. If you possess an unnaturally kind or generous disposition, then I assure you, Agatha made her way to a happy life as a beloved wife and mother, or nurse, or schoolteacher. As you wish.

10/20/2010
Dear Odelia,

There you have it. I hope the documents will be of some use in tracking better sources. I apologize again for their poor condition. The boxes in which they were kept, and discovered, were almost wrecked by water damage. They must have been in storage for decades. Don't ask how I got my hands on them. I'll tell you the whole story of my undercover operation at a later date.

As you can see, part of the introductory letter (Item #2) was torn away—top and bottom, salutation and signature. My genealogist friend has moved to Olympia, so I don't have the means to track right now. (By the way, the estate was divided for auction before I had a chance to sort through the rest of the boxes. Greedy family! More on that as well, next time I see you.)

At a guess, I'd say the professor who's addressed in the letter (Item #2) was a distant relation based at a university, but I can't explain how his belongings ended up in the garage of my sister's house in Vancouver. If you have a theory, please advise.

My (amateur) examination tells me the date on the log/journal/medical record (Item #1) is accurate, while the letter and story (as I mentioned earlier) probably date from the 1880s to the early 1890s. No need to return them. I've made copies for my scrapbook. The originals are all yours.

We have a lot to talk about next time I visit Skillute—all the best until then.

—Gloria

THE LOW, DARK EDGE OF LIFE
LIVIA LLEWELLYN

TRANSLATOR'S NOTE: *These are the only extant, unburned, and legible (for the most part) pages retrieved from what was apparently the diary of one Lilianett van Hamal, an American girl who apparently lodged at the Grand Béguinage shortly before the Great Summoning of 1878 that left much of the city of Leuven in ruins. No other items from before that event have been recovered from what is now the Leuven Exclusion Zone, which as of this date remains permanently off-limits to the outside world.*

[FRAGMENT, DATE UNKNOWN, SOMETIME LATE MAY, 1878]

and so the train serpentines its way through the Low Country, each car pulling the one behind it in an iron-fisted embrace, all of them together a chain of languid lovers moving deep into the verdant lands toward the quiet, circular town. It is an unseasonably hot day in late spring, and flocks of bright-winged birds burst up from and circle small islands of trees heavy with leaves, while glossy horses and cows nuzzle their grass-fed, brown-eyed bodies up against each other in the flat pasturelands below. Farmlands and fields roll past in an uninterrupted wave of green fecundity: everything alive revels in the warming of the world. Even with my black-tinted glasses on, even with my eyelids shut tight, the fertility of the land shimmers in my sight like the roiling surface of the sun; and over the bucolic valleys great colorless shapes float and dart and spread their death-filled jaws, and no one sees them but me. Inside the car, couples sit next to each other on the stiff velvet seats, drinking fizzing amber ale or clear cold water from bottles while pointing to white clouds colliding and colluding across the delft-blue skies. (They aren't clouds.) The sharp tang of warming cheese rises in the air: I gnaw at the red-rinded sliver of the wheel and lick my fingers and lips, then wash the taste off my tongue with the last of the warm, red wine.

(My hospital-issued, French- and Flemish-speaking handler sitting next to me spider-crawls her hands over mine, thinking I need help feeding myself because I'm only fifteen and just her stupid "charge," but I slap her away; and when she over-enunciates into my stoic face that I need her European expertise in order to ingest my own lunch and drink my own wine—which I suspect she covets for herself—I whisper and spit and hiss back into her indeterminate face: IF YOU DO NOT STOP TOUCHING MY PERSON I WILL REACH INTO YOUR CHEST AND DRAW YOUR STILL-BEATING HEART OUT AND NIBBLE-SUCK IT CLEAN LIKE THIS RIND AND I WILL GATHER YOUR SPURTING BLOOD INTO MY LITTLE FLASK AND SAVOR EVERY DROP AS I LAY IN THE ARMS AND CHAINS OF MY BELGIAN SISTERS, CHANTING YOUR NAME OVER AND OVER UNTIL THE GREAT AND VOLUMINOUS MOTHER HYDRA SPILLS OUT OF THE GATE OF MY FLESH AND DEVOUR-FUCKS YOUR TWITCHING REMAINS. Appropriately, she slips out of her seat to an empty one across the aisle.)

(Her face is indeterminate because I cannot distinguish human faces. They are the one thing I cannot truly ever see. I only see the bodies, capped with oversized, oval-shaped heads, from which out of their soft waxen folds swarm masses of fat black interdimensional bees.)

I lean back against the seat, running my hands over the ancient ancestral names and starry family symbols engraved on the silver flask. I would close my eyes and sleep, but it never happens. Excepting human faces, I always see everything, and I never sleep.

I have been put in this beautiful car, given this spacious seat, because I am the daughter of a troubled artistic woman with no power save in her family name, who abandoned me at birth for her love of sticky opium dreams but now finally finds a lucrative use for her disabled get; because I am the niece of a highly disciplined and determined woman with great power, whose deep pockets and dark desires have freed me from my lifelong imprisonment only to be delivered into a new imprisonment that will deliver untold new powers unto her and the sisters of her order; because I am a woman who has no power of her own in this world. And so the train transports me and my keeper in these ruby velvet seats from my old prison to the new: through the brilliant, bright life and hum of Europe into the ancient walled city of Leuven, Belgium, and then into my even higher-walled destination, where the gold summer sun dares not shine against abandoned black church spires, where eyeless creatures float beneath the flat brown surface of the River Dijle, where my handler will deliver me to an aunt I've never met, where I will spend the rest of my life locked in thousand-year-old timber and stone rooms and never leave, even after the absolute end of it. Every bone in my body, every wet sliver of flesh, will be put to good use in the name of my dark goddess. Or some other use, not necessarily good—the letter commanding my presence was a bit vague on that point. At any rate, the Most Holy Order of the Filiæ Solitudinus has many plans for my talents and my flesh; not all require my being alive, I presume.

In addition to being powerless, I am also, according to many learned physicians and alienists, quite impossibly and thoroughly insane—even by Arkham's impressively rigorous standards. I would say "maddeningly" insane, but that is no doubt redundant, and there's no one to tell the joke to except these dumb pages. But the doctors really are, amusingly, quite maddened by my inability to accept that I am completely, irreversibly, clinically blind, that my pupils (which I can see very well up close in a dust-free mirror, thank you) are as cloudy and white as the banks of mist that perpetually roll in off the wide white-capped waves of the Atlantic. My world should be pitch black; I should require a cane; I should walk in halting steps with my arms waving about me, naked trepidation in my face as my hitching, slithering body prepares itself for furniture or stairs or endless falls. I should be a meek, helpless, compliant child. And it is true that I have difficulty reading, that I need primers with letters as big as children's blocks. (This diary no doubt looks like it was written by a primate with a wax coloring stick.) I cannot create fine embroidered linens like other girls my age, and when I sit at the piano I cannot fully perceive all the black flecks of notes on the page. But when I slip my wrists and ankles out of the leather straps on my bed and flawlessly dart down the stairs, out the front door, and into the cosmic river of starry night, when I race across the neat hospital lawns and clamber down the steep cliffside trails and navigate the great pocked boulders and massive dunes of the thundering beaches and raise my trembling arms up to the wondrous skies, I see everything I need to, and more. My sight extends beyond.

(Those learned doctors have no idea what rolls in with those banks of ocean mist, or what peers down at us from the whorls of the galaxy. If they did, they would gouge their own eyes out, cram them in their gibbering maws, and mash them into pulp with their flat, yellow teeth, praying all the while that they might choke upon their own flesh and sink into a black and endless nothingness of death. But I've seen what peers down, what rolls in. Whether it sees me, I cannot say.)

I lean back against the stiff columns of upholstery and stare out the window like everyone else, wishing I had a bar of chocolate, wishing we could have stayed in Paris an extra day, wondering what it is all those holy men and women in the ancient labyrinthine churches of Leuven think that I shall see in their machines, wondering what it is they need to see through me

[ILLEGIBLE SECTION]

out the windows, pointing and staring ahead. The handler does the same, her moist, pudgy exterior registering no emotions as usual, although I detect a slight flickering in her pupils, a dilation that betrays her waxen bee-covered face.

(I have decided to refuse to speak or write the handler's actual name, as she does not deserve a proper name any more than does the lock on a jail cell or a cage.)

I shouldn't look out the window but I want to. Shouldn't/want, shouldn't/want. My life always narrows down to these two opposing points. The end is always the same. I hook my finger around the metal frames and pull my glasses away. Not that it matters. But when I'm horrified, I always like to be horrified to the fullest degree, without pretense or illusion. Full respect where it's due, right?

Ahead of the train and the tracks and the low, flat lands, I see—or rather, perceive—the circular beginnings of a tornado hovering like a flat brown mouth opening up over what I presume is the location of Leuven. Of course the women in the car are trembling, the children are crying, the men are gasping. These inexperienced Europeans from their small, tame towns with their small, tame weather systems, they've never seen anything like it. The handler has seen it—she was born in the vast middle expanse of the continent, raised under the gaping maw of wild American skies, skies that rip open and vomit out hectares of lightning-crowned destruction, destruction as wide as Europe itself. And those skies, that mouth, stretches all across the land, from one shining coast to the other. This small, snuffling snout of a storm? It's nothing. But I can tell even from this distance that no natural light shines down on whatever village or town it stalls over, and I can tell from the curved, sinuous direction of the cars in front of us that we are drawing ever nearer to it. How could this *not* be my destination? I shouldn't have looked up beyond the clouds, but I did, and

[END FRAGMENT]

[FRAGMENT, SAME DATE, EARLY EVENING (APPROXIMATE)]

gables, each of them the same: two small multi-paned windows topped by a roof of long, flat shingled wood. At the highest front edge of each gable, a single metal spire juts up like a sharp blade into the dark gray sky. From down on the street, all these rooftops look like armed sentinels, guarding against whatever might be hovering above Leuven. I remember reading in my primer about the friar whose torso was found stuck on the flèche of the Begijnhof cathedral, as though he'd been split in half and the leftovers tossed away. I laughed when I read that! Honestly, these gables and spires aren't really much of a defense.

The handler had the map, and although my mother made me memorize the map before I left Arkham, I dutifully followed behind for once, letting her think she was leading the way simply so I could enjoy our walk in silence. (My mother had two gifts: rolling balls of opium and memorizing maps. The woman was a living, walking cartography of this world, and others.) Away from Grote Markt, the spectacular carvings of Saint-Pieterskerk Cathedral (I forgot to mention—I can see human faces that are carved in stone!) and the bustling commercial center of Leuven (which I know I would never see again), there were walls everywhere, walls lining the narrow streets and lanes, walls to keep curious pedestrians out, to keep neighbors and scholars and clergy safe within. The walls in Leuven are fashioned of crumbling rust-red brick, one and often two stories high, and the very tops of the walls slant steep, so that it would be impossible to climb over them without sliding back down. The architecture is different from that in Massachusetts, but the intent is so very familiar that even now, writing this under the rooftop of an unlit six-hundred-year-old room, I feel like I'm

[ILLEGIBLE SECTION]

the handler said, her first words in almost an hour. "Groot Begijnhof. Gesticht rond 1232." I realized she was reading from a small sign attached to the side of a great stone arch in the wall. The arch's thick steel gates were open—beyond them, a gracious courtyard that split off into several round-edged cobblestone streets, each disappearing into a forest of medieval buildings. The Grand Béguinage of Leuven—we were finally there. My new prison. But there was warm, lemony candlelight coming from many of the windows, and I saw masses of bright flowers, thick trees brushing the rooftops, ribbons of smooth green lawns. The blanket of perpetual clouds overhead obscured the setting sun, and round black globules and spidery masses floated down the quiet streets next to the black-clad priests and nuns, but there was beauty here. I did not expect that. We picked our way across the high, slippery cobblestones over to a small bridge that look down into the Dijle, less a river here than a canal. After the vast waters of the Atlantic, I have to admit I was less than impressed. The water was light brown like milky coffee, flat and slow-moving under a canopy of willows and ivy that erupted over the continual bricked-in garden walls. I stopped and peered down. Shapes formed just under the surface, some that darted back and forth in the current, others large and lengthy, making their way in calm increments through the waters like miniature cetaceans. For one brief second, I almost thought I saw a humanlike face breaking the surface, masculine and bearded like Zeus, with unblinking black eyes.

And that's when the hand clamped around my left arm, dragging me around and away.

"Stupid girl. Get away from the railing or you'll fall in." It was a woman, clad head to toe in plain black, bees writhing in fierce circles under gray hair bound in a tight bun. She spoke in a weird hodgepodge of Belgian, French, and R'lyehian. The language of the sisters.

"Only if I climb over the wall," I snapped (in proper, pure English, because I am a proud American, and an even prouder bitch) as I tried to pull my arm from her grasp.

"You were told to wait at the station." The woman let go of my arm: and then she slapped me, so hard that my glasses flew from my face and extra black dots danced and swam in my sight, along with small sparks of light, those bright bridesmaids not of the supernatural but of ordinary shock and pain. The handler let out a small gasp—back at Arkham, I had been prodded and poked and experimented upon, but it was all done with a certain amount of trepidation and religious fear, all done in the name of knowledge and science. No one ever hit me like a common whore—because they didn't know which dark god's whore I might turn out to be.

I raised my fingers to my stinging flesh.

"There was no one at the station to greet us," I replied. "And I am a van Hamal. I don't wait."

My aunt struck me again, her skeletal fingers lashing out like bolts of dry lightning. I couldn't help but cry out. There were others gathering around us now, young women all dressed in the same severe black clothing, buttonless and seamless as though the garments had grown over their bodies like fizzing mold, their heads nothing more than ugly scratches of agitated bees against the honeycombed tablets of their faces. Behind them, some small commotion—the handler being led away into the warren of darkening lanes. As I scribble these words in the middle of the quiet night, listening to distant screams that echo out over the empty courtyards and canals of the Begijnhof, the screams that might very well be hers, I know now that I will never see her again.

(What a shame. I had hoped that I would have been the source and inspiration of those screams, perhaps after sticking my fingers deep into the sides of her heads until her brain congealed under the moons of nails, and then feeding into her scrambling thoughts visions of what it is I see when I stare at the supposedly blank walls or the supposedly empty stairs or the supposedly quiet skies.)

"I don't know what your *doctors—*" she spat the word out of her mouth like it was poison "—or your *mother* told you, but in this place you are not a van Hamal. Your name is worthless." She picked up my glasses and tossed them into the canal. "There are no individual beings in the Begijnhof, no independent thoughts. You are property of the Most Holy Order of the Filiæ Solitudinus, and you will never disobey us again."

I said nothing. If I learned anything in the asylum, it was how to pick my battles. She stepped forward, this queer, strange relative of mine, her angular face swimming up out of an evening air filled with wriggling particles that seemed to feed off the intensity of her emotions, and in shock I stumbled back against the low bridge wall and

[ILLEGIBLE SECTION]

led us single file into a quiet courtyard surrounded by two-story houses, plainer than those we had just passed. At the side of one dwelling, clear water trickled from the double-headed Janus mouths of a very large marble cistern. Despite my fear of the unknown, of my strange situation with my horrible and apparently completely insane aunt, of the ominous clouds overhead and the strange shadows that paused at the curtained windows to watch our progress, I could not help but be moved by the somber beauty of the place. There were flowers everywhere, green trees and low, thick hedges in long columns, trimmed with great care. My aunt led me through an iron gate into a private garden behind a row of attached houses, her faceless attendants following close behind. Stopping at the first door, she turned and grabbed my right wrist. I didn't struggle or fight as one of her attendants clasped and locked an iron manacle in place. And then she did something supremely clever and cruel. My aunt took a small ring attached to a chain, and slipped it onto my middle finger. She bent the finger back until I couldn't help but cry out. Only when I did so did she attach the deceptively slender chain to the back of the manacle. In this way I had limited use of my hand and could not pick the lock or remove the cuff.

And then she manacled my other hand.

"No wriggling out of this for you, I'm afraid. Orders of the order," she said, her words accompanied by the subdued hum of the bees that flew in and out of the hole of her mouth.

"I wasn't planning on trying to escape," I replied. This was true. I have always fully, even joyfully, embraced my power and destiny. Why does everyone think that every young woman who is led in chains to some terrifying end doesn't actually wish for that end, because we see that it is not an end but a beginning, an evolution? Why doesn't anyone just ask us? You would all be so shocked at how many women would be happy to walk to the Devil when you assume we need to be dragged.

"Perhaps. I don't disbelieve you. Still. Precautions." My aunt looked around the garden, as her retinue silently filed in through the rounded wooden door behind her. She grabbed the chain and yanked it—at the far end of the hedge-lined stone path, I could see it clanking out of a flywheel attached against the wall of what looked like a gardening shed, a brick box covered in waves of ivy and capped with wavy terracotta tiles. There were yards of that chain, but it only went as far as my aunt's door. I stood at its very limit, not even close enough to touch the main house. I looked through the high lead-paned window we stood beside. Inside, between the wooden slats of the shutters, I saw flashes of movement, the flicker of candle flame and fire, and smelled the savory warmth of cooking food. It wasn't my home, it would never be. And yet.

"I know my place, Aunt—"

"I am not your aunt anymore. Call me Sister."

I paused only slightly, then began again. "Sister. And I am not a dog. This treatment is unnecessary and cruel."

My aunt responded only by pointing down the path to the pitch-black opening of the shed. "It's summer, but there's a cot with blankets, so you'll be warm enough. There are two covered pots—one has candles and matches, one has bread and cheese. You're right next to the canal steps, so I suggest you eat in the dark, otherwise you'll attract flying things, and some things that do not need to fly." Even in the dark, she could see the look on my face. "We are the Daughters of Isolation, not the Daughters of Sewing Circles and Chit-Chat. It's more than they were going to allow you, until I stepped in. The van Hamal name still has a little weight, even here."

"Thank you."

"I told them you needed to be segregated from the other initiates until we've confirmed your health and virginity. We can't have the disease-riddled flesh of the daughter of an opium-addicted, syphilitic whore infecting the purity of the order."

"Thank . . . you."

(I must constantly remind myself that my aunt is a stranger, and perhaps even my enemy, even though from time to time the mask of her honey-wet bee face slips and I see flashes of the true human face beneath, one that is imperious yet beautiful and seductive. My weakness in thinking she can be understood or swayed by familial sentimentality is her strength. She does not think of me as family. I am nothing more than the thirteenth vaginal canal. Therefore, I must always remember that she is a viper with the delusion of self-relevance, and I cannot turn my back on her.)

She lifted my worn portmanteau, the one my mother had left with me at the asylum twenty years ago, after she collected her money. "Violeta's," she said, inspecting the clasp. I started at the sound of my mother's name. I hadn't spoken it myself in over a decade.

"I recognized it from when we were girls. It was your grandfather's."

"I didn't know that." I held out my free hand, praying she wouldn't take the portmanteau inside. When she held it out, my body almost buckled with the relief. "Thank you," I said as I took it. "For everything. I'll make our family proud."

"Which family?"

"The order, of course." And my mother, I think to myself, who despite her failings deserved a better life.

My aunt slipped into the house and closed the door quietly behind her. It was painted a slate blue, and probably looked cheerful and inviting in daylight, next to those windows lined with red and blue and lavender flowers. But I heard no sounds, other than footsteps and the clink of dishes.

Twelve women I'd counted, and none of them even now, in the downtime of evening, said a single word. Tomorrow or the next day or the day after, I will become one of them, I will be joined. We will all be one, all chained to each other, chained to whatever it is our joining brings up out of the cosmic deep.

I have eaten my bread and cheese in darkness, knowing full well my aunt (or someone else) has been watching from the window, and now I scratch out these words by the queer creeping light of the sky that only I can see. Outside this door, down the path, my aunt's home hulks in the dark, as do all the other ancient crooked buildings—the Begijnhof no longer looks as lovely and inviting as it had just a few hours before. Much pain is before me, and perhaps finally true darkness. But now I hear the canal on the other side of the wall, the waters rushing low and lilting like a bedtime song, and the wind rustles the leaves like a woman brushing her long unbraided hair, and I cannot help but feel th

[END FRAGMENT]

[FRAGMENT, DATE UNKNOWN (THERE HAS BEEN SOME DEBATE AS TO WHETHER THE NEXT SECTION OCCURS THE SAME EVENING OR SEVERAL DAYS AFTER THE PREVIOUS FRAGMENT—NO CONSENSUS AMONGST SCHOLARS HAS BEEN REACHED)]

[ILLEGIBLE SECTION]

standing at the edge of the chain, until the very limits of my body have been stretched so completely that I felt my bones cracking, and my little middle fingers bent back and I heard the joints creak and crack but the trail of phosphorescence that ended at my doorway, that ended at the middle of my cot, that ended in a large handprint against my cheek, led to between two small cottages and down steps that descended directly into the canal. The waters were dark and dank, and thick ivy grew all across the bottom steps, so I couldn't even see where they ended, if at all. The phosphorescence trailed off onto the leaves, into the water, and across the canal to the opposite side, like shining strands of peridots and emeralds against a slender throat, but the smell of the steps and the water was rank; and I realized that this was where the women and all the other inhabitants of the houses lining this garden came to relieve themselves, directly down the steps into the waters. Across the canal, another brick wall, covered in long strands of vegetation that bulge

outward, almost as if breathing. I stood at the top step for what seemed like forever in the night, watching creatures swim back and forth in the currents. Waiting, for what or who, I don't know.
I still taste the salt on my lips. The canal water is not salt
There is something in those waters I cannot see
I'm still trembling

[END FRAGMENT]

[DATE UNKNOWN, APPROXIMATELY TWO DAYS LATER]

me farther into the Begijnhof, past the beautiful lawns and over two more bridges and into the great cathedral. There were no pews or benches or chairs; we walked across a massive gray stone floor made up of slabs chiseled with the names of those buried beneath our feet. MARIA VAN PIVIEREN. That is the only name I remember now. She died in 1692, I think. Below her name, a small skull and crossbones was etched into the stone. There were hundreds of skulls, hundreds of crossbones, none of them sinister, most like children's etchings, with a touch of a smile in their jaws and round eyes, as if death was simply another amusement. Perhaps, after all this is over, I can return and do some grave rubbings. They would look so beautiful on my walls back home. I looked for a van Hamal, but didn't see one. (I think our people are elsewhere, where there's no need for pretense of Christianity for the sake of the rest of the world, as many Catholics still worship at this place, despite the best efforts of the order to dissuade them.) The priests led us across all these ancient bodies and back past the nave, down several flights of very small and worn steps into the catacombs, into a warren of rooms I'm still too tired to describe in much detail. Libraries of strange tomes, tiny altars clogged with delicate and profane statues of multi-limbed gods, crevasses where the mummified remains of anchorites and anchoresses sat or stood, staring out at passersby with bejeweled eye sockets and gold-plated grins, holding giant tridents or multi-bowled drinking cups in their deformed, flapperlike hands. (Well, in all honesty, those mute corpses did make quite the lasting impression on me. I've never owned a single piece of jewelry in my lifetime—it was never allowed in the asylum, the inhabitants more likely to eat or gouge out a few eyeballs with it than wear it.)

[ILLEGIBLE SECTION]

long journey, with an unsettling and entirely predictable end. A white room, three doctors, two who held me down and parted my legs, and the third who authenticated the state of my maidenhood. (When I say doctors, I mean that these were men instructed by our church to act as doctors on its behalf. These men were not doctors. SOON WHEN ALL THE SKIES ABOUT THIS WORLD ARE AS DARK AS THE EDGES OF THE MILKY WAY I WILL SHOW THEM WHAT IT IS TO BE A DOCTOR, WHAT IT IS TO INSPECT A LIVING SUBJECT, WHAT IT IS TO TEAR THE PUMPING-DRIPPING ORGANS OF A HOWLING PATIENT BY YOUR OH-SO-DELICATE TEETH AND DEEM THEM FIT TO LIVE EVEN AS THEY BEG TO DIE.) I said nothing the entire time. There was nothing to say. My aunt and two of the black-clad women stood guard over the proceeding, also saying nothing. When the moment happened, my aunt simply remarked that she was astonished that none of the many male doctors and attendants hadn't thoroughly abused me with as much abandon as the rest of the female patients. I thought the heat from my blush would have set the entire room on fire. After the doctors left the room, my aunt stayed behind, reading to me an entry, from a small New England auction catalog, describing the history of a powerful and rare grimoire while the women stripped me completely naked and proceeded to sew me into a long wool garment exactly like theirs. Even after they had finished trapping me in yet another cage, she continued reading, her low alto words accented by the thrumming wings of the bees that swarmed in agitated fury over her hidden face. I do not have the book with me, though I asked for a copy that I might transcribe those passages here in my diary, because I do not in this instance think my words would even begin to suffice. My aunt looked incredulous—rather, the bees made a waxen, misshapen semblance of incredulous disbelief over the pulsing folds—and said I was free to write what I wished, as she'd seen chicken scratches and insane scribblings that I believed in my blind state to be actual legible writing, and couldn't possibly imagine anyone ever being able to decipher a single word. I told her there would therefore be no harm in my copying the entry for my own erudition. She agreed, and left me to recover from my examination with the book on the table. I did my best to set down what I could in the half hour I was given—a very small portion of which is written below. However, the catalog would stay in the catacombs, along with the now-complete thirteen book set that had been commissioned by our ancestor, Maria van Hamal, so many centuries ago.

    I now know my exact purpose, and it is no greater or lesser than any of the other twelve women who comprise the

[ILLEGIBLE SECTION]

perhaps I am not so willing as I thought to be a part of this great work, this wondrous summoning of the great goddess of perversion and destruction. I love the ocean in all its majestic and unfathomable power, I have forever loved my great father Dagon and Mother Hydra, but I have no desire to invite them or the ocean to leave their vast beds and visit me upon the land. But my part in this ceremony is inevitable. So I sit in my chains with my fingers bent backward over my diary, scribbling in the dark as the mice come to nibble at the remains of my bread and cheese. The canal serenades me, a deep bass lullaby that recalls the majesty of the song of the ocean shores that I shall never walk upon again. How ironic that I see everything yet cannot see a wa

[END FRAGMENT]

> *TRANSLATOR'S NOTE: The book in question is* The Catalogue of the Occult Library of the recently disbanded Church of Starry Wisdom of Providence, Rhode Island, *an illustrated auction catalogue printed by the occult auctioneers Messrs. Pent & Serenade. Few extant copies of this catalogue exist today. A copy resides in Rare Books Room at Miskatonic University, but we were not allowed to view the copy, and requests to other libraries and private collections have netted no response. Lilianett van Hamal's (unfortunately) largely illegible transcription of the passage below is the only public version of the entry in existence to date.*

[ILLEGIBLE SECTION] travel journal and feverish spiral into nightmare-fueled madness, *Las Reglas de Ruina* was written sometime in the early 1500s by the Spanish friar Philip of Navarre, [ILLEGIBLE SECTION] a recounting of various legends surrounding an obscure and ancient deity, sister and bride to a chthonic god, who awaited release from her prison in the stars to wreak unspeakable, apocalyptic perversions upon mankind.

After finishing the manuscript, [ILLEGIBLE SECTION] affiliated with the Roman Catholic Church but as a northern fortress and stronghold for *Filiæ Solitudinus*—The Daughters of Isolation, an all-female religious cult with Assyrian roots, formally founded during the last days of Etruscan

Rome. There, the final version of the manuscript was hand-copied, bound [ILLEGIBLE SECTION].

In 1527, an additional thirteen copies of *Las Reglas* were commissioned by Begijnhof resident Maria van Hamal, widow of [ILLEGIBLE SECTION] records, Hamal, whose vast fortune had already paid for several private buildings and an extension of the network of canals covering the béguinage grounds, ordered custom metal bindings [ILLEGIBLE SECTION]. At the same time of the fire—and after inflicting a goodly portion of the Begijnhof sisters with a mysterious flesh-putrefying disease that [ILLEGIBLE SECTION] like rotting flowers—Friar Philip [ILLEGIBLE SECTION]

[ILLEGIBLE SECTION] "profane" variant of *Las Reglas*, remained absent from historical record for over three hundred years, until all thirteen copies resurfaced in the aftermath of the Great New York Fire of 1835, which destroyed over seven hundred buildings at the southeast tip of Manhattan. A series of subterranean rooms hewn from the island's natural rock were discovered beneath the ruins of a Maiden Lane basement, along with the unclothed bodies of [ILLEGIBLE SECTION] The other twelve have once again submerged into the unknown folds of history and time.

The profane *Las Reglas*, [ILLEGIBLE SECTION] duplicate of the text of Friar Philip of Navarre [this is yet unconfirmed]: there the similarities [ILLEGIBLE SECTION] ovoid shape has been pressed into the leather on the cover: within the ovoid, small folds of leather have been sewn as to mimic the effect of a maelstrom or whirlpool—or perhaps, it has been suggested, the most intimate [ILLEGIBLE SECTION] outer edges of the ovoid are surrounded by two Latin phrases in fading silver capital letters: IMMENSUS ASTRA INCLINANT FILIÆ, SED NON OBLIGANT FILIÆ ~ LAS REGLAS DE RUINA INCLINANT KASSOGTHA, SED NON OBLIGANT KASSOGTHA, [ILLEGIBLE SECTION]

Attached to the back of the book is a thick, leather-covered protrusion approximately ten inches in length, curving steeply upward. Five chains are attached to each side of the book. According to notes and sketches taken [ILLEGIBLE SECTION] were attached to the end of a limb, with the fifth chain attached to a bit placed in her [ILLEGIBLE SECTION] series of interlocking patterns until an entire circle of iron links was created, the center which was hollow like a portal or gate [ILLEGIBLE SECTION]

[ILLEGIBLE SECTION] ceremonial instructions have been found to date. Careful examination has revealed machinery of an electrical and [ILLEGIBLE SECTION] paroxysm in female patients suffering from hysteria. The discovery site notes reveal that [ILLEGIBLE SECTION] Removal of the books and devices from the bodies revealed numerous sharp instruments hidden within the protrusions, devices which, [ILLEGIBLE SECTION] fretwork, chains, and accoutrements reveal fine wires of an unknown geologic material woven throughout [ILLEGIBLE SECTION] "wondyrechaun" of "iron, flesh, and bone" through which Kassogtha could return. An astoundingly creative use of *Las Reglas de Ruina*, envisioned by Maria van Hamal and *Filiæ Solitudinus* so many [ILLEGIBLE SECTION].

[END LILIANETT VAN HAMAL'S TRANSCRIPTION]

[VARIOUS FRAGMENTS, MIDNIGHT THROUGH EARLY MORNING, NEXT DAY (APPROXIMATE)]

So many horrible dreams throughout the night, and yet if I had only known then what I know now, in the calm light of morning. So many moments of chilly, anxious wakefulness, hearing my own panting breath in the humid midnight air, feeling the quaking of my heart like the hooves of horses pounding against the earth. Time and time again I awoke with my crippled hands flailing against my chest, the chains clanking like Marley's ghost. Earlier in the evening, when a vestige of the sun still pounded down through the thick clouds, I had stood at the door to my aunt's lodgings, barely able to contain my dismay as she once again chained me like a beast and left me outside. "This is for what your mother did to me, and to the order," were the only words she spoke. I have no idea what transgression she spoke of, but that is of no matter.

(The bees told me a different story—even as they parted from her mouth to reveal that impossibly wide grin of her saber-toothed mouth, the ivory so overgrown and thick, the smell of her breath so foul, even as she pushed the words out with her pustule-encrusted tongue, the bees swarmed at her forehead, undulating in a multidimensional frenzy as they transmitted her thoughts into a living, winged sentence that hovered in the air: *YOU ALONE OF THE ACOLYTES WILL KNOW YOUR TRUE FATE, AND YOU ALONE WILL SCREAM WITH DELICIOUS HORROR EVEN BEFORE WE CHAIN YOU TO THE FLOOR. THE UNENDURABLE PLEASURE AND PAIN OF THE THIRTEEN IS OUR GIFT TO THE GODDESS, BUT YOUR UNENDURABLE TERROR EVEN NOW, IN YOUR EYES, IN THE SHALLOWS OF YOUR BREATH, KNOWING THAT THE ATROCITIES KASSOGTHA BRINGS ARE ALREADY BURROWING INSIDE, FEEDING*

ON YOUR SOUL—THAT IS A LITTLE GIFT TO ME.)

How stupid I have been, how naïve. In the asylum, I imagined myself a queen, and I was—a queen with no kingdom or power, save the power to believe she had any to begin with. I ruled daydreams and foolish visions; I crowned myself before a court of childish fantasies. What do I know of true power, of true sacrifice and pain? My mother, even my sad, addicted mother, knew the price of all these things.

Now I have knowledge of that price, too.

I rose from my damp blanket and cot, pacing back and forth, standing in the garden walkway like a mournful specter all in black. My once-fine traveling dress, all matted and stiff with sweat and dust and browning traces of blood, lay somewhere far beneath the vaults of the cathedral, a new home for the mice. Quietly I made my way to the very limits of the chain, this time not to the canal stairs but to the windows of my aunt's lodging. In the deep pitch of the night, under the gaping black mouth of the never-ending storm, I could see the faintly glowing Odic outlines of the women, all of them laying about the floor on thin mattresses, like chess pieces that had been tipped onto the floor, the bees on their faces silent and heavy with sleep. Will it be tomorrow that I lay with them, all of us spread out in a circle, our hands and feet entwined, all of us chained together in layer after layer like a massive web, a net to catch our uncatchable prey? If I had the power, I would silently open that blue door now, float through the air upside down over each supine body, slitting their bodies from stem to stern, watching as they sank into their own spurting, escaping life, all of them together slipping into freedom and away from the invisible chains of this terrible life. It would be no worse than what awaits them with the dawn, what awaits me.

(Oh what I would have given for a small brown ball of opium and a slender pipe of bone, then and now. Vestiges of my mother's excesses still linger in my flesh and bones, raising their heads in the most distressing of moments like Medusa's tresses, writhing through me like faint itches that cannot be scratched.)

[ILLEGIBLE SECTION]

and the hedges kept me company throughout the night, as I paced back and forth, up and down, pondering my fate, and so did the numerous black squiggling clusters shuddering in the air, the eyes of strange birds with clusters of eyes like spiders that stared at me unblinking from the high spikes and gables. And in the early cracks of the morning, as I found myself staring down the steep stairs into the canal, watching the long strands of deep green vegetation blossom and pulse against the wall, it came to me. I suddenly realized what I could not previously see before me, what was staring out at me through the phosphorescence-dappled wall of trailing ivy and willow branches, not unlike how the attendants would stand and stare behind the curtains of the communal showers at the asylum. It was the perfect vantage point, from across the waters, to see all the acolytes and sisters of the Begijnhof, all the women young and old, lifting their petticoats and exposing their notches for everything about the canal to see. Including, for the past several mornings and nights, me.

An idea, as profane as this situation, crystallized in my fretful mind.

A solution so simple, I almost laughed at the thought of it.

(I must confess I am glad for my terrible handwriting and miserable eyesight that cannot form legible letters on paper, as well as for these chains that inhibit the grip of the pen even more than usual. These events I write of would be the death of me were anyone to read them—the thought of it makes me almost sick. I may have a temper and a bit of bloodlust and a wholly unrealistic view of myself as I move throughout this strange world I both see and cannot see, but what I am about to put on these pages . . . words fail me. And yet, they cannot.)

The chains and manacles prevented me from descending to the lowest steps just above the waterline, but the trail of bright green bioluminescence from the prior night already confirmed that an underwater assignation would not be necessary. Which I was quite satisfied with, as the waters of the Dijle were quite easily the filthiest I'd encountered in my short life, especially considering what was flowing into them at all hours of the day and night. Therefore, I positioned myself on the top step, overcoming my revulsion at sitting down in such a spot by reassuring myself that I was not touching the stone with bare flesh but with a horrid and quite unflattering dress made of scratchy fabric that could only have been woven from the skins of porcupines. So it was something of a relief to lift the long straight skirt up above my

[ILLEGIBLE SECTION]

he swam toward me, his powerful arms traversing the length of the canal in a mere three quick strokes. And then in a flash he stood on the steps, his feet hidden by the curling leaves and vines clinging to the water's edge, and my breath caught in my throat, not because I had never seen a man like this before but because I had seen many of his kind before, or like him, diving and arcing through the crashing cold waters all along the eastern coast of my home country, their thick, tentacled beards and barrel-chested bodies cresting the waves like whales, eyes like flat slashes of licorice, tapered at the ends. Not the most handsome creatures, but compared to some of the horrifically deformed souls that kept me company at Arkham, I could do worse. I thought of the book, of the description my aunt had read. Yes, there was worse. My heart galloping in my chest at the impropriety, the sheer audacity of my actions, I leaned back until I could see only the cloudy sky, my legs and womanhood as uncovered as the day my mother birthed me. (My mother, who would no doubt be supremely proud of her daughter in this, her most desperate and shocki

[ILLEGIBLE SECTION]

black as pitch, as oil, and skin, so cold and slick, but the power of his movements, the power I could feel under his skin, like the roiling of my beloved stone-gray Atlantic, a power so mesmerizing that the split-second pain of his

[ILLEGIBLE SECTION]

and if he felt pleasure or joy in the act, I could not surmise beyond the obvious, his language so ancient and otherworldly that the few words he might have uttered were beyond my ken, but oh, after the first sharp shock and the rolling aching, it were as if the infernal clouds above parted; oh, the stars, so many stars, clear and bright in a sky devoid of membranous monsters plummeting down on an unsuspecting world, only stars, and our breath, and a rising tide within that I

[ILLEGIBLE SECTION]

LAP AT EVERY THROAT AND CUNT AND HOLE IN THEIR BLEEDING BROKEN SUPPLICATING BODIES AND WALK OVER AN OCEAN OF FLESH, SCOOPING IT UP WITH MY ENDLESS MOUTHS AND FUCKING THEIR REMAINS UNDER AIRLESS STAR-BLACK SKIES UNTIL THEY HAVE BEEN UNMADE INTO MY BONES, MY WOMB, UNTIL I QUICKEN SQUAT GRUNT THEM OUT AGAIN, HOLLOW THEM OUT AGAIN WITH MY FINGERS AND TONGU

[ILLEGIBLE SECTION]

nd so was I now a woman according to the customs of the day, but if so, how is it possible it that I was not before? I can say with the utmost honesty that there was no difference between the before and the after. I remained no more or less but only what I am supposed to be, even with this strange being shuddering inside me—a woman who sees all but is blind, a woman surrounded by the all the creatures of the universe but who is alone.

After a time, he removed himself from the scene, slipping back into the fetid waters of the river without a single word or glance back. I was neither glad nor sorrowful at his departure, only tired and sore, and suddenly in great need of sleep. With some difficulty, I pulled myself to my feet, smoothed out my garment as much as I could, and proceeded to make my way in small, stiff steps back down the path to the garden shed, where I fell upon the cot and slept as though dead for several much-needed hours.

And now it is morning, and I hear the door opening from the far end of the path, and I hear the hum of bees and the soft rustling of fabric and slender limbs, and the musical clinks of the keys to my manacles. So I shall put this diary away and pray to Mother Hydra with all my heart that I shall return to it before nightfall, that I shall live to see nightfall, that this will not be the la

[END FRAGMENT]

> TRANSLATOR'S NOTE: *The following is the last section from Lilianett van Hamal's diary, and the only complete entry, with no illegible text or missing sections. This section was discovered not in the actual diary, which was excavated at the Leuven Exclusion Zone during the last authorized Miskatonic University expedition (in 1976), but in the town of Bruges, over one hundred and twenty miles away. These pages have generally been interpreted as a natural continuation of the original diary, with clear indications that these are not the only entries she wrote after the event. However, despite intensive ongoing research in both Europe and North America, to date no other entries, pages, or books have been found. No additional mentions in public and*

hospital records have been found of Ms. van Hamal, and there has yet been the discovery of a final resting place. Our search continues.

Eventide, the 31st of December, 1878
(I have become an expert in rolling those sticky brown balls. My mother would be so proud. And with every inhalation, with every smoky exhalation from the furnace of my lungs, I become more proud of her, more in awe of her courage and strength, that she was able to endure and survive that terrible, mismanaged first ceremony at Maiden Lane, that she was able to carry me in her womb for such an unnaturally lengthy amount of time, giving birth to me in painful secret only after years of fighting my contractions, after decades of confusing and stunting my purpose and sight with seductive poppy dreams. But I am older now, and I have power. She did not create me, but she gave my primordial flesh its final form. When the smoke billows into my body, I know how to hold it, how to shape it into purpose, how to extrude it into the air along with all the other invisible squiggling black horrors that populate the world. This is not addiction. This is destiny.)

And smoke still rises to the southeast, a lightning-studded pillar as thick and coiled as Krakatoa, a muscular demon rising out of the volcanic center of the earth to grab and pull down the sky. When I sit at my writing desk with my diary and pen and pipe, I see it billowing up past the medieval gables and spires of Bruges through the delft-blue mornings and violet nights, all the smoldering remains of Leuven wafting back into the cosmos. I wonder how much of my aunt is above me now, how much remains below.

Forever will I feed from the look on her face, the look she gave me as the twelve acolytes—so beautifully laid out against the lush carpet of morning-kissed grass, their pale hairless limbs parted wide and draped in silver chains that formed an intricate web, copies of the profane book of the goddess Kassogtha attached at their trembling wet notches, the Odic force flowing thick and hot between them like a cyclone—all started in perfect unison, the interdimensional bees streaming away from their now-naked, sepulchral faces as they half-rose and cried out when they felt the thirteenth book with its massive protuberance inserted into my womanhood, my energies merging with theirs as I too cried out in tremulous, painful joy. My triumphant aunt, and all those smug-faced priests with their tall linen and gold caps, their bejeweled vestments, their chalices of wine and bowls of incense. All of them dancing and rubbing themselves, waiting for their goddess to rise from the tangling birthing circle of limbs and suck them off while my aunt stared on like a Roman statue, imperious and oblivious to the cacophony around her. Eyes and the eyes of her bees, only on me.

And how I will remember until the vast fecund river of time becomes as dried up as a prostitute's bottomless pit how those same eyes widened as my cries of joy and pain turned to high-pitched laughter, laughing as the twelve young women around me screamed and writhed whilst their insides were whipped into a pink gelatinous froth that spumed and sputtered out of the sides and backs of the profane books, their bodies thrashing like fish dying in poisonous tides of red; how my aunt slipped and fell backward into the sticky, flopping mess of boneless limbs as I gracefully rose, pulling the chains around me like a cloak as I bathed in the great river of dying life all about me, drank the thirst-quenching fear and thick sexual release their sad animal bodies gave off even as they collapsed like mounds of fly-specked shit at my feet. And all about us, the black speckled floaters scratched away at the pale air, and I raised my hands and they descended in swarms, pouring over the priests and dissolving their flesh to the bone. Had I seen them all these years, not knowing they had always been mine to command?

I don't recall what I said to her as I stood over her supine body, my naked body dripping viscera onto her austere black gown as she held out her arms to me and screamed the name of her perverse goddess over and over again. Perhaps I said her goddess would not save her. Perhaps I said nothing at all. Everything grew so much darker than usual, and even my limited vision failed me, the world scratching itself out as I reached down, down—and then, for the longest time, nothing. Pure black. So calm and beautiful, like a deep sleep. I awoke in sun-drenched fields, next to grazing cows, staring at my gore-covered hands.

Did my aunt see her goddess? Wherever she is, does she understand now? I wiped my hands on the grass, and then I moved on.

Bruges is a strange town, but I have cooled my heels long enough, and made myself too familiar; and there are people back in Arkham that must answer to me for all the things they have done. My birth mother thought she was finished with me, but there is a long-overdue conversation ahead of us that will crack the world in two. Tomorrow morning I will take a carriage down long, straight roads under steel-gray skies to a shore so flat and wide that the very waters of the channel seem to rise above it; and I will claim my berth upon a ship that will carry me first to England, then across the low, dark edge of life back to the New World and home, home to great wide waters and great wide spaces and room to run and scream and consume. The agent who sold me my ticket warned against travel this time of year, warned me against rough seas and rougher men; but he is a wriggling insect whom I shall someday crush then wear as a tiny bead on a necklace made of all the bodies of the human race. He is mortal and so therefore fears everything and has everything to fear. I do not fear. I bring it.

THE ANCHORESS
LYNDA E. RUCKER

If you're born at midnight, you can talk to the dead.

Avarice, born into a cold winter midnight—so she was told—was thirteen years old when her daddy gave her to the Brides of the Morning Star somewhere over the hilltop and a world away from her home. They walked all day to reach the Brides, through the woods, far from people or roads, deep into the mountains. Her first sight of the place was a tall wooden fence ringed with barbed wire. She wondered whether that was meant to keep people in or out.

Her daddy banged on the fence's wooden gate and after a long time, a small, pale, thin woman opened the door. She looked surprised—more than surprised, shocked—at the sight of them standing there. Her daddy said, "Avarice, go sit over there," and pointed to a rock jutting up from the ground some distance away. Avarice did as she was told, and as she sat there, she watched her daddy and the woman talk intently for some time. It was a hot summer's day, and the rock was warm, and she was sweaty from their long walk. It was all she could do to stay awake. She noticed that they acted like there was still an invisible door between them. Her daddy never crossed the threshold to whatever was on the other side of the fence and the woman never stepped out of the compound.

After what seemed like a very long time, her daddy turned and motioned for her to come back over. Nobody told her what was happening, not on that day and not on any of the days that followed. She walked back up to that fence and the woman said to her, not unkindly, "Come on in, child," and Avarice turned to tell her daddy goodbye but he was gone.

As for herself, Avarice already belonged to the Lord. She found God after her mother died awash in her own blood with a deformed stillborn baby lying between her legs, half in and half out of her body. This was the punishment for allowing the touch of a man in the first place. Didn't it say so, right there in the first chapter of the Bible? "I will greatly multiply thy sorrow and thy conception; in sorrow thou shalt bring forth children"—that's what God told Eve after he caught her running around with that serpent and eating those apples. Before her mother died, Avarice had thought maybe she and her little brothers had been conceived without sin, like Jesus, but here was proof that her mother was just as stained as any harlot in the Bible. Avarice understood then as well that it had been a sin of pride for her to even think that her mother was like the Virgin Mary. Maybe her sin in thinking that was even what had caused her mother to die. Avarice prayed about it, but the Lord didn't have anything to say back. That was all right. Avarice was patient, and willing to wait.

She had learned to read from the Bible at home because the school was so far away and her mother couldn't spare her, and anyway the kids at the school acted so strange around her. She tried to be nice but it was like they didn't want nothing to do with her. Still, her parents said she had to learn to read and write and do her sums so she could get by in the world someday. *The world.* They said it like they were talking about Hell, and it sounded like Hell from what she could read in the newspapers that papered the walls of their cabin and what she sometimes heard her daddy talking about after he'd been into town. Out there in the wider world it was just starvation and war, far as she could tell. At home, she might go to bed hungry sometimes and feel cold in the night, but at least she was safe.

And sometimes in the evenings her daddy would play on his dulcimer and her mama would sing along. She had the sweetest voice. Sometimes they would go out to play and sing at people's weddings or for other special occasions. Avarice never joined them, but she knew that even though they were outsiders, it was the one thing that made people feel all right about her mama and daddy. They might keep to themselves most of the time but her mama had a voice like an angel and her daddy played the dulcimer so well that people joked he must have sold his soul to the Devil to get a sound like that out of it.

Of all the songs her mama and daddy sang together, her favorite was about a woman who lived in a cave, down deep in the ground. Like many of their songs, which were often about heartbreak and murder and sometimes murder caused by heartbreak, it was such a pretty song, but when you listened to the words, you realized it was a dreadful story: someone had put the woman down in the cave because she could see and talk to the haints walking the hills, because she spoke with the dead, because she frightened them so much with her talk of older ways and of times when the walls between worlds shimmered and thinned and things could slip through. Before they put her down in the ground they made her kill her lover, and they took her children, just newborn babies, a boy and a girl.

They used to change up the story sometimes, her mama and daddy. Sometimes the woman got away. Sometimes she died down there. Sometimes she sang sad songs to people at the surface, people who gathered round to gape at her or shout questions down at her. But every version included a sad refrain:

> *And the stars they looked down, they looked down from the sky.*
> *They found her hiding place, by and by.*
> *They said lost lady, lost lady, don't you cry.*
> *Your love don't suffer, your sweet babes are nigh.*

Her mama used to tell her stories, too, about the haints of murdered and jilted lovers who walked the hills and witches who lived on the sides of mountains and men who could turn into bears. Avarice couldn't think of any reason at all why she would ever want to go away from this place, to get to know *the world* that could never be as enchanted as the mountains and the woods all around her. She wanted things to stay just like they were, helping out her mama and taking care of her little brothers and listening to songs and stories.

"You won't always think like that," her mother would say to her. "Sometime you might want to go out there and see what it's like. When you get older, you'll get a hankering for the world. You'll see."

Avarice didn't see; she couldn't imagine wanting things to change, or ever wanting to be far away from her mama and daddy and little brothers. They didn't have any other family, it was just them, and she imagined herself without them, lost and skittering across the earth like a dandelion seed. As long as they were together, she was safe.

But after her mother died screaming and cursing both the Lord and Avarice's father, Avarice didn't feel safe any longer. That labor and birth broke her mother apart, and it all broke Avarice apart along with her. She knew there was something bad wrong with her after that when the fits and the headaches and the visions came on. She tried to hide them but she didn't have any control over them.

All the same, that day her daddy gave her away to the Brides she did not cry, not a single tear, because she did long to dedicate herself to the Lord. She had no intention of bringing forth children in suffering and sorrow and dying in a pool of her own blood.

"Child, your name is Avarice?" That was the first thing the thin woman, who Avarice later learned was called Abbess, said to her. Avarice nodded, not trusting her voice. The woman put her lips together like she didn't approve, but she didn't say anything, not then. Avarice wanted to tell her that her mother had just named her that because she liked the sound of it, it didn't really mean that she was greedy and sinful, but she felt like pointing it out made her seem like she was protesting overmuch. Instead she looked past the woman and around at the compound.

At first she was comforted by the sight of cabins that were a lot like the one she grew up in. There were seven cabins in total, and between each cabin neat rows of vegetables growing. In the middle of the compound there was a stone well, and she could see three outhouses along one wall.

Just then Avarice got the holes in her vision that always indicated a fit was coming on. *Not here, not now,* she pleaded with her body and with God. Sometimes, only sometimes, she'd found she could will the fits away before they took her entirely, but she wasn't always successful. She knew her daddy had brought her here because he couldn't handle her fits, but she didn't know whether he had told the thin woman about them. Maybe when they saw her having the convulsions and shouting out the visions they would turn her out, too, and she'd be lost and walking these hills forever like the ghosts that talked to her in her dreams.

THE FIRST TIME AVARICE HAD a fit was four days after her mother died, the day after they buried her and the half-formed child who had died in her womb. Even though her family didn't have much to do with other folks, some of the women from the church they attended from time to time had come to help Avarice bathe and dress her mother and sit with her. Avarice heard them talking about her once when they thought she was asleep, saying she and her brothers were all half-wild, and then, "Well, what do you expect?" and all the women murmuring assent. That made Avarice mad; it wasn't her fault they had no other family and she didn't know what she was supposed to do. The women had instructed her to lay pieces of silver on her mother's eyes so they'd be sure to stay closed when she entered Heaven. Later on some of the men her daddy worked with came and helped him dig a grave not far from their house. Avarice thought that was nice because she might be able to sit out there sometimes and talk to her mama, and she could tell her little brothers all about her as they got older, especially Baby Tom who was still so young he might not remember their mother at all in a few years' time.

So the day she had the first fit everybody had gone home and the house was all quiet with her daddy gone and her brothers off playing somewhere. It was just her and Baby Tom, and she was spooning some food up into his mouth and the next thing she knew she was on the floor. She knew something bad had happened because Baby Tom was screaming his head off and she had wet herself. That was the worst of it. And it wasn't like she had a lot of dresses to choose from, and washing day wasn't for a while. She went and changed into an old dress that was too small for her. She was so ashamed she wanted to burn or bury the one she'd been wearing but then she wouldn't have nothing to wear that fit.

Luckily, she didn't wet herself every time she had a fit after that, and the second time it happened she was alone too except for Baby Tom sleeping. She kept them to herself but then she had one in front of the boys, and she made them swear not to tell.

That didn't last long. It finally happened when her father was home. He was crying and shaking her when she came to her senses and she pretended like it was the first time. Even then, she never imagined he would send her away because of them. After all, didn't he say she was like the little mother of the house now, that he needed her to look after her three little brothers?

But he asked her why she said the things she did when she was having the fits. She asked him what things she was saying, but he wouldn't tell her. And then one morning after a particularly bad fit the night before he told her to get dressed because she was going away. All during that long day's walk he wouldn't tell her what she had said that had upset him so much. He wouldn't even hardly talk to her at all. Her chest felt like a hand had closed around her heart and was squeezing it so tight she could barely breathe.

Avarice was determined to be brave, but she didn't fit in with the Brides of the Morning Star, and it wasn't just because of her name. The first thing she learned was that she asked too many questions, and that they were the wrong kind of questions. When she asked why they were called the Brides of the Morning Star, since everyone knew the Morning Star was Lucifer, they looked at her like she'd said a bad word. Sister Lucinda, who was younger and kinder than the others, sat her down and showed her a passage in Revelations: "I Jesus have sent mine angels to testify unto you these things in the churches. I am the root and the offspring of David, and the bright and morning star."

Avarice frowned. "My daddy said the Apostle John wrote Revelations while he was smoking jimson weed. He said it must have been growing right outside his window in that prison, and he'd smoke a little bit and write a little bit and smoke a little bit more and write some more."

She thought Sister Lucinda looked like she was concealing a smile, but Avarice wasn't trying to be funny.

"Maybe so," said Sister Lucinda, "but if I were you I wouldn't go telling the abbess that."

The other thing she couldn't understand was what kind of religion they were supposed to be. Everybody she had ever known was Baptist, but as far as she knew, Baptists didn't have sisters and abbesses and things like that. Were they Catholic? She had heard about Catholics, but in the same way she had heard about digging a hole to the other side of the world where people walked upside down; she never imagined she would actually meet one, let alone live among them. Sister Lucinda laughed and said no, they weren't Catholic and they weren't Baptist; they were just the Brides.

"Is everyone a Bride?" Avarice asked, and Sister Lucinda said no, one of them was an anchoress. Avarice asked what an anchoress was and Sister Lucinda said it was a very holy woman, one who took herself away from the world and lived a solitary life of prayer and communion with the Lord.

Then Sister Lucinda said they needed to stop talking and get back to work. They had been assigned to clean the cabin where they slept. Of the seven cabins, the thirty-odd women who lived in the compound slept in three of them. The abbess had her own room sectioned off in one of them. One cabin held a liquor still, much to Avarice's surprise, but it wasn't for their consumption. They traded the liquor for whatever they needed that they couldn't grow or make on their own. A few of the Brides were in charge of any dealings they had with *the world*, but as far as Avarice could tell, none of the others ever left or even talked to anybody from outside. One cabin was a sort of general workshop where they made their own clothes and the furniture they sat and slept on. One was reserved for cooking, eating, and food storage, while the other was for worship. That cabin had hard benches and a pulpit at the front, but no one ever stood there and preached or said anything at all. Avarice hadn't been to a lot of church services for the same reasons she hadn't gone to school much: where they lived was so isolated from other folks, and her family just didn't seem to get along that good with other people. But the few times they had gone, there had been singing, and a preacher up at the front. The Brides, in contrast, would just go and sit for hours at a time. They were supposed to be quietly communing with the Lord, but Avarice always found herself dropping off.

It was little wonder; their days were filled with work punctuated by interminable worship services. The work was hard because they were largely self-sufficient. They grew all their own food. None of the Brides were allowed to eat meat, and the abbess said it was because doing so would make them unclean. Apparently they used to keep some chickens just for the eggs but the chickens had all died and they hadn't gotten any new ones to replace them. Avarice wasn't sure how long ago that had been, though, because all the Brides talked about time in such a vague way. Everything was either happening now or had happened at some indefinite time in the past or would happen at some indefinite time in the future. How long ago or recently or soon such things were seemed irrelevant.

They worked the garden all summer long and put up vegetables for the winter. They always had sewing to do, clothes and bedding and the like. There were so many other tasks as well: drawing up enough water from the well each day for cooking and drinking and cleaning things and watering the garden, keeping the outhouses clean and relatively odor-free, and keeping everyone fed. Avarice was used to hard work, but this was something more. She went to bed tired and hungry and woke up tired and hungry. She had always been thin, "just a little thing" her mother had called her, but after a few months with the Brides she could count her ribs at night running her hand down her torso. That was all right; all the Brides were thin and pale, and she was becoming more like them. There was something beautiful and ghostly about being so thin and white and knowing that you were destined to be a Bride of Christ.

That first day, she had managed to hold the fit at bay, and she thought maybe even she had been cured because weeks and then months passed without any sign of them. What she didn't know was something worse was waiting to reveal itself.

> *The souls of sinners turn into haints, and you got to watch out for them if you walk these hills at night.*

AVARICE HAD GONE TO LIVE with the Brides in midsummer, and now they were edging toward fall. The air was getting that crisp feel to it and the dark was lingering longer in the mornings and stealing in earlier in the evenings. A day passed that Avarice marked as the six-month anniversary of her mother's death. On the following morning, she woke to find blood between her legs. Some of the other women gave her some rags to soak it up with, but she had to appear before the abbess. The abbess looked at her and said, "It seems you are well-named after all."

The abbess told her she was bleeding because she was greedy and fat and also had lust in her heart. None of the Brides bled. That was because they were pure. She said she had felt that it was a bad idea to let Avarice come and live with them in the first place but that she had prayed about it and the Lord had told her she needed to give Avarice a chance, but Avarice had let her down. She was a sinner at heart, sure as her name, and the abbess would have to think now on what she was going to do about that.

In the days that followed, Avarice found herself careening wildly from happiness to terror. She imagined herself returning home, welcomed with open arms—never mind that she didn't know the way back, or how to get anywhere at all from the compound. Baby Tom wouldn't be such a baby anymore and the other boys would be bigger as well and her daddy would have missed her so much he'd have realized his mistake in sending her away. Maybe her mother would even be back there. Maybe they had all been wrong. Mama had not been dead at all but just in a deep sleep. Other times, she imagined herself forced out of the compound with winter coming on. Her daddy had always told her that if she ever got lost in the woods, she should do three things: Go downhill to find water. Follow water to find a road. Follow the road to find people. Surely that would get her somewhere, if the Brides didn't want her any longer.

The next time Avarice was on kitchen duty, she slipped away with a paring knife. That night, under the covers, while the others snuffled and snored in their sleep, she made small cuts on her legs and arms. It felt as though she might be able to slice the blood and the potential visions that might return at any time right out of her. The pain was almost soothing, and she fell asleep pressing the knife against the crook of her arm. In the daylight she examined her wounds: they looked like tiny red shrieking mouths cut into her flesh. She had told herself the previous night that she would only do it the one time, but she had not imagined she would find the act so irresistible. Each night she scraped the knife across her skin; each night she tested herself, digging deeper and into more tender spots for a longer time to see how much pain she could endure. The agony took her out of herself, made her feel like she was soaring above the world and all of her sorrow. She took to turning aside or slipping away during the day so that she could leave little scores on her skin. She volunteered for solitary tasks like cleaning the outhouses to gain herself more time away from watchful eyes. Sometimes, she prayed as she did, it although she was no longer certain to whom: *O Lord,* she would begin, and wondered who the Lord might be. If the only Bible she'd ever seen was the one Sister Lucinda showed her in her first weeks there and nobody ever talked about who or what they worshipped, how could she be sure? And did she want to pray to the Lord who had killed her mother in so ignoble a fashion anyway? She had turned to that Lord when her mother died, but what good had come of it?

O Lord, she prayed, *to whoever out there might be listening. Take away my fits and my visions and my blood. Make me pure and worthy of you. Make me one of your Brides.*

AS FALL SLIPPED INTO WINTER and the end of the year beckoned, Avarice found she could no longer clearly remember the faces of her family. She tried to picture them and failed: her father, Baby Tom and her other brothers. Her mother's face was the most difficult of all to recall. She could not even recollect what color her hair had been, or whether it had been dark or light. How could it be possible to forget such a thing?

It all contributed to her feeling that she was fading away, right out of existence. She was eating as little as possible, and went around lightheaded most of the time. The work continued to be exhausting and the worship hours endless and dull. But she hadn't bled again since that first awful time, and it was enough to give her hope that whatever she was doing to stave it off was working.

To the paring knife, which she kept tucked beneath the thin padding of her cot when it wasn't swaddled in her clothes, she had added a larger, sharper blade. That one had been missed in the kitchen, but as far as she could tell, its disappearance had not been connected with her. Whenever she could get a few minutes alone, which was not often, she had begun to carve patterns on her flesh: spirals, especially, and the deepest cuts left scars. She slipped bits of salt from the kitchen and rubbed it into her wounds, and the pain strengthened her. She was so thin by this time that her arms and legs reminded her of the little dolls her mother had made for her out of twigs and matchsticks. One night while on kitchen duty she used another one of the large knives to hack away at her long locks—all the Brides had them—and she yanked out chunks of her hair until her scalp was bleeding. That, of course, did not go unnoticed. Sister Lucinda was the one who came in and found her.

Sister Lucinda said "What are you doing?" and Avarice said "I'm making myself more pure for the Lord," and Sister Lucinda didn't know what to say to that. She didn't go get the abbess or anything. She just sat there and watched her and when Avarice was done she tried to bathe the wounds on the top of her head, but Avarice wouldn't let her.

Before she went off duty from the kitchen she stole a pinch of salt to rub into her scalp.

That night, her visions came flooding back to her: all that she had forgotten, and new ones as well.

HER MAMA'S VOICE WAS SINGING to her in the dark, and she heard the soft strains of the dulcimer too, but quiet, quieter than her daddy had ever played it. She was so cold. Had she ever been so cold? She didn't think so. She was cold, and she was wet, and she was so hungry. And it was dark. She wondered if there might be a lamp or candle nearby, but as she rose to look for one she caught sight of the ceiling—only it wasn't a ceiling, it was the sky above, a magnificent sea of stars in a black sky. She tried to steady herself because she thought she might fall into that sea and drown, and then she was falling, and then she was shouting, and then Sister Lucinda and some of the others were holding her down and someone had a kerosene lamp and it was rocking back in forth in a way that made the face behind it look like a monster and she couldn't stop screaming until her voice was hoarse and raw and then gone altogether.

If you don't bury your hair after you cut it, a witch can get hold of it and cast a spell on you.

THEY MADE HER STAY IN bed all the next day, though she insisted that she was fine. But she wasn't; she had a fever that kept her tossing and turning and throwing the covers off even though somebody kept coming in and putting them back on her. Near dusk, the abbess came to her. Avarice could barely get the words out, but she wanted the woman to know that she knew:

"You done witched me."

"Shhh, child," said the abbess, laying the back of her hand gently across Avarice's forehead in a way that made her think somebody else must be in the room with them. The abbess wouldn't be so gentle and calm with her if they were alone.

"Give me," Avarice said, but her voice was too weak, and failed her. She wanted to say, Give me back my mother, but nothing was powerful enough to do that, was it? Not even Jesus, not even the Lord, not even the Morning

Star, whether that was Jesus or the Devil, could make somebody wake up and climb out of their grave again after they'd been dead nearly nine months, could they? Maybe after just a few days, like Lazarus and like Jesus himself. But what kind of a body would her mother be returning to all these months later? It would be rotten. She probably wouldn't even be able to walk in it. Her legs would dissolve if she tried to stand up on them. If you went to touch her you'd just push right through her like she was spoiled fruit.

"Who did you put down in a cave?" Avarice said, or meant to say, but she could barely form the words, and her breath came out stale and dead-smelling.

"What is wrong with your arm, child?" said the abbess, pulling her bare arm from under the covers, and she was running her hands over the cuts and the spirals Avarice had made there, and Avarice knew that she wasn't really asking, that she knew what Avarice had done and why, maybe even better than Avarice herself. "What have you done to yourself?" For a few moments Avarice was afraid that the abbess was going to strip her naked right there and then, and see the cuts she had made all over her body, but she just pulled the covers back up and said to the other person in the room, "Bring her some water."

After that, Avarice guessed that maybe somebody did, but she didn't know, because time went funny for a while. Different people came and sat by her sometimes and talked to her. Sometimes they were her mother and her father, sometimes her little brothers, but whenever she went to talk to them they turned into someone else, into one of the Brides. Sister Lucinda was with her the morning her fever broke. She was glad, because she didn't trust anybody there, but Sister Lucinda seemed like the one she needed to mistrust the least. All the same, she didn't let on right away that she had come back to her senses. She lay there and she waited to see what they would do, but all that happened was that Sister Lucinda went away and somebody else came to sit with her and finally she couldn't stand it any longer.

"I'm all right," she said. "I'm not going to die, I'm awake now. Go get the abbess and tell her I'm all right."

BUT THE ABBESS DIDN'T COME right away. She didn't come for hours, and when she did, it was like she wasn't even concerned that Avarice knew all about her and what she had done, how she'd witched her, and put a woman down in a cave, and lied to everybody. It was almost enough to make Avarice think she'd dreamed it, that it had all been part of the fever and the sickness rather than that the fever and the sickness were coming from the abbess herself. But weren't witches tricky that way? Wasn't that just how they got you to trust them?

The abbess said she was glad Avarice was feeling better because that night was the Winter Solstice, and it was an important time for the Brides. Avarice remembered then: "It's my birthday," she said, and the abbess looked at her, and Avarice knew what she was thinking: *Greedy. Selfish*. Or was she? Avarice was so confused now, after the vision and the dreams. It was hard to know what was real and what wasn't. Maybe it always had been that hard. After all, she had never believed *the world* was real, even when her father went out into it and came back again with stories. Maybe she *was* wrong about the abbess and everything else as well.

Avarice felt well enough to get up and dress herself, but Sister Lucinda came in and said no, she couldn't wear one of her old dresses, that they all dressed up for the Winter Solstice. Sister Lucinda brought her a long white dress—"White like the moon and the stars," she said, and Avarice thought that was a strange thing to say, almost like Sister Lucinda had come into her dreams and then stolen away with a picture of the black sea of stars. She was so weak from being ill that she had to sit down on the edge of the bed and rest halfway through changing her clothes. In the end it was easier to just keep her old dress on and pull the one Sister Lucinda had brought her over it. The new dress hung on her like it was made for three or four Avarice-sized people instead of one.

She held her arms out in front of her and she could see her veins under the scars, so thin and translucent had her skin become. Avarice found herself thinking for the first time that maybe *the world* didn't sound so bad. Could it really be stranger and more difficult than life here with the Brides? She wondered what would happen if she tried to leave. Would they stop her? Would they say she had been free to go all along? But where would she go?

Sister Lucinda came back for her then. "Drink this," she said, and handed her something Avarice thought was water but which burned her throat and choked her and made her eyes tear up. "What *was* that?" she gasped, and Sister Lucinda laughed and said it was liquor from the still, that they always drank it at Solstice, and that later that night there would be a feast and more liquor.

Avarice had thought they would just be going to the worship house and sitting for a few boring hours, but much to her surprise all the Brides were gathered at the gate. The sky was nothing like her dream. It must have been overcast, because it was pitch black. Instead, the Brides were themselves like the stars, all in white, a sea of light in the darkness.

She was still very weak. The abbess opened the gate, and Avarice wondered if they had far to go and if she would be able to walk the distance in her condition. She found herself apprehensive at the thought of stepping through the gate. She had not been on the other side of it for months, and some part of her had accepted that she would never again be on the other side.

Every year, on her birthday, her mother had told her the story of her birth. How it had just been her and Avarice's daddy and how they didn't know anything about what to expect. How the birth pains came and she liked to have died because they hurt so bad. Who could imagine women went through this to give birth? Why would anyone? How were they not all dead? How Avarice's daddy had run, run, halfway down the mountain to where an old healer lady lived and brought her back, and thank goodness Avarice's mama had a long labor and Avarice wasn't born while she was all alone up there because sure as *the world* they both would have died.

Now Avarice thought of all the questions she had never thought to ask in a decade of hearing that story: Why were they all alone? Where had they come from? Who were their people? Didn't they have mamas and daddies, brothers and sisters, a home somewhere?

She thought of the last sight of her father, standing her at the gate, as the abbess led them in the opposite direction from the one they had arrived in, along the fence, round the back part of the compound, and then into the woods. It was so dark that Avarice found it difficult to keep her footing. She found herself falling behind the others, and soon she could just see them bobbing ahead like little points of light, like ghosts. She wanted to call to them and ask them to slow down but at the same time she did not want to bring attention to herself. A slow but familiar sort of dread was building in her, a sense of something known that she had long tried to unknow without success.

She could not say how long they walked because the fever, or something, had come back, and gripped her. Or so she told herself; surely that was the reason she felt so lightheaded and imagined she heard the soft strains of a dulcimer and her mother's sweet voice.

Lost lady, lost lady, don't you cry . . .

The others were still ahead of her, but they had stopped and gathered, and she was able to catch up to them at last. For a moment she thought she was hallucinating from the fever, or a fit, for several of them had lit torches, and the sight they illuminated was that of a skeleton, chained to a tree. As she moved closer, she could see that the chains were old and rusty, and that the skeleton's skull had been smashed open.

Your love don't suffer . . .

The second thing she saw was a crevice in the earth, and some of the Brides were kneeling or on all fours around it and calling down. At the same time, she heard a voice drifting up from the cavern below, the sound of someone singing, in the voice of her mother.

It was a vicious trick, some witchery by the abbess—

But she saw their faces then, all ringed in the light, and the expressions on them were not cruel but beatific.

"Anchoress!" called the abbess. "The circle is complete! Your babes, born from lust and fornication, united themselves in unnatural and unholy union, have given their girl up to us, of their own free will, just as it was written."

Your sweet babes are nigh . . .

Avarice wanted to shout that it was untrue, that her mother had never given her up and would never have done so, that she had died, and that wasn't the same thing, but she could not make her voice work.

What kind of god did they worship in this place?

What did it even matter? A wrong god; a bad god; maybe all of them were bad.

Go downhill to find water. Follow water to find a road. Follow the road to find people.

Later, she would wonder: Had her father known, all the times he told her that? Had he been preparing her?

That was all it took: she was off, without thought, cursing the white gown like a beacon in the dark, and praising the blackness of the night as she tore the gown from her body, praising the weakness that had made it impossible earlier for her to struggle out of her old gray dress underneath that helped the dark hide her now. She was still weak. She would not be able to run far at all, and soon she would have to hide, and she might even have to crawl, and there was no point in trying to go back home because not only would they find her there but they would all be gone—her father and Baby Tom and her other two brothers—long gone, far away, into the world. Someplace safe.

But she had been born at midnight, and that meant she could talk to the dead.

And her mother made pictures in her mind, showing her where to hide. For a long time, the abbess and the Brides looked for her, calling out, exclaiming that they'd found her when they were nowhere near, and she could not breathe easily until their voices grew distant. She thought that the longest night of the year would last forever, but dawn broke at last, and again, in pictures, she saw what she needed to see: a stream nearby, and a road.

Avarice, born into a cold winter's midnight fourteen years earlier, straightened her shoulders and walked toward water, walked toward morning, walked toward the world.

SIŪLAIS IR KRAUJO IR KAULŲ
(OF THREAD AND BLOOD AND BONE)
DAMIEN ANGELICA WALTERS

A GIRL WENT INTO THE Dainava Forest. Seventeen and angry and scared, like everyone in Lithuania. Boots and trousers, provisions carried in a pack on her back. A Russian rifle slung across her chest. A comforting weight, albeit an irony. Others in her troop carried German rifles. The girl in the forest remembered how, at first, they thought the Germans would help them break free from the Soviets, and how wrong they were, then the Germans were gone and good riddance. For the rest of the world, the war was over, but it wouldn't be over in Lithuania until the Communists were gone. The partisans thought the West would help. They were wrong again.

The girl was still in the Dainava, but lost, along with her pack, her rifle, and the rest of her troop. All around her, birch and pine and spruce and black alder. Mute soldiers standing watch. Alone, the girl staggered through the trees, one hand on her belly, blood seeping between her fingers.

Her troop had known Russian soldiers were close, but they'd underestimated how close. They thought they could make it to the next bunker buried beneath the forest, less than a day's walk away. But Tadas's compass started showing north no matter which direction they headed, so they stopped to check their maps. No fire. No cooking. No sleeping. The girl put down her rifle, stepped behind a dense clump of bushes with a tangle of thorn at her back, crouched low to avoid splashing her boots with urine. And then—

Chaos, gunshots, and shouts. The girl pressed herself flat against the forest floor. Her gun, resting against the trunk of a tree, too far away. More gunshots. More shouts, but of triumph, not surprise. Screams from Lina when the soldiers discovered she was a woman. Karas padarė laukinius žvėris vyrų. *War made beasts of men.* The girl wanted to help, wanted to stop the soldiers, but she couldn't, so, not yet aware of the stray bullet, not yet aware of her wound, she slithered beneath the thorns, crawled deeper into the forest, down a small hill, hid beneath a rotting tree trunk that had fallen long ago. Heard Lina crying, cursing; heard the soldiers grunting and laughing. Another gunshot pierced the air and Lina fell silent.

The girl got to her feet, felt the blood and the hurt. Stumbled from tree to tree and all she wanted to do was curl up and sleep, but she kept moving, lost like a child in a fairy tale. And were there heavy, booted steps approaching from behind? A harsh voice calling out?

One moment, the stone building wasn't there and then it was. Gray, towering, old. The girl let out a soft sound. Moved closer. A place to hide, to wait, and, perhaps, to die. Better there than under a Russian soldier's rutting body. The girl fell to her knees. No strength left. Blood flowed warm and sticky over her fingers and pattered to the forest floor.

A woman with young eyes in an old face crouched beside her. Touched her forehead.

"Prašau," the girl said.

Please.

AUDRA WOKE TO THE SOFT tap of footsteps. When she tried to sit, pain lanced through her abdomen and a gentle hand pressed her shoulder back into the soft mattress. Windowless stone walls. Burning candles. Shadows. The scent of beeswax. The woman with the young eyes, the lines on her face deepened by the flickering light, her hair in a thick silver braid. She wore a linen dress, trimmed at hem, neck, and cuffs with dark red, and an apron bleached white.

"Where am I?" Audra said, her voice whisper-thin. "What happened?"

"You don't remember? We found you in the forest. You've been shot."

Audra closed her eyes against the memory of Lina's screams. "Russians," she said. "Soldiers."

The woman nodded. "Of course. Here—" she held out a small cup "—this will help ease your distress."

The woman supported Audra's head with a hand so she could drink. The liquid was cool and slightly bitter, but it left the faint taste of honey on her tongue; even after the first sip, the ache in her abdomen began to ebb. "Thank you," she said. "Where am I?"

"You're safe. The soldiers won't find you here. I'm Saulė."

"Audra."

"Storm. A good name for a soldier."

"My father said the same."

"Is he a soldier, too?"

"No. He's a shopkeeper. In Vilnius. Where am I?" Audra repeated. "Are we underground? Are we hidden?"

"You need to rest."

"I need to know. Prašau, how long have I been here? How bad is my wound? My troop is—" she swallowed the lump in her throat "—gone, but there will be others waiting at the bunker. I need to get back and tell them what happened."

The woman's face crumpled, first into a frown, then a strange, humorless half-smile. "The abbess will come and explain everything soon enough. For now, you must rest."

"I need . . ." Spots danced a waltz across her field of vision, her limbs grew heavy and everything began to turn gray. "What did you. . . ?"

"Shhh, rest now," the woman said. "Rest."

THE DOOR TO HER ROOM was locked. Audra pushed her shoulder into it hard enough to drive her teeth together in a painful clack, but the wood wouldn't budge. She banged with the side of her fist, shouting, "Hello?" Dimly, she heard voices, but no one heeded her call. The arms of fear gripped her tight. Why had they locked her in? The woman, Saulė, mentioned an abbess, which meant this was a convent of some kind. Before the war and the Communists, Audra went to church every Sunday; she'd never seen a nun dressed in attire like the woman. For that matter, she'd never known a nun to lock someone in a room.

She muttered a curse beneath her breath and paced the room. The stone walls were cool, which meant the building was probably underground. Vaguely, she remembered seeing a building just before she fell, but that was impossible. Even in a forest as large as the Dainava, something of that size would've been spotted and overrun with Russians by now. More than half the partisan bunkers had been found and destroyed or taken over, and those were well-hidden from view. The Russians were as determined as they were brutal.

Gone was Audra's uniform; in its place, a nightgown, the fabric soft and fine. Her fingers traced the outline of a bandage beneath, and when she undid the buttons, she found the dressing clean and dry. Perhaps she was in some sort of makeshift hospital. That might explain the drink she'd been given, but it didn't offer an explanation for the locked door.

The wound still ached, but in much the same way as a monthly cramp. She perched on the edge of the bed and carefully peeled back the bandage.

The wound was closed with seven small stitches in red thread, stark against the pale of her skin.

The door opened and Audra refastened the buttons of the nightgown as another woman, even older than the first, came in, closing the door behind her. There was no mistaking the click of the lock engaging.

The woman's face had the texture of tattered parchment. Her short hair was a mix of pale and dark gray, but her blue eyes were bright.

"You drugged me," Audra said.

"We gave you something to help you sleep, that's all," the woman said. "We mean you no harm, but you're wounded."

"You drugged me and you locked me in. Where am I? Is this a hospital? A convent?"

"I'm sorry if we've frightened you. It's not our intention. We only wish to keep you safe. You should be in bed."

"I'm not frightened, but I need to leave."

The abbess pursed her lips, her eyes inscrutable. "I'm Gintarė, the abbess here. This is the Abbey of Deivės Valdytojos, the Seven Sisters who create the fabric of mortal lives."

As a child, Audra had been told stories of the old pagan gods and goddesses by her mother, but she'd never heard of an abbey still devoted to their worship. If—*when*—the Communists found it, they wouldn't care which deities the women prayed to. She thought of warning the woman, but everyone knew the risks. Instead, she said, "I want my clothes and my boots."

"I don't think that's a wise idea yet. You should rest. You're wounded."

Audra met her gaze and held it. "Am I a prisoner here?"

"No, of course not."

"Then I want my things."

"I understand. I'll have them brought to you."

"No, I'll come with you to get them. I want to leave now. I've spent too much time here already."

After a long moment, the abbess said, "Follow me."

They traveled down a long, shadowed hallway lined with closed doors and up a small staircase to a wide landing where several hallways branched off, which made the building even larger than in her scrap of memory. The abbess led her down one of the hallways to a room with tables, chairs, and baskets of fabric. Audra's uniform was folded atop one of the former.

"We did the best we could," the abbess said.

Audra clutched the washed, but stained and torn uniform in her hands and took a deep breath. "May I have some privacy to change?"

"Of course," the abbess said. "I'll wait outside."

Audra left the nightgown on the same table and rummaged for sewing supplies, but found none. The bandage would have to suffice. Though the fabric of her uniform was stiff, it felt comfortingly familiar. If she had her pack and rifle, she'd feel even better, but she'd have to make do and travel fast. She laced her boots tight and joined the abbess in the hallway.

"Thank you," Audra said.

The abbess nodded. "This way."

They returned to the landing and down another hallway, through a large, open room, and into a smaller vestibule. At one end stood a pair of oversized wooden doors carved with swirling designs. The other woman was waiting beside the door along with two others Audra had not met, both with silvered hair and aged faces. Their gazes flitted from the abbess to Audra and back again.

"You don't have to do this," the abbess said, her eyes sad.

"Thank you for helping me. You should be careful here. There are thousands of soldiers in the forest."

When Audra pulled the door open, mottled sunlight filtered in, and she shielded her eyes with one hand. The forest was quiet and still. Saulė touched her arm.

"Prašau, come back inside and rest for a bit."

"I can't. I have to get to the bunker."

Three steps led down to the ground and Audra took them quietly. A dry leaf crackled under her foot, a twig beneath the other. She glanced over her shoulder, but the abbey was gone; where it should have been, only leaves and a scattering of fallen branches. She spun in chaotic circles, searching, her mind reeling. She stumbled away from the now-empty space, and pain blossomed in her belly, a flower with razor-tipped petals. The stitches snapped, as though they were harp strings plucked by a careless hand. Warmth followed suit; her fingertips came away red, but it wasn't blood. It was thread. Long strands of thread, all pouring from a gaping hole in her uniform. She fell to her knees, breathing out a moan. The hole grew larger, revealing neither skin nor organ nor bone, but a dark, shadowy nothingness. And from its edges, the thread continued to unwind.

The hurt spread from her belly to her limbs. She opened her mouth to call for help and—

A GIRL RAN THROUGH THE Dainava Forest. Twigs broke beneath her boots and she staggered, one hand on her belly, one outstretched. All around her the trees loomed. Voices and shouts drifted through the air like ash from a fire. All those in her troop were dead and she was lost in the forest, her pack and rifle lost too. She pressed a fist to her temple. Something wasn't right. Something—

(in a room, all chanting and candle flicker and there were needles weaving through her arms and legs and four women)

—was wrong.

One moment, the stone building wasn't there and then it was. The girl let out a soft sound and took a step toward it, then froze in place. The soldiers would find her there. She needed to hide someplace else. The girl's knees buckled and she fell, blood darkening the ground. A woman with a long silver braid crouched beside her.

"Prašau," the girl said.

THE ROOM WAS SMALL WITH windowless stone walls. A candle burned on a table next to the bed, turning the corners of the room to shadow. The woman with the braid smiled.

"Where am I?" Audra said, her voice whisper-thin. "What happened?"

"We found you in the forest. You've been shot. Here—" the woman held out a small cup "—this will help you heal."

The liquid caught the light from the candle and a cold snake uncoiled in Audra's spine.

"No. I don't want to drink. I want to—

(run)

—leave."

The woman's eyes turned sad, but she said, "I'll get the abbess."

She slipped from the room and Audra sat, feeling the edge of a bandage on her abdomen beneath the nightgown. She remembered the blood, the pain, but there was only a small ache now. A good sign. A woman entered the room, her face lined, her eyes bright.

"I'm Gintarė, the abbess here. This is the Abbey of Deivės Valdytojos, the—"

"Seven Sisters."

"You know them?"

Audra frowned and rubbed her temple. "I think my mother told me stories."

A smile curved the abbess's lips.

"How bad is my wound?"

"Saulė told me you didn't want to take the medicine she brought for you."

"No, I don't want any medicine. I want to know how bad my injury is."

"You were shot," the abbess said, not unkindly. "But the abbey let you in so we could take care of you. Are you feeling up to a walk? It will help you regain your strength."

Audra nodded. Touched the bandage again. It must not be too bad. If it were, she'd be in agony, unable to stand or walk.

The abbess led her slowly down the hallway and up a small staircase. Although distant voices echoed from arched openings to other hallways, they passed no one. They went up another staircase that opened into a large room with wooden benches and a small altar covered in linen. Niches on the wall contained carved wooden statues of veiled women. The room smelled of old incense, beeswax, and wildflowers.

"Once, this is where people came to worship," the abbess said. "Where babies were named, where the dead were honored."

The abbess guided her to the first niche, where the statue held a spindle in her hands. "This is Verpiančioji. She spins the threads of life." The second statue gripped a spinning wheel. "Metančioji, who turns the wheel. Audėja, the weaver—see the braided strands of thread in her hands?—and this is Gadintoja, who breaks the thread." The carved muscles in her forearms revealed tension.

The abbess crossed to the other side of the room. "This is Sergėtoja. She scolds Gadintoja, which is why the statues are never placed together. She also incites war." The statue's hands were behind her back, her face turned to the side. "And here—" the abbess swept one hand toward the last two statues "—are Nukirpėja, who cuts the cloth of life, and Išskalbėja, the laundress, who washes us clean." The former had a knife in one hand and a drape of fabric in the other; the latter, a small bowl.

"At one time there were fifty women beneath this roof, all devoted to the Sisters." The abbess crossed her arms and cupped her elbows in her palms "Now, we're only four, but we're not powerless." Her lips wore the ghost of a smile. "The Seven Sisters may have been relegated to old stories, but they are not powerless either."

"Why are you showing me this?"

"To help you understand."

"Understand what?"

The abbess clasped her hands together. "Understand what we're trying to do. How we're trying to help. The old ways, even those almost forgotten, still hold some power."

"The old ways. You mean magic."

"Of a sort."

"The Communists killed all the magicians," Audra said. "They killed priests and nuns, too. If they find you, they'll do the same. Kill you or send you to Siberia, which is the same thing, only it takes longer."

"I trust in the Seven Sisters to keep us safe."

"Neither god nor goddess can protect you from the Communists. Families disappear in the middle of the night, and everyone pretends not to notice because if you say anything, you'll disappear too. Everyone is afraid. If you say the wrong thing, do the wrong thing, look the wrong way, or have the wrong thoughts, they'll come and take you and there's nothing anyone can do about it."

"I think perhaps we should go back to your room. You should rest."

"I think I'd like to leave instead."

"Your wound—"

"Will be fine. The bunker is less than a day away."

"But, Audra, it's late. Wouldn't it be better to rest a bit and then leave in the morning?"

The hair on the back of Audra's neck prickled. "How do you know my name?"

"I don't—"

"You never asked me, and I never told you. The other woman, she didn't ask either."

"Let me explain. We're only trying to help. You're the first person the abbey has shown itself to in a very long time."

"No." Audra backed away, arms up and hands held palm-out. "I don't want to hear anything more. I'm leaving. I want my uniform and my boots."

The abbess opened her mouth, closed it, and sighed. "I understand. Saulė?" she called out.

The other woman arrived so quickly Audra knew she must've been standing nearby.

"Bring Audra's things."

When Saulė returned, Audra tucked her uniform beneath one arm and her boots beneath the other. The women exchanged a look Audra couldn't decipher, and a strange sensation wormed its way into her gut.

"The door is this way," the abbess said.

Keeping a safe distance, Audra followed both women down the staircase, along the hallway, through an open room and into a small vestibule with a pair of heavily carved doors at the end. Two other women stood off to the side.

"I wish you'd reconsider," Gintarė said. "We aren't sure if your stitches are strong enough yet."

Without a word, Audra shoved open the front door and took the steps. The forest was quiet and still. Leaves and twigs cracked beneath her feet. She glanced over her shoulder, and the abbey was gone. No, that wasn't possible. It wasn't—

Pain flared in her abdomen and she doubled over, boots and uniform tumbling from her hands. Red spilled from a hole in her nightgown. Not blood, but thread. She tried to push the strands back in; the hole grew larger and in its center, a vast darkness. What did the women do to her? What did they do? She cried out for help, but all that emerged was a froglike croak and—

A GIRL MOVED THROUGH THE Dainava Forest. Echoes of gunshots and coarse laughter followed as she staggered from tree to tree, one hand held against her belly, trying to stop the flow of blood. Her troop was gone. All of them dead, surprised by Russian soldiers when they paused to check their bearings. No pack, no rifle, but she was lucky—

(the thread we spin,
the life we give)

—so lucky because she—

One moment, the stone building wasn't there and then it was. The girl shuddered. She needed to hide—

(the spindle turned and the women threaded the needles and they sewed and sewed and sewed)

—someplace else. Her legs gave out, blood spattering the ground as she fell.

("I think she sees us."
"Don't be silly. She can't. Not yet, not until the final stitch."
"Maybe we should tie her down."
"We can't do that. We don't want to scare her.")

Leaves crackled as a woman crouched beside her and extended a hand.

"Prašau," the girl said.

A WOMAN WITH SHORT HAIR, a lined face, and blue eyes sat at the foot of the bed. She looked familiar, though Audra couldn't place her.

"Where am I?" Audra asked, wiping sleep from her eyes.

"We found you in the forest outside. You've been injured."

Audra closed her eyes against her memories. "The soldiers," she said. She touched one hand to her abdomen, felt the edge of a bandage beneath the nightgown. "How badly am I hurt?"

"Bad enough," the woman said. "We're not sure how much to tell you. Saulė thinks it's harmful, Meilutė and Aldona think it cruel not to, and I, well, I'm unsure. It doesn't seem to matter or to change things. Not yet anyway. Though I suppose by even saying this much, I've made my decision. Gera pradžia, pusė darbo."

Starting properly ensures it will be done correctly. Audra's mother always said the same when beginning a difficult task.

The women's names were slightly familiar as well, but not as though they were people Audra knew, but those she *might*. A shiver danced the length of her spine. "I don't understand."

"I know you don't. I'm Gintarė, the abbess. This is the Abbey of Deivės Valdytojos."

"The Seven Sisters?"

The abbess tipped her head in a brief nod. "You know of them?"

"I think so." Audra plucked a string on the blanket. An image of veiled women flashed into her mind, skittered away. "I've heard stories, or I've seen statues somewhere. I don't remember."

"The world has nearly forgotten them, but we prayed for a way to bring them back. We prayed for such a long time, and they gave us you," the abbess said. "If we can fix you, if we can bring *you* back, then we'll be able to come back, too. The abbey is the door, but you're the key."

Audra clenched her jaw. The woman's eyes looked perfectly sane, but her words were anything but.

"I know it sounds strange, but we're only trying to help. I promise. Sometimes it takes time to get things right. We were out of practice. It'll work, of this I'm sure, but it will take time. We all must make sacrifices for the greater good. As a partisan, I'm sure you understand that."

Audra swallowed. "What I understand is that I can't stay here." She slid from the bed, ignoring the ache in her belly.

"Prašau," the abbess said. "Just rest a little longer. You're not strong enough yet. The stitches need more time to set."

Audra shoved her aside and was out in the hallway before the thump as the woman hit the floor. She ran until she reached a small staircase, took the stairs two at a time. Several hallways branched off from the landing. She picked one at random, ending up at another staircase that opened into a large room with benches and statues.

Back down the stairs she fled, to the landing and another hallway. She needed to find the double doors, doors of carved wood that led outside, but how she knew that, she wasn't sure, and her feet had forgotten the way.

A voice called out. "Audra?"

Her mouth went dry. How did they know her name?

A different voice said, "I think she's already gone."

"We have to find her. She's not ready yet. Check the chapel, Meilutė. Saulė, go back down and make sure she isn't hiding in one of the rooms. Aldona, come with me."

On tiptoe, Audra crept down another hallway, away from the voices, opened a door, and snuck inside. Footsteps rushed past. She brushed hair away from her face. Hissed a slow breath through her teeth. What did the women want with her?

She retreated deeper into the room—it was far larger than she'd expected—and as she neared the back, her legs turned to rubber. On long tables lay women, half-covered in sheets. A strange perfume of wax, copper, and freshly washed linen clung to the air. Heart pounding, fingers trembling, Audra moved closer. Touched the nearest one. Not women, but dolls—twelve, no, thirteen, woman-sized dolls of woven thread—and all wore her face.

A soft moan slipped unnoticed from her lips. As though sleepwalking, she moved around the tables, her shoulders slumped, her eyes darting from shape to shape. Each doll was cold to the touch, motionless, and though she could see the delicate weave of the threads, they felt as though crafted of skin and bone. The disconnect between touch and sight left a bitter taste on her tongue, like dandelion.

The doll on the last table appeared different, though. She traced her fingers along its shoulder. Bent closer. Its skin had neither strand nor pattern. Not a doll at all, but a body. *Her* body, lifeless and still, a hole in the abdomen crusted with blood. She cried out, pressing both hands against her mouth to muffle the sound. This wasn't right. This couldn't be.

She held out her arm. Ran her fingertips along its length. Her mouth filled with the bitter taste again.

"No, she whispered, her voice hitching. "Oh, no."

"We can explain," a voice said from behind her.

Audra whirled around, tears burning in her eyes. "What did you do to me?"

"We can explain everything, child," the abbess said. "We're trying to make it right. We're trying to save you. Please, we know it's hard, but once we know exactly how many stitches we need to make, everything will be all right."

"Stay away from me," Audra sobbed. "All of you. Stay away."

She shoved past the women, and this time, her feet remembered the way. She skidded to a halt in the vestibule, wrenched the door open.

"Audra, wait!"

"No, let her go. We'll do better next time. We'll be more careful."

She half-ran, half-stumbled down the steps that led to the ground. Leaves and twigs broke beneath her feet, and the abbey and the women were gone. Laughter spilled from her lips. She was free. She was safe.

Pain shuddered through her belly, and her hands came away red. Not with blood, but with long strands of thread unwinding from a hole inside her. She threw back her head, let loose her voice, and birds took to the sky in panicked flight.

She wouldn't let the women do this to her anymore. If she was gone, let her be gone. She pulled on the threads, moaning through clenched teeth, but even as she removed handful after handful, she knew she'd never get them all; there were too many.

She thought of the candle in the windowless room. *Thread burns*, she told herself. *Remember that, if you remember nothing else the next time. Thread burns.*

Hooking her fingers into claws, she yanked harder and—

A GIRL BLED IN THE Dainava Forest. She weaved through the trees, one hand on her belly, the other pushing branches from her face. Voices rang out and she staggered. She needed to hide before—

(the thread we spin)

—they found her. Before they—

A stone building towered overhead, a building that wasn't there before, and she cried out, her feet sliding on twigs as she tried to stop. Bėgo nuo vilko, užbėgo ant meškos. *If you run from a wolf, you may run into a bear.*

She had to get away. She'd been here before—she felt it in her gut, knew it with every fiber of her being—and before and before. They'd done something—

(the life we give)

—to her. They—

Her ankles tangled together and she fell, blood pooling in the dirt, fingers scrabbling for a root, a vine, for anything at all.

(We prayed for such a long time, and they gave us you.)

An old woman with bright eyes crouched beside her. The girl tried to scuttle away, but it hurt to move and her arms and legs were heavy and awkward and didn't want to move.

"Prašau," she said. "I don't want to do this again. Let me go."

"Don't worry. We'll get it right this time, we promise. Everything will be all right."

Fear flooded the girl's veins, and she knew it would never be all right. Nothing could make this right. Tears coursed down her cheeks, and every time she blinked she saw flames and she didn't know why.

GRAVITY WAVE

NADIA BULKIN

WHEN SHE TURNED THIRTY-FIVE, IBU Indah Ratnasari decided that she wanted to add a tapol to the supernatural arsenal of the Agriculture Department of the National Secretariat of Ladies' Cooperation. She already had a sleeping tuyul in a jar, a toothy jenglot in a jewelry box, as well as a cadre of experienced dukuns of assorted specialties on stand-by—healing, harvesting, matchmaking, divination, clairvoyance, sorcery—she even knew a dukun santet who lived on the outskirts of the city in a perpetually collapsing hut, but he was risky; she had heard he did work with the General, and when she met him at midnight in that hovel of his he sneered at her, to her great discomfort.

A tapol was not a magical being per se, but it was a cursed creature, disowned by human society and thus afflicted with the most powerful magic in the world. Glowing Ibu Ayu, whose husband was director of livestock, did not follow this logic. "Tapols are stamped with absolute nothingness; what can they possibly do for you?" But Ibu Indah knew that a tapol's power—or at least its usefulness—lay in this nothingness, in the dark stamp that marked them as human waste. Ibu Murni, whose husband was deputy general inspector, did understand her vision, but objected to the use of tapol on principle. Ibu Murni also didn't know about the dukun santet. And Ibu Indah was not about to raise the tapol issue with her boss Ibu Sujati, who wanted the results of magic but not the "stain"—she'd go on a pilgrimage to the graves of the Nine Saints of Islam, but God help she who asked Ibu Sujati to have so much as an exorcist on retainer.

In the end, though, all the other ladies could do was counsel—Ibu Sujati's husband was discovered to be having an affair with a stewardess, and the General's wife had him removed as minister, sending around an anxious communiqué to the entire Secretariat about "*The Importance of Maintaining Matrimonial Fidelity for the Health of the Nation.*" Ibu Indah's husband became the new minister of agriculture, and Ibu Indah became the new head of the Secretariat's Agriculture Department. There were a few early whispers that "someone" had bewitched Ibu Sujati's husband, a dope of a man who went straight to sleep as soon as the plane started rolling, or at least the stewardess, a rather dull-witted and not particularly symmetrical girl—but Ibu Indah snuffed those rumors out. There was a new mistress in charge, she told the junior wives, and they could either rise with her or fall alone. Everyone wanted their husbands to keep their government-issued Toyotas, so everyone fell in line. And Ibu Indah found herself a tapol.

The tapol was a fourteen-year-old girl living in the slums on the banks of the Ciliwung River. She sold tapioca cakes on a road next to a hospital, and Ibu Indah's driver nearly ran her over during a minor rain spell. She smelled of mud and cigarettes, and she had gotten the signature black mark of a tapol—a lumpy, dark cloud that drooped over her head and stuck out in the hot sun like a cigarette burn on a white piece of paper—when she was only four. Her parents had infected her—spread it by virtue of genetic relation. The mother was in Bukit Duri Prison; the father was in the Buru prison colony, apparently. Ibu Indah didn't ask too many questions. Best not to know about such unpleasantness; it made for more plausible deniability. She just popped open her car door, extended her rainbow umbrella, and asked, "Do you want to get rid of that thing?"

SITI WAS A DECENT SERVANT—obsessively diligent about scrubbing surfaces until her hands were raw, but poor at basic deferential hospitality, which worked out because she was never allowed to deal with guests—but the other maids and nannies and drivers and handymen disliked her, even though she was paid the least of all of them. What they didn't like was the black mark. They never wanted to get too close to it, although they couldn't stop staring at it. The only maid who talked to Siti was the woman who did most of the cooking: she'd lash out on busy days, snapping that Siti was a criminal and a deviant and a traitor who had no right to be in the house of a government minister.

Siti understood their reactions, sort of. She supposed she wouldn't want to be around the black mark either, if she had a choice. Like a cloud, there was no touching it. Like a demon, there was no shaking it. It loitered like a halo that had spent a few months strapped to the exhaust pipe of a delivery motorcycle, soaking up the city's ashy, wasted spite. And it tended to carry smells until they rotted, besides. So she didn't begrudge the other maids. They had all worked hard, bargained, begged to get a job in a minister's mansion, hoping it would keep them and protect them, hoping that some of Ibu Indah's wealth would rub off on them just by being in her presence. The last thing they expected was to work alongside a monster like her. But in her defense, she was usually scrambling around the back innards of the house, carrying buckets and slaughtering chickens. She had never even seen the minister, only his sleek Japanese car.

Still, she got lonely talking to herself or the kitchen appliances. She missed her parents. Around Ciliwung there was always a more destitute individual who had no choice but to listen, brow crinkled and mouth agape. There were also old washerwomen who talked about "the way things were, before the world was remade," and there was even another tapol there, though he was sullen and angry because no one would take a rickshaw ride from a tapol. Who knew what a tapol would do? Siti herself didn't know the answer, maybe because she didn't choose to become a tapol and nothing had changed from one day to the next except a sudden, violent uptake in the amount of fear in her bloodstream. But at Ibu Indah's house, no one except the screaming cook would even acknowledge her existence, so much so that she sometimes had to find a mirror to remind herself that she was real and not someone else's dream. And so she began talking to the only thing that couldn't walk away from her: the black mark.

"Where did you come from? Do you have a name? Do you believe in God?" These were questions that seemed to matter a lot, on any given day. It took weeks of prodding, petting, combing through what felt like gnarly goat's fleece until it learned—or decided—to speak to her in a language she could understand. Or maybe it was Siti whose brain had unlocked another level of meaning, sitting alone in a closet-sized room and listening to the crickets as she neurotically ran her fingers through the black mark. And at first, all the black mark did was growl nihilistic words. "Nothing" and "dead" and "kill." She had the terrible feeling that its violent thoughts had somehow sprung from her body, and so she told no one. She was already barred from using knives; they all assumed she was on the brink of something terrible.

Ibu Indah was a smart woman and intuitively understood the complex dynamic at play. When she did finally tell Siti that her time had come and the mission that she had been waiting for her whole life was at hand, she did it quietly, at midnight, with a soft rap upon her closet-shaped door. The only light Siti had to go by was the starry glimmer of Ibu Indah's shark-sharp teeth, but Ibu Indah did not need eyes to see in the dark. She did not need eyes to see at all.

BACKSTAGE AT THE BISMA THEATER, the goddess Shinta was snorting cocaine. She was thinking, mostly, about her upcoming trip to Paris—her lover, who had inherited a multi-island timber operation, had decided to take her for her birthday. He asked her lazily, with his thumb tracing circles over her knee, where in the world she would go if she could go anywhere. She had thought immediately of Degas and his shadowed but glowing ballerinas. They lived in a coffee table book that an old lover—this one a diplomat, who had since moved with his family to Pakistan—had once bought her: *The Life Eternal*.

Out of the corner of her eye she saw the man playing Rama approach her from behind, mumbling something about next Saturday's performance of a Gatutkaca sequence. She inhaled sharply and told him no was no, the role of Gatutkaca the legendary warrior was going to stay with Raden Mas Nugroho. She heard the whining start up as she put away the little baggie. "Don't push your luck," she said as her dagger-sharp eyes found his in the warped mirror, and Rama fearfully bowed his head and scurried away.

There was another painting in *The Life Eternal* that she turned to time and time again: *The Magic Circle*, by a man named Waterhouse. When she first came to the Bisma she had been limited to low-level handmaiden roles even though she was descended from minor nobility, because the old miser who ran the theater said she did not have natural talent. It was impossible to believe—she was *Raden Roro Novarti*; she had been practically raised in the palace at Jogja; talent was in her blood—how dare that chain-smoking nobody insult her? Her father offered to "have a talk" with the man, but *The Magic Circle* reminded her that she could solve this problem herself. She was priyayi. She was blessed.

Under the din of the angels putting in their hairpieces and giggling about their boyfriends, Rr. Novarti heard a shuffle of feet. There was a shadow in the doorway that led out into the theater's alleyway exit, and when the shadow came into the light she saw it was a girl . . . or something that resembled a girl, anyway. The visitor looked like somebody's maid in her pastel smock and rubber sandals, and normally Rr. Novarti would have just yelled at her to leave—if not for that horrible, terrible *thing* hanging over her head. In her years practicing the inborn magic of the inner world, Rr. Novarti had seen auras of all kinds—blue, green, the occasional red crown and even rarer white halo. But never that black cloud.

It could only be evil. Frantically, she tried to think of who all could have sent it after her. The old theater director was the first to come to mind, although as she understood it his mind was porridge now—but he had children, and no doubt those criminals knew low-class sorcerers... the cheap, filthy variety that twirled their mustaches and demanded sacrifices in the form of virgins and Rolex watches. The kind that promised to remove a tumor and would multiply it instead. Sometimes Rr. Novarti picked up on the jealous rumblings of the discontent, that there was no need any more for a priyayi caste—"They're just the descendants of colonist tax collectors; they're no better than the rest of us," and so on, so forth—but this was why. This was why priyayi were needed, to keep animals from using the tools of gods.

The old half-blind woman who patrolled the back exit never had been very good at reading auras. They kept her around because she didn't care about the drugs, but... "Mbak Eni! What did you just let in?!"

The girl-demon asked, with an authentically young and uncultured accent, "Are you Raden Roro Novarti, miss?" But above her and beyond her, the black mass growled like an enormous, thunderous tiger. The dancer clapped her hand over her mouth. She was thinking, *Stay away from me*, but all that came out of her mouth was an undignified squeak of terror. She grabbed a nail file.

"I have a letter I'd like you to sign." The girl-demon extended a manila envelope and a ballpoint pen.

"A letter? A letter to who?"

"The General," the girl-demon said. As she said his name the black cloud above her head shuddered and curled its tendrils like the leaves of a bashful plant.

Rr. Novarti frowned and wondered if this had something to do with her lover, the timber tycoon. She herself had never met their nation's leader. Tommy had and found him impressive, though he sometimes complained about the arbitrariness of the General's decisions. "The people are mad," she would whisper to him in the middle of the night, when he came to her bungalow complaining about whatever new tax or edict or arm-twisted contract. "But he's a mad king," Tommy would sigh. She should have been relieved that this wasn't about her, but truthfully it left her hollow. "Is this about the plantation in Pontianak?" she asked. "Because I don't know anything about that. That's Tommy's business."

"Please just read the letter," the girl-demon hissed. She walked forward slowly, as if hypnotized, and once she got close enough, the black cloud's growling became as audible as words. It was calling her shocking, vile names that didn't make any sense—"*witch woman*," and "*goblin queen*." It stung.

It left her speechless. She thought she could see half-formed hands and eyes emerging from the cloud and she quickly ripped the envelope open, cutting her fingers. The letter was just a jumble of racing, pounding words. She caught a few block-font phrases here and there that deeply frightened her—*no longer fit to lead the nation* being the worst. Did this girl-demon know what happened to people—or spirits—in possession of that kind of language?

Her trembling fingers reached for the little baggie of cocaine.

"*Sign the letter, sorceress!*" The cloud's noise blocked out everything—all the gilded gold, the oil paint, the incense and silk that defined her graceful genealogy—except for the gush of lava that poured out of the cloven earth like blood . . . in that glorious year that the world was remade. That year her parents had held her close and said that the fire would only burn the sinners, the bad ones, but "Everything gets burned," the cloud said, "Everyone gets eaten."

Rr. Novarti wiped her nose and looked up at the girl-demon. "This letter is treason," she whispered, and the black cloud exploded in a bitter laughter.

ONE OF THE FEW PEOPLE in Ibu Indah's employ who wasn't scared of or disgusted by Siti the tapol was Pak Garto, the medium. He was only around on occasion—Ibu Indah and the Agricultural Department of the National Secretariat of Ladies' Cooperation had little use for a clairvoyant. But sometimes a farmer's death might leave behind a massive land ownership dispute, or a family might become convinced that their irrigation system had been poisoned by the spirit of a vengeful neighbor, and then Pak Garto would roll up on his puttering motorcycle and light some candles and comb the world of the dead for the truth.

One afternoon, he asked Siti to buy him a pack of cigarettes from the little stall down the road. She watched him light a Marlboro, waiting for him to avert his eyes and tell her to get out of his sight, but he never broke eye contact. "I see the dead all the time," he said when she asked why. "So I don't care about that mess on your head. I've seen much worse."

When he wasn't performing psychic counseling, Pak Garto worked at a company that made batteries. His knuckles were as knobby as tree knots. "Someday we'll be making televisions," he said. "And after that we'll start making cars. That's what the General says, anyway."

"He says a lot of things," Siti said, thinking about the weekly Sunday night broadcasts that Ibu Indah always watched and clucked her tongue at.

"Yes," said Pak Garto, inhaling deeply.

It was sunset. Somewhere in the neighborhood, a dumpling vendor was singing and banging on a tin pan to ply his trade. "Do the dead say a lot of things?"

"Most are quiet. There are always a few loudmouths roaming around."

Eventually Siti got up the nerve to ask him about her parents. It wasn't really that she wanted to speak to them. She had no idea what she would say except that she was "okay"—her mother made it clear before Siti left Bukit Duri Prison that she and her father only cared that Siti "just survive." It was more that Siti wanted confirmation that they were dead. It was the last thing she needed to turn her heart completely to stone—sometimes she still daydreamed about running into her mother and father in the soft neon glow of a night market, falling into their comforting embrace, crying that she thought she would never see them again. And she needed her heart to be stone, to be just as hard and barren as the remade world.

She had to wait another four months before Ibu Indah needed Pak Garto's services again. He was in a hurry; he said something about a son being sick with tetanus. But she begged him to at least tell her whether he was picking up her parents' signal, somewhere in the misty void of the afterlife.

Pak Garto stared hard at her, then tightened his lips and said, "Child. I know what it is you want. And I'm not going to go there. You know perfectly well that your parents were swallowed by a dark that even I won't touch. There's not a dukun in Java that would try to talk to a pair of . . ."

He wouldn't say the word. Nobody would. He just fumbled with his motorcycle helmet. Fifteen years ago, everyone had said it so many times—or screamed it, or sobbed it, at the edge of a knife—that the world caved in on itself, and now they were all too gun-shy. They knew now that even whispering the word risked summoning an iron-fisted power that none of them could control, not Pak Garto and the dukuns, not Ibu Indah and her demonic dolls, and certainly not a hapless little cursed girl like Siti. She and the black mark were, after all, living proof of the undeniable power of the curse.

So her heart kept beating and bleeding for a while longer. "How much money does it take to curse somebody? Like a really bad curse. Snakes coming out of their stomach and stuff."

Pak Garto chuckled and fastened his chin strap. "More than you'll ever have, little one."

THE CITY'S MOST PROMINENT CLERIC had been gone for a month. His wife, Dr. Aisyah Alawiyah, insisted that he was not missing, only on a holy pilgrimage. She wasn't lying. He was meditating alone in a dark cave on a blessed mountain, waiting to hear the trickling, dripping word of God. But the fact remained that when six young Muslim protesters were killed defending their right to invite whomever they wanted to speak at their mosque—including a kiai who did not approve of the secular heathen-state that the General had built—the cleric was not there to smooth over the scars, to pencil in the apologies. The task of responding to the anxieties of his flock was left, as it had always been left, to his wife.

She was not particularly good at calming them. She had always been a bit too incendiary. "Had too much schooling," her husband's snippety friends said. Her temptation, to be frank, was to tell their herd that yes, the General had abandoned his faith, and the General had declared open war upon political Islam—this had been obvious for years, ever since the Muslim parties had been forced to merge into one enormous, toothless, state-controlled entity. Ever since the joke that was the National Mosque Council was born. The General had tried to wrestle God like God was just another wild, non-state element that had to be roped into the bounds of state control. As she sat at her plastic-lined, fruit-adorned dining room table, Dr. Aisyah found herself getting angry. If her husband was here he would have rubbed her shoulders and patted her head and blithely said, "Yes, I know, sweetheart, but think of what's best for the nation."

But he wasn't here. He had tapped her on the arm in the middle of the night and excitedly whispered that the spirits had come to him in a dream and told him he had to go to Gunung Semeru now, and he had no idea when he would be back. "The spirits?" she'd hissed. "Can't you tell them to call you back?" It wasn't that the spirits never spoke to her; they just seemed to give her much more practical advice. Such as, *This agitation at the mosque is going to get messy. Maybe try not to leave the city.*

When her servant Rini and her driver Andi came shuffling into her purview she assumed that another angry imam was at the door, demanding that her husband make a stand against the General's tyranny. "Tell them he's in very deep consultation with God," she muttered, and scribbled out another line of a religious harmony communique for the National Secretariat of Ladies' Cooperation.

"Madam, it wants to see you."

She turned her head. "It?"

"A tapol."

The corner of her eye twitched. "Well, get rid of it. Tell it this is a house of God."

"It says it has a letter that it wants you to sign. Something to do with the General?"

Dr. Aisyah almost wanted to laugh. Her instinct, again, was to tell them to sweep it away—with force, if necessary, although she was loathe to make them touch a tapol—but a whispering rational voice that sounded much like her husband's suggested that it might be best to control this situation quickly. "All right, bring it in," she told them. "But be careful."

She turned back to the communiqué for ten minutes. The General's wife—that lady's *gall*—had asked her to write it after the protests, the deaths. "Ibu Aisyah, talk to them about the importance of making sure the goals of our religious community are in line with the goals of the state." Masyallah. When she married a cleric she had no idea how much she was going to have to lie. She heard scuffling sounds from the hallway and in a moment Rini and Andi had thrown the tapol down onto the living room floor, just centimeters away from the authentic Persian rugs they had brought back from the hajj.

Dr. Aisyah had seen only a few tapols in her life, and never close-up—a monstrous shadow begging on the side of the road as Andi drove her to Parliament; a crippled beast selling water on the beach that overlooked the smoldering silhouette of Anak Krakatau—Krakatau's child, borne out of Krakatau's violence. She had heard that it was acting up this year, Anak Krakatau, spitting rocks and lava and frightening the birds. She hated to look at it. Hated that beach. And now that she was so close to its human equivalent—the black pumice cloud, the noxious gas, the grotesque reminder of what they had all been forced to do in order to save the world—Dr. Aisyah thought she might vomit.

"You are truly hideous," she said. "I'm surprised no one's done their civic duty and put you out of your misery."

The teenaged girl beneath the black mark looked up from the floor with a hurt expression. *Oh good, so now they've learned how to fake human emotion.* Dr. Aisyah snorted. "Oh, don't be mad at me, girl. Blame your godless parents. They must have been truly wicked to leave you with that much of a stain."

The black mark shuddered and flared its tendrils. "*Fascist bitch*," came its reply. Anything less coarse would have been a disappointment. "*Just wait till you see what's waiting for you down in Hell.*"

Her servants were horrified, but Dr. Aisyah was unfazed. She might not have the tact to deal with spineless bureaucrats and the frightened ummat, but fighting evil was what she'd been raised for. She had pointed them out, the year that the world was remade—the year that houses were emptied, then refilled; the year that rivers stopped flowing, then gushed with blood. She went through community lists with her husband, who brought the lists to the Army, and said, "There be monsters."

"Be quiet, Satan," she said now. "I helped kill enough of you monsters in 1965. I'm not scared to do it again."

That shut it up—or rather, reduced its voice to a howling, incomprehensible babble. The way even a wild dog knows to cower when it's been beaten with a pipe.

"So what's this letter?"

Rini handed it over. Dr. Aisyah read fast, her face contorting more with each increasingly seditious line. It was worrisome that someone out there thought she would sign this letter; even more worrisome that she agreed with most of it. She thought she had been very careful about expressing her opinions of the General. "Who sent you? Who wrote this?"

Neither the girl nor the black mark answered. Dr. Aisyah nodded at her servants, who began to take turns hitting the tapol with their open palms, then their fists. They were due to be married soon, in Rini's home village, and would make an excellent couple. The tapol girl tried to shield her head and eventually keeled over on the floor, but wouldn't speak. Dr. Aisyah wondered if the girl's godless parents had done the same, when they were interrogated on account of planning a coup against the nation.

"All right, that's enough. She's probably been enchanted. She probably *can't* say."

She looked again at the anonymous letter. It had some formidable signatories already: Raden Roro Novarti, logging magnate Tommy Hassan. Respectable people, not some squalid, unwashed rabble of "democracy" agitators, fresh out of a European university education. They were patriots. Of course her husband might not like this; he was somehow more patient with the General and his rages. Maybe the waterfall kept him calm. Kept him blind. "Just give it time," he said, but that was how they ended up colonized by the Dutch for three hundred years. If this letter had legs, maybe they could finally be rid of—

"Please sign the letter."

Like a wound that wouldn't clot, a volcano that wouldn't die, the tapol girl was now bleeding on her freshly mopped floor. "You have no right to speak to me," said Dr. Aisyah, and when she closed her eyes the spirits washed her eyes in the color red.

Ibu Indah found Siti washing her wounds in the servants' bathroom—the dark one downstairs by the laundry room, with the light that didn't work— and rested her head against the eave of the door. "I hear you wanted to talk to me," she said. "What happened to you? I can smell the blood."

"I had a little accident." The black cloud, her only friend, was hiding just how bad and purple she looked. Just like it had hidden her from everything—people who didn't want to admit she existed, jobs she didn't dare ask for. Life. Sure, she wouldn't be anywhere near glamorous Ibu Indah or pure-blooded Raden Roro Novarti or sanctimonious bitch Dr. Aisyah. She'd probably never wear fancy, formal blouses with gold brooches and extra embroidery to fancy, formal events. But maybe she wouldn't be beaten. Maybe she'd spend her off-hours strolling through an air-conditioned mall, a flash of the life she saw in soap commercials.

Siti turned off the tap. "Ma'am, you said you would get rid of this mark, if I got those signatures."

"Yes . . . and I thought you had one left."

"I wanted to ask if you would swear it on an unbreakable oath, ma'am." The black cloud made a mournful sound. It didn't want to go. It loved her, in its own way. But her parents wanted her to survive.

Ibu Indah jerked her head back in shock. "You don't trust me," she whispered, as if in this terrible jungle of a world she really didn't grasp why such an oath might be necessary. "Haven't I taken care of you?"

Siti held her breath, heart pounding, keeping her eyes glued to her bloodstained fingers. Ibu Indah might be bound up in clothes so tight she could only hobble to and fro on her little sandal heels, but she was a dangerous woman, Siti knew, and an even more perilous employer. She had recently taken out a dukun's eye—just straight reached over and snatched it out of his head with her long patriot-red nails—because he had tried to cheat her out of five hundred thousand rupiah. So modest, so graceful, so *high-class*. Just how the General's wife liked it.

Ibu Indah took a small knife out of the folds of her waistband, sliced her finger open, then grabbed Siti by the chin and smeared her reddened finger against one of the open, pulsing cuts on her forehead. The pain bit her like a hot needle. "Fine. I swear . . . that I will get rid of that black mark . . . after you collect the signatures you need. . . ." Ibu Indah licked her finger, sealed the wound. Wouldn't do to go unto her husband with blood on her hands. "Happy now?"

"*Watch out*," the black mark growled in her ear, so only she could hear. It was such a jealous little god. "Thank you," Siti said, and the corner of Ibu Indah's painted mouth curled up: not pleased, but pretending to be satisfied.

SITI WENT TO COLLECT HER last signature armed with all she had: a butter knife stolen from the kitchen, a safety pin, and the dread determination of a convict who had finally had a glimpse of the sunlight beyond the bars. A hunger that alarmed her.

The black cloud, afraid of being left behind as she ran for puttering cross-town mini-buses in the heat and the smoke, wrapped itself around her head like a jilbab. She snarled at it. It trembled in confusion. "*Don't you love me anymore?*" the black mark said, and of course the answer was no. She never had. There was a difference between loneliness and love.

The final signatory lived in a house in a new development complex. It was riddled with scowling, fingerless construction workers plucked from the slums who didn't care what Siti was as long as she could pay them to shuttle her on the backs of their motorcycles past the half-built stores and banks and restaurants, rising slowly from the red dirt. She was dropped at a neighborhood checkpoint, but the guard was sleeping and only stray cats watched Siti creep under the gate. She wandered through a grid of identical streets named for birds that didn't roost there until she found the right house. There was a young maid around Siti's age, but she was busy watering a weedy lawn, and Siti waited for her to drag the hose around the corner before grappling her way over the fence.

The police chief's sister was resting on the couch, watching a spider descend from the ceiling, when Siti came in through the front door. As soon as she saw her—this skinny, bug-eyed tapol—the woman started to cry. "I've been expecting you," she said. "I've been seeing you in my dreams for a week."

"So you know why I'm here," Siti said, pondering that she wouldn't need to use the knife and perversely finding herself a bit disappointed. She extended the letter in the manila envelope. "Sign it."

The police chief's sister sighed and eased herself up, her face glowing now with sadness. "My child, do you even know what that letter says? Do you know what would happen if you were caught with it?"

She had read it, as soon as she was alone with it; Ibu Indah had generously allowed her to learn to read. She had been mostly pleased to know that Ibu Indah had not lied about its contents. It was a letter to the General, expressing gentle concerns about his rash decisions and the violent heart that seemed to drive them. *For the good of your humble, grateful people . . . might you consider setting aside the throne?*

"It doesn't matter," Siti said. "I'm nothing. I'm a tapol."

"You're not nothing," said the police chief's sister, and wiped away a tear. "Don't you see you're always the most important person in the room? You're the scar. None of us can look away."

The spider landed on the coffee table, and Siti wondered who all this woman had killed. She had asked Ibu Indah—"Where were you when the world was remade?"—and had received a drifting, lilting answer about her having just gotten married and being pregnant and laying low, waiting for the rage to blow over. Siti had already known that there was no way Ibu Indah had seen her father dragged out of the house and put into a truck and hurtled away. There was no way that she had sat on her mother's lap as a man in camo shouted at them both, understanding nothing but her mother's tremors beating against her skin.

"Where were you," she asked now, again, "when the world was remade?"

The police chief's sister stood up without answering and went to a little china cabinet. Siti thought for sure she was going to pull out a gun—perks of being the police chief's sister—and weighed the knife against the safety pin until unclipping the safety pin from her dress—but the thing she retrieved was not a gun. It was a small sepia photograph cradled in a pewter frame. The woman in the picture was still more of a girl in a school uniform, looking upward and out toward what must have been a beautiful horizon. She was smiling broadly, showing more in the way of teeth and boldness than would have passed for decent now.

"My sister-in-law," said the police chief's sister. "My brother's wife. His only wife. She was, well, one of you. A Communist."

Siti's breath hitched in her throat. She didn't know what she expected to happen—the roof to collapse? The floor to give way? The world to be cleaved in half and folded over like batter, again? But nothing happened. In this room, the curse just hung listless in the air and then slowly melted away.

The police chief's sister shrugged with a grunt, as if the entire world was sloughed around her shoulders. "My brother had just started out. He wasn't very political. He wasn't happy that she was in the Communist women's group but he didn't really care. He said, 'Just don't get in trouble.'" Like Siti's parents said: "Just survive." "But then, after the purge started . . . they showed up at the house. His fellow policemen. We were hiding her but they said, 'Let us take her; it'll be better for you that way.' He didn't want to, but what could he do? He knew what they would have done to me."

The girl in the photograph seemed to wink, as if to say, *And now you lie in the grave that is your bed.* And her sister-in-law shuddered and took the photo away. "I hate it when she does that."

The spider had jumped off the table and was crawling among the cushions. When the police chief's sister sat down again it was startled and bit her; she watched it patiently. Something in Siti wanted to say that she did not have to sign the letter that would expose her, forever, as an enemy of the

General, but the police chief's sister brushed the spider away and signed the letter before Siti could make up her mind to speak.

"Are you excited? Tomorrow is the first day of your new life."

The black mark was going to be removed tonight, and then Siti's world would once again be remade. This time, she had made Ibu Indah swear, she would end up free. In honor of the occasion, Ibu Indah gave her a new white dress and even touched her up with a dab of jasmine perfume. In the bathroom mirror the ugly black mark hung like perpetually dripping tar.

She nodded. "I can't wait."

They walked down a tile-lined hallway in a part of the house she had never seen, drenched in a gravity-altering, stomach-churning half-light. Ibu Indah seemed to be tilting, and Siti had to lurch toward her a few times on the long trek toward a little room with an old wooden door. Ibu Indah gave her the long, pleased look of a parent about to unveil a present, softly knocked three times, then led her in.

The room was dark but filled with candles and the smell of patchouli and cloves and something musty and old, like an opened coffin. Several other women who Siti recognized as part of Ibu Indah's Secretariat were gathered around three chairs that sat in a triangle facing each other. On two of the chairs were two old full-size mirrors, and Ibu Indah urged Siti to sit in the third. As Ibu Indah lit a final candle in the center of the triangle, the other women hummed a repetitive and increasingly anxious sequence of four or five notes and kept their eyes clamped shut and their feet rocking back and forth from heel to toes. Siti wanted to ask what they were doing when she noticed in the two mirrors a familiar sight that she thought to be long-gone: the faces of her parents, hovering overhead where the black mark used to be. They looked haggard and weather-beaten and half-starved, but they were smiling.

Siti jerked from her chair, but Ibu Indah pushed her back onto her seat. "Why are they here?" Siti asked, suddenly feeling sweat rise and pool over her skin. "Where's the black mark?"

Ibu Indah brushed back her hair. "The same as always, dear one. They are your black mark. You said yourself that they had passed it down to you."

"But . . . I don't understand . . . my parents were . . ." She didn't have too many memories, but what she had, she clung to. Her father sitting on the back porch, cross-legged, telling her a ghost story as she sat on his lap in the fragrant, chirping night. Her mother giving her all her food when they were detained in Bukit Duri, hissing, "Eat, eat" so sharply that Siti stuffed the rice in her mouth out of fear. "My parents were good!"

That didn't register on any of their blank, claylike faces. The Secretariat kept chanting and Ibu Indah kept brushing, though her strokes were becoming painful. "Your parents are in Hell," she said, sternly, in the same matter-of-fact way she might say, "Your parents are picking you up at school." So they were dead. Siti had expected that but the news still sank like an anchor inside her. "And all you need to do is break the mirrors. You can do it with your bare hands if you want, but I brought you a hammer."

One of the other women, Ibu Ayu, sweetly slipped a rusty hammer into Siti's right hand—in her shock Siti nearly dropped it on her foot. "What happens if I break the mirrors?"

"Well, you break the bond. You cast them off of you and send them scuttling back into the dark."

Like cockroaches, Siti thought. *She thinks they're cockroaches.*

Ibu Indah squeezed her shoulders. "What are you waiting for, child? Did you do all this for nothing?" She gave her a little shake. "That black mark is going to be the death of you. You've seen how people look at you. Spit at you. Do you really want your dead heathen parents to keep you from everything, forever?"

My parents didn't do this to me.

But still, she lifted the hammer. She lifted it to her father's face, and then her mother's, and watched as their faces lit up when they saw her coming and then recoiled—and then, finally, screamed in agony. A shard hit one of the ladies of the Secretariat in the leg but no one stopped her. She saw in the broken glass the skin and flesh that her parents had given her being pulled from her bone, leaving only an anonymous skull, but she didn't stop herself. Everyone in the room knew the price of magic. She smashed each haunted mirror until her parents were lost in the web of splintered glass, and cried, "I denounce you! I denounce you!" because Ibu Indah was right. The black mark would be her death. And her parents wanted her to survive.

IBU INDAH RATNASARI HAD PLANNED everything perfectly. The economy was in a slump, though the General's friends were still speeding around in Ferraris; a popular minister had been removed from his post for disobeying the General; rumblings of discontent were surely but quietly spreading. There was an election coming up, and those circus shows—peppered as they were with the illusion that there was such a thing as choice—always fried everyone's nerves. She whispered to her husband and then assembled the strongest among her signatories to accompany them to a special legislative session. She could tell some were afraid, but she had their oaths in writing—they and their men were sworn to her just like the rest of her psychic menagerie.

"We would like to present a letter to the General," her husband said, clearing his throat, and Ibu Indah could not have been more proud. She could see heads—nearly all male—turning toward them, and bodies—half in military greens and blues—shifting in their seats. They were all anxious for a way out. They only needed someone to show them the way.

But about midway through her husband's speech, there was a startling, disrespectful rustling in the chamber and a high female voice shouted, "Communist!"

It was like someone dropped a corpse on the legislature floor. Representatives held their breaths, careful not to inhale the stench of political death, and Ibu Indah's husband froze, awkwardly hitched between, "We humbly suggest that the General," and the words that should have followed: "consider the introduction of term limits." Ibu Indah craned forward, anxious to see who on God's Earth would have dared utter the great unspeakable curse in her presence, against her husband. And a little part of her wasn't surprised to see the little tapol girl, now no longer besmirched by the black mark—now a true nothing in a crisp white government blouse and gray pencil skirt.

As soon as they made eye contact, a chasm cracked between them. Ibu Indah was silently willing her to be quiet, to repent, but the tapol girl plunged the knife in deeper: "The minister's wife is a Communist."

"Little snake," Ibu Indah whispered, and stood. Ready to do battle. Last she heard, the ungrateful bitch was sitting pretty at the Agency of Agricultural Research and Development, typing away at her little meeting minutes and answering the call with a cheerful, "How may I help you?" She had turned out. And what was she doing to the woman to whom she owed everything? "You are the Communist, brat. Your father was sent to Buru and your mother died in Bukit Duri and you laugh in the face of God!"

But there was a reason that this curse—this particular, toxic curse, worse than *imperialist* and *counter-revolutionary* had ever been—had once been used to remake the world, acre by burning acre: it was free. Anybody, anywhere, could pick it up and wield it. Of course you still had to pay to play (and if you miscalculated, you paid in full), but not in rupiah nor gold nor labor. And as everyone knows, the cheaper the curse, the harder it is to control. The tapol girl smiled in her emptiness and innocence, because her emptiness was innocence, and that emptiness brutally bounced the curse right off.

People get swept away all the time. Waves crash. Houses fall. That day, in the special legislative session of the People's Representative Council, the earth yawned and swallowed Ibu Indah. She and her cadre of supporters, including the businessman's mistress and the cleric's wife and the police chief's sister, were dragged away with their respective men, and never seen again.

SITI VOTED IN THE ELECTION. She was a government bureaucrat now, so she was required to vote for the General's party. She cast her meaningless ballot with her new meaningless name and walked back out into the sun, trying not to overthink it. Sometimes she worried that she had made the wrong decision. Sometimes she wondered, when she looked up into the General's portrait that hung in every room of every government building next to the ruthless tick-tock-ing clock, what a different face might look like.

But only sometimes. Usually, she knew that any successor appointed by the Agricultural Department of the National Secretariat of Ladies' Cooperation would have just slid comfortably into the halls of power like an old man slipping under a blanket, and become the General, Second Variation. He would have started with some niceties about being "the people's voice" and then stuffed another gag down their throats. And at all times Siti knew that there was nothing to be helped than to help herself survive.

So she caught up with the other secretaries from her office, linked arms with them, and when they teased her about the young research clerk who made eyes at her when he had to drop off communiqués with her boss, she smiled. After all, that boy was a budding scientist. He was going places.

THE VEILS OF SANCTUARY
SELENA CHAMBERS

From: embarton@[REDACTED].edu
Date: Thursday, August 27, 2015
To: chj[REDACTED].edu
Subject: J'arrive!

Dear Dr. J—,

    I have made it to Paris and am settling in. My appointment for the Bibliothèque [REDACTED] isn't until tomorrow, and so I have spent these past few days exploring and getting to know my neighborhood. My apartment is on the crooked Rue de la Montagne Sainte-Geneviève, and the hour is marked by the ancient bell at Saint-Étienne-du-Mont.

    It isn't exactly what I expected . . . champagne does not flow from the fountains, the people here are very serious and preoccupied with getting to and from the office, and the cafés are full of tourists who ignore the truth behind the history they attempt to recreate. The Latin Quarter is especially disarming because it is donned in medieval drapery. The mornings have a morbid pall, and the slate-white of the tall, crooked buildings on Cardinal Lemoine do not seem like the heart of Lost Generation frolics, but more like teeth jutting from a gaping jaw. This makes Paris seem like a corpse, doesn't it? If so, then I am the maggot crawling and devouring its ruins.

    No . . . it isn't a corpse . . . it is more somber than that . . . Paris is like a church filled with the sacred relics of culture and history, and it constantly craves communion and sacrament. Is this why you sent me here? So I could commune with my personal idols?

    Of course, I've always wanted to come here. In high school, I used to make little lists of things I wanted to do with my life—live in Paris was always number one. While I can't say I've achieved that list, thanks to your belief in my work and the Arnold Fellowship, I can now cross it off as a dream half-realized, which is more than I've been able to afford in the way of dreams.

Just from my commute from CDG alone, have I already found myself pausing in reverie before Pont Neuf and gazing down into the murky river where Beatrice Vail drowned herself.

That's what everyone else maintains, anyway. I, of course, don't believe it. But so far in scholarship, there's been no figure present that would have wanted her dead.

Then again, there is so little scholarship about her that almost her whole life is a mystery, making her footsteps especially elusive to follow, more so than those of the more famous peers she walked with in Montparnasse.

Mina Loy, Djuna Barnes, Natalie Barney, Dolly Wilde, Isadora Duncan, Colette—but even their footsteps, prominent as they are, are buried under a century's worth of trash, traffic, and tourism kitsch.

I suppose in my mind there would be actual footsteps, like on Sunset Boulevard, where I could slip my feet into their feet, hold hands with their petrified phalanges, and through this cosmic parallel feel their power flow through me. Isn't that what communion is all about?

Well, enough reverie for now—I must unpack and find supplies—then tomorrow off to the Bibliothèque [REDACTED].

Fondly,
Elise

From: embarton@[REDACTED].edu
Date: Thursday, September 3, 2015
To: chj[REDACTED].edu
Subject: So far so good

Dear Dr. J—,

I have spent the past few days sitting in the magnificent reading room of Bibliothèque [REDACTED]. The archivists are a bit stiff and terse, but they give me the boxes and leave me alone.

I am not so down on this place as I was in the last email. I have found that, in Paris, there is no limit to what one can imagine and then realize from the imagining.

For instance, I imagined that based on the few footnotes found on Vail's work as a poet and performer, that somehow she was following in, if not recreating, the molpe practices of Sappho and her followers who performed their poetry with music and dance as the first instance of transcending realities through ecstatic expression.

While it does seem like she performed, no account of any performance exists. The committee, as you know, told me she was less than a historical specter, and have never supported my thesis. Only, you, Dr. J—, have dared to imagine with me, and here we are, holding hands at the séance.

Speaking of, I do think exploring the theory that she was involved in some sort of espionage is interesting and is a thread worth seeking in this research. It is interesting how almost all of her contemporaries—Isadora Duncan, Maud Allen, Colette, and Mata Hari (who was actually executed!)—were eventually persecuted as strongly as they had been adored, and how at the center of these parallels lie the discarded veils of Salomé.

I did find one letter from Maud Allen telling Vail she was too intellectual and "people will think you hate men. Silly girl, men are the money." So perhaps she was not welcomed in the dancing halls. She was, however, welcomed at the salon of Natalie Barney—where it seems she gave an exclusive performance complete with sets and costumes based on "several conclusions I have drawn about the seven gates of Ishtar and discoveries of unknown writings of the Tenth Muse," she writes to Barney. It seems Barney was over-the-moon at the performance.

And still . . . nothing has been recorded by those who witnessed this performance that sounds like a forerunner to myth-punk.

You don't have to bother responding to this one, because I can hear your reply now: Keep digging.

So I dig,
Elise

From: embarton@[REDACTED].edu
Date: Tuesday, September 8, 2015
To: chj[REDACTED].edu
Subject: Vail's Performances

Dr. J—,

I just can't even concentrate now, I am so excited. In box 5, I found several loose-leaf sheets of paper stuffed in an envelope that appears to be a draft of Vail's Sapphic performance. It has everything: poetry (she claims to be singing some unknown Sappho poem about Medusa, what!?), music, and dance . . . it is feminist theory made theatrical and while it is only one example of her mind . . . it deserves to be studied along with Elsa von Freytag-Loringhoven's sound poems and Mina Loy's manifestos.

The Bibliothèque will not let me make Xeroxes, and is something we will have to arrange when I return. I thought about taking pictures with my phone, but her handwriting is erratic and it'll just be easier if I go ahead and transcribe it. See below.

This is getting exciting! I hope you enjoyed your long weekend.

—E

(Enclosed)

The curtain opens upon an execution scene among the mountains. Note that the construction of the stage should be such that the audience can see beneath the floor. Will have to talk to N— about a special construction.

I am the firing squad's target and draped solely in black but for my eyes. As the music begins, a soldier offers me a blindfold and I refuse. No one moves as the music crescendos and builds. After a minute of this, the loud staccato of a dozen bullets shoot off and disturbs the audience and the scene. I let my body tug against the lead now imagined in my flesh. I crumble to the ground. The leading officer walks over to my prostrate body and presents to the audience his sword, which then falls upon my head. He grabs the head by the hair and presents it to the stage and to the audience.

Then he tosses it into a pit—the second half underworld of the stage—and the lights fade as all the dancers transfer and get into position in the pit.

The stage lights rise again like the morning sun and the audience will see that the pit is a cavern with a giant marble slab segmented into three beds. Three dancers dressed as beautiful Gorgons sleep. The soldier, who has traded in his fatigues for a Grecian skirt, but has kept his sword, sneaks into their lair. He dances a dooming minuet around the slumbering sisters. He has targeted the middle sister, and he pulls her up and out of the bed by her thick, curly hair that must be adorned to shoot around her like a writhing, serpentine halo. He then cuts her head off (will need to hire a papier-mâché artist to recreate our heads, and get advice from H— on ways to produce these guillotine-like illusions). He reaches into his leather satchel slung on his side and pulls out a large jorum. Into this, he places the sister's head. The surviving sisters are awake, screaming and wailing—the orchestra should match this emotive cacophony á la Stravinsky—and writhe around him. He swings at them, he abuses them, but he cannot win. He avoids their gaze, but still weakens from it. They disarm him. They disrobe him. They look into his eyes. He turns to stone. He drops the jar. The orchestra stops playing.

The audience can only hear the two dancers' battle gasps, but they are soon drowned out by raspy, high-pitched frequencies reverberating throughout the theatre. From the mouth of the cavern, I make my grand entrance. I am still swathed in black, but my head and torso is unveiled. I walk slowly toward the sisters, dragging a huge Aeolian harp behind me (may have to see if Marcel can assist or direct me to someone who could construct such a thing).

My dance is composed of poses that progress with the frequencies of the wind, and I stare at the audience as one frequency takes up the melody of another. When I finally reach the sisters and the statue, I sing the Gorgon's song by Sappho with this added refrain: "The only way/they let us win/is when we kiss their lips."

I then swing the harp up and over the assassin, knocking his petrified head clean off. Ideally, it will fly into the audience. The impact, I imagine, will make the harp's vibrations wobble between octaves, and I will resume my song: "The truth lies beneath/the veils of/sanctuary./Lifted,/the truth becomes/a different story."

Then my Dance of the Seven Reveals. By its end, one of the dancers will have stealthily retrieved the stone head from wherever it falls and returned it to the stage so when the next-to-last veil drops, I will pick it up, kiss it, and as all the Gorgons dance around me, present the head to the audience. When I cast my last and most voluminous veil—my headpiece with the long train—high up in the air until it seems to fill the entire cavern with its umbrageous cumulous tucks and folds, among them will rise the Medusa's stricken head, and she shall float over my own. The stage lights will fade until only the Medusa is illuminated, and she shall dominate the entire stage like Jokanaan in Moreau. We all sing one last refrain:

"He came to us in the night."

The curtain falls.

FROM: embarton@[REDACTED].edu
Date: Friday, September 11, 2015
To: chj[REDACTED].edu
Subject: Undiscovered Lee Miller photograph . . . of VAIL

OMG Dr. J—,

I have to say, I am surprised about your sudden skepticism. Do you really think she made the Sappho/Medusa thing up? I mean, the possibility of her having discovered such a thing is as great as her not having done so. But, then again, the loose papers lack proper context other than what I presumed to give them. Maybe they are nothing but a lark, a joke to a friend . . . but I don't think so, as you'll see. (The plot thickens!)

There aren't many boxes and I am down to the last one. They saved the most mysterious for last, it seems. It is just a single book, a photograph, and a jewelry box. The photograph is striking, not only because it is the first time I, or any other scholar for that matter, as far as we know, have set eyes upon our subject, but . . . she has such a command of presence it is a wonder she wasn't the Queen of the Orientalists. Furthermore, based on the signature on the back, it appears to have been taken by Lee Miller.

As you can imagine, I ran over to the head archivist and began babbling in my terrible French about the find. In their signature style, they were unamused and unconcerned. How can they be so blasé about this? And, of course, immediately I became curious as to what other buried treasures laid in this place's collection. Do they even know? It is quite careless . . . I mean, aren't they worried about theft? Without an inventory, how will they ever miss such a thing? Who is to say half of their inventory hasn't already gone missing?

The image is breathtaking. It immediately summons the lines, "Darkness comes in variegated shades and hues like any other color," from her one published poem "The Coupé Obscura," that appeared in *The Little Review*.

She is entirely veiled in "variegated" shades of black and gray silk except for her breasts and arms, and the gradations are put to ultimate effect under Miller's unique chiaroscuro. On her head is a crown of silver snakes, and they writhe around her dark, wild, loose hair and pale forehead like diadems. She is posed like a goddess on a Grecian urn—in something of a lunge, with an impressive Aeolian harp resting on her planked thigh. She stares at the camera from smoldering eyes, and her inky, bee-stung lips are parted as if caught in mid-cantation. In her free hand, she holds a stone head and presents it to the camera almost as tribute to the viewer. She is the femme fatale personified, beautiful and monstrous, and this . . . this is her vision of Sappho! Not some gentle poet singing songs over the Luecadian cliffs . . . but a goddess who'd eat Ovid and Virgil for breakfast, and poop Homer out as part of her green smoothie cleanse.

Barthes writes about the astonishment phenomenon one feels when discovering an unseen image of a historical figure . . . I am looking at eyes that looked upon them all, and rather than look enthralled with her youth and her age as the flapper is often illustrated, she looks . . . fucking pissed.

It's disjointing . . . and it makes me want to look away, but again with the Barthes, when I close my eyes, I see her even more clearly in the context of what I feel must have been her being.

She is wearing one piece of jewelry in the image: a demure pearl necklace that adorns the same wrist offering up Perseus/Jokanaan/whoever. I assumed I'd find it in the jewelry box, and I found part of it, I think. There were two individual pearls resting within its velvet clamshell. It must have broken after the performance, and this was all that was salvaged.

I feel the fatigue of fragmentation. I will have to look at the book after the weekend.

—E

From: embarton@[REDACTED].edu
Date: Monday, September 14, 2015
To: chj[REDACTED].edu
Subject: Marguerite de Châtillon

Yet, possibly, another great discovery! The book is an *ex libris* it seems from some institution of yore with a bookplate sporting a Sphinx as its main emblem. Over her head, the eight-pointed star of Ishtar sparkles in a night sky, and in silhouette are seen figures night traveling to and from the Sphinx.

There is no title page, it seems, but just a warning: "*Quicumque furatus eum fuerit anathema sit.*" Which I think translates as "Whoever stole this book is anathema." So what happens when one becomes anathema?

This warning has been crossed out by a pen, and the arabesque scrawl of Beatrice Vail reads: *The thread you seek.*

Did I not just write you that same sentiment days ago? I did! (I just checked my sent box). Creepy.

Disqualifying my ego and resisting the urge to imagine specters hovering over my shoulder and pointing their skeletal fingers toward clues— Who is "you," I wonder? Is she writing to herself? Or, perhaps the rumors are true and she was delivering messages to the Germans, ye old accusation thrown at her peers such as Mata Hari.

I can't help but harken to the prescience of the "you." Is it me, or any page-worn wanderer who would one day try and excavate her ashes from pulp and dust? That one line was not the first effacement of the book. It seems Vail took to translating the text and writing the English in-between the lines. From what I can gather, it is some sort of doctrine, or manifesto of a loose network of female intellectuals. However, the doctrine, which seems to have been written around the end of the 15th century by a young girl, is solely in the future tense.

In the back, Vail, I am assuming as it seems to be the same kind of dark blue ink, has drawn a map of Greece. There are a few dots on certain places, some around Lesbos and Crete, but what they are marking exactly I cannot tell and now I am feeling a bit overwhelmed and anxious. I am unsure that I have time for all these unexpected findings . . . to translate, make sense of, then place into context. But Vail's inscription keeps harkening to me—now it is she who is telling me to keep digging to find the thread I seek.

From: embarton@[REDACTED].edu
Date: Tuesday, September 15, 2015
To: chj[REDACTED].edu
Subject: Re: Marguerite de Châtillon

Check this out: The text alludes to "the Library of the Sphinx, where all our experiences will be added to the Grand Narrative." Are you thinking about Mina Loy now? Is it possible she didn't coin this term alone for her essay, but appropriated it from conversation with Vail? If Vail knew of this text, had stolen it, as it seems, would she not have out of pride or scholastic spirit shared it with a few of her contemporaries? Were they even that good of friends, you think? Perhaps Loy accessed another copy in her earlier travels in Florence or in Munich, perhaps even Mexico. I cannot recall exactly when it was Loy wrote that essay—. You are, of course, the Loy expert, so I will leave that to ferment for a while.

In any case, it seems the Library of the Sphinx was some kind of spiritual place . . . the mecca to this sisterhood where each "soror has within her a Passage" that would eventually lead to the Library of the Sphinx. What I can't quite figure out is where the Library of the Sphinx might be, if it is in fact physical. Based on Vail's translation, the doctrine may be advocating a more internal journey:

> *Within our mind is the temple*
> *Draped in the veils of sanctuary.*
> *For those who look too long into*
> *The past and beyond the surface of the world,*
> *Within the Library lie all*
> *The secrets of stories untold by their retelling.*

Sounds like our kind of place, huh, Doctor? Do you know of any of this? Have you heard of Marguerite de Châtillon or any sort of organization like this? Salons or academies that took to calling themselves the Library of the Sphinx or....?
More more more,
Elise

FROM: embarton@[REDACTED].edu
Date: Tuesday, September 15, 2015
To: chj[REDACTED].edu
Subject: Marguerite de Châtillon—The Fifteenth Century Helen Heck?
Dr. J—,
More about finding the Passage to the Library of the Sphinx—.
"With the swallowing of the elixir spheres,/the humors are tamed for travel."
And then there are a bunch of recipes . . . mostly written in alchemical symbology that I am unfamiliar with.
Consciousness...expansion? If so, wouldn't this be the first documentation of, I don't know, natural philosophers, mystics, quacks (?) recognizing the brain had chemicals that could be manipulated by other chemicals?
I still can't make heads or tails of it, but somewhere in all this is the answer to all of Vail's mysteries—I can feel it so much that it is transforming Paris around me.
You haven't responded to my last few emails. I'm sorry if I am blowing up your inbox with novel-length texts, but you did ask me to keep you updated and abreast of what I found and there is a daily news break almost every five minutes here in this archive. Believe me, no one is as surprised at how fruitful the archive has been as I am. But, I do worry I am letting myself get bogged down in the discoveries—one answer begets a question, and when I leave the archive, I do feel as though I've stood before the Sphinx and survived her riddles, only to be quizzed again the next day.

FROM: embarton@[REDACTED].edu
Date: Thursday, September 17, 2015
To: chj[REDACTED].edu
Subject: Access denied—why?
Dear Dr. J—,
I have just been informed by the archivist that I would no longer be welcomed to continue my research here. They said it was made so by your

request. And yet, in your last email, you made no mention of being displeased with me and my research, much less revoking my privileges. Maybe it wasn't your choice—have you told the committee of my findings? Could you please contact the archivist and give me a few more days' access? I have the thread and will rip it out with my teeth, if need be.

Sincerely,
Elise Barton
YOUR doctoral candidate, still, I hope?

FROM: embarton@[REDACTED].edu
Date: Thursday, September 17, 2015
To: chj[REDACTED].edu
Subject: Re: Access Denied—why?

C[REDACTED],

I have stopped pretending days ago that these are faint footprints in the dust of time. From the moment I opened this box, I have felt that these are all messages for me . . . and I can't quite find the key to unlock the encryption.

In the middle of the book, scraps of what appears to be ancient papyrus have been glued to the pages. They are blank, but strip after strip has been methodically placed on about ten pages. I almost drove myself crazy trying to deduce if the Marguerite de Châtillon text left exposed composed a message or not, and I don't think it does. I think at some point the message was within the scraps. . . .

I just need a few more days. You've helped me come this far—please—tell the archivist it was a mistake. These findings could change the world of many fields of study—if I don't finish following the thread, all this knowledge will just rot away here, like an underprivileged, unrealized genius in an unmarked grave.

Your Resurrectionist,
Elise Barton

FROM: embarton@[REDACTED].edu
Date: Sunday, September 20, 2015
To: chj[REDACTED].edu
Subject: Re: Access Denied—why?

Dear Dr. J—,

You know how I said I used to make lists as a kid? Well, living in Paris was one of the things, but I was embarrassed to add, based on its utter improbability, that also on the list was to find undiscovered fragments by Sappho. But when I wrote that, I imagined I'd be some kind of Egyptologist invading tombs and finding the scraps within the jaw of mummified alligators or something. Not as an English graduate student going through archives in a private library in Paris. But I have.

I think I have.

Not that any of you seem to care.

It was an accident. I was drinking wine and turned the glass over onto the text. Worried that the wine would seep into the pages and run the ink, I held it over my radiator for a few minutes. When I looked at the page to assess the damage, I saw that developing on the papyrus scraps were letters... words... a cryptograph that I thought was more of those alchemical symbols I saw in the recipes, but I realized were Greek. Aeolian, actually.

Invisible ink?

Invisible ink!

I have spent the past few days translating, and what I believe these scraps are, what these scraps compose, is the Medusa song Vail alludes to in the "Veils of Sanctuary" draft. I believe this is a transcription of some sort on Vail's part, which not only points to her having made a grand discovery, but also to her skill and knowledge in espionage (who else used invisible ink; let's see, Mata Hari, right?). Even so, I don't think she spied for any government, but for this Bas Bleu sisterhood I keep seeing referenced in the text.

If my Latin (and Lord, my Greek, too) is correct, this is some sort of secret society that collects intelligence, keepers of forbidden and lost knowledge. Why else glue these scraps in this text? Where are the originals? How on earth did Vail discover them? It seems dramatic, but is this the kind of stuff that compelled her to make her own grave?

You are wondering then: Did Elise steal the stolen book? With my access revoked, it was the only choice I had. I did what I believe Vail would have had me do. What I believe Vail was compelled to do. I am following in the footsteps like I was sent here to do; I can't help where they lead.

It is the thread I seek.

If I had been really smart, I would have taken the pearls and photograph, too. Perhaps I have. If you wrote back, perhaps I'd tell you.

—E

From: embarton@[REDACTED].edu
Date: Thursday, September 24, 2015
To: chj[REDACTED].edu
Subject: Re: Your flight AF[REDACTED] on September 25, 2015 from Paris-Charles de Gaulle

Ever since I discovered these fragments, I've found reality growing fainter—as if piecing these adventitious fragments together is unlocking my inner mind to spill out onto the world, or worse yet, for the secret world to flood in. I cannot tell which.

I believe the "elixir-spheres" are the pearls in the box . . . they are pills of some kind . . . and I think they helped whoever took them to break through "the veils of sanctuary," as Marguerite de Châtillon writes. And I am certain that Vail possessing them indicates she was part of this clandestine coterie and perhaps it was by taking these pearls that she made her discoveries. . . . There is no record of her traveling anywhere from her Midwest origins other than straight to Paris. Nowhere else . . . on the surface, at least.

Ishtar's journey to the underground was very much on her mind, and how through the first four gates she died, then through the next she was reborn—"thus the knowledge of the Sphinx was revealed to her, and it is this knowledge that is always shorn by the sword."

These tickets are your blade, then? I am to leave tomorrow . . . I had three more weeks . . . I do not want to go. I feel I have found her footsteps . . . I want to follow, but if I can no longer conduct my research, then what is the point?

See you soon, I guess.
Anon,
Elise

From: embarton@[REDACTED].edu
Date: Thursday, September 24, 2015
To: chj[REDACTED].edu
Subject: Re: Re: Your flight AF[REDACTED] on September 25, 2015 from Paris-Charles de Gaulle

Finally, a response from you. Why do you evade my questioning about the Bas Bleu? You say it is unimportant? It seems like the most important thread, does it not, to Vail's work and life? And I am certain this is a lost poem of Sappho. I am in the Church . . . this text is my bible, these pearls my communion.

Beatrice Vail's footsteps glow on the streets of Paris and end at the bottom of the Seine—it is the first gate and I must dance and dance some more for the Gatekeepers to let me in.

    I danced for them once. I danced for you. But now I realize it was you.... You came to me in the night, C—, but you will come to me no more because now I know about the Power.

    I wear the veils of sanctuary.

    Just the thread that leads to the temple.

    The Power that tries to silence us all.

    I have been contacted by a greater source, and I intend to follow them toward the rest of my research until my thesis is complete. I am seeking the different story now.

Editor's Note: On Friday, September 25, 2015, Elise Barton did not check-in for her flight back home to Boston, or to anywhere else in the U.S. or another country. All items in her apartment were gone and the place had been cleaned. Her passport has not been used, nor any of her credit cards. It is suspicious that a woman named Beatrice Vail purchased a train ticket to Rome on Saturday, September 26, but any other leads as to her whereabouts, or Elise Barton's, from that point soon grow cold. The last correspondence Dr. J— received from her student came in the snail mail, postmarked September 30, and is reproduced in full below. It is Barton's translation of what she claims is the undiscovered Sappho poem found and performed by Beatrice Vail in 1924. Because it is believed Barton is still in possession of this manuscript, no verification of the origins of this poem or its veracity can be obtained until Barton, and we believe the original manuscript, can be found:

> He came to us in the night while we laid, most
> vulnerable, upon our altar of life.
> We were there to protect the fading blooms of
> wisdom; to polish [
>
>
> the tarnish fallen upon the golden age
> of understanding. He was there to destroy
> it, preserving the black tar that dripped like a
> spent candle upon [
> [   ]
> the surface of the world.

[   ]
[   ]
We laid, unarmed, swathed in darkness. Swathed in the blinking eyes of our conspirators—
[   ]

He had been sent by Athene, with special
shield and sword, to kill Medusa the Gorgon,
Who slept in-between her serpentine sisters.
He was to kill her [

Not only for her envied beauty and wit,
but for her power, and her mortality.
[   ]
[   ]
          ] in the middle of their chamber,
all vulnerable but for her eyes.
Were she to awake, he would be turned to stone.

[   ]
          ] he must
return with her head!
[   ]
He was promised the hand of a maiden, and
Respect of all MEN. For Medusa and her
sisters had tyrannized and petrified them
for too long.

[   ]
[   ]
[   ]
Such prospects, he could not refuse, and
eagerly obeyed the Gods.

[   ]
[   ]
                  ]   O, Metis
[   ]
        ] Euranies severed

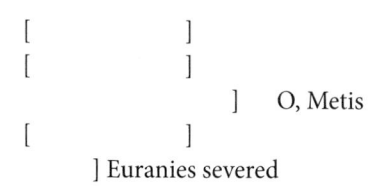

He saw within the shield her dying head and
saw no malice, but only confusion sweep,
through her gray-eyes—she was the most beautiful
creature ever seen.

More beautiful than the goddesses,
                    ] the promised wife
more beautiful than the world's admiration.
And he had killed her.

The rest, then, was legend.
The truth [
                ], the truth [
different story.

THE SISTERS OF EPIONE

ALISON LITTLEWOOD

The clinic was a small, mean building clad in sludge-green wooden panels that were peeling and stained. Inside its double doors, two rows of sunken chairs faced a small reception area with a fist-proof plastic screen, cracked across its center. The smell was of bleach and faded hopes, and it brought everything back to Cathy at once; it was as if she'd never been away. She used to work in a better area than this, but it still had that same smell. It hadn't bothered her then and it didn't now, not with Nathan's sweet milk scent lingering on her uniform. She could still feel the warm, heavy weight of him, the threads that bound them stretched by separation but always unbroken. She took a deep breath, fending off the nerves that fingered the edge of her consciousness, and forced a smile. She was there because she cared. Caring is what she did.

She flashed her new ID card at the receptionist, who buzzed her through to the staff area for the community nursing team. Her footsteps were loud on the linoleum and the figure standing at the end of the corridor turned to face her.

Cathy froze. The woman looked like a patient: sallow, sick-looking, bent under whatever illness she had. *Haggard* was the word that came to mind, and it took her a moment to realize that the woman wasn't old, wasn't even a patient. Her uniform was the same as her own, neat and gray.

A door burst open and the matron who'd interviewed Cathy hurried from it and toward her stricken colleague. The woman hadn't moved; she looked as if she might faint. Cathy started forward but Matron stepped in front of her, supporting the woman, cutting her off from view.

There were hasty whispers, the words unclear, and Cathy caught: "Are you carrying?"

Matron twisted back to her, snapping out the words, "I'll be with you momentarily." Her tone stopped Cathy dead, making her feel like a trespassing schoolchild. She watched them lurch away, Matron toeing the door closed behind them.

It opened again almost immediately. Her face appeared in the gap, overwritten with a professional smile. "Welcome, Sister!" she said. "You should get started straight away."

"But—your colleague. Should I help? Would you like—?"

"It's kind of you, my dear, but it happens all the time. She'll be fine in a moment." Her voice rose on the final three words, as if she could cover the low moan that emerged from her office. Her expression never faltered. "All the time."

"Is she ill? Or—?" *Pregnant*, is what Cathy was going to say. *Are you carrying?*

"Now, my dear, it's none of your beeswax. I must ask you to focus on the task ahead. That will be quite enough, I'm sure." She held something out: brown cardboard folders, just like the ones at her old job, as if she'd never moved at all; as if she'd never had Nathan. Matron thrust them toward her. They were thin files. Nothing too demanding for the new girl.

"As soon as you like," Matron prompted.

Cathy forced herself to return her smile before heading back toward the locked door and the waiting room and her car. Suddenly all the apprehension she might have felt, probably should have felt, came flooding in. She hadn't done this for what seemed like a long time. What if she'd forgotten? She might let someone down. And yet the certainty was there beneath it all, the iron-hard sense that this was her place. *I care*, she thought. *Caring is what I do.* That was why she'd been given the job. She had said those words at the interview, said them with conviction, and Matron had looked deeply into her eyes to see if it was true before giving a single nod.

And yet the uncertainty made her hands shake as she unlocked her car and made ready to start on her rounds. It wasn't the thought of the files that was so unsettling. All she could see as she slipped into her seat was the doubled-over woman she'd seen with Matron; the moment when she'd met her eyes and Cathy had seen what was in them, the emptiness, the pain, and the way Matron had turned to her and covered everything over with a smile.

She'll be fine.

But Matron was right, it was none of her beeswax. She had other people to care for now. She patted the files on the seat next to her and tapped the first address into her satnav.

Do a U-turn where possible.

Cathy smiled, and she did.

THAT NIGHT, CATHY SAT WITH Nathan on her lap and he opened his blue-gray eyes and stared at her. His cheeks were pink and he was sated, smelling of the milk she had given him. Her love dragged at her insides like something physical. Still, soon he would sleep, and there would be only the burbling television, the wailing of "EastEnders" or another soap, families living in their little boxes while she sat in hers. It was less than a year since her husband had died, beaten and abandoned at the side of the road. They had never found who'd done it; they had never discovered why.

She gripped Nathan a little more tightly and he squirmed. She leaned in and rubbed her nose against his, his skin so soft and so new it made her want to cry. Then she shook herself and straightened. She had things to do. This was why her new job was so important. It wasn't merely something to occupy her, to make her move forward once again, to earn money for Nathan and for her; it also allowed her to see that it could always be worse.

Her first patient hadn't been so bad. The old lady's complaints were as strident as her blue-rinsed hair and her doorbell, which played "The Blue Danube" at top volume. The loud ones never were that bad, in Cathy's experience. But then there was Mrs. Benson, a modest old dear who'd had nothing to eat until she arrived because her hands, gnarled and knuckled, failed to grasp even her specially adapted tin opener. She'd been cold, too; she'd managed to slip one arm into a cardigan but had to keep pulling the rest around her because she couldn't fasten it.

"I do try, dear," she'd said as Cathy stepped in to help, and she hadn't mentioned the pain but it had been there, imprinted on her face, and frustration had risen inside her; did it always have to come to this, eventually?

That made her think of the nurse she'd seen that morning, her eyes so much younger than Mrs. Benson's but still full of pain. Cathy had met her properly later that afternoon, when she'd returned to the clinic to file her reports. The woman hadn't looked sick any longer. She had stood tall, her brow unlined, her eyes clear, and she had smiled and held out her hand as if nothing had happened. Cathy's eyes had flicked to her belly—*Are you carrying?*—but Sandra was stick thin, nothing on her at all. Cathy began to ask after her health and Sandra forestalled her, waving her words away. She had only leaned in closer, so that Cathy could feel the breath on her face as she said: "Maybe one day, you'll know."

Cathy frowned, but the memory was subsumed as she carried Nathan upstairs, feeling the rise and fall of his chest, everything pushed into the background by the breathy sound of him, his clean and lovely scent.

IT WASN'T UNTIL SOME WEEKS later that Cathy really spoke to Sandra again. She'd fallen into a routine, no longer feeling strange when she was buzzed through into the clinic but just like one of the others, exchanging pleasantries and laughing together. On that particular day Cathy hadn't laughed. She hadn't felt like it, though her lip twitched when she saw Sandra. The woman was in mid-flow, telling another of the sisters how one of her old men had tried to show her the tango, and she'd caught Cathy's eye and her smile faded.

Still, when the woman saw Cathy in the parking area and waved, Cathy felt a sudden urge to pretend she'd left something inside and edge away. There was something in the way Sandra looked at her, as if she had something momentous to impart, that turned Cathy's stomach cold: had someone complained about her? But Matron had said she was doing so well, had said it loudly and in front of the others, as if to signal that her verdict was not to be questioned.

Sandra came over, pausing to glance left and right as if to make sure they were alone. She leaned in close and Cathy tried not to recoil from her coffee-smelling breath. "You feel the pain, don't you?" she whispered. "I knew you would. That's why she picks 'em. She always does. She sees it in their faces."

"What on earth do you mean?"

"There is one, isn't there? It's always the way. There's one that gets to you. Seen 'em today, have you? Upset you, has it?"

"Oh—oh." Cathy had suddenly known what the woman was talking about. An image rose before her: Mrs. Benson. The old woman had insisted on opening a packet of toffees for Cathy's visit that morning; she'd wanted to show her appreciation. She hadn't been able to smother her hiss of pain when the packet ripped and the sweets spilled out, her hands too twisted and slow to catch them. She wasn't the worst of her patients but Cathy still couldn't shake the memory of her disappointment when they had fallen to the floor.

"You do know what I mean," Sandra said. "I'll tell 'er you're ready, shall I? Next time I'm carrying."

Cathy had no idea what she was supposed to say. She only stood there as Sandra walked toward her car. Cathy stared down at the files she carried, as if they held the answer. She had been gripping her keys far too tightly; the metal had carved deep red lines into her fingers.

CATHY DIDN'T HAVE TO WAIT long before she came to understand Sandra's words. A couple of days later she was out on her rounds—she'd just attended a lad barely into his twenties, dying at home in a specially adapted bed that now filled the front room of the house, barely leaving space to squeeze past the television so that she could monitor his medication. He nodded to her, his naked scalp catching the light as she left the room and her mobile phone began to ring.

"If you want to see, you need to come now." It was Matron's voice. There was a click and the line went dead.

Cathy stared down at the screen, which turned dark as she watched. She headed back to the car, her legs suddenly unsteady, though she did not know why. She had nothing to fear from her boss. She'd been nothing but approving. And yet . . . why so mysterious? She found herself thinking of the expression she'd seen in Sandra's eyes that first time she'd seen her; the blurry pain that filled them. *Are you carrying?*

She touched her hand to her belly, hardly conscious of doing it. But of course, she wasn't carrying. Nathan was fine. He was out in the world, safe at nursery, all smiles and curling golden hair.

She had other visits to make, but instead she headed straight back to the clinic. As soon as she reached it, lights flashed from across the car park. It was Matron's Mondeo. Matron was behind the wheel and Sandra was sitting beside her, her face waxy in the dull afternoon light, the sun blocked out by a thick mantle of gray cloud.

What Cathy wanted to do was get back in her car and drive away as quickly as she could. She wanted to go to her son. She wanted to hold him and bury her face in his hair and let the smell of him carry everything away. Instead she walked over to the car and when Matron gestured to her, she opened the door and slipped into the back seat. The sound of Sandra's labored breathing filled the small space.

Matron spoke, but not to Cathy. "Don't worry, Sister," she said. "We'll be there in a jiff." She started the engine and pulled out onto the narrow streets.

They grew narrower still as she drove, not toward the town center but away from it, deeper into the suburbs. The red-brick terraces stretched long, everything lidded over by clouds that grew darker as they went, as if at any moment it might turn to rain. Sandra's gasps gave way to a moan. Cathy peered around the seat and saw that her face was running with sweat. She reached out to touch her shoulder, almost crying out when Sandra reached out too and grasped her hand, seizing her fingers, squeezing hard.

"There soon," Matron murmured, turning into a lane that was narrower still. The car rocked and jolted over potholed concrete. They were closed in by walls that were darkened with rot and layered with indecipherable graffiti, everything running with damp. There was no sign of human habitation; the place seemed long abandoned. For the first time, Cathy felt a stab of fear. She had expected a hospital or some other kind of clinic and she could not fathom why they might be here, in a back alley hidden deep in one of the worst parts of the city.

"Soon over." The handbrake squealed as Matron tugged on it. She turned and her lip twitched; it was not quite a smile and Cathy somehow knew that this wasn't a place for smiling, wasn't a place where happiness could live. There was something deeply wrong. It wasn't their isolation or the fact that anything could happen. It just felt wrong, as if the place was a sinkhole dragging her down, a dark heart that blackened everything it touched. Infectious, she thought, and did not know why.

Matron helped Sandra from the car. She pulled keys from her pocket with her free hand and Cathy realized there was a door set into the wall, a plain wooden door faded to gray, bearing only scraps of peeling paint.

"But why—?" Cathy began, falling silent when she saw Matron's expression. Sandra did not even look up. Her face was gray.

Matron started to help her toward the door and said over her shoulder, "Are you sure you're ready, Cathy?"

Cathy pressed her mouth closed against her retort. She hadn't asked to be here. She didn't know what they were doing and wasn't sure she wanted to. Still, she couldn't find the words.

Matron nodded, as if silence was the right answer, and Cathy followed, helping to support Sandra as the door opened onto blackness. At first she thought it was full of shadows, but as she looked past the doorway, she didn't feel so sure. It looked thick, that darkness. It looked as if it might taint her with its touch. She didn't like the thought of breathing it in. For a moment there was silence as the three of them stared into it.

"No good waiting." Matron's voice was resigned as she stepped over the threshold. Cathy's hand shot out, wanting to pull her back, and then she let it fall. She only stared as they shuffled away from her, and she took one step and then another until she was standing inside. She caught one last glimpse of Matron's shining silver car. It looked as if it could have landed there from another world entirely.

"Just pull that door to, Cathy." Judging by the dry scraping, Matron was running her hand across the wall. Cathy winced, thinking of spiders, or worse, someone waiting there in the dark, their own hand outstretched. She took a deep breath and pulled the door almost closed behind her. She couldn't bear to shut it entirely but the darkness flooded back anyway, moving in close.

A sharp click and Cathy winced as an overhead bulb flickered on, the filaments visible in its yellow heart. Ahead of them was only a stairway, leading down.

"Slowly," Matron whispered.

Cathy did not know why she followed them. All she wanted to do was get out, to run, and yet she couldn't have said why it was so bad. The air was musty but not choking. The wooden steps were worn but not broken. She was not given to daydreams. Life was real; she had always known that. She had seen its beginning and she had seen its end, and yet on some level, she knew that here was something different, something she did not understand and probably never could.

At last, the stairs ended. They had not been so many after all, though she felt she was standing deep in the earth. Another click and a second light came on, illuminating the room in which they stood.

The walls were bare of pictures or markings or doors. At one time they had been painted but the color was now a filthy ochre, patchy and stained. The room stood empty except for a single object at its center, and Cathy stared at it. It made no sense.

The thing was a crib. It was large and old fashioned, the fabric peeling away from the metal struts beneath. It had possibly once been black, though now it had faded to a moldering gray. The canopy was raised and it was festooned in filthy cobwebs. There was nothing else, and no sound, none at all.

Matron and Sandra stood in the silence with their heads bowed. Cathy had the impression of deep concentration, almost reverence; then they began to step toward the crib, very slowly and with their eyes still lowered, as if they did not dare to look at it directly.

There was a sound, barely audible, as something stirred within the crib. Cathy's breath froze in her lungs. The soft slither came again. It wasn't right, that sound. It wasn't natural. And something emerged over the side of the crib and she almost cried out.

Fingers. They were like a child's and yet unlike. They were small and gray and loose, as if its tendons were as rotten as the crib, and they were too long, and the knuckles were too small. The skin was mottled and smooth, like a reptile's. Where the fingertips touched the side of the crib they *flattened* somehow, and when they withdrew Cathy thought she could see the shine of liquid deposited there. She raised her own hand, wanting to keep the cry that rose to her lips inside, not wanting to rouse that *thing*. She didn't want to make it lift its face; she didn't want it to open its eyes and turn them on her.

Matron stopped and let Sandra go on alone. Cathy moved at last, stumble-stepping toward her, as if she could bring herself to do anything to stop the woman approaching the thing in the crib.

Sandra didn't flinch from whatever lay inside. She leaned over it and drew back her sleeves and reached in. Cathy let out a dry breath, like the air escaping a tomb.

She could not see the thing that Sandra lifted from the crib. She could only hear it: a wet inhalation, then a brief silence before an awful sucking noise began.

Cathy covered her eyes. She could not be here, seeing this. She could not be hearing it. She thought for a moment of Nathan's gummy mouth latching onto her, feeling the warm pull as the milk left her and nurtured him, giving him life. It was right. It was *pure*. This thing was nothing but a parody, an aberration; it was obscene.

She took a deep breath, knowing she had to take hold of Sandra and pull her away, but a hand grabbed her arm. Matron tugged her back. She still had her head bowed, as if in prayer, or as if she didn't want to look. And then Sandra straightened and backed away from that awful thing, and she turned and Cathy saw the shine in her eyes.

It was Cathy who felt weak as they ascended the stairs once more. Her legs shook. She scraped her shoes against every rough step, though as she rose she began to feel better; perhaps the thing's influence was weakening. When she walked through the doorway and felt daylight on her face, she wanted to sob. She felt as if she could breathe again, as if the fist that had closed around her heart had loosened.

"It's hard, the first time." Sandra was no longer bent; she wasn't sick. "Once it feeds, it's better. It becomes your own, in a way. And you'd become one of us, don't you see? You'd be truly one of the sisters."

Cathy turned to face her. She felt the blood draining from her cheeks. Sandra didn't appear to notice. It was Matron who quietly got them into the car, twisting in her seat to reverse out of the narrow alleyway without meeting Cathy's eyes. She did not try to explain, not then, and Cathy didn't care. She didn't think there was anything they could say that would make her understand.

"THEY CALLED US THE SISTERS of Epione, once," Matron began. They were back in the office, Matron sitting formally in her chair with her ankles crossed, Sandra leaning against the wall, smiling, while Cathy sat opposite the desk, sipping hot, sweet tea.

"No one knows how far back we go. One person hands it on to the next; it's always been that way. They had different names, too. The Sisters of Solace, some called us. It's all the same underneath. Epione was a Greek goddess—the goddess of the soothing of pain. I don't know about that. We live to serve. It demands respect—you'll have felt that yourself—but, really, it just wants to feed."

Cathy looked at Sandra. *Feed?* The thing didn't seem to have bitten her.

"It feeds on pain," Matron continued. "And that is why we don't just leave it to wither. It means we have a choice, you see. We can take the pain away. I think that's why we were chosen by the ones who came before us—because we care. Because we are in the perfect position to help. Our patients suffer. They need us. But . . . Sandra, why don't you tell her what it's like."

Sandra started forward, eager to interrupt. "There's this boy," she said. "He's only eleven. He's terminal, and the pain relief only helps so far. It's awful. But when I hold his hand—when I'm touching him and I close my eyes and think of the god, the pain leaves him and goes into me. It feels bad, but it isn't for long. And I carry it to the thing you saw. It drinks it in. It thrives on it. Then the pain's gone, and Lee has some respite, at least till it builds up again."

Cathy closed her eyes. She could see, in her mind's eye, another room: a sweet, yellow-painted room, lined with soft toys and mobiles and pretty things, with another crib at its center. A hand, appearing over the side . . .

"I know it's not nice. No one ever said it was," Matron said. "You knew this job wasn't nice, not really. But you took it because you can face things, didn't you? You took it because you're strong enough. And you wanted to help."

Suddenly it wasn't Nathan's room Cathy saw. It was another room entirely, one in a colorless hospital ward staffed by people whose faces were carefully blank. Only her husband's was twisted. He had been left for dead at the side of the road but he hadn't died, not straight away. She had seen the pain burrowing into him, pulling at his insides.

"Your Mrs. Benson," Matron continued. "You said you wished you could do more. You said you wished you could take her pain away."

Cathy looked up. She met Matron's eyes and saw that, despite the woman's harsh tone, her eyes were soft.

"You have a choice," she said. "The least you can do is try."

THE THING INSIDE CATHY WAS cold. She hadn't expected it to be like that. She'd assumed there would be pain and there was, but when she'd put her hands on Mrs. Benson's and thought of the god, silently asking it to draw what it needed from the woman, she hadn't thought that she would feel the burden growing inside her. It was horribly akin to being pregnant, but the weight settled differently, and it was cold instead of warm. It was a chill, writhing, tentacular thing, and she could feel it probing her from the inside, as if her body was a cage it longed to escape.

She tried to stand and she staggered instead. Mrs. Benson had roused herself at once, her eyes clouding with confusion. "Are you all right, dear?" she'd said, and she'd reached out to steady her before staring at her own hand with a puzzled expression. She tightened her grip on Cathy's arm. She hadn't been able to do that for a long time.

But Cathy hadn't been able to stay and share the old woman's joy. She had made her excuses in a small voice and tried to walk to the door, grabbing onto the jamb to hide her weakness.

It was fortunate that Matron had parked her car outside. Cathy had said she needn't bother, and Matron had only smiled and shook her head. Now Cathy knew why. She wasn't sure she could walk; she felt too dazed with pain to drive. She was glad Matron was there, the stolidity of her ready to shore her up, not so much like a colleague but a friend; a sister.

The cold thing inside her began to stir. It made her want to be sick, to purge herself of it, but she knew there was only one way to do that. It wasn't something she had allowed herself to think about until the old gray crib was standing in front of her.

"Just reach in," Matron said. "You don't need to do anything else."

I have to bear it, Cathy thought, but she did not speak. She forced herself to go a step closer. There was a smell. It was the mustiness of unclean rooms and unwashed clothing and rancid milk, like the opposite of home, the things she loved. She could see the thing in the crib, its too-smooth, mottled skin covered only by a filthy cloth. She could not bring herself to look at its face but she could see those strangely flattened fingers opening and closing, reaching. Reaching for her. The cold inside was squirming; it could sense the closeness of its god. She couldn't stand it being inside her any longer. She reached out her hands and thrust them over the side of the crib. It latched on at once. She could not look but she felt its lips probing her skin and she squeezed her eyes closed as the sound began, that awful, greedy, sucking feeding, the thing pulling and straining for what she had to give. Its breathing grew louder, anxious, and breathy, and it echoed in her chest, as if they were connected somehow; as if that dreadful thing was joined to her. She fought back her revulsion and opened her eyes. Its sides pulsed in time with its gulping, its whole body rippling with peristaltic motion. And yet something inside her was easing. She took a deeper breath. The coldness flowed through her, draining away at last, the burden being lifted by this hideous thing. As she thought the word *hideous*, its eye opened a slit. A dark pupil rolled toward her, rimmed by a child's ordinary soft blue-gray iris, and it was so full of pain that for a moment Cathy almost pitied the foul thing.

She felt such lightness as she walked away that it was only the press of Matron's arm in hers that kept her from running up the stairs. It wasn't until she stepped outside that weight began to return, her body feeling like it belonged again, and it was only then that she realized something else had changed. The connection was still there, inside her. It was the same way she'd felt when her son was born, the birth not just of his body, but of a new bond; one that might stretch thin but would never, ever break.

THAT NIGHT, SHE FED HER son. She held him close and felt her heart was breaking. The scent of the room was of cleanness: his new skin, the milky sweetness of his head. It was like that other smell, but uncorrupted. It was the scent of innocence. And yet, whenever she looked at the crib she found herself expecting to see it, those flattened fingers, the color of decay, creeping over its edge.

It becomes your own, in a way.

She shook her head and focused on Nathan's face, shutting out the thought of that hungry, sucking thing. She felt the weight of her son, felt the life, the *joy* of him, and she let it bring her back; she let it restore her.

IT TOOK A WEEK FOR Mrs. Benson's pain to begin to come back. The old lady didn't say anything, but Cathy knew. She saw her grimace when she fumbled the pen trying to sign a form. Cathy snapped out her hand to catch it and met the woman's eye. That look told her everything. It wasn't the pain that hurt, not really: it was the sadness. It was the sadness of someone who had thought their constant companion banished, only to realize it was not.

It would only grow worse; Cathy knew that too. She pictured that thing in her mind's eye, its sides pulsing with its greed, its breathing resonating in her own chest. Mrs. Benson would suffer. She would remember the day that Cathy had taken her pain away, and she would despair; unless Cathy ministered to her again. And there were other patients, people who were worse off than Mrs. Benson. She felt the walls of the sisterhood closing around her as she thought of them, close as comfort, tight as a trap.

They called us the Sisters of Epione, once.

That night, she Googled "Epione." The Greek goddess of the soothing of pain had been married to the medicine god, Asklepios. Cathy had never studied such things in school, had never before heard the names, though there was something noble in the sound of them. She scrolled down the page of unfamiliar words, exotic as sunshine on a sandy beach, and then she stopped.

The Algea, she read. *The three spirits or daimones of pain: Lupe, Ania, and Akhos. They were considered to be bringers of weeping and tears. Their opposite numbers were Hedone, a bringer of pleasure, and the Kharites, also known as the Graces or Joys.*

She shook her head. It hadn't occurred to her to wonder if the creature had a name. She hadn't considered where it might have come from. She wondered if that was because, in a way, she felt she knew. The touch of its skin made her think of the rotten filth in a long-blocked drain. It was the color of the dank hairs trapped in a plughole, the musty stink of folds of skin never caught by the sponge, the sourness of liquid seeping from a dustbin. It was all of these things and none of them, but somehow she'd had the sense of it being not created but *accrued*, taking to itself all the cast-off and unwanted parts of humanity.

Algea. It was far too grand a name. Perhaps, too, was the Sisters of Epione. She thought of the women at work, their coarse laughter, their blunt ways, but it was Mrs. Benson's face that rose before her, the awful need in her eyes. And something else she'd read came back to her, the words circling in her mind: *the bringers of weeping and tears.*

But it wasn't, was it? The creature in the basement took such things away. It consumed them, and it thrived. Wasn't that a good thing—even, in a way, a beautiful thing? Even if Cathy had to suffer its presence, its touch, its *taint*, in order for it to feed?

She shut down the computer and sat there, staring into the depths of the dead screen. After a while she stirred, realizing she was wiping her fingers against her blouse, over and over again.

THERE WAS SOMETHING WRONG WITH the man leaning against the wall. Cathy didn't know what it was, but she didn't want to go any closer. She didn't know why—he had no visible trace of sickness, no rash, no fever—but she almost felt that what he had could leap through the air between them, could settle on her skin; *inside* her skin, maybe. She looked around at the red brick, darkened and stained as if it were rotting away. She thought of the thing hidden in the basement somewhere beneath their feet and shivered. The man stood with his back to that filthy-looking wall and she wanted to tell him not to touch it, but he didn't appear conscious of her presence. He stared down at the concrete. *It's all around us*, she thought. *He doesn't know, but he can feel it too.* It was rising from the ground, an almost visible miasma.

She had already been inside—*donated*, as she had come to think of it. This time she had gone alone. It had become easier to bear the burden of what she carried and so they had given her a key. When she met her new patient and found she couldn't resist helping, she'd come straight here. The patient was a woman in her forties with a tumor they couldn't remove and two kids who couldn't bear to see her suffering. She had only been half aware of anything that passed around her: the bright voices trying to bring cheer, offers of food or succor she couldn't eat or didn't want. She had looked up, though, when Cathy put her hands on her arm. For the first time, she had smiled.

After her visit to the basement, Cathy hadn't wanted to get straight back into the confines of her car. She'd wandered around the corner to be free of the high walls shutting out the light, and had only found herself circling around the place. Now she peered at the man. She could hear someone else approaching. The *tap-tap-tap* of footsteps was joined by the high, tinny sound of headphones and a lad came into view, white wires snaking from ear to pocket. Cathy tensed, but he did not look up. Did anyone, here?

The man pushed himself away from the wall. She tensed, ready to call out a warning, but the only cry that came was the boy's as he was suddenly punched: once, twice, three times. He doubled over, wheezing, struggling to pull in each breath. Cathy hurried toward him. The man was already walking away, his hand pressed against his head, as if he was the one who'd been hit. He hadn't even stolen the lad's iPod. It was still there, one earbud dangling from its cord, spinning some kind of rap into the air. The words were indecipherable.

Cathy murmured questions: Did it hurt? Did he know that man? The boy wrenched his hand from her grasp and pulled away. His face was empty. He drew back his arm, and she met his washed-out eyes. That was when she felt it, the creature's miasma creeping into her, and she knew exactly why the man had wanted to hit the boy; she knew because she wanted to hit him too, to drive her nails into his sunless skin, to rake it from his flesh. She wanted to stick her thumbs into his eye sockets and rend. That would be best; that kind of pain would last. It would never leave him.

The lad spun on his heel and started to walk away, one hand clutched to his stomach, cradling the pain he had been given. His gift.

Cathy closed her eyes and stumbled to the rotting wall. She leaned on it. She gazed at the ground and she took one breath after another and she did not look up for a long time.

"It doesn't disappear," she said later. Matron didn't reply. She had been in the middle of a pile of paperwork and she stared down at it resolutely.

"The pain," Cathy insisted. "The Algea doesn't consume it. At least, it doesn't *neutralize* it. Nothing disappears, it's just—recycled. You can feel it, can't you? You must have felt it. That whole area. Apparently it didn't even used to be such a bad place to live, but it's getting worse. Turning into a no-go zone. It's being poisoned."

For a moment, Matron did not look up. Then she did. Cathy did not like the message she read in her eyes. They were gray and flat and hard, like rain-washed zinc. "It's taken away," she said.

"Yes, but it's fed back again. It's passed on. The pain only goes to someone else."

"Our patients need us." Matron's voice was laced with sanctimony. She bowed her head, like a priest bestowing some benediction. "We take it from those who can no longer bear their load. It is given to those who can."

Cathy thought of the lad she'd seen, the flat emptiness in his eyes. "But it's not for us to choose. Don't you see? We can't play God. Someone could die." An image: her husband kissing her one last time, nothing more than a quick peck. *I'm just going for a walk.*

"But it is for us to choose." Matron straightened and gave a slow smile. It was cold, that smile, and there was no comfort in it. When Cathy moved to speak again, Matron raised her hand: *stop*. Then, quite deliberately, she returned to reading the file on top of her desk.

Cathy stared a moment longer. Then she turned to go. There was nothing more that she could say, nothing the woman did not already know. She had another appointment in half an hour and her patient was expecting her. She could not let her down. She remembered who it was that she was going to visit, and shrank inwardly. She could already see the need in the old woman's eyes, feel her grasping hands on her arm. She remembered the words she'd spoken, the last time Cathy had helped her: *My savior.*

LATER, SHE SAW SANDRA IN the car park. Cathy had waited for her; she thought she might listen, though when she saw the woman get out of her car, she knew at once that she would not. Sandra tossed her head in acknowledgment, her face carefully blank, and headed into the building. Perhaps Matron had already warned Sandra about their sister, the one who was asking questions, the one who didn't fit. But surely Sandra couldn't know what was happening. She couldn't know about the pain, about the violence they were unleashing into the streets.

Cathy's husband hadn't yet turned thirty when he died. He had never held his son in his arms. Cathy put her hand to her cheek, the place he had last kissed her. She had barely said goodbye to him that day. She'd been too busy, preparing for Nathan. And now she had her son to care for, but there was no one to care for her. There were only the sisters.

She paused, torn between going after Sandra and turning away, letting it all go; then she followed her into the building.

Almost at once she caught the murmur of voices. She found herself stepping more quietly. The lights had been switched off; there was only the lurid glow of exit signs and a clearer light spilling from Matron's office. The door was open a crack. As Cathy approached, she heard a low moan.

Sandra was supporting herself on the desk, her head bowed, her cheeks drained of blood. Cathy couldn't understand why—Sandra had looked fine when she'd come in—and then she saw Matron seated behind the desk, one arm outstretched with her sleeve rolled up. Her nostrils flared as she breathed in deeply, savoring the air, a half-smile written across her features. The worry lines on her forehead had smoothed over. She looked transported; her expression was something approaching ecstasy.

Her eyes snapped open. "Did you hear something?"

Air rattled from Sandra's lungs. Cathy backed away, slowly, silently. No one followed. No other sound came until she heard Sandra's murmur, the words faint as she struggled to speak. "No, I—is that better? Does it hurt anymore?"

CATHY HURRIED THROUGH THE BLIGHTED alleyway. This time she had seen no one, but she could still feel the pull of the creature below the streets. The bringer of weeping and tears. Perhaps they should never have used those words of the god; it's how they should have described its servants.

She remembered Matron's beatific expression after Sandra had leached away whatever kind of pain it was that filled her. She would never give this up, Cathy knew that now. The woman would never stop. They would be on their way here, Matron wearing that sanctimonious smile on her face as they prepared to feed the creature that waited in its crib.

Cathy raced to the door. Her feet knew the way; she did not stumble on the stairs.

The creature's fingers opened and closed, opened and closed. It lay fat and swollen, its skin moist, coated in some awful birth fluid. Cathy forced herself to move closer. She could not afford to waste time. She ignored the smell, realizing it didn't seem so bad anyway, now. She was inured to it, the way she'd gotten used to changing dirty nappies.

She slipped her arms underneath the creature and lifted it to her breast. It was the exact same weight as Nathan, but it didn't sound like him. Its breathing had the resonance of a cat's purr. She felt it more than heard it. The thing wasn't warm, didn't mold itself to her shape. She held it more tightly. She could feel its waiting—its greed, its expectation. Excitement, even. She closed her eyes and rested her cheek on its blunt head. All at once she felt it rushing from her, and she thought of the gift she had brought, letting it flow. The thing squirmed in her grip. Its damp fingers brushed her face but she did not flinch.

When it stopped moving, she laid it down in the crib. She did not look at it again, not even to cover its face. She turned and hurried up the stairs, moving back toward the air and daylight. She hurried around the corner to where she had left the car, out of sight of the door. The rumble of an engine was growing closer. In her mind, she could already hear the cries of horror; it wouldn't be long until the shrieking began.

ONCE SHE WAS HOME, WHAT Cathy had seen and done began to take on the quality of something she might have once read in a book. Still, she felt there was something she was supposed to be doing, something she was supposed to know. She busied herself around the place, getting everything straight, and only then did she turn toward the stairs and slowly walk up them.

The crib was there. Its canopy was raised: clean white cotton in place of the moldy, faded black hood she had half-expected to see. She moved closer. For a brief, sickening moment, she thought it was empty; then she heard a breathy cry and saw a flailing fist, the skin healthy and pink, the knuckles each marked with a soft little dimple.

She swallowed. She walked over and looked down at her son. She felt that she should smile, or speak, or touch him, but she did none of those things. She simply watched as he looked up at her with his blue-gray eyes, and she tried to remember what it was she was supposed to feel.

The Algea, she thought. *The daimones of pain. Their opposite numbers were Hedone—pleasure—and the Kharites, graces or joys.*

She hadn't fed the Algea with pain. She had given it the opposite—warmth, and light, and love. She had given it her joy. She hadn't had much of it to spare since her husband had died. She had been alone, and then there had been the sisters, but she had turned her back on them.

There was only Nathan. She put out a hand and stroked the baby's cheek. She remembered how good that had once felt. The little spark when he smiled at her or when he laughed. Her delight at the softness of his skin, the warm weight of him. The depthless joy of taking care of him, bathing him; her pleasure in the knowledge that she had met his every need.

It had been all there was and so she had given it, all of it, pushing it into the creature until it couldn't even breathe. She had killed it with her joy, and now there was only this: a wriggling thing in a crib. It looked up at her and she felt sure it knew her for what she was. It began to cry.

She lifted it, hefting its weight, as strange now as it was familiar. She rocked it—*him*, she reminded herself. Even his scent had faded. It had felt more real when she'd touched the damp gray skin of the pain-eater. *She* had felt more real.

Her son lay heavy in her arms. The touch of his skin had taken on the quality of something she might have once dreamed. The connection between them was broken. Where it had been there was nothing, only a floating emptiness that she couldn't forget and knew she couldn't fill. *I care*, she thought. *Caring is what I do.* Now the thing she had cared about had gone. In some ways, that came as a relief.

She closed her eyes and pictured her husband's face. She hadn't cried for him when he died, hadn't been able to allow herself that, but she did now. *The bringer of weeping and tears,* she thought. And it was; its name was aptly given after all. She just hadn't realized that it would be her weeping. She hadn't known that it would be her tears.

RED WORDS

GEMMA FILES

That quote by Anne Carson—the one about patriarchal culture putting a door on the female mouth by linking female sound with "monstrosity, disorder, and death"—constitutes your thesis statement, more or less. Your advisor approved it, then sent you straight over to the Connaught Trust, whose Rare Texts Collection has been a godsend, especially in terms of witch trial transcripts and obscure murder cases. It was there you first drew the cognitive line of descent between the cleansing of the town of Chatouye, that long-lost nest of poisoners and self-acclaimed demon-spawn, and the tome you currently spend your days visiting, copying out section by section, while simultaneously studying all other reference material you can find on its existence: the semi-legendary *Testament of Carnamagos*.

"I started out tracking the use of gag restraints in trials with female defendants, pre-nineteenth century," you tell Amaryllis Ho, as the two of you shiver through a much-needed break outside your nighttime "day" job, warming yourselves internally by blowing great defensive plumes of cigarette-smoke into the crisp autumn air. "Then scold's bridles, sewing up lips, tongue extractions . . . Most witch-hunters love the Question as a concept, the call and response aspect of torture; just like Kramer and Sprenger—those two guys who put together the *Malleus Malleficarum*, the *Hammer of Witches*—they're looking to quantify, to record, get things down in as much detail as possible, if only so whoever comes after knows what to ask. So whenever you get cases where no one seems to've wanted to talk to the people involved at all before burning them, you know something really bad had to be going on."

"Like what?"

"Well . . . how much do you know about the Middle Ages, exactly?"

"Assume 'nothing.' That'd be close enough."

"Okay, so—it's the middle of the Hundred Years' War, give or take, about 1356, just after the Black Death passed through Europe, and shit's chaotic, to say the least: like this guy Jean de Venette says, 'All went ill with the kingdom and the State was undone.' Thieves everywhere. The nobles hated each other and they hated the peasants, whose goods they pillaged at will. They did worse to the peasants themselves." You pause. "People called it the time when God and His saints slept."

"Right before Joan of Arc and all that? Cool, consider me temporally GPSed."

"All right. So there's this town, Chatouye, on the border between France and Flanders. And like with a lot of places where war's been going on for generations, there aren't a whole lot of able-bodied dudes left anymore, just very old men and very young boys, but a whole big-ass spread of ladies—maidens, mothers, crones—yet the town itself remained reasonably sound: walls intact, occupants unmolested; that alone must've seemed kind of suspect, in context. Not to mention the place was located at the intersection of two huge plague pits where everything for miles around had been burnt over and over, so it wasn't immediately apparent how the hell these chicks were even managing to keep themselves alive, especially after almost forty years of continuous occupation by one army or another...."

Amaryllis gives a little chuckle, more dry than humorous. "I'm guessing whoever was in charge didn't like *that*," she says, to which you just nod again.

"They do tend not to," you agree, silently calling to mind the details of the incident you have been studying, seemingly forever:

The Scouring of Chatouye, as it later came to be known, was chiefly the work of one Guillaume Corniche, acclaimed by his peers as the foremost witchfinder of his age. Raised in the Church but trained as a lawyer, Corniche had already assisted in twelve separate witch-purges by the time he was sent to Chatouye, his lucky thirteenth. He'd written a fairly popular text on the subject, *Libre des Damnées*, but since all known copies were eventually collected and destroyed in the wake of Corniche's own excommunication, researchers have had to mostly rely on other people's descriptions of what the book might or might not have contained. That said, it seems Corniche may have been pursuing a very particular heretical bugaboo in his persecution of Chatouye's denizens, above and beyond the simple devil's ass-kissing and what-not usually associated with most covens.

The silence between you and Amaryllis stretches into the margins of awkwardness, so you quick-search your memory for something, then begin to recite: "'I feel I do not exaggerate to claim these women dangerous far beyond anything seen before, a remarkable and notorious complement of sorceresses, even in this God-forsaken age.' That's how the witchfinder Guillaume Cornîche described the women of Chatouye in a letter he sent to some witchfinder colleagues."

You check to see if your audience is still with you, and to your slight surprise, she is, so you continue.

"Some scholars believe—*I* believe, anyway—that the letter repeats some of the text from Cornîche's lost book. It would be the only surviving material from *Libre des Damnées*." You shift your stance slightly, unconsciously, and finish the recitation: "'Nor can I forbear from warning that though they themselves are mere peasants, utterly without education, their diableries show a clear descent from far older, more pagan horrors. It is this legacy which has gifted them with a power to curse that is unparalleled, necessitating my order to silence them by force, cutting their evil words off at the source— for thus has that creature they name the Red Girl built her empire, here in the heart of a corpse-filled midden, and thus has she many times boasted she may trust her foul blood to maintain it far into the future, even after her body has been burnt to ash.'"

"'The Red Girl,'" Amaryllis repeats, lighting a second smoke from the burnt-down coal of her first. "Wow. That's like some sort of . . . evil Disney princess-type shit."

You shrug. "I didn't make it up. Cornîche, either. That's literally what people for miles around called her."

The Girl's actual name, supposedly, was Sépultrice Fillette-du-Raum, a noted *voulteuse* or doll-maker. Described as "seemingly young and fresh, small and well-made, with odd eyes of two different colors and an exceedingly wicked smile," she was of unknown age and origins, but was said to have settled in Chatouye sometime before the Great Death began, along with her mother, aunts, and grandmother. By the time Cornîche blew into town, however, the only family Sépultrice had left were those she'd given birth to herself, in the interim—five daughters and a son, aged three to sixteen, all by different yet equally anonymous fathers.

"She used to wear a cloak made from uncured hides, dyed red," you tell Amaryllis, "which probably stank to high heaven, but was definitely metal. Even more so when you factor in that it was also covered in needles, which she supposedly used either to torment wax images or kill unwanted babies she midwifed, by slipping them through their fontanelles."

"Jesus, seriously?"

You shrug. "Hard to tell. It's a fairly normal charge, with witches—child sacrifice, procuring miscarriages, cursing with barrenness, abortion. Getting people pregnant, or getting them un-pregnant; all good when it's men on women, but not so much the other way 'round. Like the Supreme Court versus Planned Parenthood."

"What sort of last name is du Raum, anyhow?"

"Um, nonexistent? I found the name Raum Goetim on a list of demons summoned by black magic; he's a Great Earl of Hell, commander of thirty legions, a fallen angel who takes great pleasure in destroying cities and 'men's dignities.' He officiates at the witches' Sabbat, often in the shape of a crow, and also loves children ... not just 'cause they're good eating or whatever, but because he has a lot of them, our gal Sépultrice apparently included." Now it's your turn to light one more, checking your watch. "Probably her mom just got knocked up at some orgy, had sex with whoever wore the devil-mask that month and got pregnant. Like Lisa Bonet with her voodoo child, in *Angel Heart*."

"Uh huh. And she does the same with *her* kids, etcetera."

"Witch-cults are matriarchal, so yeah. Another reason for dudes like Corniche to find them threatening, along with the whole murder-for-hire thing." Explaining, off her stare: "By which I mean the final thing the Girl and her bunch were accused of was brewing up a potion made from mushrooms grown on plague corpses and selling it to local widows-to-be, so they could inherit all their husbands' wealth; charge number three, completing the trifecta. 'Cause just like Eliphas Levi says, witchcraft is above all the science of poisoning."

"Eliphas *who*?"

She's pretty, Amaryllis, you only just now seem to realize—head cocked slightly as she listens, hair back in two pigtails, one slightly more uneven than the other. The cold brings out just a hint of pink to her pale face, outlines her temples and the tops of her cheekbones, like she's using blush for eyeliner; her eyes are clever and kind, lips always skewed sidelong, like she wants to smile. But much as you'd love to go on, to see that happen again, there's maybe five minutes left to pee before you both have to get back down to business: time and money, money and time. Never enough of either, in this world.

So: "Well, that's all for now, looks like," you tell Amaryllis, squashing the second cigarette under your heel. "Have to catch you up on the rest tomorrow night, I guess—if you want me to, I mean. 'To be continued....'"

Cheap Tarantino quote, all that. But it does the trick, or seems to.

"Hope so," Amaryllis replies, doing the same with her cigarette. And lets that hidden grin bloom once more as she turns, bumping your shoulder with hers, to hold the door open for you both.

SOMETIMES, WHEN THINGS GET GRIM, you take a sort of comfort from the idea that somebody as screwed up as you ever got a job counselling other screw-ups, albeit anonymously, over the phone. Even if it was your own former therapist who actually tapped you for the job in the first place.

U of T's gone through a plethora of help lines over the years, both on campus and off. Outcry, the current employer of yourself, Amaryllis, and at least twenty other call jockeys, definitely falls into the second category—they've been incorporated for less than a decade, ministering specifically to QUILTBAG—identifying students whose mental health issues might be interfering with their academic standing. Your former therapist got in on the bottom floor, right after being downsized from the Ontario Institute for Studies and Education Health & Wellness Centre, which is when she promptly started cherry-picking her habitual walk-ins list for potential trainees; you're the only one who made it through who's still on the floor, as far as you know, which speaks to you having either a nice bedside manner or no real life, besides getting this fucking thesis of yours sorted, to interfere with taking almost any shift they care to throw at you.

Probably help if said thesis wasn't taking so damn long to sort, of course. But that's where the anxiety and the OCD come in, ebbing and flowing like tidal waves of barely controllable chaos, along with the sad fact that since your parents cut you off after the first two degrees—half because you wouldn't start teaching already, for God's sake, and half because you finally told them the likelihood of you ever bringing a guy home was only fifty-fifty—you're responsible for everything else in your life as well, on top of all the creepy mystery collation. The "bi-" part in bisexual doesn't mean all too much to Mom and Dad, you've found, since what they were really banking on was you being straight.

They told you point-blank at the time of that last, worst argument that if you left, you wouldn't ever be coming back; that you were dead to them, essentially, as well as to their checkbook. And you left anyhow, which certainly felt good at the time, but keeps you up at night if you allow it to . . . that terrible clutch of existential fear always lurking 'round every corner, just waiting for your guard to drop. It's why you so desperately need to make your own money in order to keep going, just like you need it in order to graduate, no matter how slowly, and none of that's likely to change anytime soon. Thank God for this job, in other words, however occasionally stressful it is to be treating other people's ills when your own remain firmly uncured: giving advice without taking names, passing them up along the chain of psychological assessment and evaluation like some long-distance pseudo-medical traffic director . . .

. . . for as long as you can stay solid enough to keep it, at least. Which is an obsession in itself.

Across the room, Amaryllis has her headset on already, finger poised over that first blinking light, but you're still having a hard time shaking free of today's research: the *Testament* itself, nonsensical and oblique from its untranslatable main text—a trove of oral wisdom inscribed, phonetically, from some unidentifiable original language, first into crude Roman Latin, then Coptic Greek, Hebrew, and back again into Mediaeval High Latin, with additional scribblings in Angevin French. Not to mention a whole file full of subsequent notes, jottings, commentary from all sorts of different sources, the many scholarly collections the book has passed through since Guillaume Cornîche's time; so much stuff to sort through, and all so contradictory. Why would a coven of illiterates keep a copy of a book they couldn't read, for example—merely to venerate it, use it as a prop, an (un)holy relic? And why, having gone to so much trouble to destroy it, would Cornîche apparently then insist on trying to reproduce it by hand a mere two years later, before murdering his family and hanging himself?

You'll have a lot to talk about with your advisor at tomorrow's meeting, as well as with Amaryllis, next break. For now, however, it's time to be helpful: pick up your own headset, punch your own button, settle back. Sound nice.

"Outcry, here for you in crisis, twenty-four hours a day: safe, discreet, supportive. How can I help?"

There's a lag on the line, a soundless sort of click, a not quite hum; fairly normal for clients to wait a minute, consider their options—though, granted, you can usually hear them breathing while they do so. When no voice follows, however, you give a bit of a sigh yourself and ask: "Hello?"

Nothing.

"This is Outcry," you repeat. "Are you still there?"

More nothing; the silence stretches like blood in your head, hissing. You glance over at Amaryllis, chatting away, then past her—catch the eye of the floor monitor Eve and point to the line in question, tapping your headset, raising a brow. She checks the line, shrugs, gives a thumbs up:

there's *somebody* on there. That's what you're meant to take away, you can only assume. But . . . you still can't hear them, no matter how you strain. Not a peep.

"I'm sorry," is all you can think to say, eventually. "Must be something wrong on our end. Please try again later."

And without giving yourself time to think about it, you switch lines.

"We need to talk about what happened tonight," your ex-therapist says as you're putting your coat on, so you hang back, watch Amaryllis wave and walk off, and brace for what comes next. "Sit down, will you? Now, I know we haven't spoken in a while—"

"Yeah, that's okay; I'll stand. Is this about that call at the top, after the break?"

"You know it is, Zohra, just like you know the rules—you're in our top percentile, which is why we're so surprised, but I'd say this to anyone, regardless: This is a help line. We need to be consistent, pleasant, patient. Which is why you can't just hang up on people."

And here it comes, all at once, in a wave: lapping up from behind, surrounding and submerging you, reducing you to nothing more than impulse. The fear, fear, fear, whispering with every strangled heartbeat—

I need this job, I can't lose it; need to keep my place, to graduate, get my degree, to prove I'm not trash. So whatever I have to do to make that happen is justified, completely . . . anything, everything. Anything at all.

You have to bite down on it, sharp and hard, before you can even trust yourself to answer. Pointing out, as you do: "There was nobody *there*, Helen."

"According to Eve, the line was live, so there obviously was." No answer to that, so you just wait, well aware you're supposedly proving her point; Helen sighs and continues, gently. "Sometimes people are shy; you need to wait, let them come to it at their own pace. I seem to recall at least one of our sessions where you barely spoke at all, but that didn't mean I told you to leave and come back when you were feeling more talkative."

"Are you really supposed to discuss that?"

"If you were anybody else, I wouldn't. But you're not my patient anymore, are you? We're past those days. You're my colleague, now, my friend—"

"—Your employee, I get it. Look, I'm not lying, and I'm kind of upset you'd think I would be: the line was dead, empty air. I know what a live line sounds like."

As does Eve, you can see her thinking, but not saying. "All right," she says, finally. "We'll drop it, for now; agree to disagree. But if it happens again . . ."

"It won't."

That night, you lie awake far longer than you should, mind-numbingly tired yet unable to drift off, for no immediately discernible reason. Your eyelids droop; every yawn cracks your jaw. Something pricks your temples all the way around, sandpaper discomfort spread thick everywhere it touches—a crown of invisible thorns, dug tight and lit, burning.

In the morning you wake face-down and dream-sick, hot with sweat, bruised by your own back-circling, infinitely intricate nightmares. You have dim memories of arguing with a faceless man inside a decaying building on the sea, cliffside; he was wearing a long-skirted robe made from some sort of dark material, collar stiff and white, hair curling to his earlobes but crown of the head shaved high, almost into a tonsure. Bits of the building around you kept breaking off and falling into the surf below, a pounding basin where bloated bodies could be seen surfacing amongst paddling swimmers, pale intruders to be brushed aside—no one seemed to notice them, or the lowering sky, the mounting tide. Lord, here comes the flood.

Red light in the sky, drifting down dim, like dried blood, like dust. Dust everywhere, but not from here: cold dust, musty, alien at its smallest grain. Dead as light from some distant, long-extinguished star.

We must cut down the tree, he told you, quick and low, as though trying to convince himself. *It cannot be otherwise. Extirpate it, utterly; tear it up by the roots and then burn it; that's only proper. For a burnt offering is pleasing unto the Lord, isn't it? Yes. Yes.*

Our god thinks differently, Maître, you told him, not knowing why. But you don't think he believed you.

"So," your thesis advisor begins, "how're you liking the Connaught? Nuns treating you well?"

"Great, thanks. I mean . . . they're pretty quiet."

"Yeah, that's their stock in trade, basically. Not that they take a vow of silence or anything—but, hey, it *is* a library. Right?"

". . . Right."

She's a bit of an oddity, all told, Professor Nan van Hool. Though that's probably no surprise, given her area of expertise: psycholinguistics, an interdisciplinary field of study based around language comprehension and production, but her particular interests lie in trying to track down and reconstruct dead languages like the one the *Testament* must have been—well, not written in, not at first. Spoken in? Dictated from?

Impossible to tell, as with so much else.

(It was Helen who first pointed you toward Nan, you'll remember later, when it doesn't matter anymore. She was the one who first asked you what really drew your interest, during your initial counselling sessions, back when you were still gearing up for the career teaching English as a Second Language your parents wanted you to have; the only one who made it clear how important it was to live your life for you, not others, at the most difficult point in your own development. Which is probably why you still feel so attached to Helen, so loyal to her, even now. Why you'll do almost anything to please her, aside from the most obvious reasons: pure practicality, cash for cooperation, so you make sure you don't need to worry over paying your way, along with everything else.)

"The *Testament* can be hard going, at first," Nan remarks, as though she's read your mind. "That language, or what remains of it—they call it the Red Speech."

"Uh huh. Who does?"

"Ah, well: nobody, I suppose. Not anymore. That's what the sources Cornîche found called it, though, and he translates it in his letters as *les mots rouges*, red words, *l'esprit des portiéres*. Doorkeepers' jargon."

"He told his superiors Sépultrice Fillette-du-Raum could speak it," you say, "that it was the main component of her spells, but she could not read it. Even though she supposedly had a book written in it, or close as whoever wrote the book could come."

Nan wags her finger at you approvingly, teacher to gold-star pupil. "Mmm-hmm. And that was the reason he gave for having her tongue cut out, right at the start, along with the tongues of as many of her coven-mates as he could get his hands on."

For a second, you find yourself wondering what that many tongues would look like, all piled together—but that's a truly horrible thought, copper-tasting, far too bright for comfort. So you make yourself ask, instead: "Yeah, right—so here's what I've been wondering, actually: Given Cornîche burnt the only previously known copy of the *Testament*, and the present copy—the one at the Connaught—is probably the one he wrote afterward, from memory . . . then how can we be sure the present *Testament* bears any resemblance whatsoever to the original? This Red Speech of yours could just be, like . . . gibberish. Something Cornîche came up with in a dream, before killing his whole family."

Nan nods. "Good point, and totally understandable that you'd go there, Zohra. To be frank, I'd've been disappointed if you hadn't; it's Logic 101, really. Well done."

"Um . . . thanks, I guess."

She smiles. "C'mon, don't be insulted. Let me show you something."

Moments later, you're hunched over her computer, watching in fascination as she clicks through a series of high-resolution .jpgs so large they can't even be laid side by side, just on top of each other. She flips from one to another skillfully, almost too fast for you to track: each with one more translation than the next, moving backward through history. "It's not that there isn't more than one edition of the *Testament*, thankfully," she says, "though they're hard as hell to come by, and almost all of them seem to be reproductions of one sort or another, with Cornîche's being one of the earliest. So I've tracked keywords between versions, from Greek to Latin, Latin to French, even into English—this is a translation made *from* Cornîche's, around 1780, Angevin French to eighteenth century Dutch, possibly by Hoek van Monster, the guy who wrote *On Varying Heresies*. And this one's in English, dated 1860-something, the old m-dash reach-around. My thesis advisor thought the person who wrote this might've been Gael Sidderstane of Ontario, who took over van Monster's collection. Notice anything?"

You peer at the list of keywords, consider a moment. "The words . . . stay the same."

"Across versions, yes. After Cornîche, but also before Cornîche." Nan flips back to a .jpg of a page from said book, one you recognize from days poring over it in the Connaught. "If he was simply making it up, or even just trying to reconstruct it from memory, he'd most likely get *some* of the keywords—literate people had a better memory for vocabulary, back then, and even we can still memorize short sections—but he surely wouldn't know to use *all* of them. Would he?"

"No," you agree, quietly, even though it isn't really a question. Your eyes never leave the screen. "No, he wouldn't."

The list of keywords is longer than you expect, running the gamut from obvious (*the, she, worship, sacrifice*) to very much not (*knockers, intruders, portals, flesh, treader, orb*). Plus other things too, here and there—different on top yet similar underneath, or so they seem, unrecognizably rendered though they might be—

(they could be names)

"This one's the oldest," Nan tells you, pointing. "A scroll, papyrus-based rag, wax-treated. Found in Gharbia Governate, in Egypt, near Khotoor—

that's where the last stronghold of an order of Coptic Alexandrine nuns was located, before it was burnt and its backbone membership massacred during the Muslim invasion of 641. You know what they called themselves, these ladies? The Red Sisterhood."

"Red like the Girl, in Chatouye."

"Exactly."

You take a minute, consider this carefully. "From nuns over here to witches over there," you comment, finally. "That's an . . . unpredictable sort of transition."

Nan shakes her head. "Not really, in context; the Church didn't like nuns all too much either, especially once they worked out how many of them took vows essentially to escape the patriarchy. Unlike secular women, mediaeval nuns were expected to educate themselves, mastering all sorts of skills they'd never even have had access to on the outside. There were nun-composers, nun-physicians, nun-artists . . . abbesses such as Saint Hildegard of Bingen wrote books and practiced law, ruling their nunneries like tiny cities where they acknowledged no authority but the voice of God Himself, whose glory they sought to magnify through their otherwise unnatural actions." A pause. "But of course, the Red Sisters were never really nuns."

"What do you mean?"

"Oh, that they started out as pagans, much like Constantine the Great, the Roman emperor who adopted Christianity personally and then passed it on to the Empire like a head cold." Nan's dismissive hand flip grates on you, for some reason, but you say nothing. "Just like Corniche suspected, the Red Girl's coven had been active in France since before Paris was Lutèce, well-lit jewel of the Gallic Roman occupation. And that's where the Red Sisterhood came from, too: they were Roman cultists, worshippers of the goddess Carna, right up until Emperor Theodosius I decreed the Eleusinian Mysteries officially closed in 392, and they were forced to rebrand themselves 'under new management.'"

"Carna." You sort mentally through your (rudimentary) Latin. "Goddess of . . . meat?"

"That'd be Carnea." Nan pronounces it Carn-ee-yah, like *Narnia*.

You realize her pause is an expectant one, so you rack your memory for another guess, finding only the obvious one comes to mind. "As in *Testament of*—?"

"No, but I can see how it's confusing." If Nan has a fault, this cheerful obliviousness to her own more-than-occasionally patronizing tone is it. "Carna is conflated with the Roman doorkeeper deity Cardea, of the hinges, through the adjectival form of *caro, carnis*, which means 'of flesh, of meat'—Carnea would be the feminine nominative singular. So *Carna Magos* means, um . . . 'High Priestess of Carna,' basically, though 'woman shaman-leader' would be more accurate."

"All right. . . ."

"So Carna was an obscure pre-Etruscan goddess brought into Rome with the rest of the pantheon, one of their smaller deities; her realm was that of the liminal, defining what was inside from what was outside, what could be let in from what needed to be kept out. She was one of the *ianitores terrestres*. In other words, a demarcator of sacred spaces—not so much a gate-warden like Janus as a gate-*builder*, the person who defined the boundaries of the earth, and where, when, and how to pass them. Not to mention that through the association with *caro*, flesh, she was also supposed to guard entry and exit from the human body." Nan pauses. "Her cult was considered an innately female concern, the same way Mithras the Bull—the soldiers' god, focal point of the Legions' own personal mystery religion—was considered an innately male one. And the cultists liked it that way, apparently. No one with a penis need apply."

This sounds familiar. "Like the mother-goddess, right? Cybele. All those priests who—"

"Ripped their junk off in ecstasy, threw it on the pile, and went full eunuch? The Carnans were even more exclusive, or so rumors went. If any men tried to insert themselves where they weren't wanted—lit or fig—they risked getting pulled limb from limb, like Orpheus amongst the Bacchae." She straightens up a moment, cracks her back. "So for hundreds of years the Carnans kept to themselves, passed all their wisdom down mouth to ear, secrets traded strictly from teacher to student, where no dirty male might be able to overhear anything truly important. But by the time Christianity started to crowd them out, they must've become afraid that if they didn't tell *someone* what the deal was, they might run out of teachers entirely. Which is where the very first *Testament* came from, the original."

You shoot her a glance. "Don't suppose you've got a .jpg of *that* lying around here, somewhere."

Nan laughs, half amused, half sad. "Nope, that one's lost in the mist of time, I can only think. And everything after is just a copy of a copy of a copy—but as you've observed, they all tell the same story, using pretty much the same language. Red Speech full of red words, perfect for drawing big red circles 'round the places where the walls of the world are rubbing thin, breaking down. Ready to give way and let something bad come through. . . ."

"'Doorkeepers,'" you repeat, out loud. "And where were these doors supposed to open, exactly?"

"Anywhere and everywhere. In walls, in floors, in ceilings, trees—the earth, the rock, the sky. Inside of people, even."

Carna vs. Carnea, you think; doors vs. flesh. Or maybe, given the association with bodily ins and outs, doors *into* flesh—*of* flesh—

And again, you feel your eyes drawn back to the screen, picturing that .jpg of Cornîche's *Testament* you know is lurking four or five down from Nan's Khotoor scroll, and the words you've studied so recently rewrite themselves across your mind's blank page in a homicidal/suicidal witch-finder's spiky brown script: *To repel and guard against Those Outside, Those Others, the Knockers and Intruders, who poison and degrade all they touch....*

Whoever the hell *they're* supposed to be.

(*the names?*)

Out the corner of your eye, you vaguely notice just how dusty this place is, Nan's office. Much like your apartment's been looking lately, along with every almost other place you go these days. Motes set swarming in every sunbeam, tiny as gnats, and the light itself reddish, dimming, lending everything it touches the same ill hint of decay. A feeble, poisoned glare, borne across space from some distant, equally ominous star.

The hairs on your arms start to stand up all of a sudden, and you're damned if you know why.

"In hindsight, I suppose the funny part is that the people who wrote the Testament, while never truly the sort of Christians Cornîche might have wanted them to be, were still trying—in their own way—to do something constructive, literally so," Nan continues, musingly, apparently immune to the sensations currently making your teeth grit and your skin crawl. "Of course, he must've heard rumors the Red Sisterhood once practiced human sacrifice, but those are endemic to any cult, especially one so gynocentric; easy enough to apply those facile, unproven assumptions to the various gradations of murder the Chatouyenne coven actually practiced, once he'd identified that book they pulled out at rituals as the *Testament*. Even so, his real mistake was trying to destroy the book in the first place."

"What do you mean?" you ask, wrapping your sweater closer.

"The *Testament* protects itself. That's the legend. Yes, the original text itself is lost—not written but *told* in Red Speech, a language only those who are part of the Red Sisterhood itself can learn, or speak, or maybe even *hear*, depending on which source you refer to. But whenever a copy is destroyed, somebody somewhere is essentially *forced* to write another copy, a curse that starts with the book-burner him- or herself. Like hypergraphia, or a form of possession via automatic writing, even to the point of compiling a special ink for the purpose, whose ingredients include the author's own blood."

"*Seriously.*"

"Oh, sure. Sister Encratia could tell you about the analysis on the Connaught's Testament: written in gall, wormwood, and 'animal protein,' which was their polite euphemism for blood of some sort. Determining whether it's Corniche's would take something a bit more elaborate—but then again, there are descendants of his family in the States, under the name of Cornish, at least two of whom recently escaped from jail. So it's not like their DNA isn't in the system."

Wouldn't be hard to test for a genetic marker, then, your brain suggests, as you're sure it's meant to. But you guess Nan hasn't yet been able to argue anyone at the Connaught into it, which makes sense; by all appearances, the OSP aren't exactly a rich order.

"Um . . ." You get up, not quite able to keep from shivering. "Y'know, I'm gonna have to go pretty soon, Professor. I need to get ready for my shift."

"At the chat line?" *Help line,* you think, nodding. "Oh well, absolutely; sorry to keep you. At any rate, your work looks good, thus far. Keep at it."

"Thanks. I will." You turn to go, but pause, because the question's suddenly welling up behind your teeth at a truly unmanageable rate, hot and fresh, unavoidable as bile. "Uh . . . I was just wondering . . . are you expecting me to *use* any of what you just told me? In my thesis?"

You wonder if you should be a bit more circumspect, or clarify what you mean; *some* of it's likely to be useful, obviously. The true stuff, everything that can be even vaguely proven. Not all this—other crap. This sheer speculation.

Nan blinks up at you, mildly.

"Not unless you want to," she says, eventually.

"You seem weirded out," Amaryllis observes, during your next smoke break, and you are, a little. Or more than. So you find yourself telling her about your meeting with Nan, possibly in far more detail than you need to. Still, it feels good to say this stuff out loud.

"I like her a lot, Na—Professor van Hool," you say, almost as if it's an apology for betraying someone's confidence. "But . . . when she gets going, when she starts talking about this stuff, sometimes it's like . . . she *believes* it. Like she thinks it's true."

"Well, you do too, don't you? I mean, these nuns *did* write the book that the Chatouye witches ended up with, right? Thought that was the whole point of the thesis."

"No, more like—she buys them *being* witches, *real* witches, in the first place. You know. Like what the Red Sisterhood thought they were doing actually worked. Like magic's real, or some shit. And all the stuff that goes with that, too: spirits, demons, the Devil . . . maybe even God with a big-ass G."

Amaryllis shrugs, takes a drag, expels a great cloud of silver-gray smoke. "Most religions believe what they're based on is real, Zohra. They kinda have to, by definition. That's why their membership keeps on being religious."

"Yeah, and I get that, I do. I just . . ."

"It's creepy, right?"

"*Really* fucking creepy, yeah."

Amaryllis grins. "Creepy can be good, though. Fun. I mean—*I* like creepy, anyway."

"You do?"

"Yup. I like it a lot."

You feel your face heat—catch a spark, maybe mutual. Or is that simply wishful thinking? As you look away, glance aside, you spot something vaguely disturbing curled just beneath the shadow of a nearby bush: a desiccated animal corpse or a plastic bag full of picked chicken bones, some twigs bound in wastepaper, whatever. You can't tell which from this angle, and on some level, you don't really want to know. Better to switch back to Amaryllis, comfortably uncomfortable as that may be, and deal with the way she makes you feel head-on.

So: "Well, I'm not *totally* against creepy, on principle," you admit, managing a brief smile, as you swerve back to the subject at hand. "It's just that it'd be easier if I had the option to walk away when things got a bit too rich for my blood, but right now, I just don't. Won't, for a while."

"Thesis and all."

"And all."

Amaryllis nods sympathetically, apparently not bothered by your less-than-stellar attempt to return what you can only assume—what you *want* to assume—was a form of flirtation on her part. "Tell you what," she says, after a moment. "Wanna hear another kind of weird tale, just to take your mind off? It's not *non*-creepy, but it does have absolutely nothing to do with anything red, aside from the strictly biological." Another smile. "Trade you for a smoke."

"Okay, sure; *mi nicotina es su nicotina.*" You dig out your pack, tapping one onto her offered palm. "Shoot."

"Thank you, madame." Amaryllis lights up, breathes deep, and plumes out the rest, a tiny, hot-eyed dragon. "You know how I do some work for CreepTracker.org, right? Local website, run out of the Freihoeven Institute for Parapsychological Research; it was put together by this dude Ross, who used to run some kind of ghost decon operation downtown."

"Not really my thing, but sure."

"All right. Anyway, I'm what you'd call a stringer, I guess, for Toronto and the downtown core; I keep a lookout for current events, oddities, unexplained mysteries, and write them up—sometimes they'll contract me to do a whole article. Takes a bit of data-mining, because this is the kind of shit that doesn't exactly make the front page, but 'luckily. . .'" —and here you can all but see the scare-quotes forming midair, even without her attendant gesture— ". . . I happen to have an ex in the coroner's office who told me about this cluster of deaths they're keeping out of the media somehow, mainly 'cause on first look they don't even seem connected. Even on second—well, they're pretty sure they *are*, just can't figure out *how*. Which makes it interoffice gossip at the most, right now."

"Going to need a few more details, I think."

"But of course." Theatrically, Amaryllis looks around, then beckons you closer; you lean in, unable to help yourself. "The autopsies," she goes on, voice low, "revealed severe internal organ damage, absolutely fatal injuries—like there's no way any one of these people would've survived, no matter how fast they got to a doctor. We're talking muscles, liver, kidneys, gallbladder, spleen, all ripped open from the inside, but the skin of the body itself is intact everywhere. No way to tell how it happened. I know, I know—what if you inserted something sharp up inside somebody, through the obvious entry-points? Nope, still wouldn't work. You'd leave traces, and there just aren't any."

Her eyes sparkle as she says it, like it's cute, like it's nothing. People torn apart as though they've swallowed a fragment of black hole, guts unfurling 'til the skin dents and then locks back down at the last possible second, leaving barely a bruise on top—

The fuck, the *fuck*. Where is this coming from? Not *you*, surely . . .

. . . but then it clicks, somewhere deep inside your brain; pops up like a slide, brown words on buff, lit from behind. *For when the doors we keep open themselves, they do so without warning, in every sort of wall. Yet through our speech are the world's thin places shored up with prayerful words, each a spoken key. Thus do we bend our lives to the world's life, locking out sickness, plague, and sorrow.*

Carna into *carnea*, flesh irises smashed open then barricaded shut once more, bricked up, sealed over: no wonder they all died, if that's what happened. Which it obviously couldn't have; that's just Nan's crazy-talk implications bouncing off Amaryllis's Grand Guignol tabloid gossip, surely, the aftereffects of too much *Testament*-reading still rattling around in the blank space between your ears. Since you very definitely *weren't* thinking any of the above, because who the hell ever would? Jesus!

Well, Amaryllis, apparently—at least in terms of speculating that these things might have a slightly less concrete cause than some kind of toxic agent, or a necrotizing fasciitis that only starts metastasizing when it reaches your innermost areas, or a previously unknown form of decompression sickness causing air bubbles large enough to displace whole organs, a supersized dry-land version of the bends. Which is a problem, or *should* be, surely; should render her suddenly unattractive, or you un-attracted. Except that it doesn't.

You're just not that good of a person, you guess.

So instead of calling her out, you smile, sickly. And it's as though she sees right on through to the horror underneath, because suddenly her glee is gone, smile quick-fading. "Zohra? You all right?" She touches your arm. "Look, I just wanted to get your mind off things, but it's no big deal—it's probably some bullshit Kai spun my way, anyhow, to keep me on the hook. Nothing to worry about."

You nod shakily, taking a gulp and holding it a breath or two, before judging yourself calm enough to answer. "The people with big gaping holes inside them might beg to disagree," you suggest, attempting to keep it light, and failing.

"Probably, yeah. You okay, though?"

"Oh yeah, yeah. No problem." You check your wrist. "Hey, is that the time? We should go back inside, don't you think?"

"Um, sure." As you both turn back toward the call center door, she throws in: "So: you don't think this Prof. van Hool of yours actually thinks those things are *true*, not really? Do you?"

"Oh, hardly. That'd be *crazy*, and I'm not. Her either, that I know of."

And this is irony, too; karma, if of an oddly petty kind. Because it only now occurs to you that Amaryllis is looking at you exactly the way you must have looked, from the corner of your eye, at Nan van Hool—side-eyeing her narrowly, hard enough to choke off any emotional presentation beyond the most rudimentary, the most deeply shallow. But at least Amaryllis is honest enough to do it openly.

"'Cause magic doesn't work," she says, gaze holding fast on yours, prompting your response.

"No," you agree, at last. "Of course not. 'Cause there's no such thing as magic."

"Right."

"Right," you repeat, more rote than persuaded. And let it drop.

THE SHIFT GOES BY FAST enough after that, measured out in rambling conversations and hapless stabs at solving other people's problems long-distance, giving out advice that'll almost certainly end up ignored. But you keep at it, give it your full attention, not least because you want to scrub your brain clean and this will probably do as well as anything else to fulfill that particular ambition: a pumice-stone pummeling, enacted aurally.

Entering zero hour, however, it happens again—you click the button on a seemingly dead line, then grit your teeth; stay on it as long as you can stand and longer, one eye firm on Eve's silhouette, bent to her panel, obviously listening in. There isn't going to be any friendly but threatening "chat" with Helen tonight, not if you can help it.

As the seconds eke by, though, something on the other end starts to . . . well, *clarify*, is one way to put it: widens, deepens. The lack of tone becomes a slight tremble, the barest hint of static, white noise washing up like a very slow tide, too stagnant even to lap. In the distance, you can almost hear an echo of movement, followed by sounds so dim they could be the infinitesimal cartilage pop of your own jaw shifting as you bite your tongue, concentrating hard enough to court a headache.

(*what?*)

Eve's signaling you, from the sidelines; you turn and squint, see her draw a finger across her own throat, as though broadcasting *No, it's okay. You can stop now. You were right. Nothing there, so you're wasting time. Just call it a night and move on—*

Which is when you hear it, of course, at last: bell-clear, if far away, and cryptic as hell. Coldly sharp, too, yet malleable; every syllable carved from ice, melting on contact with the speaker's lips, evaporating in a cloud of mist.

Is there dust where you are? it asks, or seems to. To which you have no answer but a gape.

Soon enough, this gives way to a click, two beeps, and someone else's voice entirely: "Hi, is this Outcry? I'm, uh—never mind. I just . . . I need to talk."

"I'm here," you reply, fast as you can process it, with only a half-moment's lag.

Later, as you're packing up, Helen approaches, looking sheepish. "Sorry you had to go through that again, Zohra," she begins, "but it does look as though you were right after all; someone's crank-calling us. Nothing to do about it but wait them out, I suppose."

"You mean that last call, with the—?"

"Total gibberish? Suppose it beats deep breathing and the sound of one hand clapping, but, yes. I'll talk to Martin about changing that line out and see what we can do to block the number. You know how we can back-dial and record those if we need to, for security purposes?"

". . . I didn't, but that makes a lot of sense."

"Yes, well. In the meantime, I think it'd be best if you switch places with someone—Amaryllis, maybe. You two do know each other, right? No problems there?"

That betraying dryness returns, parching mouth and throat, a silly little heart-flutter. It's like her name alone spikes your system, flushes it with adrenalin, makes you giddy.

"Um, no," you say, struggling not to trip over your own tongue. "No, no problems. We get along fine, Amaryllis and me."

"Then it's settled," Helen announces, disappearing once more. Leaving you where you stand, even as you can't begin to keep yourself from thinking: But . . . *it wasn't gibberish. I understood it all, perfectly. Like it was nothing more than, than—*

(*words*)

THE NEXT MORNING YOU WAKE stiff and hot once more under sweat-sodden sheets, tongue sharp-feeling as a well-kept razor blade, fit to split your own mouth open. Taste metal on your tongue as you try to cough, as you hawk and spit in the sink, expecting blood—but none comes.

(Not a surprise, no; thankfully, for your sanity's sake. But a relief, nonetheless.)

Your apartment seems even dirtier than usual, abruptly unsuitable to bare feet, with every surface lightly gray-furred, suspicious clumps lurking in all the corners and hair-spiders kicked up as you cross the rug. Something glints on the bathroom floor, crunching under-sole like mica or sand. The taps groan when you turn them on, and that first cold gush is red-tinged, rusty.

Outside, you shrug your coat tighter and walk quickly to the corner. A baleful sun stares down, barely fist-sized at its apogee, slit like a skeptical eye.

At the Connaught, when Sister Encratia slides the *Testament* across to you, you clear your throat, making her pause mid-move. "Something you want to ask, miss?" she asks, softly, her voice a bare, dry murmur in that paper-burnt air.

"Um, yes. . . ." Too loud, by far—you hear yourself echo in the stacks, bass notes thumping, and redden, head dipping. "I, uh . . ." In a whisper: ". . . don't want to cause any disturbance. I mean, if I am."

The nun swivels her headscarf sidelong, checking to see if you're still alone together, then gives the faintest of faint shrugs once it becomes all too painfully obvious absolutely nothing has changed. "The likelihood of your disturbing anyone seems—low, at best," she says, drily, "but we could talk in my office. Bring the book, if you like."

Nuns can't hear confessions or give absolutions, but it's clear Encratia's training overlaps more than somewhat with your own counselling seminars: she sits you down in her tiny office, makes tea on a hot plate and dishes it out like a gentle maiden aunt, though you doubt she's even ten years your senior. Recognizing the technique doesn't mean it doesn't work, though.

Sister Encratia sips her tea, sighing in pleasure, then sets it down and leans forward. "Tell me your troubles," she says.

"I don't think we have that long."

Encratia nods. "Would it help if I told you being disturbed by our books isn't uncommon? Researchers are driven by a combination of imagination and obsession, both of which make them vulnerable to the texts we guard. Some very black parts of the human soul are recorded here."

"Oh, well . . . I don't really believe in all that, Sister."

"Which doesn't help either, sad to say. But go on."

You sip your own tea, mostly to gain time. "Look," you begin, at last. "How much do you know about the *Testament*?"

"The basics," Encratia replies. "Guillaume Corniche is held in high esteem by my order, sad fate aside, and his descendants likewise. We've also spent some time tracking *les Chatouyennes*, Sépultrice Fillette-du-Raum's get—one of whom escaped Mennenvale Women's Prison along with Dionne and Samaire Cornish, as it happens." She chuckles slightly. "That family is a curse."

Which one? you wonder. But ask, instead: "Unlike those for a lot of witch trials, Corniche's records clearly show actual crimes being committed at Chatouye—that ring of poison-murders the Red Girl assisted with, for example."

"Somewhat like Catherine Deshayes, *La Voisin*, in the Burning Court Affair of 1682, yes. What about them?"

"I was wondering if any of those records detail the effects of Sépultrice's mushrooms, beyond mortality—like an autopsy? Unusual findings in the bodies?"

"Well, dissection wasn't actually prohibited at the time, but no, that wasn't regular practice; this wasn't that far away from the Black Death, so people tended to avoid corpses, if they could. Burnt them, too." She casts you a look, shrewd and penetrating. "You know all this already, though. What you *want* is something you haven't found in our collection . . . not yet, anyhow."

You nod. "Organ failure, on a massive scale. Degradation so bad it'd look as though a bomb went off when you opened them up, basically."

Though Encratia's poker face is near-seamless, you see her fingertips whiten on the teacup's handle. "There *are* legends of deaths like that occurring in the vicinity of the *Testament*," she says, "but nothing like reliable evidence, of course."

"The book, protecting itself?"

"So some say. Nothing in Cornîche's materials details anything similar in Chatouye, however."

"Which is odd, right? I mean, if the Red Girl and the Red Sisterhood were 'red' for the same reasons—" Here you stop, mid-spoken thought, suddenly struck by another sort of revelation entirely—one you start to sound out as Encratia merely watches, eyes mild, attitude patient. "Except . . . what if they weren't? If the Chatouyenne coven had no affiliation with the Red Sisterhood whatsoever beyond *venerating* the same text, or maybe not even venerating it—if they appropriated and misused it, instead, the same way Satanists supposedly appropriate and misuse holy symbols in the Black Mass—"

"There's no 'supposedly' about it," Sister Encratia puts in, tartly. "No reason to profane and ridicule Church doctrine except to refute the entire concept of sanctity, to literally defecate on the idea of communion, absolution, and redemption."

Unable to sit still, you rise, begin to pace. "From Cornîche on down, everybody's assumed the Red Girl was just the Red Sisterhood's latest Carna Magos, that the presence of the *Testament* signified an unbroken chain of descent—but what if that's not true? What if the Chatouye coven was deliberately subverting those traditions, desecrating them, corrupting them? The whole point of the *Testament* is to, hang on—" you flip to a page in which you've tucked a slip of paper, from your previous study sessions "—'keep closed the doors around the world.' So maybe Fillette-du-Raum was trying to do the exact opposite."

"To open them." Encratia purses her lips. "For what purpose?"

"Well, why does anyone open a door? To see what's on the other side, find what you can get out of it. Make a deal." You flip to another slip-marked page. "Take these . . . they look like names to me: the spelling changes, but there's something recognizable in all of them, isn't there? Same combination of vowel sounds, here and here—and here. *Kvaashl ohtuss, kuhweshell ochtaysh*, uh . . . *kacheel oothowss.* . . ."

"Quachil Uttaus, the much-feared Treader in the Dust," says Encratia quietly. "Of whom the *Necronomicon* says, 'Seldom is he revealed: for he dwelleth beyond the outermost circle, in the dark limbo of unsphered time and space. Dreadful is the word that calleth him, though the word be unspoken save in thought: for Quachil Uttaus is the ultimate corruption; and the instant of his coming is like the passage of many ages; and neither flesh nor stone may abide his treading, but all things crumble beneath it atom from atom.'" She turns over another page, then points. *Yamil Zacra-yoomell zukkragh, eiumill zoocreh.* "'Accursed forevermore is Yamil Zacra, star of perdition, who sitteth apart and weaveth the web of his rays like a spider spinning in a garden. Even as far as the light of Yamil Zacra falleth among the worlds, so goeth forth the bane and the bale thereof. And the seed of Yamil Zacra, like a fiery tare, is sown in planets that know him only as the least of the stars.'"

As Sister Encratia finishes, looking up, the last few words seem to rise as well and hang in the office's warm, close light like pollution, a stain on the soul. "These are only two of those entities the Sisterhood called Knockers and Intruders," she says, "though the *Testament* contains descriptions of many more. These two outrank them all, however—old gods, if small. In the war between good and evil, they might be reckoned commanders, *generals*, rather than foot soldiers."

Again, you seem to hear last night's call in your head, that voice. Oddly distant, yet so clear.

Is there dust where you are? Is the light red and dim?

Can you hear us?

Can you hear us, knocking?

(Remembering how you wanted to snarl, the first time you heard that same "empty" line: *Look, do you even want my help or WHAT?* To which the answer might apparently be, now that you can actually hear it: *Yes, we do, and very much so—open the door, please, Zohra. Open it. Open, open . . .*)

. . . *or re-lock it once more, forever.*

Every word of the Red Speech is a key, after all, as Nan van Hool said. And keys work either way.

And perhaps the nun can see it on your face now, this uncomfortable revelation—that or something else, no doubt equally disturbing. Because although Sister Encratia may not be on her feet too, as yet, you can still see her shift slightly in her seat, thighs tensing; one hand presses flat to the desk as the other subtly reaches toward the heavy teapot's handle, ready to grasp and throw.

In the meantime, however, she waits, thankfully. For you to explain yourself, to yourself.

"Does anyone know how the Red Girl got her copy of the *Testament*, in the first place?" you ask at last, voice gone hoarse.

"Ah," Sister Encratia replies, mouth twitching upward once more, as though pleasantly surprised. "That *would* be the question. Though you might not believe how few actually think to ask it, given the context."

"I'll bet Cornîche had a theory." You take your seat again, listening intently.

"He did, yes. After discovering an empty yet red-smeared bottle amongst Sépultrice's effects, he formed the opinion that she had *invoked* it, somehow, by brewing her blood into ink and setting quill to paper, opened herself up to it, perhaps through meditation, then transcribed the results automatically."

"That doesn't sound very effective."

"Oh, on the contrary. Cornîche's closest associate on the case, Bouwen van Maartensbeck—who copied down a portion of the Chatouyenne *Testament*, so he could check it against the version in his family's arcane library—claimed that aside from some small differences he put down to misspellings, it matched not only the existing text but also that which Cornîche later produced, in the grip of his own deadly reverie." She taps the book. "This text, right here."

"That doesn't . . ." . . . *make any sense*, you want to protest, but why state the obvious? So: "Any *Testament*'s just a transcript, though, right? Even its oldest sections, it's just an approximation, not a Rosetta Stone. So how could the Red Girl use it to learn the Red Speech in the first place?"

Encratia gives you a long look. "You said you didn't believe."

"Do *you*?"

"I'm a nun, young lady, and by choice; this order is my vocation, not just my job. One could argue that believing in things without visible proof is my *raison d'être*."

"Oh, that's just sophism—"

"I'll thank you not to presume to tell me what my faith 'is,' or isn't." Not angry, but her tone is curt, final; it shuts you up, like a slap across the face. And all at once, here comes the fear again, a thick, drowning rush:

What if I've insulted her so much she cuts off access to the Trust, the stacks, the Testament? If she separates me permanently from this book I hate and fear but nevertheless need *so distinctly, in order to make the kind of points that'll keep me in Nan van Hool's good graces?*

There are far worse things than being banned from studying the Testament, or so you increasingly suspect. But your gut doesn't know that—or even if it does, it doesn't believe it.

Breathe, Zohra. Breathe. Make your heartbeat ease its hammering by slow degrees; make this whole too-bright, too-loud world around you run gently down, stabilize and fade, like a dimming, reddening evening light. Let it rise, and fall, and settle yet again, softly, softly. Like falling ash, like snow . . .

. . . like dust.

"Think of it empirically, if that helps," Sister Encratia continues, slowly, "using the same basic methods, if apparently applied outside the scientific realm. We observe effects and presume the cause retroactively, always; all physical laws work this way. Because we know, provably, that every object consists of infinitely reducible components, we assume a force that holds these components together, even though the force itself is imperceptible, invisible, verifiable only by inference. The work of things unseen."

"I don't—"

"Don't you?" She sighs, then softens. "Meaning, in this case, that when there's no other information readily available, sometimes you have to go with what's presented to you, no matter the source—check it against the facts, see if it resonates. Decide what, if anything, sounds likeliest. When you have eliminated the impossible . . ."

. . . whatever remains, however improbable, must be the truth; even if everything that remains is equally impossible, magical thinking, literally. You can't help but think that Sherlock Holmes—or better yet, Sir Arthur Conan Doyle—wouldn't have approved. Still, you find yourself playing it through nevertheless, out loud: "So if people can rewrite the book without a source copy, as if the very act of writing the book *teaches* you how to write it . . . then speaking the Red Speech must, somehow, teach you how to speak it. Right?"

"Oh, right and wrong have little to with this particular black miracle, I think, sadly. It simply *is*." Encratia lets out a breath, the same sound a cliff-diver might make, preparing to leap. "Yes, exactly; the *Testament's* indices, which I can only assume you haven't reached as yet, tell us outright how mere possession of the book itself teaches the Speech, osmotically. So the more one studies it the more one understands it, often without knowing what it *is* now being understood; one moves by degrees toward a place where you will be able to read the Red Speech, even speak it, without ever perceiving that one does so. Thus the reader becomes an outgrowth of the book, a member of the Sisterhood by proxy, ensuring that the order and the book it exists to maintain—not to use, so much, as to be used *by*—will continue their mutual work, protecting our world against those who would penetrate and pollute it."

The silence that follows this declaration stretches out, long and longer, until at last you lunge to your feet, pushing your chair back so hard it falls to the floor.

"This . . . you're . . . that's *crazy!*" you spit. "Why would you let anyone else read it, if that's what happens? Expose them to it, instead of just . . . destroying the thing?"

"Not our call," Encratia responds. "Besides, as Corniche's own case teaches us, destroying the book is useless. Even trying to conceal it ultimately fails, since anyone given that charge will—sooner or later—become victim to its pull, and if no one is told of it then sheer chance inevitably brings it to light once more. The *Testament* is a key those beings outside the world's doors keep on sliding underneath to us, again and again, hoping one day someone will use it. And the only solution, however theologically problematic we find it—" she grimaces, as if biting metal "—is to exert what little influence we can over who picks it up, and why."

It's the weary, almost miserable way Encratia says these last words that robs you of your fury, peels it back to expose the ice-cold, sick-sweat fear underneath. You swallow, clear your throat.

"How—how would someone know if this was happening? If they were. . . ?"

". . . developing this ability?" Encratia looks straight into your eyes. "Is that what you think is happening, Zohra? To you?"

For a second, taken aback, it occurs to you that you've always assumed she didn't know your name, though she must have watched you sign it fifty times over on the Restricted Access sheet. "I'm not sure," you reply, eventually.

She nods. "Then the main thing to ask yourself is how you intend to use the Speech, if so—for good or for evil? It's a choice, after all. Your choice."

Which really counts as the funniest single moment in this whole lunatic conversation, in hindsight: the idea you've got a choice, of any kind. That you *ever* have had.

TIRED, SO TIRED—EXHAUSTED, AS if you haven't slept in days, and restless too, like there's a current running through you. But there's no time to go home before shift, so you set up in Kali's Coffee instead, headphones on and blasting, typing frantically. Got to get it all down, make sure you remember everything, before it leaks out the corners of your sticky, drooping eyes like tears. Then you pause for a moment, sign onto the shop's dicey Wi-Fi and check your email (nothing relevant) before absently punching the link for local news headlines: upcoming federal election, traffic accident, Turkish earthquake charity fraud trial enters third week—

And there it is, halfway down, small and simple, as befits the web-based equivalent of what used to be the bottom of page five. *SIXTH DEATH FROM "UNESTABLISHED CAUSES"*; *"We have no way of proving beyond a shadow of a doubt exactly why these people died," Chief Coroner for Ontario Richart de Kerck admits, of the latest in a string of unexplained Toronto mortality cases.*

"They scooped you, Am," you hear yourself mutter without meaning to. But the words turn in your throat, cut sideways, draw a thin, hot thread of pain, and for just a second the screen seems to flicker in front of your eyes, to pixilate and pop, as though jammed mid-signal.

In the women's bathroom, you stand in front of the mirror transfixed, studying the shape of your own lips and swallowing, reflexively; your throat feels raw, abraded, almost feverish. Your eyes shine, mouth gone flushed 'round the edges, slightly swollen. When you put one hand to your chest and cough, meanwhile, something gives slightly beneath your palm with a soft, twisting click—a bone key, turning in some invisible cartilage lock.

No.

You watch your too-pink mouth shape the word, but nothing comes out. Not that you can hear, anyhow.

That evening you barely speak to anybody without your headset on—not Amaryllis, who watches you with a worried look from the middle distance, trying and failing to catch your eyes, and not Eve or Helen, either. Instead, you bury yourself headfirst in the work, quite possibly giving the best advice you ever have, not that you remember any of it afterward; everyone you deal with certainly seems satisfied, by the time they ring off. Like you've stumbled on a magic formula, a template to fit all ills alike, along with their sufferers—some sort of universal balm, commonly inaccessible. The same words they sometimes hear in dreams, transposed somehow to bitter, grimy reality without losing a jot of efficacy: salving grief, clarifying confusion, soothing away hatred. Flipping the telescope right way 'round at last, de-magnifying their troubles, then making them forget.

Or maybe it's not so much *what* you're saying, in the end, as . . . the *way* that you say it.

When break-time comes you stumble outside, drag so hard on your cigarette you can feel your lungs stain. Amaryllis follows, treading softly, lit and fig.

"You all right?" she asks. You just nod, not trusting yourself to speak. Not to her.

She passes you a candy bar from the store downstairs, warmed by her hand; you bite in, deep. Feel it melt on contact with your fever-spiked tongue. Breath and smoke steam on the freeze-dried pocket of cold air that surrounds you both, meanwhile, pluming up into the night sky: darkness behind, too-bright step-towers of unnecessary light in front, leaking brilliance everywhere. Paling the black to gray and then dimming again as though on a timer, an endless Ouroboros loop.

"Don't have to talk tonight, if you don't want to," she assures you, voice pitched low, so sweet it almost makes you want to cry. "'Cause we can be comfortable together just like this, right? You and me. Now that we know each other a little better, I mean."

But: *I don't know a thing about you, Amaryllis,* you realize, without much resentment. *Not really. Not where you live or where you come from. Not about your family. Not even if that ex of yours—Kai?—is a girl or a boy or what, or if it matters, either way. If I even have a shot.*

Back inside, behind you, Eve and Helen have their heads bent together now, whispering intently. You wonder what's up with that, but only for an instant; you have other things to worry over, other fish to fry. That voice in the back of your head to shove down as it pops up, quick as any whack-a-mole, telling you: *Eyes on the prize, Zohra, get back in the game, shape up or be shipped out. You lose this job, you lose your place in school, your degree, your future—might as well lose your life and be done with it. Might as well slide on into the bathroom, break the mirror, and slash your wrists for real, this time, 'cause you are* done.

Remembering your mother's eyes at the hospital, aimed anywhere but at you; your father's one hand, white-knuckled on your bed's railing. How they sat there for hours, heads bent, but only as long as they thought you were still asleep. How the minute they realized you weren't they were up and out that door like a flash, not a single glance back and never to return.

Actions have consequences, Zohra, your father always seemed to like to say, back when he still acknowledged that you exist. *Words are seeds, and you reap what you sow. A girl must keep a tight door on her own mouth in order to make her way through this world, locked and bolted with the key well-hidden, and not where any fool can find it. A girl must be* careful.

To which you'd just snort, mostly, refusing to be drawn in; his ridiculous old-country ideas weren't worth the effort to disagree with until that last disastrous dinner, when you simply couldn't keep your lips together anymore. When you yelled out loud, right to his face: "But what if I don't, huh, Abba? What if I never do, not ever again? What's the worst, the absolute worst that could happen?"

And now you know; the worst has come and gone, long since. You're living it, here on the edge of the Abyss, hanging on for dear life with both bloody, torn-nailed hands.

Now it's top of the second half. You sit down once more, headset sliding into place, take a breath, and punch the button, mouth already open. Only to hear—nothing, not even a tone. Dead air.

(*oh God, no*)

Eve is on the floor, but turned away. Helen you can't track; in her office, maybe. That same tone as before is rising, abrading the inside of your eardrums, dim and red like a conch shell's furl. You can feel something inside your chest again, slipping between the top two ribs, deft as a key-edged knife and starting to turn, to crack—tumblers trembling, waiting the signal to fall. To open up, become a pink meat flower in full bloom.

Amaryllis on your left side, reaching for your shoulder as you gasp, one hand on your sternum: "Zohra, what? Zohra, let me help you, please. . . ."

While at the same exact time and on the line's other end, the red words croon: *Please, Zohra, yes, help US. Let it happen. Let what must be—be.*

The turn, the creak. The click, giving way, poised to pop.

Let us IN, the red words bark, croon sliding fast to growl. As you find yourself already barking back, in turn—

"Just get off the *line*, goddamnit! You *get off the line, and leave me the* hell ALONE!"

The words come out like bullets, hard and fast; they come out caustic—hot, like touching them would burn; they come out poisoned, strong enough to kill. They come out . . .

(*red*)

The whole room's gone numb, shocked silent. Inside the receiver's bell, something echoes, distantly: a gasp, sharp, like you've stuck your own phantom blade in. As you recoil, slapping the headset off so hard it bounces on the desk, you see Helen's office door slam open and her come bounding out—but she doesn't get the chance to tell you you're fired or whatever's about to happen. Instead, Amaryllis slings both of your packs over one arm and pulls you forward with the other, toward the hall. Eve makes a weird little lunge toward the two of you, trying to interpose, but Amaryllis's glare is enough to deflect her; she skitters to Helen's side, even as Helen blurts out: "Zohra, what the hell! You didn't have to—"

"Sorry," you reply, already halfway out the door. "I tried, I can't—sorry."

"We need to address this, Zohra. You can't just—"

"Yes, she can," Amaryllis snaps back. "Doin' it right now, just watch her. Step aside, man."

Helen turns to Eve: "This is very unprofessional, to say the least, and if she leaves, I won't be able to explain what's happened in any way my bosses will understand." To you: "You do understand that, don't you? Keep going and you'll end up fired, effectively. I won't have any recourse."

"Sorry, Helen," you repeat, meaning it. It makes no difference, though—for the first time ever, the threat doesn't mean anything. All you can feel is the words, burning inside you; Red Speech in your throat like a funnel, narrowing the port of entry 'til you think you'll puke, or choke. Your tongue gone dry, leathery, and everything else gone suddenly dim and red and suffocating, the whole inside of your esophagus spasming, all the way down to the voice box.

Get me to a sink, I'll spit up dust, you think, dazed, as Amaryllis turns you bodily, threading her arm through yours. "Guess you just lost us both, then," she tells Helen, flashing her teeth in a strained, grim grin, and elbows the elevator's "down" button.

Though Amaryllis's apartment is smaller than yours, she's made it look spacious through clever use of feng shui: replacing the door to the kitchen with a hanging curtain of bead-strings, using some of the thinnest frames you've ever seen for the art on her walls and employing a futon as both couch and bed in the living room, so her bedroom doubles as office and all-purpose storage. You've been sitting on that futon for what seems like hours with her comforting arm 'round your shoulders, going back and forth between fits of shuddering and outright weeping; when the knitting-needle pressure in your throat at last eases, it's mostly due to nothing but sheer exhaustion.

You'll take it, though. Take just about anything on offer, at this point.

Which is probably why—despite being vaguely aware this is a bad idea—you make no resistance when Amaryllis turns your face to hers and kisses you, gently. She is delicate, almost diffident at first, giving you every chance to speak up, protest, force her away. You don't.

Presently, things become less delicate.

Let go! she urges you, at one point, in between other actions. *Stop being so strong; I'm here, I'm here for you; let me help you, please. Cry, scream—say what you need to, whatever. Don't be afraid, Zohra. Say the words, the words, the words . . .*

(*those red, red words*)

But even at the height, you clamp your mouth shut on anything beyond the occasional breathy moan or wordless shout. Because the Speech is still there in you, lurking patiently, edges barely dulled by physical distractions. You don't want to know what might happen if you let it slip, cried it out loud, especially in such an uncontrolled—uncontrollable—moment.

At the last, you're both silent, Amaryllis draped over you, tiny and hot and snoring so lightly as to be almost a purr. You're not sure when you realize that you're already dreaming, but it seems to have been going on for a while: there's a sense that you've been wandering this building for hours, upstairs, down hallways, through massive empty chambers and tiny cubbies packed full with rotting furniture, dust-dry wood, or mossy stinking stone, all of it lit in shades of dim and weary red. Everywhere is the susurrus of tide and surf, a constant rushing whisper, yet it still shocks you to turn a corner at last and be confronted by sky, that same cliff's edge above the same ocean, a huge, bloody star glaring above. On the horizon rolls a strange, heavy darkness, closing in with inexorable, dreadful slowness, but the sea beneath is bleached almost white, as if flash-frozen to absolute zero—an alien landscape, like Plutonian ice or the Oort cloud's comets, lost far beyond the familiar sun's last light.

Across the open chamber, at the precipice, stands a man who turns as you approach. You know that face: broad and strong-jawed, long hair in a pseudo-tonsure. His eyes are a startling blue, weariness-bruised and red at the rims; he shivers, wringing his big, scarred hands and clutching his robes about him, skin bleached pallid with the bitter cold of the dry air, the dead red light of the sky.

Too late, child, he says mournfully. *You cannot defy them; the words are in you now, scribed deep, emblazoned upon your own blood's smallest atomies. I fought, and my family died. Refuse the charge and you too shall see everyone you love dead before you too succumb, like as not by your own hand—if you are so fortunate as to find such an end, that is.*

But I don't love anyone, you reply, after a long moment of silence.

His face softens, and for some reason that frightens you more than anything else has thus far: what can you possibly have said to make the pitiless Guillaume Cornîche pity you?

Though that may confine your suffering, he says, *it will not lessen it.*

And here another voice entirely intrudes, quiet yet familiar, words strung together loosely, barely intelligible: *Wake, sister, now, please, now. Zohra. Sister.* (*wake*)

The dream breaks up, pixelates, resolves to black; Amaryllis's apartment flickers back in overtop as you sit up, blink, shaking your head clean of shadows. Your eyes focus so slowly it takes an extra second to recognize both women standing over the futon, especially given how completely unexpected is it to see them here.

"Eve?" you finally choke out. "*Helen?*"

Helen kneels down, and it's like you're back in therapy again.

"Hi, Zohra," she begins, keeping her voice low, as though she doesn't want to disturb Amaryllis. "I'm sorry we scared you; sorry about your job, and about everything that's happened. But nobody expected the Speech to come on you as strongly as it did, so we had to get you out of there in a way that wouldn't provoke questions. If you want to get your clothes back on, we have a place you can stay 'til all this is a bit more under control...."

You cut her off, gripping her wrist, your grasp's force sharpened by all the fury you don't dare trust your voice with, right this second. She winces, doesn't move. "How did you get in here?" you demand, similarly quiet.

"I'm not sure that's the most important—"

"Shut up!" She does, eyes on yours, watchful. After a moment, you breathe: "So you knew all this time? Knew what's been happening to me?"

"What was likely to, yes. If you read the *Testament.*"

"Just like Nan did," Eve puts in, which makes your heart jump sharply, your system spark. "We were all in the Ordo once, Zohra, just like Encratia—we've been exposed. Thing is, though, the Red Speech isn't just a language but a ... *potential,* for lack of a better word; a talent, a knack, one that comes at different speeds to different people. And while Nan and Helen had enough to guess you might eventually make a more powerful speaker than any of us, none of us could predict *exactly* how you'd react."

You drop Helen's wrist and retreat, shaking your head, unable to process what Eve's just said. "I, I don't—I just, I don't, *why*—?"

Helen sighs, half sad, half something else; you're not quite sure what. "Because—if there's such a thing as a Red Sisterhood, these days—" she looks at Eve, who shrugs "—then we're it, I guess. And now, you are, too."

"Just like that, huh?" You want to weep again, to scream, to punch both their oh-so-dreadfully earnest faces in. "No matter what I have to say about it?"

"*None* of us asked for this, Zohra. Some people think that's the entire point of the *Testament*'s setup—that if you *could* choose the Speech, too many would seek it out for the wrong reasons, while the truly trustworthy would refuse it outright. Like the book, the Sisterhood maintains itself, protects itself; we look for those born to replace our own when they die, facilitate their introduction to the *Testament* however we can."

Eve nods. "It doesn't always work, either; for most people, the book will never be more than an incomprehensible oddity, like the Voynich manuscript. But when it does—well, we don't have a choice, any more than they do." Her voice goes quiet, but hard. "And even less so now, Zohra. Because we have enemies, and we're under attack."

Which is when you start to understand, finally, much though you don't want to.

"Those mystery deaths," you say, hoarse. "Holes opening up, inside; uncontrollable lesions. The victims must've been Sisterhood."

"Most, yes, with enough innocents mixed in to confuse the issue; speakers like us plus those who sign on to help with our great work, friends and family, colleagues. The fewer of us who remain, the easier to subvert the *Testament* to selfish or malicious ends. But . . ." She frowns. "Nothing was reported; we made sure of that, first thing. How'd you find that out—through dreams, the dead? The words themselves?"

"Proof of her power," Helen suggests. But here another voice intrudes, disagreeing.

"Not quite," it says, from beside you, "though she is powerful, or will be. She knows, because I told her."

Amaryllis, of course. Who else?

Oh, baby, no.

Startled, the two women—the sisters—recoil as she sits up as well, slings her arms 'round you from behind, casually possessive; you feel her bare breasts press into your back. She brings one small hand to rest, palm flat on your breastbone, just over the sudden snap-click insubstantial penetration that feels like nothing so much as a key slotting neatly into your chest, digging deep. Poised and ready to turn at the barest tap.

"Had to help you guys along, right?" she adds, conversationally. "I mean, I'm willing to do my part, for the cause. Just—not yours."

Whose, then?

Helen slaps up one hand, fingers twisted like she's throwing gang signs, which you suppose she sort of is; Eve opens her mouth, lips snarling back, and starts to say something—"*Aroint ye*," is *that* it? You can tell it's not in English. But Amaryllis is already cutting her off, a disdainful bark: "Shut *up*, old woman." To which Eve doubles up as if stomach-punched and retches black blood, clapping palms to mouth over a tongue split suddenly crosswise—lets slip with a horrid gurgling scream that chokes off halfway, becomes a muffled, liquid whine—

(And: *I will give you back your curse, word for word*, the Red Speech murmurs, inside you. *The sword of your mouth shall I turn against you, shut and lock your throat like a door, thus saieth She who we alone celebrate....*)

"Not alone, though," Amaryllis corrects, however, her hand twisting in the hollow of Eve's heart. "Not always. For a key turns both ways easily enough, and shapes itself to any willing hand."

With a violent shove, Helen thrusts herself forward even as she pulls Eve back, leaving her friend to double over further and let her hands drop, revealing the full, awful truth of her transformation: Eve's lips have sealed, literally; blood hardened like epoxy, stitching her mouth into one bold scar, cries smothered as her jaw works beneath, strains in useless effort.

You, meanwhile—you can't move. The Speech, as voiced by Eve and Amaryllis alike, ramps its pressure up throughout your guts, your lungs, your voice box. It wants out. At the same time, Amaryllis leans in close, lips against your ear, whispering so quietly her words read as thoughts forming inside your own skull: *Let it happen, you feel it, speak, open the door. The Girl waits for you on the other side, along with our friends, our masters....*

Blood spews out Eve's nostrils, thickening as you watch, closing off her last airway; she tears at her throat, like she's trying to perform an emergency self-tracheotomy. She crumples to her knees, face going red, then blue, then gray. Her eyes bulge, rolling senseless; her heaving chest falters, goes still. Helen pounds at Eve's chest a moment, futilely, before rising with eyes ablaze to turn on Amaryllis, throat puffing like a howler monkey's: the Speech cascades from her, fresh and hot as bile. Amaryllis meets it in kind, yells a sentence that sounds like an animal buzzsaw—jointed, metallic-wet, and bone-cracking—whose meaning alone makes you want to retch. Those Red Words translate themselves across your mind's screen, appearing one brand-strike at a time, as letters burnt in meat.

You caryatid, sentinel, gatekeeper and gate in one, lay down your call; stop your ears, silence your mouth. Yield in duty to they who end all duties.

Render up your flesh as a bed for the Treader, a tapestry to glorify Perdition's Star. Let fall the gate, make straight the Way, and end your journey in all journeys' ending.

You see it written in jagged, browned Angevin French beside glyphs that encompass whole verses in two, perhaps three symbols—words no mere *man* can ever speak, more deplorable than any sin, original or otherwise. Words that are, in the end, nothing more than the sound . . .

. . . of a key, in a lock. Turning.

At its touch, Helen buckles, smashed to her knees as though a great weight has fallen across her shoulders, pinning her down. She twists, writhes, jerks; the blood that spurts abruptly from her pores and darkens her worn skirt with awful intimacy—before and behind her—is less the black ichor still strangling Eve than hot, bright red heart's blood, aerated, fatal. It almost seems to glow, filling the apartment with heat fiery enough that the wall behind Helen ripples, like a curtain. Then it dims and flares back up, a flashlight illuminating the hand cupped around it, the silhouette glimpsed through the scrim drifting forward, shrinking, sharpening as it collapses: slight and waifish, bony body swathed in stiff fabric fringed with spikes, a thread-thin needle halo.

A friend on the other side, and one whose name you know already, Zohra, Amaryllis says, smiling, and each word emerges as a red mist-bubble, a jagged red jewel, a half-formed blood-clot popped in turn. *See how eager she is to meet you, at long, long last. See how impatient.*

Here the figure lifts its hand in turn, distorts the wall outward, pressing against some interdimensional membrane the same way a baby tests its mother's womb-wall; five points jutting outward, sharp as bones. The Red Girl printing herself on this world once more, if only metaphorically, after five hundred long years of exile: Hell and damnation, the dull red light of our universe's utter end, all ash, fossil-grit, and dust.

Unselfconsciously nude, Amaryllis strolls past Helen—lying jackknifed on the floor, now, as she bleeds out—and raises a hand to the wall herself, lays fingertip to fingertip. She gives you a dreamy, back-thrown smile over one shoulder, beckoning you on, and in the wall's red light you can suddenly see how her lovely eyes are actually two different colors: one the same caramel brown as ever, the other an unnaturally light hazel, almost amber-hued. Some kind of illusion, you can't help but wonder, or a simple contact lens?

But: *Oh, Zohra,* you can all but hear her croon, shaking her head at your silliness. *None of that really matters now, does it?*

"Guess not," you make yourself answer, out loud. "So, that being true, why don't you let them go? Eve, I mean. And Helen."

Amaryllis's dreamy smile doesn't change, and even in this nightmare—even without opening her mouth—she *sounds* just like she always does, mischievous and cheerful; flirtatious as ever, even under the very worst of circumstances. *Oh, but they don't matter either. You, Zohra—you're the only one who matters here, in the end. Don't you know that yet?*

And the thing is, terrible as it might be . . . you do, kind of. Want to, at any rate.

What would you rather be, after all? she continues, smiling even wider. *A slave to time, flesh-imprisoned—some ridiculous oxygen-waste, addicted and doomed, like those fools we counsel—or so much, much more: chosen, singled out. A vessel, a priestess, a god. . . .*

Some god's slave, you mean, you think back, coldly, clearly. *Maybe two gods at once, like the Red Girl was, or only one, depending. Because much as I may not owe Yamil Zaccra and Quachil Uttaus shit, if Carna thinks I'm going to spend the rest of my life worshipping Her just because She gave me her Speech like a fucking STD then She maybe has another think coming, too.*

Amaryllis's eyes widen slightly; this isn't exactly what she was expecting, probably. But at least she does try to keep on being charming.

Just open the wall for me, Zohra, she wheedles. *Do what you need to—let the Girl out, her masters in. Then, when that's done, we can talk about the rest.*

No, we won't.

The glyphs are alive, burning your mind. It's almost as if you don't have to speak them at all; the red words ride your breath, bursting forth in a pyroclastic burst, a geyser's billowing jet, a flash flood. *For the doors we keep open themselves without warning, in every sort of wall,* you cry, barely able to recall having read this particular passage. *Yet through our speech are the world's thin places shored up with prayerful words, each a spoken key. Thus do we bend our lives to the world's life, locking out sickness, plague, and sorrow.*

Amaryllis's eyes widen further, to their outer orbits, and bulge like the wall, shadow-tainted, brightening from behind. If her expression looks like anything, in that last second, it's the flesh equivalent of a *WTF?!* Emoji; she literally can't believe what you just did. No time for much else, after: her face is already crumpling, skin sucked tight to skull, gone leathery, sere. Tugged backward from the waist, her body bends over and cracks, folding in half-slips sideways, into the wall itself. At the same time, you see the figure behind the wall's needle-fringed robe flare up, a lizard's raised crest; it punches its fist out through the crumbling flesh of Amaryllis's corpse, red-taloned and acrid brown, stinking like an open grave.

It jerks back and forth, a blind fish's proboscis blurred by its own stuttering movement, the intersection of two distinct types of gravity. It puppets what's left of its votary, your betrayer, in a clumsy, blurring circuit before lunging back inside, leash yanked just as the half-formed door slams shut, doomed long since to pay the price for its masters' disappointment forever.

The last of Amaryllis hits that barrier hard, bursts apart on contact: poof, gone, a spray of something so fine it barely hangs in the air a half-pulse before sifting away. Those lips, those eyes, that everything—nothing left of her now, not even the lies. *Nothing.*

One last indrawn breath, burning lungs you had fleetingly thought you might never use again, and your knees knock together bruisingly, bend, collapse. Your ass hits the floor, sitz-bones first. But you can't quite drag your eyes from the wall, which seems to be solidifying with a dangerous slowness; it hurts to look at it, like an image viewed through someone else's prescription glasses. *Have to do something about that,* you think, unable to guess what, as you realize with a sick lurch exactly how little energy you have left.

That's when you feel Helen's hand, her fingers knitting with yours. Hear her voice shape those same red words, that double invocation, Speech running through her like a current and into you, up your arm, into your chest. Then out once more through your throat, over your bloody tongue, out from your open, panting mouth . . . cooking the breach closed, healing yourself if not her, the same words spilling from both your lips at once:

> *thus do we bend, our lives, we bend them thus*
> *our lives, thus, to the world's*
> *our lives for life, thus*
> *the world*

Helen, clinging to her last few flutters of life, shaping your Speech with her own. And so the ritual concludes, wall grown firm again, shored up like brick and mortar; the red light fades; the dust settles. Those bright shadows recede, 'til all that's left in their wake is dead Eve, Amaryllis's absence—her complete, nauseating lack—and Helen, gulping shallowly on the floor. Knowing soon there will be two dead bodies instead of one, you crawl to her, run your palm down her side and gasp in sympathetic pain, because a touch tells you what only an X-ray would, otherwise: that whatever hole Amaryllis ripped open inside her is far beyond your skill to close, or anyone else's, either.

Put a hand to her cheek and she opens her eyes, roused by contact; her gaze finds yours, and holds. You see an apology there she won't have time to get to, not if she wants to tell you even half of what you need to know.

Your life is changed from now on, utterly. There are choices to be made, after all: you have to keep yourself from the coven's clutches, the dregs of Chatouye, the Red Girl's get; Amaryllis can't have acted alone, not entirely. But can you really trust yourself to Nan van Hool and the rest of the Sisterhood, knowing how they intentionally infected you with a power you barely understand, something whose parameters you haven't even begun to map? Sister Encratia and the Ordo might be a better bet, but then again, they might not; she's complicit as well, in her own way. A perfect storm of unreliability, everywhere you look.

With the Speech, though, all things are possible. You could even go home for the first time in years, sure no one even slightly acquainted with your life would ever expect you to take refuge there; knock on your parents' door without fear, secure in the knowledge that you can tell them how things will be from now on, and always. Loop the Testament's red words 'round their necks and then bid them burrow deep through their bodies, your mother, your father—a second nervous system, fail-safe, permanent. It's awful, obviously; you do understand that, still. But . . .

. . . the ethics of it are more theoretical than anything, and getting ever more so. As the fever spreads, you watch all the parts of you that object to using other human beings like tools start to boil away, accordingly, and it simply doesn't strike you as all that bad. Quite the opposite.

Instead, it feels only right, proper, practical. *Appropriate.* To bend their lives in service to this greatest of all causes, as you're already so entirely, inevitably willing to bend yours.

This is the world we're talking about, after all: Gloria Mundi, splendor of creation and center of all universes, God's crowning work and charge: first, and last, and only. That jewel of infinite price, with which no one person's freedom ever can, or should, compare.

So:

"*Tell me everything you can,*" you order, Speech sparking in your mouth, to make absolutely sure that Helen does. Then lay your ear to her quick-cooling lips and listen, for as long as it takes—

—exactly as long in the end, it ensues, as she has left to give.

CONTRIBUTORS' NOTES

NADIA BULKIN writes scary stories about the scary world we live in, four of which have been nominated for a Shirley Jackson Award. Her stories have been included in volumes of *The Year's Best Horror* (Datlow), *The Year's Best Dark Fantasy and Horror* (Guran), and *The Year's Best Weird Fiction*; in venues such as *Nightmare, Fantasy,* and *The Dark*; and in anthologies such as *She Walks in Shadows* and *Aickman's Heirs*. Her debut collection, *She Said Destroy*, was published by Word Horde in August 2017. She grew up in Indonesia with a Javanese father and American mother during the last decade of the Suharto regime. She now has a B.A. in political science, an M.A. in international affairs, and lives in Washington, D.C.

SELENA CHAMBERS is author of the Weird feminist collection, *Calls for Submission* (Pelekinesis), and co-author (as S. J. Chambers) of the critically acclaimed and best-selling *The Steampunk Bible* (Abrams Image). She's been translated in France, Spain, Brazil, and in Turkey, and has published in the U.K. and Australia. Her work has been nominated for the Pushcart, Colorado Book Award, Best of the Net, as well as the Hugo Award and World Fantasy Award (twice). Recent bylines include *Literary Hub, Beautiful Bizarre Magazine, The Debutante: Women Surrealists Art Journal,* and an essay in Desirina Boskovich's *Lost Transmissions: The Secret History of Science Fiction and Fantasy* (Abrams Image). You can find out more about Selena at selenachambers.com or on Twitter @BasBleuZombie.

Former film critic, journalist, and screenwriter turned award-winning horror author **GEMMA FILES** has published a Weird Western trilogy (the Hexslinger Series: *A Book of Tongues, A Rope of Thorns,* and *A Tree of Bones,* all from

CONTRIBUTORS' NOTES

ChiZine Publications), two collections of short fiction (*Kissing Carrion* and *The Worm in Every Heart*), two chapbooks of speculative poetry (*Bent Under Night* and *Dust Radio*), a story-cycle (*We Will All Go Down Together: Stories of the Five-Family Coven*), and *Experimental Film,* which won the 2015 Shirley Jackson Award for Best Novel and the 2015 Sunburst Award for Best Novel (Adult Category). She has published over eighty short stories, five of which were produced as episodes of *The Hunger*, an erotic horror anthology TV series created by Tony and Ridley Scott; she wrote the scripts for two of those herself. She is married to Stephen J. Barringer, with whom she co-wrote "each thing I show you is a piece of my death," a story since reprinted in multiple venues. She is currently hard at work on her new novel.

ALISON LITTLEWOOD's latest novel, *Mistletoe*, is a seasonal ghost story with glimpses into the Victorian era. Her first book, *A Cold Season*, was selected for the Richard and Judy Book Club and described as "perfect reading for a dark winter's night." Other titles include *A Cold Silence, Path of Needles, The Unquiet House, Zombie Apocalypse! Acapulcalypse Now, The Hidden People,* and *The Crow Garden*. Alison's short stories have been picked for a number of year's best anthologies and published in her collections *Quieter Paths* and *Five Feathered Tales*. She has won the Shirley Jackson Award for Short Fiction. Alison lives with her partner Fergus in Yorkshire, England, in a house of creaking doors and crooked walls. She loves exploring the hills and dales with her two hugely enthusiastic Dalmatians and has a penchant for books on folklore and weird history, Earl Grey tea, fountain pens, and semicolons. Visit her at alisonlittlewood.co.uk.

LIVIA LLEWELLYN is a writer of dark fantasy, horror, and erotica, whose short fiction has appeared in over forty anthologies and magazines and has been reprinted in multiple best-of anthologies, including Ellen Datlow's *The Best Horror of the Year* series, *Year's Best Weird Fiction*, and *The Mammoth Book of Best Erotica*. Her first collection, *Engines of Desire: Tales of Love & Other Horrors* (2011, Lethe Press), received two Shirley Jackson Award nominations, for Best Collection and for Best Novelette (for "Omphalos"). Her story "Furnace" received a 2013 Shirley Jackson Award nomination for Best Short Story. Her second collection, *Furnace* (2016, Word Horde Press), received a 2016 Shirley Jackson Award Nomination for Best Collection. You can find her online at liviallewellyn.com, and on Instagram and Twitter.

PENELOPE LOVE is an Australian writer whose Cthulhu fiction has appeared in *She Walks in Shadows (Cthulhu's Daughters), Heroes of Red Hook, Tales of*

CONTRIBUTORS' NOTES

Cthulhu Invictus, Madness on the Orient Express, and *Cthulhu's Dark Cults*. She has written *Call of Cthulhu* scenarios since 1986 and her publications include *Horror on the Orient Express, De Horrore Cosmico,* and others.

S.P. MISKOWSKI is a multiple Shirley Jackson Award nominee whose stories appear in numerous magazines and anthologies, including *Supernatural Tales, Black Static, Strange Aeons, The Cabinet of Dr. Caligari, Looming Low, Haunted Nights, Tales from a Talking Board,* and *Darker Companions: Celebrating 50 Years of Ramsey Campbell*. Her series the Skillute Cycle is published by Omnium Gatherum. Her novel *I Wish I Was Like You* is available from JournalStone, and her story collection *Strange is the Night* is published by Trepidatio, an imprint of JournalStone.

LISA MORTON is a screenwriter, author of nonfiction books, Bram Stoker Award-winning prose writer, and Halloween expert whose work was described by the American Library Association's Readers' Advisory Guide to Horror as "consistently dark, unsettling, and frightening." She has published four novels, over 150 short stories, and three books on the history of Halloween. Recent releases include *Weird Women: Classic Supernatural Fiction by Groundbreaking Female Writers 1852–1923* (co-edited with Leslie S. Klinger) and *Calling the Spirits: A History of Seances*. She lives in the San Fernando Valley, and can be found online at lisamorton.com.

NATE PEDERSEN is a writer, librarian, and historian in Portland, Oregon. He is the co-author of *Quackery: A Brief History of the Worst Ways to Cure Everything* and the upcoming *Patient Zero: A Curious History of the World's Worst Diseases,* from Workman. His previous Lovecraftian anthology, *The Starry Wisdom Library,* was published by PS Publishing in 2014. His website is natepedersen.com.

LYNDA E. RUCKER grew up in a house in the woods in the southeastern United States full of books, cats, and typewriters, so naturally she had little choice but to become a writer. She has sold more than three dozen short stories to various magazines and anthologies including *F&SF, Nightmare Magazine, The Year's Best Horror, The Mammoth Book of Best New Horror, The Year's Best Horror and Dark Fantasy, Supernatural Tales,* and *Postscripts,* among others, and has had a short play produced as part of an anthology of horror plays on London's West End. She won the 2015 Shirley Jackson Award for Best Short Story, collaborated on a short horror comic that appeared in the anthology

Outsiders, and is a regular columnist for UK magazine *Black Static.* Her first collection, *The Moon Will Look Strange,* was released in 2013 from Karōshi Books, and her second, *You'll Know When You Get There,* was published by Ireland's Swan River Press in 2016.

ANN K. SCHWADER's latest collection of weird verse is *Dark Energies* (P'rea Press 2015). Her next, *Unquiet Stars,* is forthcoming from Weird House Press. She is a two-time Bram Stoker Award Finalist for Poetry Collection, and a two-time Rhysling Award winner. In 2018, the Science Fiction & Fantasy Poetry Association named her a Grand Master. Her poems have recently appeared in *Spectral Realms, Weird Fiction Review, Star*Line, Dreams & Nightmares, Abyss & Apex,* and elsewhere. She is an Active member of SFWA and HWA. Learn more at schwader.net.

신선영 SUN YING SHIN was born in Seoul, Korea, during 박 정 희 Park Chung-hee's military dictatorship, and grew up in the Chicago area. She is the editor of *A Good Time for the Truth: Race in Minnesota,* author of poetry collections *Unbearable Splendor* (winner of the 2016 Minnesota Book Award for poetry); *Rough, and Savage*; and *Skirt Full of Black* (winner of the 2007 Asian American Literary Award for poetry), co-editor of *Outsiders Within: Writing on Transracial Adoption,* and author of bilingual illustrated book for children *Cooper's Lesson.* She lives in Minneapolis.

MOLLY TANZER is the author of the novels *Creatures of Will and Temper, Vermilion,* and *The Pleasure Merchant,* and the novella "Rumbullion: An Apostrophe." She is also the editrix of *Mixed Up* (with Nick Mamatas), a book of cocktail recipes and flash-fiction. For more information about her critically acclaimed novels and short stories, visit her website, mollytanzer.com, or follow her @wickedmilkhotel on Twitter or @molly_tanzer on Instagram.

MONICA VALENTINELLI writes stories, games, essays, and comics in her Midwestern studio. She's an artist, a former musician of twenty-plus years, and a graduate of the University of Wisconsin-Madison's Creative Writing program who now writes full-time. Find her anthology, *Upside Down: Inverted Tropes in Storytelling,* available wherever books are sold. For more about Monica, visit booksofm.com.

CONTRIBUTORS' NOTES

KALI WALLACE studied geology and earned a PhD in geophysics before she realized she enjoyed inventing imaginary worlds more than she liked researching the real one. She is the author of science fiction, fantasy, and horror novels for adults, teens, and children, as well as a number of short stories and essays. After spending most of her life in Colorado, she now lives in southern California. Find her at kaliwallace.com.

DAMIEN ANGELICA WALTERS is the author of *The Dead Girls Club, Cry Your Way Home, Paper Tigers,* and *Sing Me Your Scars.* Her short fiction has been nominated twice for a Bram Stoker Award, reprinted in *Best Horror of the Year, The Year's Best Dark Fantasy & Horror,* and *The Year's Best Weird Fiction,* and published in various anthologies and magazines, including the Shirley Jackson Award finalists *Autumn Cthulhu* and *The Madness of Dr. Caligari,* World Fantasy Award finalist *Cassilda's Song, Nightmare Magazine,* and *Black Static.* She lives in Maryland with her husband and a rescued pit bull named Ripley. Find her on Twitter @DamienAWalters or on her website at damienangelicawalters.com.

Shirley Jackson Award winner KAARON WARREN published her first short story in 1993 and has had fiction in print every year since. She was recently given the Peter McNamara Lifetime Achievement Award and was Guest of Honor at World Fantasy 2018, StokerCon 2019, and GeyserCon 2019. Kaaron was a Fellow at the Museum for Australian Democracy, where she researched prime ministers, artists, and serial killers. She's judged the World Fantasy Awards and the Shirley Jackson Awards. She has published five multi-award-winning novels (*Slights, Walking the Tree, Mistification, The Grief Hole,* and *Tide of Stone*) and seven short story collections, including the multi-award-winning *Through Splintered Walls.* She has won the ACT Writers and Publishers Award four times and twice been awarded the Canberra Critics Circle Award for Fiction. Her most recent novella, *Into Bones Like Oil* (Meerkat Press), was shortlisted for a Shirley Jackson Award and the Bram Stoker Award, winning the Aurealis Award.

THE LEAVES OF A NECRONOMICON

EDITED BY SHIRLEY JACKSON AWARD WINNER JOSEPH S. PULVER, SR.

The Necronomicon. For centuries, scholars of the occult have sought out the darkly fabled tome, hoping to gain insight into the secret workings of the universe—or simple brute power. What the book offered them instead was, more often than not, madness and devastation. Under the guidance of Shirley Jackson Award-winning editor Joseph S. Pulver, Sr., *The Leaves of a Necronomicon* traces the impact of a single copy of the mysterious work on its owners and those around them as it passes from hand to hand across the decades. The history is told in braided novel form, with chapters contributed by a gathering of outstanding horror and dark fantasy authors, including S. P. Miskowski, Michael Cisco, Damien Angelica Walters, Nick Mamatas, Anna Tambour, Jeffrey Thomas, and more.

ISBN 978-1-56882-408-6 - **available spring 2021** - trade paperback